PRAISE FOR WENDY CORSI STAUB

The Fourth Girl

"Staub . . . [doles] out key details with a steady hand before walloping readers with a surprise ending. It's dark, satisfying fun."

—*Publishers Weekly*

"Distinctive voices add depth and flavor . . ."

—*Kirkus Reviews*

Windfall

"A winning lottery ticket, a haunted California mansion, and raging wildfires provide the tense and atmospheric backdrop for Wendy Corsi Staub's riveting and engrossing new thriller. I devoured this novel about the price of friendship and the things we'll do for love and money in one breathless sitting. Rocket-paced and full of unexpected twists, *Windfall* is a knockout! A summer must-read!"

—Lisa Unger, *New York Times* bestselling author of *Secluded Cabin Sleeps Six*

"I couldn't turn the pages of *Windfall* fast enough in this twisty thriller that has it all—three friends who wrongly assumed they knew each other's secrets, a life-changing lottery ticket that could change their complicated lives for better (or worse), all in a Gothic setting on deadly cliffs shrouded by smoke from California wildfires. Nail biting, tense, and rich—in more ways than one!"

—Sarah Strohmeyer, bestselling author of *We Love to Entertain*

"A tense and moving exploration of women's friendships and lives. Reading *Windfall* is like winning the lottery of suspense writing!"

—Carol Goodman, *New York Times* bestselling and award-winning author of *The Bones of the Story*

"When money and old secrets collide, someone has to pay. It all comes due at *Windfall*. Compelling, atmospheric, and deliciously twisted. Suspense at its finest."

—James L'Etoile, award-winning author of *Dead Drop*

"Masterful and utterly compelling, *Windfall* is an examination of four scarred women and how the dreamlike opportunity for them to escape the unique, richly layered complications of their lives is hardly an escape at all. Staub lands every aching and triumphant emotional moment she aims for and, as the novel rushes forward, delivers a master class in page-turning suspense. Destined to be revered by readers and studied by aspiring and experienced writers alike, *Windfall* is the work of an author at the top of her game, showcasing all of her considerable skills."

—E.A. Aymar, bestselling author of *No Home for Killers*

"What's scarier than a small slip of paper holding a billion-dollar lottery win to be split between three old friends? Add in a haunted mansion on a Pacific cliff surrounded by California wildfires, no phone/internet service, and you'll get a scream in the night and someone going missing. This is not just a perfect table setting of mystery elements; it's also a complex story of three women's lives, old college friends who find themselves lost in midlife, wondering what happened to all their youthful dreams and desires. Wendy Corsi Staub is at her best with *Windfall*, keeping the reader on edge to find out who really wins it all in life and whose luck has run out."

—James Conrad, Golden Notebook Bookstore, Golden Notebook Press

The Other Family

"Great psychological suspense with a wallop of a twist."

—Harlan Coben, #1 *New York Times* bestselling author

"A twisty ride steeped in betrayal. The perfect winter read!"

—J.D. Barker, *New York Times* bestselling author of *A Caller's Game*

"Creepy families, big secrets, and lingering questions come together in this twisty page-turner that will have you speed-reading to try to figure it out."

—Darby Kane, #1 international bestselling author

"Wendy Corsi Staub has always been one of my favorite writers, but she surpasses even her best work with *The Other Family*. A chilling and addictive novel of suspense, it also speaks deep truths about family ties—and how they can support or destroy us. I really loved this book."

—Alison Gaylin, author of *The Collective*

"Dark, twisty, and irresistible, *The Other Family* is domestic suspense turned up to eleven, the gripping tale of one family's cross-country move to Brooklyn—and the explosive revelations that follow when one woman is finally forced to reckon with her past. From her pitch-perfect characterizations to her unerring sense of plot and pace, Wendy Corsi Staub displays a command of the form that's not merely masterful—it's practically diabolical."

—Elizabeth Little, *Los Angeles Times* bestselling author of *Dear Daughter* and *Pretty as a Picture*

THE LOST SUMMER

OTHER TITLES BY WENDY CORSI STAUB

Haven Cliff

The Fourth Girl

Stand-Alone Psychological Suspense

Windfall
The Other Family
Dying Breath
Dead Before Dark
Lullaby and Goodnight
Kiss Her Goodbye
Most Likely to Die
Don't Scream
The Final Victim
She Loves Me Not
In the Blink of an Eye
The Last to Know
All the Way Home
Fade to Black
Dearly Beloved

The Lily Dale Mysteries

Nine Lives

Something Buried, Something Blue

Dead of Winter

Prose and Cons

The Stranger Vanishes

Dog Days

Toil and Trouble

The Foundlings Trilogy

Little Girl Lost

Dead Silence

The Butcher's Daughter

The Mundy's Landing Trilogy

Blood Red

Blue Moon

Bone White

Social Media Thrillers

The Good Sister

The Perfect Stranger

Cold Hearted (e-novella prequel to *The Perfect Stranger*)

The Black Widow

Nightwatcher Trilogy

Nightwatcher

Sleepwalker

Shadowkiller

Live to Tell Trilogy

Live to Tell

Scared to Death

Hell to Pay

WOMEN'S FICTION

Written as Wendy Markham

Stand-Alone Titles

Hello, It's Me

If Only in My Dreams

The Best Gift

Love, Suburban Style

Mike, Mike & Me

Thoroughly Modern Princess

The Long Way Home

"Slightly" Series

So Not Single (formerly *Slightly Single*)
Confessions of a One Night Stand (formerly *Slightly Settled)*
Did Someone Say Fiancée? (formerly *Slightly Engaged*)
Happily Ever After All (formerly *Slightly Married*)
What Happens in Suburbia (formerly *Slightly Suburban*)

Chickalini Family Series

The Nine Month Plan
Once Upon a Blind Date
Bride Needs Groom
That's Amore

YOUNG READERS

Stand-Alone and Short Stories

Scream and Scream Again
Witch Hunt
Halloween Party
Summer Lightning
Real Life: Help Me
Turning Seventeen: More Than This
Turning Seventeen: This Boy Is Mine
Charmed: Voodoo Moon

Lily Dale Series

Lily Dale: Awakening
Lily Dale: Believing
Lily Dale: Connecting
Lily Dale: Discovering

Teen Angels Series

Mitzi Malloy and the Anything-but-Heavenly Summer
Brittany Butterfield and the Back-to-School Blues
Henry Hopkins and the Horrible Halloween Happening
Candace Caine and the Bah, Humbug Christmas (coming soon)

College Life 101 Series

College Life 101: Cameron
College Life 101: Zara
College Life 101: Kim
College Life 101: Bridget
College Life 101: Allison
College Life 101: The Reunion

The Loop Series

Getting Attached
Getting Hitched
Getting It Together

Voodoo Series

Obsession (written as Wendy Morgan)

Possession (written as Wendy Morgan)

THE LOST SUMMER

A NOVEL

WENDY CORSI STAUB

This is a work of fiction. Names, characters, organizations, places, events, and incidents are either products of the author's imagination or are used fictitiously. Otherwise, any resemblance to actual persons, living or dead, is purely coincidental.

Published by Thomas & Mercer, Seattle

www.apub.com

EU product safety contact:
Amazon Media EU S. à r.l.
38, avenue John F. Kennedy, L-1855 Luxembourg
amazonpublishing-gpsr@amazon.com

ISBN-13: 9781662523823 (paperback)
ISBN-13: 9781662523830 (digital)

Cover design by Ploy Siripant
Cover images: © Evelina Kremsdorf / ArcAngel Images;
© justinemt17 / Shutterstock

Printed in the United States of America

For my cousin Kristin Lee Curry Casalino,
with whom I've spent the better part—the best parts—
of a lifetime, laughing, dancing, singing, eating,
drinking, and laughing some more.

For my cousin Felicia,
the founding Italian Daughter of Staub,
who carries on with strength and love.

In loving memory of her husband, my cousin Tommy Staub,
without whom nothing—especially Thanksgiving—will ever be the same.

And always, always, for Mark, Morgan, and Brody,
with love.

Here's to the good old days, to better ones ahead, but mostly, to Right Here, Right Now. (Go Bills!)

August 16

CHAPTER ONE

The email came in overnight.

It's short. Unambiguous.

Still, he reads it several times on his phone, then opens his laptop to go over it again, as if it might suddenly yield additional information.

> I'm trying to find my birth family via DNA testing on the genealogical website Lost and Found. My results identify you as a close biological relative. I'm aware that this is a potentially sensitive topic, but if you're willing to discuss this further, I promise complete discretion.

That's it. Nothing more. No signature, not a hint toward gender, age, or location.

He copies the email address and plugs it into Google.

It doesn't get a single hit.

That's to be expected. The Lost and Found website recommends that users create a new address strictly for genealogical research purposes. It's right there under the FAQs:

While connecting with DNA matches can lead to rewarding relationships, providing personal information to strangers—even those who share a bloodline—may occasionally lead to unhealthy or unwanted communication.

There's only one way to uncover this person's identity.

But he'd have to risk revealing his own.

That would be dangerous.

Not for him, as much as for the stranger who sent the email.

Hands poised on the keyboard, he weighs his options.

Then he begins to type.

August 29

CHAPTER TWO

"Thanks for letting him off the hook, Sergeant Kennedy."

"I just hope this won't happen again." Midge tucks her iPad under her arm and glances from the weary-eyed woman on the doorstep to her young teenage son, picked up for an illicit swim on a sweltering summer afternoon.

Midge may be law enforcement now, but she experienced her share of backyard pool hopping with her older brothers and their friends back in the day. They just never did it in broad daylight.

Ninety-seven degrees, humid, sun-searing broad daylight.

And they never got caught, because there were no home-monitoring devices like the Ring camera that alerted the vacationing homeowner to an intruder on his property today.

When the call came in, Midge was already in the neighborhood, chasing down a greyhound puppy that had escaped its leash.

Dog days, indeed.

Within minutes of the intruder call, she was on the scene, still breathless and sweat soaked, armed and prepared for anything . . .

Well, anything but a scrawny fourteen-year-old splashing around wearing Hawaiian-print swim trunks and rubber goggles. She'd gladly have jumped into the sparkling pool to apprehend him, but he climbed out as soon as he saw her, apologizing profusely.

Now he stares at his flip-flops until his mother nudges him, saying, "It won't happen again, Sergeant Kennedy. Right, Jacob?"

"Right." He lifts his head to meet Midge's gaze. His blond hair is still damp, his face goggle-imprinted.

"Good. Because next time, there *will* be repercussions." She maintains an appropriately stern expression, blotting sweat from beneath the brim of her police cap, and tucks back unruly coppery strands.

If her friend Kelly were here, she'd say Midge is *frizzled.* She coined the phrase this summer, with Midge perpetually frazzled due to stressful workdays, her hair frizzy from the humidity.

Fortunately, Midge is one of those people who gives little thought to her appearance, while Kelly is one of those people who's never looked frazzled, frizzy, or *frizzled* in her life.

Her phone buzzes. Checking it, she sees an incoming call from Walter Jackson, Mulberry Bay's police chief, who's been out on medical leave all summer. He probably wants to discuss his scheduled return next week, and none too soon. She sends the call to voicemail as Jacob's mother tells him to go to his room.

"And no video games," she adds as he disappears down the hall.

A door slams. The woman shakes her head, fanning herself with a supermarket flyer advertising organic heirloom watermelon.

"I'm really sorry about this, Sergeant Kennedy. I don't know what to do with him. He's been giving me trouble ever since his dad walked out. I can't—"

"Mom! Where the hell is my uniform? I'm late!" A teenage girl appears, wearing a sports bra and skimpy panties. She has long blond hair; tanned, lanky limbs; and a pretty face. Seeing Midge, she turns to her mother. "Why are the cops here? Are you trying to have Dad arrested or something?"

"This has nothing to do with your father. It has nothing to do with you, either, Taylor. Go put some clothes on."

"I can't find my uniform!"

"Well, I saw it in the laundry yesterday. So unless you washed it, it's probably still there. It's time to start taking care of your own—"

"But I'm late! What am I supposed to do?"

"Get dressed and go to work."

"In a *dirty uniform*?"

"I guess so."

Taylor stalks away.

Her mother returns a weary gaze to Midge. "The world revolves around her, and the rest of us are just here to serve her. You know how it is with teenage girls."

Midge doesn't know—not from a parenting standpoint. And when she looks back on that time in her own life, she only remembers her friend Caroline Winterfield's prom-night disappearance, and how it impacted every aspect of her own life. That summer, and for years after. Even now.

Especially now.

"Jacob is tough, but Taylor's impossible. And my ex is no help. Do you have a husband? An ex-husband? Kids?"

"None of the above."

"Yeah, well, no wonder. Being a cop, I'm sure you see the worst of them all."

Midge nods, though the pool escapade is hardly the worst of what she's seen in her twenty years on the Mulberry Bay police force. It's far from the worst thing she's seen in a summer that began with the village's first homicide in over a decade.

"Good thing school starts next week," Jacob's mother says. "It's been a long summer—not in a good way, you know?"

Hell yes, Midge knows.

"Mom!" Taylor hollers from somewhere in the house.

Her mother looks at Midge. "I swear I'm going to strangle her."

"Ah, I'll let you go."

"Wait, you know I didn't mean that, right? I wouldn't really—"

"No, I know."

"She's just—"

"I get it." Midge flashes a smile over her shoulder. "No worries. Good luck."

Heading for the sunbaked car at the curb, she shoots a wistful glance at the sprinkler spritzing the lawn next door.

This development may be called Shady Grove Acres, but trees—even the town's insidious mulberries—are conspicuously absent amid the cookie-cutter ranch homes.

With the windows rolled down and the air-conditioning on full blast, Midge finishes entering the report details into the iPad, mounts it on the dashboard, then checks the time.

She'll be off duty in half an hour. She has dinner plans with friends later this evening, but she might have time to head down to the lake for a quick swim. By then, the sun will be lower, an added bonus for a fair-skinned ginger like her. Not that burns and fresh freckles have been much of a concern this summer.

In years past, she's slathered herself in the highest-available SPF and devoted every nonworking, nonsleeping hour to outdoor recreation. But this summer, for Midge, there's been no swimming, kayaking, hiking, playing softball and tennis. There's barely been time for sleeping.

She returns Walt's call as she heads back toward town, reminding herself that he's due to return after the holiday weekend. Maybe she'll be able to salvage what's left of the summer after all.

After a few rings, a reedy voice answers the phone.

She hesitates. "Uh . . . Walt?"

"It's me. Good to hear from you, Midge. Keeping cool?"

"Always."

A warbled chuckle. "The coolest gal in town, hands down. Listen, Midge, I hate to do this to you, but my doctor says I'll be laid up awhile longer. Do you think you'll be able to—ah, I hate to ask, but . . ."

"Walt, I've got everything under control for as long as you need me. You just focus on getting better."

"I'm . . ." He clears his throat, and her heart sinks. "Yeah. I'm really trying. And thanks, Midge. If it were anyone else standing in for me, I'd be on the job, dragging this damned IV pole. But with you, well, that's one less thing for me to worry about."

She does her best to sound chipper. "I've got you, Walt. For as long as you need me."

So much for salvaging the summer. But as long as nothing happens in the next half hour, she can still go for that predinner swim. She has a bathing suit in the gym bag she keeps at the office, along with running shoes, ever optimistic that she'll manage to squeeze a workout into these busy days.

Tourist traffic builds along Route 28 as she nears the town proper. This was once a wooded country byway with sweeping Catskills vistas. Now it's a four-lane thoroughfare lined with condos and town houses, chain stores and restaurants.

Like many Ulster County towns, Mulberry Bay's economy fluctuated for the better part of the last century, with most of this one devoted to a renaissance. Business is booming, and a burgeoning population has led to soaring real estate prices and ongoing construction. Controversy abounds, with developers, summer residents, and newcomers frequently battling longtime locals at town zoning board meetings.

She passes Wildgreen, the upscale supermarket that replaced the old A&P, and a frequent source of such contention. All summer, it's been the scene of protests by old-timers who consider it a health-food store, overpriced and sorely lacking in Kellogg's Rice Krispies and Hostess Ho Hos.

On this sweltering afternoon, there's not a picket sign in sight—just a crowded parking lot and a massive bin of organic heirloom watermelons with a big yellow sale banner.

Midge's mouth waters. What she wouldn't give for a wedge of cold pink watermelon, served up with ribs, corn on the cob, potato salad . . .

There have been no backyard barbecues for her this summer. No hot dogs on the grill, no toasting marshmallows for s'mores, watching fireflies flit beneath a starry sky.

Maybe this weekend, though. She's hoping for some downtime. Her friend Talia is coming to Mulberry Bay with her family, staying at Haven Cliff with Kelly.

Despite the heat wave on this Thursday before Labor Day weekend, the town hums with activity. Locals, summer residents, and tourists are out en masse, clogging the streets with vehicles, bikes, or skateboards. Double-parked delivery drivers unload crates onto hand trucks. Pedestrians carry shopping bags, push strollers, or have dogs on leashes.

A line stretches along the sidewalk beneath the pastel-pink-striped awnings at Get the Scoop, where a hand-printed banner advertises a *heat wave special.* The ice cream parlor, located on the first floor of the old *Mulberry Bay Daily News* building, is presumably far more lucrative than the newspaper, which went from a daily to a monthly before folding altogether in the early 2000s, and is now tentatively back in print as a weekly.

In the grassy commons across the way, every tree-shaded bench is occupied, and a few sweaty souls are actually using the jogging path. Midge, a lifelong athlete, wouldn't dream of it in oppressive weather like this.

The police station is located at the corner of Main and Center Streets. With four floors, a clock tower, and an 1890 cornerstone, the granite building presides over the town square. Municipal offices, meeting rooms, and the historical society occupy the main and upper floors, with headquarters on the subterranean level.

As always, Midge feels a flicker of gratification as she parks in the spot designated **Chief Only, All Others Towed**. It's a perk she'll miss when Walt comes back.

She grabs her iPad and climbs out of the car. There's a garbage truck near the outdoor stairway, giving off a sickening stench and making a deafening racket as it backs up toward a dumpster.

Descending the steps, she can see the front desk through the glass doors. Allie, the temp who's covering for the regular receptionist on maternity leave, is scrolling on her phone, leaning back in her chair, crossed feet propped on the desk. She's wearing a tank top and dangly earrings, and Midge notices a purple streak in her brown hair that wasn't there on her first day.

Midge wishes she'd played a more active role in the hiring process. Surely they could have found someone more presentable for a forward-facing position in law enforcement.

Spotting Midge just before she steps through the glass doors, Allie straightens and shoves the phone into her pocket.

"Hey, Midge."

"Hey, Allie. All good here?"

"All good. It's been quiet. I guess the bad guys are too hot to commit crimes."

Midge flashes her a smile and moves on to her office. Yeah, *she* might not have had purple streaks in her hair at eighteen, but at least Allie isn't lying to everyone she knows, including the authorities, to cover up the truth about her friend's disappearance.

Caroline wanted the world to think she was dead and extracted a promise from her best friends never to reveal the truth. To this day, Midge, Kelly, and Talia have honored their word.

But Midge wrestles with guilt and always will.

In her office, she wraps up her reports with an eye on the clock. The room is warm. On a day like this, central air can only do so much.

But even this late in the season, the lake, fed by Catskills streams, will be icy. She needs that swim, needs to wash off the sticky, smelly, uncomfortable day.

Five more minutes to go . . .

Two . . .

The desk phone rings.

It's Allie. "Yeah, Midge, I've got a lady on the phone who needs to talk to you. She says it's urgent. Her name is Sarah . . . something."

"Sarah *something*? Allie—"

"I tried to get her last name, but she's, like, hysterical. She wants to report a crime, but she said she won't talk to anyone except Detective Sergeant Imogene Kennedy."

Midge doesn't know anyone named Sarah, and no one in her personal life has called her by her given name in decades.

She tells Allie to put the call through and checks her watch, hoping Sarah will make it snappy.

A voice comes on the line, shrill and loud. “Hello? Hello? Is this Imogene Kennedy?”

Midge winces, holding the phone a few inches away from her ear. “Yes?”

“It’s Sarah Greene! My daughter! She’s disappeared!”

CHAPTER THREE

"Mommy?"

Talia, in the front passenger's seat, turns to six-year-old Caleb, buckled into the back.

He looks so small, despite the booster car seat. He's always been in the bottom height and weight percentiles for his age. He acts young for his age, too, radiating sweet innocence, needing endless reassurance.

His sister, also in the back seat, is the opposite. Hayley is fearless, the kind of kid who went off to kindergarten without a backward glance and was the first in her age group to dive off the board and swim across the deep end at the town pool.

She turned twelve in July, but she looks at least a few years older. Her shorts and cropped tank bare long tanned limbs and a maturing figure. An earbud peeks through strands of thick brunette hair that hang past her shoulders. She appears to be lost in whatever she's listening to, oblivious to her parents and brother.

"What's up, buddy?" Talia asks Caleb.

"How many more minutes now?"

She glances back at the map on the dashboard screen. When they left home in Westchester, the ETA to Mulberry Bay had been just before five o'clock. It's been pushed later every mile they've traveled. As of now, they won't get there till after seven.

She just smiles and says, "It won't be long, sweetie."

"But how many minutes?"

"We're not counting in minutes," Ben says, behind the wheel. "We're counting in *hours*."

"Wait, *what*?" Hayley removes one of her earbuds. "Mom said this place is only, like, two hours from home."

Ben shrugs. "Mom was wrong."

Talia bites her lip to keep from pointing out that she made the trip in under two hours back in June.

That trip is the reason her ordinarily laid-back husband has been in this dark mood all summer.

This trip was intended to bridge the chasm that's been growing between them ever since she confessed the truth about where she'd really been that weekend.

"This *stinks*!" Hayley shouts. "You tricked me!"

"Nobody tricked anybody," Ben says.

"Mom tricked me! She's a liar!"

Ben says nothing on the subject. He doesn't have to. He said it all in June, when she confessed that she hadn't been away on a yoga retreat, as she'd told him.

No, she was in Mulberry Bay, reunited with Midge Kennedy and Kelly Barrow on the twenty-fifth anniversary of their friend Caroline Winterfield's prom-night disappearance.

"I'm *not* a liar, Hayley," Talia says, then clamps her lips between her teeth to keep from saying anything more.

This definitely isn't a conversation she feels like having right now. Or ever.

"Yes, you are, Mom! You said we had to leave tonight because there will be too much traffic tomorrow."

"I'm sure there *will* be too much traffic tomorrow. A lot more than there is today."

"That's hard to imagine," Ben mutters, eyes on the rearview mirror, right turn signal on.

"I was supposed to sleep over at Chloe's tonight because I haven't even seen her all summer because she was at sleepaway camp and then she was on vacation with her family and Mom said I can and then she said I can't!" Hayley gasps a breath and rails on, "It's not fair! I'm not even going to see her until school starts next week!"

"Because *you're* on vacation with *your* family," Ben points out.

"I don't want to be on vacation! I want to sleep over at Chloe's!"

"There will be other sleepovers."

Oh, Ben. Wrong thing to say.

"I don't care about other sleepovers! I care about *this* sleepover! This sleepover is epic!"

Ah, Hayley's word of the summer. Everything—from podcasts to bathing suits to quinoa bowls—can be, according to her, *epic*.

Except for the things that are not. Like her parents, her brother, and family vacations.

"Chloe's mom even said I could stay there all weekend instead of going on this stupid trip, and that's what I want to do, and it isn't fair that I have absolutely zero say!"

Ben turns toward Talia. She attempts to catch his eye and mouth a warning: *Do not engage!*

But he's looking past her, craning to see out her window as he edges the car toward the right lane, saying, "Hayley, you're being completely unreasonable."

Wow. Good job, Ben. That's a perfect thing to say to a twelve-year-old girl at a time like this.

"*Unreasonable?* I am not! How am I being unreasonable? *You're* being unreasonable, and so is Mom! You're the most unreasonable human beings in the world, ever! *Ever!*"

"Because we wanted you to spend a fun weekend with us instead of leaving you at Chloe's for four days?"

"Her mom wants you to leave me there! And so does Chloe!"

"Come on, you don't want to miss out on seeing Mommy's hometown."

Oh yes she does, Talia thinks.

"Yes I do!" Hayley says. "I don't care about some stupid place in the middle of the stupid Catskills!"

"That's not a nice thing to say about Mommy's hometown," Ben says, eyes on the rearview mirror.

"Don't call her *Mommy*! I'm not a baby!"

"Nobody said you're a baby. Dammit!" He slaps the steering wheel. "What the hell is wrong with people? What happened to common courtesy?"

He gestures at the traffic in the right lane. It's moving now, rolling slowly past them as they remain at a complete standstill in the left lane behind a red ribbon of taillights.

"Just wait for a truck," Talia advises. "Truck drivers always let you merge in front of them."

"They don't in my experience."

"They do in mine."

"That's because you're a woman."

"What's *that* supposed to mean?"

"Forget it."

It isn't like him to make comments like that. He's Ben—loving husband, lifelong best friend, father of her children, and the one person who believes in her.

Until lately, anyway.

She's been job hunting ever since she got laid off from her marketing position during a postpandemic corporate downsizing. Yesterday, yet another company with which she'd had multiple interviews informed her—via what felt like a cut-and-pasted email—that they were moving ahead with a different candidate. When she told Ben about it, he just sighed and shook his head.

It feels as though the man who's always encouraging her not to give up has given up on her himself.

"Mommy?" Caleb says.

"Mm-hmm?"

"I have to go to the bathroom."

She looks at her husband. "Ben—"

"Yeah, I heard. What would you like me to do?"

"Can you hold it for a little bit?" Talia asks Caleb. "Just till we can get to a rest stop?"

"How far is it?"

"About three miles. I saw a sign."

Hayley unplugs one earbud. "So that means, like, three hours. I hope you're wearing a Pull-Up, Caleb."

"I don't wear Pull-Ups! Pull-Ups are for little kids!"

"Yeah, well . . ." She shrugs and puts in her earbud again.

"Let's play the alphabet game, Caleb," Talia suggests.

"We already did that."

"Then we'll pick up where we left off. How many things can you spot that start with the letter *c*?"

"We already did *c*."

"Then *d*."

"Um . . . dump truck?" he says as Ben attempts to merge into the right lane in front of one that speeds up to close the gap.

"Dammit," Ben says.

"Dammit starts with *d*," Hayley comments.

Talia shoots her a look. "Are you playing?"

"Nope."

"Daddy? Can you play?" Caleb asks.

"Not right now, buddy. I'm trying to merge."

Ben tries to merge, Caleb names *d* words, Hayley sulks, and Talia wonders if she and Ben are ever going to get past this thing.

"Marriage limbo," her friend Mei-Xing said when they had lunch last week. "That's what they call these little rough patches with couples like you and Ben."

"Couples like me and Ben? What does that mean?"

"You know—couples who are going to stick together no matter what because they love each other and they're good together, aside from whatever caused the problem. As long as the problem isn't an affair. Then, all bets are off."

"No one had an affair!"

"That's what I mean. Ben will get over it."

It: Talia's lie.

He was the one who suggested that she go to a yoga retreat, perhaps feeling a little guilty about his own frequent business travel and golf outings.

She was torn. But Caleb, recently diagnosed with a separation anxiety disorder, was so attached to her that his child psychiatrist had been urging her to spend a night or two away from home.

It wasn't easy to lie to Ben about that trip. To lie to her children. But she did it.

Just as she'd lied all those years ago to the police, to her own mother, and to Caroline's.

At that age, if your friend asks you to do something—makes you promise not to tell—you do it. You promise.

At that age, your friends mean everything to you.

She turns around to look at Hayley.

She's glowering, arms folded over her bare, tanned midriff.

"Hey, Hay?"

It's a thing in their family. Cheerful, fun. *Hey, Hay,* Talia and Ben say to her, and if she's in an agreeable mood, she smiles and answers, *Hey.*

If she's in a bad mood, Talia and Ben sometimes greet each other with a heads-up: *Hayl-storm warning.*

They haven't done that in a while, even though Hayley's good moods are few and far between. This hasn't been the summer for good-natured banter.

Either Hayley doesn't hear her, or she's ignoring Talia.

She waves at her daughter.

Hayley removes one earbud. *"What?"*

"I'm sorry."

"For what?"

"The sleepover. I know it meant a lot to you."

"It did! I haven't seen Chloe in forever. This was the worst summer of my whole entire life."

It may not have been the worst of Talia's—that distinction belongs to the summer of 1999, when Caroline disappeared—but it's right up there.

"I really am sorry. Let's just try to make the best of it, okay?"

Hayley rolls her eyes and replaces the earbud.

Talia turns back to Ben—so familiar, and yet not. He works as an advertising sales executive in Manhattan, the type of man who always looks neat and pulled together.

Even back in their college days, Talia teased him about his preppy style and expensive taste in clothes.

Today, he has a hint of beard stubble, and he's wearing black Wayfarers, a T-shirt, shorts, and sneakers. They're spotless white canvas, and the T-shirt and shorts are Brooks Brothers and neatly pressed, because Ben is Ben, even dressed down.

But there's a stubborn set to his jaw, and she knows it isn't just because of the traffic.

"What kind of person *are* you?" he asked her in June, with tears in his eyes, looking at her as if she were a stranger. "What kind of wife does something like this? Lies to her own husband? What kind of parent lies to their children? How could you?"

"I'm sorry," she said, over and over. "I'm so sorry."

Ben has yet to accept, or even acknowledge, her apology.

He's still trying to get his head around the fact that she kept so much of her past from him.

When they met, they lived in the same residence hall and hung out with the same group. He had a hometown girlfriend, and Talia was focused on the present and the future. They were just friends—well, occasionally friends with benefits—when he noticed the four letters indelibly inked over Talia's heart since 1999.

T-I-C-K.

When he asked about the tattoo, she said it was a reminder that the clock is always ticking, that time can run out before you know it.

It's true.

Tick . . . tick . . .

It's just not the whole truth.

T-I-C-K: Talia, Imogene, Caroline, and Kelly.

Throughout her childhood and high school days, they were an inseparable quartet: Talia, Imogene "Midge" Kennedy, Caroline Winterfield, and Kelly Barrow. The tattoos were a group Christmas gift, intended to seal their friendship before they graduated and left for college.

But that last summer didn't work out the way they'd planned. For Caroline, there would be no graduation. No college.

For Caroline, time was quickly running out the June day when she asked her friends, "Can you keep a secret?"

Talia always assumed that things had worked out for Caroline the way she'd planned. She wanted to believe she'd run away, become a mom, maybe a wife. That she had grown up and was growing older like the rest of them.

Now she knows it's just another lie in the string of them that tethers her to the past, some of which—many of which—were told by her.

Riddled with guilt, haunted by memories, she knows, too, that just because you can keep a secret doesn't mean you should.

CHAPTER FOUR

"She's not picking up her phone or answering texts! Oh, Lord. Oh, please. Please, Sergeant Kennedy, you have to help me!"

"I'm going to help you." Midge props her own phone between her shoulder and ear and reaches for her iPad to access the state's Integrated Justice Portal. "What's your daughter's name?"

"I told you! Sarah! Sarah Greene."

"I'm sorry, I thought *you* were Sarah Greene."

"I am. I'm Sarah, she's Sarah."

"Got it." Midge types it into her report.

A mother and daughter, both named Sarah . . .

Why is that familiar? *Sarah . . . Sarah . . .*

Midge knows her, or them, or maybe just *about* them. A recent connection, something unpleasant, flits at her mind's periphery.

When was it? Where was it?

"How old is Sarah, Mrs. Greene?"

"Sixteen."

Midge thinks of the impetuous Taylor and her weary mother.

The world revolves around her, and the rest of us are just here to serve her.

She asks for Sarah's birth date, height, weight, physical description, and whether there are any other identifying factors.

"What do you mean?" her mother asks.

"Any birthmarks?"

"No."

"Any scars, tattoos, that sort of thing?"

"Tattoos? No!"

"And no scars?"

"Absolutely not."

"What is she wearing? Do you know?"

"Of course I know. It's a short-sleeved, knee-length pink dress."

"Shoes? Jewelry?"

"White ballet flats and a gold cross."

"Anything else? Glasses, a watch, earrings?"

"No."

"When and where did you last see her?"

"Today! At home! She was heading for her Bible study youth group."

"What time was this?" Midge asks.

"Around noon. I mean, it was supposed to start at noon, but that's when she left, because she was late starting her chores."

Chores. Midge types the word, feeling the phone slipping as her sweaty skin slicks its screen. *Chores* makes her think of farmhands, or kids in historical novels.

"And you've tried to reach her? She has a cell phone?"

"Yes. She always answers calls and texts right away."

"Are you able to track her phone?"

"What do you mean?"

"A lot of parents have access to their kids' phone locations."

"We've never needed that. Sarah always tells us where she is, and she lets us know if she's going to be late. This isn't like her!"

"Okay, we have to consider that she might have lost her phone or it was stolen. Maybe that's why you haven't heard from her."

"But where *is* she?"

"Did you check with her friends? Or other family members? Sarah's dad?"

"My husband is in Georgia. Well, almost. He's driving our son back to college. When I got ahold of him, they were somewhere in South Carolina. He told me to call you. He knows this isn't like her."

"Okay, well, how did she get to her meeting? How was she planning to get home? Did she drive?"

"She's *sixteen*! She doesn't even have a driver's permit yet."

"Did she get a ride with a friend?"

"She walked."

"Alone?"

"Yes, alone. It's not far. It's . . . I don't know, half a mile? In broad daylight! Right here in town! What could have happened to her? This is Mulberry Bay, not . . . not . . . some *city*!"

Mulberry Bay. Where nothing bad ever happens.

Right.

Staccato tapping her fingers on the desk, Midge thinks of Caroline Winterfield.

"When were you expecting Sarah, Mrs. Greene?"

"She should have been here by one forty-five. Two o'clock at the latest!"

Barely two hours ago. And she's sixteen. At that age, kids are so easily sidetracked.

"Where does the Bible study group meet?" Midge asks.

"They usually meet at the Hardys' house because they have three teenagers who are all in the group. They live in the red-and-pink Victorian on Center Street, and there's plenty of room for everyone. Do you know them?"

"I know the house. So that's where Sarah was headed?"

"No, the Hardys are away at the retreat, so this week's meeting was changed to the church."

"*Which* church?"

"Congregational Memorial!" Mrs. Greene says, as if there's no other.

There are plenty, their steeples rising from historic white clapboard and fieldstone here in the heart of town.

But Congregational is ostracized to an old industrial neighborhood of warehouses and freight yards. The yellow brick rectangle was built in the seventies without a hint of vintage small-town charm.

It was Caroline's church. Her parents are still members. It has always been the center of the Winterfields' lives—spiritual and social. Caroline met her high school boyfriend Gordy Klatte at the youth group, and—

Light bulb moment.

Sarah . . . Sarah!

"Mrs. Greene, does your daughter date Michael Klatte?"

"She did, until . . ."

"Until . . . ?"

"Until *June*."

The word is pointed.

June. That's when Midge investigated Gordy Klatte's death in what appeared to be an accidental fall.

Even now, she can hear his wife's inconsolable keening and see her pristine white nightgown stained with his blood. She can see his teenage sons, pale and shaken. The younger, Noah, did his best to answer Midge's questions. The older, Michael, leaned on his girlfriend . . .

Sarah.

Sarah Greene.

Sarah's mother, also Sarah, was one of the church ladies who flocked to the house with prayers and casseroles as Midge asked the routine questions that accompany any unattended fatality.

"They broke up? Sarah and Michael?" Midge asks.

"I wouldn't put it that way. Amy and the boys left town as soon as school let out. They've been in Pennsylvania all summer, staying with her parents."

"Your daughter and Michael didn't break up, then? They're just apart for the summer? Are they still in touch?"

"No, they're not. Michael's not coming back. Amy's going to put the house on the market. And finding my daughter has nothing to do with the Klattes. Please, I just need you to help me."

"We're going to find her. Did you call the church? Maybe she got held up there after the meeting, for a project or—"

"I tried calling the office. No one picked up. Reverend Parker left this morning, and he won't be back until Monday."

"He doesn't teach the Bible class?"

"No. It's not a class. There's no teacher. It's a social group, all young people. They meet every Thursday afternoon."

"How about your daughter's friends? Did you check to see if she's with any of them?"

"Most of them are away at the retreat."

"How about their parents? Maybe check with them and see if—"

"It's a family retreat. A lot of people are there."

"Then maybe there was no Bible study today," Midge suggests. "Maybe Sarah didn't realize it had been canceled."

Or maybe she knew and didn't want to tell you, so that she could do something more fun on a beautiful summer afternoon.

"It wasn't canceled, just moved to the church. Shouldn't you be putting out an all-points bulletin, or . . . What is it that you do?"

Midge hesitates, weighing her words. "It's not—"

"An Amber Alert, right? Isn't that it?"

"There are parameters for doing that, Mrs. Greene. It has to go through the New York State Police SVU—that's Special Victims Unit. They have to review the request to confirm reasonable cause that there's been an abduction, or evidence that a child is in imminent danger. We—"

"My daughter is missing! Of course she's in danger! She's not the kind of girl who . . . she's a good girl. You *know* her."

Midge met Sarah only once—at Gordy Klatte's house on the day he died in what appeared to be an accidental fall down a flight of stairs.

"I can put out a BOLO, Mrs. Greene."

"What is that?"

"It means *be on the lookout.* It gets the information to other local law enforcement and other agencies."

"The FBI?"

"At this stage, I don't—"

"Please! This isn't like my Sarah. She's been kidnapped. I just know it."

Midge opts not to voice her disagreement, nor to mention the Occam's razor problem-solving principle. The simplest explanation is usually the most likely. Don't reach for far-fetched, convoluted hypotheses—like kidnapping.

Sarah Greene is sixteen. She probably lied about Bible study group and is instead hanging out with friends, or a boy. Or maybe she went to her group but stopped off in town afterward to return a library book or buy nail polish, or whatever teenage girls buy, and lost track of time. Maybe she's up to something her mother wouldn't approve of. Maybe she's trespassing in someone's backyard pool.

Maybe.

But maybe not.

Midge considers the connection to Gordy Klatte, whose death occurred on the twenty-fifth anniversary of his high school girlfriend Caroline Winterfield's disappearance.

Multiple coincidences often turn out to be evidence. Midge has since become convinced Gordy's death was no accident. His hands showed evidence of a struggle. Presumably, forensic tests will soon confirm his attacker's DNA under his fingernails.

Midge is certain that attacker won't be a stranger. Not to him.

Not to Midge.

Now his son's girlfriend—ex-girlfriend—is missing?

"Where do you live, Mrs. Greene?"

"Twenty-five Valley Avenue."

"Okay, I'm on my way over. You can tell me more in person."

Midge disconnects the call, already on her feet.

CHAPTER FIVE

Kelly Barrow checks her watch—not the Rolex her first ex-husband gave her on their first and last wedding anniversary, but her late father's TAG Heuer Chronograph. It's too big, even with several stainless-steel links removed, and the face doesn't quite match the blue of her eyes as it did his, but she likes to feel close to him. Especially when she's dealing with her mother's failing health.

The neurologist is running late, as usual.

They arrived forty minutes early for a three thirty appointment, and it's past four now. The crowded waiting room is close and stuffy. Her makeup is sweat smudged, and her linen shift is damp and rumpled. She's queasy, thanks to the doxycycline she took on an empty stomach because she didn't have time for breakfast or lunch.

Her mother, seated beside her, is reminiscing about the day she was born. She does that a lot lately, recounting old memories as the recent ones grow more elusive. Kelly is well aware that it's the disease, but sometimes, it wears on her—the constant questioning, the repetitive stories, the light in her mother's eyes flicking on and off like an electrical short.

Every time they come here, Kelly drills the neurologist. He always says there's not much, if anything, that can be done to slow the progression, but she's holding out for a magic bullet.

All around them, other patients and their caregivers flip through magazines, scroll their phones, or are engaged in quiet conversations of their own.

Directly across from Kelly, a pleasant-faced woman about her own age, mid-forties, is accompanied by an elderly man wearing hearing aids, jeans with suspenders, and a blue-and-gold navy veteran hat.

"That dentist had better hurry up," he tells her, holding up his left wrist and tapping his watch with his right forefinger.

"Dad, this isn't the dentist. We're here to see the neurologist. And your appointment isn't for another twenty minutes. I told you we didn't have to leave so early."

"Early? It's almost time for lunch."

"No, Dad, we already had lunch."

"What?" He cups a hand to his ear.

"Never mind. It's not important. It's almost your turn." She goes back to her magazine.

Kelly wishes she could do the same as Beverly's monologue continues. She told the same story in the car, twice. The fifty-mile drive to Albany took twice as long as it should have, and the ride home will likely be even more painstaking, with so many weekenders getting a head start on this last summer getaway.

". . . and we were going to call you Frankie because Daddy wanted to name you after his father and because he really wanted a son," her mother goes on, unfiltered as always these days. "But I was the one who went through forty-seven hours of labor, not Daddy. You were a beautiful blue-eyed princess, so I decided to name you after one. I always loved Princess Grace of Monaco. But Daddy thought Grace sounded like an old lady. Before Princess Grace married Prince Rainier, she was an American actress named Grace Kelly, so you were Kelly. Princess Kelly Barrow of Mulberry Bay. But Princess Grace died on September 14, 1982. That was just, let's see, just four months before your second birthday."

"Mm-hmm," Kelly agrees, lamenting the injustice—Bev's long-term memory, sharp and rife with impractical details as the disease ravages the short term.

There are moments when Kelly believes it would be easier if Beverly were too far gone to remember anything at all. Moments when she asks where her husband is, as if he's at the office or running an errand. At first, Kelly broke the news of his death all over again and comforted her mother as she grieved anew. Now she goes along with the office or the errand because Beverly will soon forget the answer *and* the question.

The woman seated across from them says, "Excuse me, did you say Kelly Barrow? Mulberry Bay?"

"I'm *Beverly* Barrow of Mulberry Bay," Mom informs her, looking pleased at the acknowledgment, or perhaps just that she knows her own name and hometown, which isn't always the case.

The woman holds up the magazine she's been reading. It's the July issue of *Hudson Valley Home*. An attractive blue-eyed blonde beams from the glossy cover, above the caption *Can Kelly Barrow Reverse the Haven Cliff Curse?*

"Is this you?" she asks Kelly.

"That's me."

Though maybe she should say, *That* was *me.*

The woman on the cover is fresh from the salon, chic in Hermès cashmere, flashing a carefree smile.

She was photographed and interviewed for the piece last winter, back when she was still contentedly reconstructing the long-abandoned mansion from its ruins. And yes, when she was still optimistic about reversing the so-called curse that's dogged the woodland property since an 1894 double homicide.

But now?

Yeah, no. Not so much.

Eight months later, she's sweaty and disheveled, her hair pulled back in a basic ponytail with a coated rubber band. She's recovering from a summer of debilitating illness.

At the onset, terrified that a few of her symptoms mimicked her mother's dementia, she submitted her DNA to one of those online genealogical sites that tests for hereditary markers. She was relieved when the doctor diagnosed Lyme disease, and even more so when the DNA results revealed that she hadn't inherited anything more troubling than ties to a couple of unsavory ancestors.

She musters a smile for the woman clutching *Hudson Valley Home* with her old self plastered on the cover, wishing there was a polite way to extract herself from the conversation.

"Wow! I can't believe this. I mean, I'm sitting here flipping pages and there you are in the magazine, and *here* you are in person. What are the odds?"

Kelly points to the low table between them, where an issue of *People* shows Jennifer Lopez on the cover. "I mean . . . I wouldn't expect JLo to walk through the door, but hey, you never know, right?"

The woman returns her smile. "It's amazing what you've done to the house. The article says you've re-created the interior to exactly how it was in the eighteen hundreds?"

"Well, I didn't do it all by myself. My decorator, Linden, is a genius. He used old photographs we found in the historical society archives. It's almost identical to what it looked like when the Winterfields lived there."

"Did the property come with their original furniture too?"

"No, but I've tracked down a lot of it."

The property *did* come with the Winterfields' great-great-granddaughter Caroline's remains, unearthed in June by Kelly's pool excavators.

"Have you always been interested in renovating old houses?"

"Not necessarily."

"Then why this one?"

She seems like a nice person. Kelly, who isn't always, doesn't feel like making small talk with strangers. Especially not in a place like this, when people around them can hear every word they say.

Or not.

The old man nudges his daughter, pointing again at his watch and shouting, "They're late."

"No, Dad, you're *early*. And guess what?" She points at the magazine cover, then at Kelly. "This is her!"

"She's the dentist?"

"No! She's Kelly Barrow. She's renovating the old Winterfield place in Mulberry Bay."

He lights with recognition. "Mulberry Bay! *I'm* from Mulberry Bay. George Hamlin. This is my daughter, Cindi with an *i*." He shakes Kelly's hand, then her mother's.

Beverly turns to Kelly. "Who *are* these people?"

"This is George, Mom. He just said. And this is Cindi with an *i*."

"Do you know the Winterfields?" George asks Kelly.

Now there's a loaded question.

Kelly says, "I know their *house*. Since, you know, I *own* it."

"Which house is that?" Beverly asks her.

"Haven Cliff, Mom."

"Oh yes. The insane asylum."

"That was when I was a boy," George tells her. "Now it's abandoned."

"No, now it's a beautiful home again, see?" Cindi folds back the magazine to show her father, then Beverly.

The first photo is a vintage sepia shot of a pillared granite mansion set on a wooded bluff above Mulberry Lake, with the Catskills rising in the distance. There's a horse and buggy at the hitching post out front, beside an elaborate garden with a splash-blurred marble fountain.

The second image is equally monochromatic. It's of the same house, but framed by bare branches, its twin turrets rising against a milky winter sky and misty mountain peaks. No horse, buggy, or hitching post—just snow blanketing the wide stone terrace and dusting the frozen fountain.

Before-and-after shots, snapped 130 years apart. Images from the in-between years would have shown the same building as a tuberculosis sanatorium in the early nineteen hundreds and then, yes, a so-called "lunatic asylum" through the eighties. After that, the mansion was abandoned to crumbling ruins until Kelly bought it three years ago.

Beverly examines the photos intently, as if she's been asked to identify a suspect in a lineup.

"My grandfather did some of the masonry at Haven Cliff," George comments. "He said that pretentious New York City tycoon built the damned thing right on top of an old burial ground. He didn't care. Just went ahead and did what he felt like doing. And now look."

"Dad—"

"Cindi, you know that's how these people are."

"Pretentious New York City tycoons?" Kelly asks.

"Filthy-rich summer people. They show up and think they can take over. Throw their money around and get whatever they want."

"Dad! Sorry, Kelly. He's not talking about you. You're not, uh . . ."

Oh, hell yes, she *is* filthy rich, thanks to a pair of ex-husbands.

She says, "No, I'm definitely not a summer person. I grew up in Mulberry Bay, just like you, George."

"See that, Dad? Kelly, I think it's great that you never left your hometown."

Kelly sees no reason to correct her or admit that when she was growing up, Mulberry Bay was a bleak, dying town.

"I can't wait to escape this wasteland," she remembers grumbling to anyone who'd listen.

Her friend Caroline was a great listener. "If all the good people leave, it's only going to get worse."

"No one ever called me a good person."

Caroline, who always saw the best in people, said, "Well, you are, deep down inside. And you should stay forever, like me."

"Forever? Why?"

"Because I'm going to make it better. And because it's home."

Oh, Caroline. You never got that chance.

Kelly shoots a glance at the door to the examination area, wishing the nurse would summon her mother.

"I can't believe anyone would buy Haven Cliff after everything that's happened to that family," George says. "Not unless . . . Have you heard about the lost treasure?"

Ah, the treasure. According to legend, a robbery at the Winterfields' New York City mansion was instrumental in their decision to build a summer estate in a remote location. Reportedly, they installed a hidden vault somewhere in the rocky, wooded terrain surrounding Haven Cliff and tucked away their remaining valuables.

Long before Kelly and her friends started partying up there as teenagers, they'd traipsed around the ruins looking for the treasure, as had every other kid who grew up in Mulberry Bay.

Still, she feigns ignorance, in case old George knows something she doesn't. "Wow, there's a lost treasure?"

He nods. "Asa Winterfield didn't trust the locals."

"Maybe because the locals didn't trust him? They can be awfully insular."

"The Winterfields?"

"The locals."

"Yeah, I don't know about that. So Asa built a secret vault somewhere in the woods up there for their jewels, artwork, silver, cash, you name it."

"Gold doubloons? Cryptocurrency?"

His daughter snickers.

A door opens behind the reception desk, and a scrubs-clad man appears with a clipboard. "Beverly? Beverly Farrow?"

"Right here!" Kelly touches her mother's arm, so scrawny beneath the long-sleeved hoodie she insisted on wearing this morning despite the heat wave. "Come on."

She shakes her head, rooted on the brown vinyl sofa. "He said Beverly Farrow. I'm Beverly *Barrow*."

"He means you."

"Farrow? I think I know my own name!" She's indignant.

Maybe it's the disease. Maybe she's just in the mood to be difficult.

With a sigh, Kelly walks over to the nurse and says in a low voice, "My mom's a little confused. Would you mind calling her again, please? And the name is actually *Barrow*."

"So sorry." He peers at the clipboard and nods. "Beverly? Beverly Barrow? We're ready for you now."

Her mother heads for the door like an Academy Award winner sailing to the stage.

Aware that it will be at least another twenty minutes before the doctor comes in, Kelly tells the nurse she'll join them then.

Avoiding eye contact with George and *Cindi-With-An-I*, she exits the suffocating waiting room, and then the building.

So much for fresh air. The outside world is glaring sun and steamy asphalt. She sits on a bench and checks her phone. No new messages on the group thread with Midge and Talia, but Linden has responded to her earlier text asking whether the cleaning service left the house spotless and the catering team is there preparing the evening meal. Yes, and yes.

He's been at Haven Cliff all day, putting the finishing touches on a welcoming space for Talia's little boy, who suffers from separation anxiety and won't want to be far from his parents in a strange house. After consulting with Talia on the details, Kelly directed Linden to transform the largest guest suite's windowed walk-in closet into a cozy bedroom similar to Caleb's own.

Linden sent a few photos of the end result.

You've outdone yourself! Kelly texts back. Can you stick around for dinner?

He responds with a GIF of a bosomy, Botoxed woman—undoubtedly one of the *Real Housewives* stars—lifting a glass above a "Woo-hoo" chyron.

Kelly grins and writes: See you soon!

She's sure the others won't mind having Linden join them. He's witty and interesting and can always be counted on to keep the conversation going. That will relieve a bit of hostess pressure from Kelly, who isn't sure how much Talia's husband knows about her past in Mulberry Bay. Linden, who wasn't a part of it, either, will keep the focus on other topics.

As this long, terrible summer draws to a close, Kelly wishes she could put everything behind her, move on, truly begin to heal.

It's just . . .

For weeks now, she's been going over the facts they've pieced together about Caroline's last days, and the secrets she'd confided in them. They just don't add up. Something is off.

She hasn't mentioned that to Midge, because Midge is a cop. She has to follow the law.

Kelly isn't bound by such restrictions.

Scrolling down on her phone, she sees a text from Toby, the private investigator she hired to do some sniffing around into Caroline's past, and her family's.

Found some new information. Call me when you can talk.

CHAPTER SIX

The address Sarah Greene's mother provided is just beyond the business district's perimeter, so close and yet so far. Crawling along Main Street, Midge realizes she could have walked over from police headquarters and gotten there faster.

If this were an emergency, or a response to a crime, she'd turn on the siren, but . . .

Sixteen years old. Two hours late?

For all she knows, Sarah is among the gaggle of teenage girls clustered in front of the Chic Boutique's plate glass window, admiring the mannequins' fall fashions. Or perhaps she's hanging out in the gazebo with a group of teens who appear to be smoking weed and hiding the joint as Midge's squad car crawls past. Or maybe she's already home and her mother is caught up in being relieved and/or grounding her for being late.

Maybe.

Because she isn't *missing*, missing. She can't be.

Not on a beautiful summer evening.

Not in Mulberry Bay.

Not like Caroline.

At last, Midge turns onto Valley. More lane than avenue, it winds up, away from town, toward distant Catskill ridges kissed by late-day sunshine. Split-levels and raised ranches are set back on sloping lawns.

She parks on the road beside a mailbox marked 25. Its red flag is up, signaling that it holds outgoing envelopes for the carrier to pick up tomorrow.

In nearby Kingston, thieves have been raiding curbside boxes for checks enclosed with bills, altering them to steal the funds. The crimes have been well publicized, but idyllic Mulberry Bay has its guard down.

Midge steps out of the car into hushed, sodden air. Butterflies flutter above a curbside bed of black-eyed Susans and purple coneflowers.

Unseen insects keep up a steady whir as she plods up the steep driveway toward the house. It has tan vinyl siding and brown vinyl shutters, bordered by shrubs and beds of pink and white impatiens. An American flag hangs from a bracket beside the door, lank and motionless. A gray Nissan is parked in front of the closed garage.

Sarah hasn't come home yet. Midge can feel it.

The door flies open before she can ring the bell.

She instantly recognizes the slender blonde on the threshold—not just from glimpsing her around town over the years, but specifically, from the group of women at the Klatte house in the aftermath of Gordy's murder. They all had beauty parlor hair, wore skirts or dress slacks with gold crosses or pearls, and spoke in sweet, restrained, girlish voices.

Now Sarah's flaxen waves are mussed, her sleeveless petal-pink blouse is damp with sweat or tears, and her big blue eyes are red rimmed and mascara smudged.

"Sarah Greene? Detective Sergeant Kennedy with the MBPD." She quickly flashes her badge.

"Yes, I know. Thank you for coming."

"Your daughter isn't home yet?"

"No, she's not . . . no." She presses a fist to her mouth, scanning the yard behind Midge as if the girl might be hiding among the rhododendrons. She's clutching her phone in the other hand.

"Mind if I come in?"

"Please." Sarah opens the door. "Sorry, I'm forgetting my manners."

"You're fine."

Midge steps inside. Bright sun pours through the west-facing windows. As at police headquarters, the air-conditioning isn't set nearly low enough for her taste.

"Would you like something to drink? Lemonade?"

Midge would love nothing more—well, other than an ice-cold beer—but she says, "No, thank you."

"Are you sure? I made a pitcher this morning. It's no trouble."

"I'm sure, but thanks."

"If you change your mind, let me know."

You learn a lot about people when you walk into their home while working a case.

Typically, there's some degree of domestic disarray—maybe a few dishes in the sink, crumbs by the toaster, dust. Nothing out of the ordinary.

Once in a while, though, you encounter hoarded garbage stacked to the ceiling, dozens of cats, thousands of roaches. Or the residents are scrambling to conceal drugs, illegal weapons, stolen merchandise. Sometimes it's far worse—a skittish spouse with a black eye, a wailing toddler clad in nothing but a dirty diaper. Midge has seen it all.

The Greene house offers nothing jarring.

Sarah Greene, though, offering a pitcher of homemade lemonade and remembering her hostess manners at a time like this . . .

Well, that gives Midge a bit of pause. It could be that etiquette is deeply ingrained in this woman. Or it could be a red flag.

Midge's gaze falls on a pair of large, gilt-framed formal photographs on the wall. An earnest young man gazes out from one. In the other, she recognizes a slender blond teenager with a sweet smile. Sarah Greene looks a lot like her mother.

"Are you from Mulberry Bay?" Midge asks.

"No, we grew up in Poughkeepsie."

"We . . . ?"

"My husband and me."

"Oh. Right."

"We moved up here ten years ago, because . . . Well, where we lived, things were changing. It didn't seem safe. We wanted to raise the children in a small town, but . . ." She trails off, looking troubled.

"You chose a good one," Midge assures her.

"I hope so. But I keep thinking about that girl who went missing—the one who used to go to our church. She just walked into the woods and never came out."

Midge sucks in a breath.

Caroline.

"I mean, Elizabethville isn't that far away, you know?"

Not Caroline after all.

Sarah's mother is referring to Junia Stanton, a seventeen-year-old from a neighboring town. She went hiking in April, never to be seen again. The family has plastered the region with posters, and they're offering a hefty reward, but so far there have been few concrete leads.

"She went to your church?" Midge asks.

"Years ago, when she was a baby. But then they moved. I think they joined a congregation in Phoenicia."

"Do Sarah and Junia know each other, then?"

"Not at all. Why?"

"I'm just wondering if there's some connection."

"There isn't! Why would you ask that?"

"It's routine, not—"

"I know, I know, and I'm sorry. I didn't mean to raise my voice. I'm just worried sick about Sarah. She's so trusting. What if . . . I can't even say it."

She doesn't have to. Midge knows how the question concludes.

What if something terrible happened to her?

CHAPTER SEVEN

Slumped in the back seat, Hayley isn't listening to music. But her family thinks she is, and for the most part, it keeps them from talking to her and makes them think she can't hear what they're saying, which is a great way to eavesdrop.

Not that they're talking much now, in the car. They're just listening to their stupid playlist from last summer's Outer Banks vacation.

That's what it's called: *Outer Banks Vacation*.

So original.

When they made it, though, she thought it was epic. They asked her for song contributions, and of course she added Taylor Swift's "Carolina," which they loved. She wasn't even annoyed when they learned all the lyrics and sang along, even Caleb. It actually seemed kind of fun, the four of them on the road together. But that was over a year ago, when she was just a little kid.

Now she's a lot older and wiser, and if this trip had a playlist, she could think of a few other Taylor songs that fit, like "Cruel Summer" and "I Hate It Here." But there's no playlist, and no one's into this trip even though Mom and Dad are trying to act like they are. Like everything's normal.

Nothing's been normal since June, when Mom came home from a weekend yoga retreat that turned out to be a secret visit to her hometown.

Of course, no one told *Hayley* that, but she overheard her parents arguing about it. A lot. Like, all summer.

They don't fight in front of her and Caleb, but she can hear them in their room or down in the kitchen.

She told Chloe about it a few weeks ago, when Chloe got special permission to call Hayley from camp to wish her a happy birthday.

"Are they going to get a divorce?" Chloe asked, and she sounded kind of hopeful. Her parents are in the midst of a divorce.

"No! They're just going through some stuff."

"That's what my parents said when my dad got his secret girlfriend."

For a while last year, Chloe was sure the secret girlfriend was going to turn into her stepmother, but now her dad, T. J., has a new girlfriend who isn't secret at all. He just moved in with her, and Chloe and her mom still live in their house in Westbrook.

"My dad doesn't have a secret girlfriend, Chloe."

"Maybe your mom has a secret boyfriend. Or girlfriend. You never know."

"I do know. She doesn't," Hayley said, feeling a little bit relieved that Chloe only had five minutes of phone privileges at camp.

Still, it was really nice of her to call and say happy birthday.

Chloe had already turned twelve back in May.

Maddie Miller, who's sleeping over at Chloe's house tonight because Hayley can't come, is still only eleven and she will be until almost Halloween.

"Dammit!" Dad shouts in the front seat. "That jackass just sped up so that I couldn't get in!"

He's been trying to merge into the right lane, which is moving, while their lane is not.

Dad waves his hand at a car that speeds up to the one in front of it so that he can't get in. "Another jackass! Look at this! Do you see this, Tal'? Do you see what they're doing?"

Mom opens her mouth like she's going to tell him not to say bad words in front of the kids, but then she closes it.

Hayley rolls her eyes. It's not like she hasn't heard him dropping f-bombs when he and Mom fight about how Mom lied about where she was in June, and how she didn't tell Dad some other stuff that happened before she met him.

One thing Hayley found out is that her grandfather, Oliver, who died when she was four, wasn't Mom's father. Granny Nat married him when Mom was in college. Mom's real father was some random guy Granny Nat never married, and Mom never even knew who he was. She still doesn't, and she told Dad that she doesn't care and doesn't want to know.

Hayley definitely wants to know, because what if he's rich and famous, maybe even a prince? That exact thing happened to the girl in *The Princess Diaries*, which Mom and Granny once let her stay up late to watch because it was their favorite. For an old movie, it was pretty good.

There's a book too. Mom gave Hayley her copy. The spine was broken, and the cover was torn, like she'd read it a million times. Hayley promised she'd read it, but she mostly just likes to read stuff on her phone.

When she told Chloe about Mom's dad being a total stranger, Chloe said she could find out who he is and Mom wouldn't even have to know, because it's all online. "All you have to do is send some spit to this genealogy website, and they tell you everyone you're related to."

"How would I get my mom's spit without her knowing?"

"You send your own spit! You're related to him too! You just need to pretend you're an adult, because otherwise the company won't let you do it."

"How do you even know all this?"

"So many people are doing it."

"Like who?"

"Like my counselor—her mom made her do it to see if her dad cheated on her."

"How would it tell her that?"

"You know . . . if he'd fathered other kids without them knowing. Like, if she had half siblings out there."

"Well, I'm just looking for my grandfather."

"Right. So you should totally do the DNA thing."

"I totally will."

The car swerves as Dad starts to pull into the right lane in front of an SUV.

It almost slams right into them. The driver blasts her horn and gives them the finger.

Dad gives it back, along with a bad word Hayley can hear loud and clear through her headphones.

Ordinarily Mom would have something to say about that, but she folds her mouth so that her lips are inside, between her teeth, like she's making sure she doesn't slip.

Hayley goes back to the article she's reading on her phone. It's about Caroline Winterfield, Mom's friend who disappeared on prom night in 1999. She was last seen at Haven Cliff, the creepy old house where they're spending the weekend. Mom made it sound like a beautiful fancy mansion when she told Dad, Hayley, and Caleb about it.

She didn't mention that it's haunted and cursed. Hayley found that out on her own, by googling, along with other interesting facts. Haven Cliff's original owners, Asa and Edith Winterfield, built the house on an ancient burial ground. They were super rich, and they supposedly hid treasure somewhere on the property back in the eighteen hundreds. A lot of people have looked for it over the years, but no one has ever found it.

Asa and Edith were killed in the house by an axe murderer in 1894, and it's been haunted ever since. Maybe not just by them, because the mansion turned into a hospital and an insane asylum before it was abandoned, so bad things happened to a lot of people there over the years.

Especially their great-granddaughter, Caroline Winterfield. There's a picture of her in an article headlined "Haven Cliff Curse

Strikes Again." She vanished from Haven Cliff during a prom night party in 1999.

She was Mom's friend.

Hayley was eavesdropping when Mom told Dad about it, but she didn't give him many details.

Like, she didn't say whether she was there the night Caroline went missing. According to the article, most of the senior class was at the party, and a lot of kids were swimming in the lake.

And Mom told Dad that Caroline drowned, but it turns out, that's just what everyone thinks. Her body was never found.

Hayley goes through all the photos she can find online, enlarging every group shot of search parties and vigils, looking for her mom's face. She isn't in any of them, but that doesn't mean she wasn't there. She told Dad that Caroline was one of her best friends.

If Chloe ever went missing, Hayley would do everything in her power to find her. Like, she'd go on TV and have news conferences and talk to podcasters, and she'd even call the president if she had to.

Maybe people didn't do stuff like that back then.

When Hayley gets to Haven Cliff, she'll look for some clues. And for the treasure. And of course, for her grandfather.

It's a lot more interesting than hanging around with her family, or with a bunch of boring old people her mother used to know.

The car swerves, and Dad shouts, "Yes!" He waves at the driver of the eighteen-wheeler that let them into the right lane at last.

It's slow going, but at least they're moving forward again.

CHAPTER EIGHT

Midge discovers there's something jarring about the Greene house after all. Just not in a hoarder-drugs-roaches-or-worse way.

She takes in the sprigged wallpaper, intricately patterned rugs, doily-topped tables, fringed lampshades, lace curtains, all of it in pink and white. It's not what she'd expect to find in a boxy, earth-toned raised ranch.

Seeing Sarah Greene's expectant expression, she says, "Nice room."

"Thank you. I love pretty, feminine things, don't you?"

Midge most certainly does not, but she nods, noting that this woman *is* a pretty, feminine thing—almost like a character in an old movie. *Pollyanna*? *The Stepford Wives*?

The air smells of bleach, and of flowers—though not fresh-cut ones. Looking for the source, Midge spies a clump of pink potpourri in a cut-glass bowl, something she hasn't seen since the obligatory 1990s visits to her father's aunt in a gingerbread-trimmed house built a century before that.

She hasn't thought about Great-Aunt Mairéad's parlor in years—the perfumy smell, the bric-a-brac on every surface. She and her siblings were frequently reprimanded for roughhousing, though they were merely jostling to reach the butterscotch disks Mairéad kept in a biscuit jar *her* maiden aunt had brought from County Waterford. Yes, the hard candies were gummy with age, with sticky yellow-orange cellophane wrappers, but a treat is a treat on a boring Sunday afternoon when you'd rather be outside playing sports.

Sarah Greene doesn't remind her of Mairéad, though. She isn't a prim old biddy with a fierce independent streak. Midge's father always said his aunt had never married because she didn't want to take care of a man—or worse, have people thinking she needed a man to take care of her.

This woman is giving the opposite impression.

For Midge, she's reminiscent of Caroline Winterfield's mother, who had the same demure demeanor, the same breathy, high-pitched inflection in her voice. That last year of high school, even Caroline herself had taken on that strange, delicate way of speaking.

Midge hadn't really noticed until Kelly brought it up to her and Talia one day.

"It's like she's going backward," she said. "Like she's trying to sound like an *itty-bitty* girl instead of a grown-ass woman."

"What do you mean?" Talia asked.

"Come on, you can't miss it. Lately, pretty much everything she says is all soft and syrupy. You've heard it, haven't you, Midge?"

"Maybe when Gordy's around, but . . ."

"Gordy's *always* around."

That was another frequent complaint of Kelly's, although even dreamy, romantic Talia agreed that Caroline was seeing way too much of Gordy, and not nearly enough of her friends.

Back in June, when Midge met Gordy's family at the house after his death, she noted the striking resemblance between his teenage boys and their father at that age. She also noted the dynamic between the older son, Michael Klatte, and his girlfriend Sarah Greene—the way she hovered by his side and seemed to defer to him. It was a brief encounter and under difficult circumstances, yet the young couple reminded Midge of Gordy and Caroline.

In retrospect, the comparison brings an uneasy twinge.

If Caroline hadn't vanished—if she'd settled in Mulberry Bay and married Gordy—is this what she'd be like now? Would she be living in a claustrophobic pink house, referring to herself as *we*, as if her identity is tied to the marital unit?

"I really appreciate your coming right over, Sergeant Kennedy," the woman says. "Or should I call you Chief Kennedy?"

"Pretty much everyone in town calls me Midge, so feel free."

"Midge—that's a nice nickname for Imogene."

"Yes, I got it back in elementary school, from . . . a friend."

From Caroline, who'd bestowed K. K. on Kelly and Tally on Talia.

"You can call me Sadie, if you like."

"Is that your childhood nickname?"

"No, my husband chose it for me when I was pregnant with Sarah. We knew she'd be a girl, and it made things easier, since there are two of us."

"I can see why. It would be confusing, having two Sarahs in the house. Even with the nicknames."

She shrugs. "We're used to it. My husband and son are both Andrew, but we call our son Drew. Naming firstborns after the parents is tradition in a lot of families."

Including Midge's own. Imogene was her maternal grandmother's name, handed down to Midge's mother, who goes by Gena, and then to Midge. And her oldest brother is Robert, after their dad, but they all call him Robbie—much to his middle-aged consternation.

"Please, sit down."

Midge eyes a velvet sofa and bentwood rocker, feeling like a gangly klutz about to shatter some heirloom. She opts instead for a carved wooden chair. It creaks beneath her weight as she settles into it. She winces, reminded of the time her brothers dared her to straddle one of Great-Aunt Mairéad's antique dining chairs backward and it splintered and collapsed beneath her.

Sarah's mother sits across from Midge on the sofa, smoothing her skirt and crossing her legs at the ankles. She's wearing white pumps.

"After I talked to you, I notified other agencies and put out a BOLO," Midge says.

She also has someone checking into the Greenes' background—protocol—though she suspects they're not going to find anything.

She's growing more certain by the moment that this woman—Sadie, a name chosen for her by her husband—isn't orchestrating an elaborate cover-up.

No, she's simply a docile and ladylike throwback to another era, like Caroline Winterfield's mom.

"Thank you. And I got ahold of Ginny Livingston. Her daughter Rebecca is in the Bible study group too. They didn't go on the retreat because Ted—he's Ginny's husband—is recovering from knee surgery."

Midge nods, taking notes. She knew Ginny years ago as Virginia Shade, and Ted as Teddy Livingston. They were younger than Midge, casual friends of Caroline and Gordy's from church.

"Rebecca saw Sarah, then? At the meeting?"

"No. Ginny said when they got to the church, there was a sign on the door saying it was canceled."

"So it *was* canceled!"

"Yes. Last-minute cancellation, because the air-conditioning isn't working. Ginny said no one else was around. She's always punctual—well, early. They were probably the first ones to arrive."

"And Sarah was running late, you mentioned?"

"Yes, because she was dawdling on her outdoor chores. I told her she should have done them earlier, before the sun was so hot, but she can be a little . . ."

"Stubborn?" Midge suggests.

"No, not stubborn. She's . . ."

"Difficult?"

"No." Her tone is firm. "Sarah's a good girl."

"I'm sure she is. But at her age, I'm sure there are moments when you just . . ."

I swear I'm going to strangle her, she remembers Taylor's mother saying.

Sarah's mother shakes her head. "She's a good girl. But now that Drew's gone back to school, she has his chores too. It takes longer."

"What are the chores?"

"Inside? The usual cleaning."

"And outside?"

"Weeding and watering the garden, picking the fruits and vegetables, hosing down the patio and driveway. Oh, and the trash is picked up on Thursday mornings, so the cans need to be scrubbed and disinfected."

Midge nods, remembering the truck in the parking lot back at headquarters, the overpowering stench of rotting garbage in the heat.

"Finally, I just told Sarah to get going to study group and finish later," her mother goes on. "But I'm sure Ginny and Rebecca were long gone by the time she got there."

"*If* she—"

Midge catches herself before she can complete the sentence.

If she got there.

"—was walking," she says instead. "If Sarah was walking . . . maybe they passed her. Did they say they did?"

Yeah, no. She just told you two seconds ago that they didn't see her.

Midge sees the irritation in the woman's eyes, sees her jaw tighten. Someone else, in this situation, emotional and stressed out, might have snapped at her, with good reason.

Midge is off her game. It's the heat, weariness, feeling out of place in the fusty room. It's the connection, however tenuous, between the Greenes and Gordy's death and Caroline.

"Ginny and Rebecca wouldn't have seen Sarah walking unless she was right by the church," Sadie tells her. "They live out on 28, so they would have come and gone from the opposite direction."

"Right. Did you try to reach anyone else who might have been there?"

"I don't know how many others in the group were planning to attend today. Like I said, quite a few families are away at the retreat with Reverend P."

Midge blinks, hearing Caroline's voice echo back over the years, making introductions to the stranger at her birthday party. "This is our new minister, the famous Reverend B.!"

She can still picture Reverend Bauer, handsome but *old*, the girls thought back then. Yeah, probably about as old—*young*—as Midge is now. He was married, with a bunch of kids from her own age on down. He resides in her memory as one of those well-meaning but annoying people who tries too hard to seem cool and relate to teenagers, though she could see why Caroline spoke so highly of him. A lot of adults in her friend's world—particularly men, like Caroline's father, and the former pastor, stodgy Reverend Statham—had a tendency to talk down to women. Especially young women.

Reverend B. was different—charismatic, with an engaging smile and easy conversational skills that made you feel seen, heard, relevant.

"Reverend B. is back?" she asks, pretty sure that he left Congregational a year or so after Caroline disappeared.

"No, I said Reverend *P.*," Sadie says. "Reverend Parker."

Right. Reverend Parker. She met him at Gordy's house. He showed up shortly after Midge got to the scene and had been visibly moved at the sight of Gordy's broken body lying at the foot of the stairs.

"Where is this retreat?" she asks.

"Way up north, somewhere in the Adirondacks. It sounds heavenly—no electricity, no indoor plumbing, no roads in or out. You have to hike there."

"Heavenly for some," Midge agrees, "but it's probably hellish for others."

Judging by the woman's expression, she might as well have made a satanic pledge.

"The point is to get away from all distractions and focus on prayer and spiritual enlightenment! We've gone in the past. It's truly a wonderful experience. Sarah especially enjoyed it. But like I said, my husband had to get Drew back to college."

"And you wouldn't have gone without him? You and Sarah?"

"Without Andrew? Of course not! It's a family retreat."

"So Sarah was disappointed about that?"

"What do you mean?"

"If she was disappointed that she couldn't go on the retreat this year, is there any chance that she . . ." Seeing the woman's narrowed eyes, Midge pauses.

"That she what?"

Taking a different approach, Midge says, "You and Sarah didn't have an argument, did you? Anything that would make her want to . . ."

"Want to what?"

"Run away?"

"She'd never do anything like that! She's a good girl!"

"No, I know, but what if she . . . Would she have gone on the retreat without you?"

"I keep telling you, it's a *family* retreat."

"Right. Maybe she went somewhere else, then, when she found out class was canceled?"

"Without telling me?"

"It's so hot out. She could have stopped off in town on her way home to get a bottle of water, or ice cream."

At that, something sparks in Sadie's eyes. "She was just talking about ice cream this morning. She said Get the Scoop has a special—two-for-one cones. She thought maybe we could go over later, you know, after she finished her outdoor chores, or as an after-supper treat, but . . ."

"But?"

"But it would be wasteful. I have ice cream right here in the freezer."

"Did that upset her?"

"She understands that we have to be careful with money, with her brother in college. My husband's paycheck will only go so far."

"And you don't work, yourself?" As soon as the question is out of her mouth, Midge realizes her mistake.

"Yes, I *work*! I'm a wife and mother, and I have my hands full running this household!"

"I'm sure you do. Can you access Sarah's phone log online?"

"What do you mean?"

"Sometimes if you go to the carrier's website, you can check a phone number for incoming and outgoing calls and messages."

"I wouldn't know how to do that."

"If you pay your carrier bills online, you can usually just log in and see that information."

"My husband pays all the bills. He mails checks. He says the internet isn't private and you should never send money that way, because—"

She breaks off as her cell phone rings.

"That's him now," she tells Midge before answering with a harried, "Hello? Andrew?"

The call isn't on speaker, but his voice is loud and clear. "Is she home yet?"

"Not yet. The police chief is here with me now."

"Put him on."

"It's a woman. Imogene Kennedy. Remember, I met her at the Klattes' after Gordon died. She knows Sarah, so I thought it would be best to talk to her instead of . . . someone else."

Instead of a man.

"Fine. Put her on."

Sadie turns to Midge. "He'd like to talk to you."

"Sure." She accepts the phone. "Mr. Greene?"

"Please, ma'am, can you find my daughter?" His voice cracks, and he pauses to clear his throat. "It's, uh . . . it's going to be getting dark soon, and . . . she needs to be home before dark, okay? Young ladies shouldn't be out alone at night. I always tell her that. Because nothing good happens after dark. You must know that, too, doing what you do. I'm sure you've seen a lot."

Yes.

Twenty-five years ago, she saw her friend Caroline walk into the midnight woods at Haven Cliff, carrying a pink Walkman.

This summer, she saw the same pink Walkman lying in the dirt, alongside a skeleton.

Officially, the remains have yet to be identified. The medical examiner is still awaiting forensic test results.

But Midge knows. Deep down, in her heart, she knows it's Caroline. That something unspeakable happened to her that night.

"I'll do everything I can," she promises Sarah Greene's father, fighting the impulse to add, *I'm sure she's fine.*

She isn't sure at all, and he's right.

Nothing good happens after dark.

CHAPTER NINE

Talia is behind the wheel when the familiar wooden signboard comes into view at last.

WELCOME TO MULBERRY BAY

It's painted in shades of purple to reflect the distant Catskill peaks and the abundant berries that ripen each spring, and blues as deep as the mountain lake looming ahead beside a cluster of rooftops and steeples.

"Look, everyone! We're here!"

No reaction from her family.

A glance in the rearview mirror reveals that Hayley is wearing earbuds and focused on her phone. Caleb is asleep, resting his tear-stained face against the open window.

He had an accident earlier, before they made it to the bathroom, so all the windows are down despite the high temperature. Poor Caleb was mortified, especially when Hayley reacted as if she'd been sprayed by a rabid skunk.

"For the love of God, calm down! It's just pee!" Ben shouted at her as he pulled onto the shoulder so that Talia could comfort their sobbing son.

At the rest stop, she found shorts for him to change into while Hayley sulked in the car and Ben bought potato chips and chocolate bars for everyone. He asked Talia to drive the rest of the way so he could answer some emails.

Now he's in the passenger's seat with his laptop open, hands poised on the keyboard.

She'd put on a playlist she'd made for last year's road trip to the Outer Banks. It's filled with upbeat summer songs, reminding her of better days that weren't so long ago. Maybe it will remind Ben, as well . . . if he ever stops working and starts listening.

"Hey, Ben? We're in Mulberry Bay. See the sign?"

He glances up only briefly, distracted. "Okay. I'll wrap this up."

When she first revisited her hometown back in June, Talia was struck by how much has changed around here. Particularly this landscape at the edge of town, decidedly rural when she was growing up.

On the radio, Ed Sheeran is singing about old country lanes and going home to the friends who raised you.

Talia remembers the four of them together, riding their bikes out here when it was a road lined with fields of wildflowers and scattered houses.

She and Caroline were always in the middle of the pack, keeping pace side by side so they could chat. Midge, of course, was in the lead, standing as her muscular legs pedaled hard, urging the others to keep up. Kelly was perennially way behind and complaining about everything—too hot, too cold, too thirsty, too tired.

She stops at an intersection where a massive modern gas station/convenience store gives no hint to the rickety wooden garage that once stood on the site. There were only two pumps, both full service, manned by a grumpy attendant whose name slips her mind, but she can see his tobacco-stained front teeth, the way one slightly crossed over the other. She can see the soda vending machine that was perpetually out of order, or if it was functioning, was out of everything except Crystal Pepsi.

She hasn't thought of that in years.

Or the creek in the woods way back behind that old gas station, with cold water and slippery flat rocks and tadpoles that swam around your bare feet.

Or the big meadow with wildflowers. They'd pick bouquets for their moms. Well, everyone except Caroline, because her mother thought she was at the library or doing some other acceptable activity.

The Winterfields had strict rules about where and when and with whom she could ride her bike. Rules about everything, even visiting Talia, who'd lived right next door.

The car behind them beeps. The light has turned green. Talia drives on, pointing at a fenced modern sports complex where a girls' soccer team is practicing. "That used to be a softball field. My friend Midge played there. No lights, no bleachers, no locker rooms."

Ben glances up from his laptop. "Well, it's come a long way. Midge is the one we're staying with, right?"

"No, that's Kelly. Midge is the cop. Well, sergeant detective. Or is it detective sergeant? Actually, right now she's the chief, just like her dad."

"What about yours?"

"My what?"

"Your dad?"

Her hands grip the steering wheel. "What do you mean? You know I didn't have a dad. Just my mom."

"No, I know. But being back here . . . does it make you wonder about him? Who he is, if he's still around here?"

"Not really."

How easily she slips back to lying to Ben. But now isn't the time to admit that she has been wondering about her birth father, not just because she finally ventured back here after all these years, but because . . .

What kind of person are *you*? Ben asked. *What kind of parent lies to their children?*

Maybe she gets it from her father. For all she knows, he's made a mess of his life too.

Then again, what if he hasn't? What if he grew up to be a wonderful person? What if he regrets not being there for Natalie, for his daughter? What if he's been searching for her?

"I thought you never wanted to come back here or even talk about the past because of him," Ben says.

"Really? I didn't realize you even thought about that."

"Of course. Your mom used to invite us, remember?"

She nods.

It was the topic of her final conversation with her mother on a muggy July morning two years ago. They stood on the train platform beneath an overcast sky, Natalie's enormous rolling suitcase between them, the northbound train rumbling near, blasting its horn.

"I really would love to have you up to visit over Labor Day," her mother said. "With the kids, and Ben. Don't you think it's time?"

Talia did not. Back then, she was convinced it would never be time.

Back then, she was also convinced that she and her mother had lots more time together. That Natalie would live to a ripe old age.

"Promise you'll at least consider it, Talia. They've never been to Mulberry Bay. The lake is warm and beautiful then."

"The lake is never warm, Mommy!"

Looking back, she has regrets. Had she known what was coming, she'd have responded differently. She'd have promised to visit on Labor Day, with her family.

Now it's happening, but Mommy isn't here.

Maybe they shouldn't be either.

Maybe introducing Ben and the kids to her hometown, to Midge and Kelly, to Haven Cliff . . .

What if it doesn't resolve anything? What if it only serves to amplify the fact that she kept so much of her past from them?

But she did it because she was trying to protect her family.

Come on! You were trying to protect Caroline. And yourself.

Maybe not in that order.

Talia can add that guilt to the quarter century's worth she's been dragging around ever since Caroline, then seventeen, asked, "Can you keep a secret?"

CHAPTER TEN

After leaving the Greene home, Midge stops at her own, a three-bedroom cape where she and her brothers and sisters grew up. She bought it from her parents a decade ago, when they retired to Myrtle Beach, but they continue to spend summers here with her.

Ordinarily, they'd head south right after Labor Day, but her father had hip replacement surgery a few weeks ago, and they'll be here through at least October.

Their car isn't in the driveway when Midge parks and heads for the house. Her mother is out, but her father is definitely here. She can hear screeching tires and wailing sirens blasting from the television through the closed windows.

Bobby Kennedy—not *that* Bobby Kennedy—was Mulberry Bay's police chief for decades before Walter assumed the position. Now he enjoys watching old cop shows and reading crime fiction.

"I've got to keep my mind sharp," he says, often. "And you know what? I always figure out whodunit."

Midge finds him in the living room, snoring in front of a televised car chase. He's in the recliner, leaning all the way back, with her tabby cat, Charles, curled up alongside his legs.

"Dad?"

Charles opens his green eyes, looks at her, and yawns before closing them again.

Her father doesn't stir. He suddenly seems like an old man, wearing a robe and slippers, with a walker alongside the recliner, and what's left of his hair gone from ginger to gray.

"Dad!" She grabs the remote and mutes the volume. That does the trick.

He starts, looks around, and grins. "Hey, kiddo."

Ah, perhaps not such an old man after all, she thinks, noting the sweat-beaded beer bottle on the table beside him as she pats his still-muscular arm. "Hi, Dad. Feeling okay?"

"Feeling great for an old coot."

"Good. Where's Mom?"

"Picking up Chinese food for dinner. She should be back soon. She's getting that soup you like. The hot and sour kind, is it?"

"It is, but soup? In this weather?"

"Is it warm out?"

She laughs, shaking her head. "This is one day you can be glad you're laid up inside, Dad."

"You don't have to have soup. There will be plenty of other stuff."

"Thanks, but I can't stick around to eat. I've got dinner plans later, and I'm on a case."

"Yeah? What's going on?" He sits up straighter with an intrigued expression and a wince.

Charles awakens and jumps off the chair, coming to rub against Midge's legs. She picks him up and strokes his soft fur as she tells her father about Sarah Greene. She's brief but includes the connection to the Klatte family. He knows she's investigating Gordy's death as a homicide, but not the details.

"Wait, Midge, you think *that* has something to do with *this*?"

"I don't think that at all. It's just, I met this girl at the Klattes' in June. She was very sweet, but even the sweetest teenagers can run into trouble. They aren't where they say they are, they don't come home when they're supposed to, they don't answer their phones when their mothers call . . ."

"I raised five kids," he says. "You don't have to tell me that."

"Right. Though I don't think anyone would have called any of us Kennedy kids 'sweet.'"

He grins. "Good point."

Charles squirms in her arms, and she sets him on the floor, telling her father, "I'm going to go over to the church. Maybe she's still there."

"At church? Doing what?"

"Praying? Hanging around on the steps smoking weed? Who knows. I'll see what I can find out." She hesitates. "Hey, do you remember that girl who disappeared from Elizabethville last spring?"

"Junia Stanton?"

"Wow, Dad. Pretty sharp memory for an old coot."

"It's only on the tip of my tongue because Annie stopped by to see me this morning."

Annie . . .

Ah, Ann Webster, a close friend of her father's, is a police detective in Elizabethville.

"You discussed the Stanton case?" Midge asks.

"We did. Ann's got new information that's making her lean more toward runaway. According to Junia's best friend, she recently found out that she was adopted as a baby."

"And the Stantons kept it from her?"

"It seems they kept it from everyone. They never even mentioned it when she went missing."

"It didn't turn up in the background check?"

"If it was a private adoption, the records are sealed. But they didn't volunteer the information, and they didn't tell the investigators that they were having trouble with Junia before she disappeared. They claim everything was fine."

"And it wasn't?"

"Not according to Junia's friend. She claims there was a lot of friction in the household because Junia wanted to find her birth parents and the Stantons were against it. She says Junia had gone behind their backs and was looking for them anyway."

"Are the Stantons under suspicion?"

"No. Ann says they checked out okay. No domestic incidents, nothing like that. It's just strange that when Junia disappeared, the parents didn't mention any of this."

"The discord or the adoption?"

"Both."

"Well, a lot of people feel that it's best to keep messy household incidents to themselves, even when it might help in an investigation."

He nods. "One of the most frustrating aspects of the job. Anyway, Junia's friend says she was planning to lie to them about going on a hike that day, and that she was supposed to be going to meet someone."

"Her birth parent?"

"Or maybe just someone who had a lead. The friend didn't know the details. And Junia had sworn her to secrecy, so she kept what she knew to herself for four months, even though her friend was missing."

At that, Midge's breath sticks in her throat.

She clears it and asks, "Does the friend—Junia's friend—does she have any idea where she might be?"

"She says she doesn't, but who knows?"

I know, Midge thinks.

She knows because she did virtually the same thing for Caroline. She lied to her father, to the investigators, to the Winterfields, to everyone who cared about her. She went through the motions of participating in the search efforts, of mourning when Caroline was presumed to have drowned during a midnight swim.

She, Kelly, and Talia knew the truth—maybe not about *where* Caroline was going, but why.

They'd vowed to Caroline and each other that they'd never share her secret.

In return, Caroline promised to meet them back at Haven Cliff exactly one year after her disappearance.

It was wrong. So wrong. All of it.

But at that age, you do what you have to do to protect your friends.

Maybe you do the same at this age.

Midge continues to hold the secret. Not just for Caroline's sake, but for Kelly's and Talia's.

Her father goes on, "The thing is, Junia turned eighteen a few months ago. She's a legal adult. There's not much anyone—including her parents—can do if she's chosen to live somewhere else."

Midge shakes her head, thinking of the girl, her parents . . . her best friend. Exactly what Junia shared with her—that she was in touch with a birth parent, or that she was planning to run away—might never come to light.

"I'd better get going, Dad."

"Sure you don't want to stick around and eat?"

"No. I need to get over to Congregational Memorial, and then I'm going to Kelly's, so please don't wait up."

"I won't."

"Yes, you will."

"Yes, I will," he agrees. "Old habits die hard. Isn't Congregational the same church your friend Caroline Winterfield belonged to?"

"It is. And Junia Stanton's parents belonged, too, years ago." Seeing his raised eyebrow, she adds, "It's hardly a staggering coincidence. A lot of people go to that church. Junia Stanton hasn't been there since she was a baby. And you just said yourself that she's presumed to be a runaway."

"Let's hope that's the case. Because if not—if something happened to the Stanton girl—then we're talking similar victimology. Congregational aside, they're teenage girls in the same geographical area."

"Victimology means that there's a victim. And I'm going to bet that Sarah's heading home right now."

"Well, I'm going to pray that you're right and that she turns up soon."

"She will," Midge says, hoping her words sound more confident to him than they do to her own ears.

CHAPTER ELEVEN

Beverly Barrow still lives in Kelly's childhood home, a three-story brick Colonial in Pine Ridge, which until recently was Mulberry Bay's only private development of luxury homes. Now there's a new gated community of McMansions on the opposite side of town, and several others in various stages of planning and construction.

"Mrs. Verga?" Kelly calls, ushering Beverly into the formal entry hall.

The housekeeper appears, wiping her hands on a dish towel. Stout with a gray-streaked bun and flinty eyes, she greets Kelly with a disdainful expression before turning to Beverly with a smile.

"How was your appointment?"

"Appointment?"

Kelly answers for her mother. "It went well. We're going to try a new medication. It will be ready at CVS tomorrow morning. I can arrange for delivery, unless you'd prefer to pick it up before you come?"

"Delivery would be best," Mrs. Verga says, even though she drives right past CVS on her way over every morning. "There are too many people around town right now."

"Well, at least that's good for the local economy, right? Listen, I need you to stay until Mom's overnight aide gets here. Please tell her I'll call later to check in. Thanks! See you tomorrow, Mom."

She presses a quick kiss to her mother's cheek and is out the door without giving the housekeeper an opportunity to protest.

Mrs. Verga will do anything for Beverly, but she was never a fan of Kelly, whom she considered a spoiled daddy's girl from day one. Their frosty relationship became downright frigid after Kelly failed out of Dartmouth freshman year, then ran off to marry the ne'er-do-well scion of a wealthy New York family.

Never mind that it all unfolded amid her friend Caroline's disappearance and her estrangement from Midge and Talia. Or that she'd never wanted to attend her parents' Ivy League alma mater or law school—their goals for their only daughter.

That Kelly did eventually go back to college and earn her law degree meant nothing to Mrs. Verga, because her perceived neglect of her parents far overshadowed her achievements. She expected Kelly to drop her own life and move back to Mulberry Bay after her father's unexpected death in 2010, even though her mother was in excellent health at that time, still her competent, active self. Kelly was a practicing attorney at a large San Francisco law firm, married to—well, about to divorce—her second husband. A wildly wealthy Silicon Valley tech genius, he didn't just leave her for another woman—he left her set for life.

Now she can afford just about anything her heart desires.

Like Haven Cliff.

Like private investigators.

Toby's latest discovery weighs on her mind as she races home on back roads to skirt around the traffic in town, doing her best to keep the speedometer within fifteen miles per hour of the limit and keeping an eye out for cops.

Midge scolded her the last time she got pulled over in town, even though the nice patrol officer let her off the hook because she dropped Midge's name. Even after all these years, Midge sometimes still perceives Kelly as the scofflaw she once was. And yes, Kelly sometimes resents Midge for always doing the right thing and making it look easy.

Almost always.

What they'd done that summer, with Caroline . . .

That had been a lot harder on Midge than it was on Kelly and Talia. Her father was the chief of police, and she already knew law enforcement would be her own career path. Kelly and Talia convinced her that it didn't mean she should betray Caroline's trust.

All these years, Kelly had believed Caroline really was out there someplace in the world, living her life on her own terms. That she would come home someday to Mulberry Bay for good, just as Kelly had.

Until those bones turned up in June, Kelly had expected to welcome her old friend over the threshold of her ancestral estate, restored to its Gilded Age glory.

She'd hand her the keys and say, "It's for you, Caroline. You're the reason I bought Haven Cliff. It's all yours. A gift from me."

Instead, every day since June, Kelly confronts the gaping hole in the ground where her friend was buried all these years, right under her nose.

Now it turns out there might be far more to the tragedy than anyone, even Midge and Talia, would ever imagine.

There's a chance that Toby's latest bombshell has nothing to do with Caroline, that it's meaningless.

But if it isn't . . .

Midge and Talia need to know, and Kelly's going to tell them. Tonight.

CHAPTER TWELVE

Back in the car, Midge learns that, as expected, there's nothing in the Greene family's background to suggest there's more to Sarah's story than her mother has revealed to Midge. Without so much as a parking ticket among them, both parents and her brother have sterling reputations. So does Sarah herself. Honor roll, church choir, volunteers once a week reading aloud to sight-impaired nursing home residents . . .

She's definitely a good girl. On paper, anyway.

But that's exactly what people would have thought about Mary Beth Winterfield back in the day. The third Winterfield sister was the family's spirited rebel, but she didn't get into significant trouble as a young teenager. That came later—the significant trouble, like robbery and drugs. But the worst was yet to come.

Even now, the mere thought of her makes Midge's stomach churn.

She drives along Shore Street, keeping an eye out for Sarah. This would be the most direct route between her house and church, and it's a main artery in Mulberry Bay, parallel to Main Street, along the water. It can be a little desolate, depending on the season and time of day. But right now, on the cusp of a holiday weekend, the area is full of people.

If Sarah walked this way to and from Congregational, someone would have seen her.

At the waterfront park, families are setting up coolers and barbecue supplies in the timber-and-stone pavilions. Charcoal grills waft fragrant smoke that permeates the car's closed windows. Ribs, steaks . . . is that sausage and peppers?

Midge's stomach growls. She wonders what Kelly is planning for dinner. She texted earlier saying she's still at a doctor's appointment with her mother, and that her decorator, Linden, is at Haven Cliff and will let them in if they get there before she does.

Talia wrote back that traffic is heavy, and her ETA keeps getting pushed back.

On a case so I may be a little late myself, Midge wrote.

Stopping to let a gaggle of pedestrians cross in front of her, she notes that the pebbly town beach is lined with umbrellas, the sparkling water teeming with bathers. It would be so nice to have a swim before the beach closes at dusk, but she has a job to do.

She drives on, past the Dive Inn. It's one of Midge's favorite haunts even now that its long-peeling white clapboards are freshly painted pink, the dartboard and pool table have been banished to make way for cushy banquettes, and the old graffiti-scratched, permanently sticky wooden bar top has been replaced with white marble. A rollicking indoor-outdoor happy hour is underway. Midge scans the outdoor patio and porch. Long gone are the days when she knew every patron, and patrons were few. There are no familiar faces in the horde of summer residents, weekenders, and trendy-looking young people who could be reality TV stars.

The waterfront municipal parking lot is packed. Midge sees license plates from neighboring states as well as Florida, and even a few from Canada. Mulberry Bay tourism has come a long, long way from the ghost town years of her childhood.

At the Landing, people are already milling around outside, waiting to be seated. Formerly a diner/coffee shop where both Talia and her mom Natalie waited tables, it's been resurrected as an upscale restaurant with a yacht club vibe downstairs and a tiki bar on the outdoor deck above.

On the adjoining pier, anglers are fishing as boats come and go. Musicians are setting up for this evening's concert in the bandstand, and a few early birds are facing the stage in lawn chairs.

Parked nearby, a couple of carnival food trucks are doing a brisk business. Cotton candy, funnel cakes, snow cones . . .

Midge imagines Sarah, backtracking through here after a long, sweaty walk to church and discovering that her Bible group had been canceled.

She would have definitely been overheated. Probably thirsty, possibly hungry.

Now that Midge has some distance from the Greene house and the reminders of Caroline and her family, the situation seems a little less ominous.

Sarah isn't Caroline.

Sarah isn't Junia Stanton.

Sarah is a teenage girl who's likely just taking her time getting home on a hot summer day. She's probably cooling off in an air-conditioned store or restaurant or lounging in a shady spot by the water. Yes, and she's lost track of time—accidentally, or on purpose.

Her mother's words echo back to Midge. *I have ice cream right here in the freezer.*

Okay, maybe her daughter respects the frugal practicality, but she must have been disappointed on some level. And wouldn't even the most obedient teenager be reluctant to rush home to scrub out garbage cans on an afternoon like this? Not just the heat wave, but who wouldn't want to have a little fun on one of the last days of summer?

At Congregational Memorial Church, she follows the short driveway around to the large parking lot. There are two vehicles: a black sedan in the far corner, and a white van close to the side entrance, where the offices are.

Midge pulls up alongside the van. Its sign reads Hot Cool Guys HVAC. The back doors are open, revealing tools and equipment.

She exits her car and glances around.

It's peaceful here—so quiet compared to the bustle she left behind on Shore Street. There's a large grassy area behind the building. She can see picnic tables, a swing set, and a life-size statue of Jesus perched in a rock garden, surrounded by plants with chewed leaves and decapitated flower heads.

Deer are responsible, Midge knows. They've done the same to the flowers in her own yard.

A familiar mucky dampness wafts in the humid air. The lake is back there, beyond the tangled vines and tall grasses at the property's woodland edge.

Whirring wings dart from the dense foliage, iridescent in the sunlight. A dragonfly.

Midge eyes an opening in the undergrowth. A trail? It must lead back toward the water. Could Sarah have decided to go for a swim after discovering class was canceled?

There's a No Trespassing sign posted at the edge of the woods, and a closer look tells Midge that there's no trail. It's just a slight opening where a couple of twiggy branches are snapped and the long grass is trampled, probably courtesy of deer accessing the rock garden buffet.

Trail or not, Sarah Greene doesn't strike her as the kind of girl who'd go off into the woods alone.

Not like Caroline.

Not like Junia Stanton.

Then again, there's more to both their stories than anyone suspected.

Maybe there's more to this one as well.

CHAPTER THIRTEEN

"Who wants to see where I used to live?" Talia asks, flipping her turn signal as she brakes for another light, this one at the intersection of Main and Fourth Street.

No reply from the kids. In the rearview mirror, she sees Hayley is still wearing earbuds and focused on her phone, and Caleb is still asleep.

"Ben?"

"Hmm?" he asks, absorbed in his work email.

Or, no, when she glances at the screen, she sees that he's doing a *New York Times* puzzle.

She bites back what she really wants to say. "Yeah. It's tough today."

"Hmm?"

"Wordle. I did it this morning. It took me all six guesses to get it."

He looks up. "Don't tell me anything about it."

"I won't. But we're almost there, so you might want to put that away. I want to show you my old house . . . unless you're not interested?"

"Why would I not be interested?" He snaps the laptop closed. "Of course I'm interested."

She makes the turn onto Fourth Street. She can see it now, mid-block, beyond the newly restored or newly built homes that have replaced the decrepit ones from her childhood. Back then, the three-story Victorian with twin cupolas and a fish scale mansard roof had ranked high among the eyesores.

Now it's a stately painted lady in shades of cream, rose, and moss green. She points it out to Ben.

"*That's* where you grew up? The way you and Natalie always talked, I thought you were dirt poor."

"We were." She slows and pulls up at the curb. "We lived in a third-floor apartment, and it didn't look like this back then. All the houses on the street were run down and neglected."

"Like that one?"

He points at the house next door. Though it, too, was built in the nineteenth century, it lacks architectural embellishment, as devoid of charm and character as Talia considered Mr. and Mrs. Winterfield themselves.

"That was my friend Caroline's house," she tells Ben.

"The one who disappeared?"

"Yes."

"Wow. I don't know if you mentioned that she lived right next door."

Her parents still do, but the house doesn't look occupied. Earlier in the summer, they were overseas on a church mission. Maybe they still are. Or maybe they're visiting their older daughters.

Eve and Joanna, twins, married right out of college to seemingly interchangeable guys named Jim. They moved away soon after Caroline went missing, and of course, Mary Beth was long gone by then.

That left Caroline's parents alone in Mulberry Bay.

Talia was forced every single day to confront Caroline's physical absence and its impact on her parents. She saw the lights on at all hours, saw Mr. and Mrs. Winterfield grimly coming and going, heard them talking, praying, and sometimes weeping through the open screens at night.

Once, in the beginning, Natalie sent her over there with a meal. Talia remembers it clearly—cutting across the yard with a foil-wrapped tray, hoping she'd find no one at home even though the cars were in the driveway.

Mrs. Winterfield came to the door immediately, almost as if she'd been watching for her. Or no, watching for Caroline. Or for someone to come and tell her that her daughter had been found alive—or not.

She must have been desperate for answers.

Did Talia comprehend that even then, long before she became a mother herself?

Maybe. But now that she *is* a mother . . .

Well, now she can't comprehend how she managed to carry off the charade all that summer. How she could have handed over the casserole and asked Mrs. Winterfield if she'd heard anything, as if she might know more than Talia did.

Maybe she'd reminded herself that the Winterfields had been terrible parents, convinced herself that they deserved to suffer. That if they'd been better parents, their daughter—their daughters—wouldn't have done what they did.

Or maybe she simply hadn't questioned any of it. Caroline's secrets. Her own lies.

"This must be hard on you."

Ben's comment jerks her back to the present.

"I mean, being back here, seeing where you used to live," he says. "It must make you miss her even more. It makes *me* miss her, and I've never even been here."

Confused, she looks over at him.

He's pointing at her house, not the Winterfields'. He's talking about Natalie, not Caroline.

"I wish we'd visited her up here the way she wanted," he goes on. "It's my fault. I thought Florida was a more appealing vacation option than upstate New York. Beaches, Disney, golf . . . I was thinking of myself, and of the kids. I'm really sorry we never got here while your mom was alive."

Uncertain whether to let him accept full blame for not visiting, she shrugs. "We were always so busy with work, commuting, the house, the kids. My mom understood that."

"Still, we should have come back." Ben reaches across the console between them and touches her arm. "But I'm glad we're here now."

She forces a smile. "So am I. It's going to be a great weekend."

CHAPTER FOURTEEN

Midge makes her way toward the church office, footsteps crunching on the gravel parking lot. There's an electronic keypad on the door, and a handwritten sign taped on the glass window: *Bible Study Canceled—AC Broken.*

She knocks, then tries the knob. The door opens, and she steps over the threshold. Yeah, no. There's definitely no air-conditioning here.

She's standing in a small entry hall, furnished with a wooden bench and an enormous painting. It depicts Jesus standing on an altar, surrounded by angels. A veiled bride is before him, reaching for his hand.

Midge is reminded of the "purity ball" Caroline told her friends about at some point during their senior year. She said it was organized by Reverend Bauer, and she made it sound like fun, reminiscent of a wedding: young women dressed in white gowns, escorted to the waiting pastor by their fathers, vows sealed with gold rings.

Midge, Talia, and Kelly were taken aback when she revealed that each girl was asked to pledge, in front of the congregation, that she'd preserve her virginity until her wedding night. They saw it as a bizarre ritual. Caroline was defensive.

She assured them that it wasn't unique to this church, that she had no qualms about making such an intensely private matter public, that Gordy was completely supportive.

Yeah, sure he was. Caroline got pregnant within months of taking that chastity vow.

Midge hears a clanking like a hammer on metal from somewhere below.

A male voice calls, “Bro, grab the needle-nose pliers, will you?”

“Hello?” she calls. “Hello?”

“Yes?” someone answers from nearby, and a man pokes his head from a doorway.

Not an HVAC guy.

It’s . . . Reverend Bauer?

But then he steps out into the hall and she realizes that no, it can’t possibly be him. Reverend B would have to be pushing seventy by now.

This man appears to be in his mid-thirties. He’s clean cut with blue eyes, square jawed and fair complected. He’s wearing a short-sleeved white dress shirt, black slacks, and a worn blue bucket hat that doesn’t quite fit—his head, or the setting.

“Officer! Can I help you?”

Midge shows him her badge. “Do you work here?”

“I’m filling in this weekend for Reverend Parker,” he says, with a hint of a Southern accent. “He’s away leading a retreat.”

He introduces himself as Joseph Nielson, an associate pastor at a congregation in a neighboring county.

She gestures at the sign on the door. “I understand the teen Bible study group was canceled this afternoon?”

He nods. “There’s an issue with the AC, as you can probably tell.”

“And you’re the one who made the cancellation? You were here?”

“No. I was home, working on my sermon, and I got a call from Al.”

“Al?”

“He’s the part-time custodian here?”

It’s a question. Midge shrugs.

“He’s local. He said he lives nearby?”

“I don’t know him,” Midge says. “Go on.”

“Al’s mostly off this week because there’s nothing going on here. A lot of people are away.”

“Right,” Midge says. “The retreat. And . . . ?”

"And he came by to open up the building for the Bible group and found out the AC wasn't working. He called me, and I told him to cancel the group and get someone in for a repair. He'd called around, but it's been a busy day for HVAC."

"I'm sure it has."

"This is record heat so late in the season."

"I'm sure it is."

"It is. I heard that on the car radio."

"Yeah, well . . . global warming," she says, and steers him back on track. "So Al set up a repair . . ."

"Right." He gestures at the floor, the workmen in the basement. "He found these guys, but they said they couldn't get here until after five. Al couldn't wait around because he has to coach his daughter's soccer practice. He has four children. He's a good family man," he adds, and pauses for her reaction.

She nods. Family Man Al. Four kids. Got it.

Joseph seems to be one of those people who meanders to the point. In Midge's experience, it's a quality often found in liars and in creative storyteller types. As a man of the cloth, Joseph would fall into the latter category, like her mother's brother, a priest. Uncle Father Tom's homilies are rich with detail, and Midge enjoys listening to them.

On the job . . . yeah, not so much.

"He didn't want to leave the building unlocked after hours, so he asked me if he should give them the code for the door. I didn't think that was a good idea, so . . ." He shrugs. "Here I am. And here *you* are. You were asking about Bible study group?"

"Yes. I'm trying to locate one of the students, Sarah Greene. Do you know her?"

"I don't. But as I said, I'm just pinch-hitting for Reverend Parker. Is something amiss?"

Midge sidesteps the question with one of her own. "Do you know who might have been in charge of the group this afternoon?"

"I don't."

"Well, do you have any information about it? A list of participants, something like that?"

"There may be something around here someplace."

"Would you mind checking?"

"Not at all." He gestures her to follow him into the adjacent office. It's furnished with the basics—desk, chair, shelves, file cabinets.

It's a corner room with windows on two walls. They're open. On an ordinary afternoon, there's probably a nice cross breeze. Today, all is still, and stifling.

Record heat. Yeah, she doesn't doubt it.

She wonders whether Joseph's sermons are as inspiring as her uncle's. Probably not. Uncle Father Tom, for all his verbosity, is a big-hearted, loving presence.

Something about this man is giving her pause.

As he riffles through papers and folders on the desk, she tries to put her finger on what it is she doesn't like about him.

Maybe it's because he vaguely reminds her of Reverend B., whom she definitely found off-putting.

Or maybe it's because he's here, at Caroline's old church.

Midge has nothing against organized religion. She herself was raised Catholic, and though she's far from diligent about making it to mass, when she does go, she still finds comfort in the familiar rituals.

Caroline was bolstered by her own faith for most of the years Midge knew her, but toward the end, especially after that purity ball, her church's influence over her seemed more and more oppressive. Repressive.

Or maybe that was just Reverend B., along with Caroline's parents, more than the church itself. In Midge's memory, they're all intertwined.

She really needs to let that go. As a detective, you have to compartmentalize, set aside preconceived notions and pay attention to the details as they present themselves. The Winterfields' connection to Congregational has no bearing on Sarah Greene's whereabouts, or with this man.

She turns away, reminding herself that a lot of people rub her the wrong way. That's on her, not them. For all she knows, Joseph Nielson is as competent a temporary pastor as Allie is running the desk at the MBPD.

Beyond the window that faces the backyard, a pair of deer are grazing on what's left of the flowers in the rock garden. From here, the opening in the undergrowth is barely visible.

"Sorry, ma'am, I don't see anything here about Bible study."

It's not ma'am. *It's* Detective Sergeant.

Swallowing the impulse to correct him, Midge suggests, "Maybe it's in one of the cabinets?"

"Maybe." He opens a drawer and starts thumbing through file tabs. "Can I ask why you're looking for this young woman? Is she not where she's supposed to be?"

"She's not home yet. Her mother asked me to look into it. She has some concerns."

"Right. Well, you know how teenagers are. I've got a few myself."

"A few concerns?"

"A few teenagers."

"Wait . . . you *have* teenagers?"

"I do. I've got two. But I'll have four in October when our twins turn thirteen."

"*You* have *four* kids? Just like Al, huh?"

"Al has four. I've got six."

"Six! Wow. You seem too young for that."

"And you?"

Midge deliberately misinterprets the question with a wry, "Oh, I'm not too young for anything anymore."

"I meant, how many children do you have?"

"None at all," she says, informing a stranger that she's childless for the second time today.

This time, however, the response catches her off guard.

"I'm sorry," he says with a slight frown.

Sorry he asked? Or sorry she doesn't have kids?

She shrugs, hating that she feels obligated to say, "No regrets here."

Hating even more the long look he gives her in response, followed by a thoughtful nod, as if he's drawn his own conclusion on the matter.

She almost wishes he'd say something else, something infuriating and judgmental, so she can tell him that he shouldn't make assumptions about other people's lives.

But he goes back to his file drawer without comment.

Midge checks her phone and is surprised to see a text from Nap Moreau, the medical examiner. Maybe the test results are back. Ordinarily, he calls, but . . .

Oh. It's not about the tests. It's about . . .

What, exactly, is it about?

Hey, Midge. What are you up to?

That's it.

She frowns, wondering what it means and why he's asking.

"Ah, here we are. Youth Bible study." The pastor pulls a folder from the drawer. "Here's this year's file."

Midge quickly pockets her phone and holds out a hand. "Mind if I take a look?"

"Of course not." He gives it to her.

She opens it and glances through the contents, disappointed to find that it's mainly pamphlets and handouts. The only document specific to the current group is a schedule that lists the meeting dates.

She closes the folder and returns it to him. "Thanks. I don't see anything I can use. Sorry to make you do all that digging."

"It's no problem." He gives her a closed-lipped smile. "You wanted a list of group members, is that it? So that you can ask them to help track down the missing girl?"

The word hangs in the air.

Missing.

"She's just late getting back, and her mom wanted to see if she'd gone to a friend's house or something."

"Has she tried calling her?"

"She didn't answer calls and texts."

"She probably lost her phone and she's afraid to go home and face the music. My daughter's done that." He shakes his head. "Kids that age . . . You wouldn't know, but trust me. Even the straight and narrow ones run into a scrape now and then."

"I wouldn't know," Midge agrees, and heads for the door. "Thank you for your time."

"No problem, ma'am. Good luck!"

She offers her parting words without a backward glance. "It's Detective Sergeant Kennedy."

CHAPTER FIFTEEN

Watching the squad car pull out of the parking lot, he exhales.

With luck, that annoying woman—*Detective Sergeant Kennedy*—has concluded that Sarah Greene isn't in trouble and will return home when she's good and ready. That maybe she has indeed lost her phone and/or gone off with friends who shall remain nameless for the time being.

He returns to the cabinet, opens the drawer, and finds the list that had been right on top when he opened the Bible study folder. With the cop distracted by her phone, it had been so easy for him to slip out the sheet of paper and tuck it behind the last hanging file.

He considers putting it back now but decides against it.

He doesn't like the detective's demeanor. She asked too many questions. Looked at him in a way that made him talk too much, as he does when he gets nervous.

What if she was suspicious? What if she comes back? What if she figures out—

"Sir?" a voice calls from the hall, and he quickly shoves the paper into his pocket. "I mean, Father? Or . . . sorry, I'm not sure what—"

"It's fine." He steps out of the office to find one the HVAC repairmen. He's young, with wavy dark hair, a scruffy beard, and a gold stud in one ear. His rolled-up uniform sleeves reveal tattooed, muscular forearms. His name patch reads *Johnny*.

Hot Cool Guys indeed.

"We figured out your problem. Should've checked the thermostat."

"There's a problem with the thermostat?"

"Two problems. First, you got a couple of loose wires. Second, you got no backup batteries in there. Maybe they died and someone pulled them out and was planning to replace them and forgot. You gotta have backup batteries. That way, if something happens to the wires, the damned thing still works. Sorry." He winces, covering his mouth. "Didn't mean to curse in front of a man of the cloth."

"No worries. I'm glad you figured out the problem."

"Yeah." Johnny whips out a red bandanna and wipes sweat from his handsome face. "Whoever found the dead batteries must have yanked on the wires, because they're way out of whack. People should be more careful, you know?"

"They absolutely should."

"Chad's fixing it, and you'll be back up and running, but it might take a while for things to cool down in here. If I were you, I'd find somewhere else to go until it does."

"Will do. Thank you."

He waits until Johnny has retreated to rejoin his partner, then pats his pocket.

He definitely has somewhere else to go.

He steps back into the office, closes the door, picks up the desk phone, and hits redial.

The line rings several times before a male voice answers. "Hello?"

"Yeah, Al? It's Joseph Nielson. I'm here at the church." He can hear kids in the background. A whistle blows. Soccer practice.

"Right. Any news on the AC?"

"It's all fixed."

"Already? That's great. So you don't need me to come back there?"

"No, I'll lock up. You have a good night."

He hangs up and places another call.

This time, it's answered on the first ring. "Joseph Nielson."

"Hi, Pastor. It's Al again—the custodian at Congregational Memorial in Mulberry Bay?"

"Al, of course. Did the repair service get over there?"

"They sure did, and it's all taken care of."

"They fixed the air-conditioning already?"

"Yep. There was a problem with the wiring. Nothing complicated. No need for you to come. I've got it all under control."

"Thanks a million, Al. You're a lifesaver."

He hangs up with an ironic smile.

A lifesaver?

Some might say the opposite about him.

CHAPTER SIXTEEN

The first time Talia returned to Mulberry Bay, to Haven Cliff, she was filled with nostalgia. Back in June, she'd viewed it all from the perspective of who and what she'd been when she lived here. Child, teen, daughter, friend, student . . .

Everywhere she looked, the past came alive again, for better, for worse.

This time is different. This time, she's seeing it all through her family's eyes.

The mansion, grand and imposing, rises three stories with a rectangular turret at either end. A pillared terrace runs the length of the facade, filled with antique wicker furniture and graceful potted palms. Along the foundation, restored formal gardens are filled with blooms and trimmed hedges, bisected by bluestone paths.

Climbing out of the back seat, Caleb regards it with the same expression he had when he saw the roller coaster at the annual carnival, shrinking back against Talia.

"Do I have to go on?" he whispered then.

"Of course not," she assured him, and they sat on a bench watching Ben and Hayley go on it, once, twice, three times.

Today, Caleb looks up at her, alarmed. "Do we have to stay here?"

"We do, and you'll love it. I promise."

Ben is in efficiency mode, unloading the car.

"Come on, Hayley. Everyone's going to carry their own bag into the house. I'm not the bellhop. Let's go."

In true Hayley fashion, she lags behind as they ascend to the pillared terrace, doing her best to act blasé about the place—seen one glorious stone mansion, seen them all.

Then the door opens, and Kelly is there, looking like she stepped out of *Vogue* in heeled sandals and a simple black sleeveless dress with her blond hair in a high ponytail.

Talia sees Hayley's instant admiration. Effortlessly cool, Kelly's always had that effect on people.

She throws her arms around Talia, enveloping her in a cloud of French perfume. "I can't believe you're really here!"

"I can't either."

Kelly turns to Ben and the kids. "How was the drive? Long? Boring? Traffic?"

"All of the above. I'm Ben." He extends a handshake.

Kelly hugs him instead. "I feel like I already know you. I've heard so much about you."

Talia catches Ben's barely perceptible raised eyebrow before he says, "Same."

Kelly introduces herself to Caleb and Hayley, then leads the way inside and up the stairs. "I'll show you your room first, Caleb, but we have to cut through your mom and dad's to see it."

She opens the door to a guest suite, then to what was a walk-in closet when Talia visited in June. Now it's a replica of Caleb's room back home. Kelly bought the same red-and-white bedding and curtains and filled the space with familiar stuffed animals and his favorite books and games.

Talia catches Kelly's eye and mouths, *Thank you*, with a lump in her throat.

They move on down the hall to the sumptuous room where Hayley is staying. She seems to have forgotten the angst of her missed sleepover, whipping out her phone to take photos of everything, including the white marble bathroom that looks like a luxurious spa, stocked with every imaginable high-end toiletry and cosmetic. "Wait till Chloe sees this! She's going to be so jealous!"

Back on the first floor, they follow Kelly through elegant rooms filled with antique furniture. Ben asks about the house and its history.

His superpower is the ability to find common ground with anyone he meets and have affable conversations. It serves him well in sales, and it serves him well here, especially when they meet Kelly's decorator, Linden, in the conservatory, arranging cut flowers in an enormous vase and sipping a margarita. His wavy blond hair is streaked pink, he's wearing clamdiggers and espadrilles, and he's prone to gesticulation and screeching laughter.

"Is it happy hour already?" Kelly asks, indicating his drink.

"It's *always* happy hour. The pitcher's in the fridge."

In the kitchen, a bearded middle-aged man wearing an apron and a hairnet over a mostly bald head is sautéing something on the six-burner stove. Kelly briefly converses with him in French as a young woman dressed in black pants and a white blouse assembles individual salads on a row of white plates, making them look like artwork with floral garnishes.

"You have your own chefs?" Hayley exclaims.

"Just for special occasions." Kelly takes several margarita glasses from a cabinet. "Okay, I've got everything I could think of that you guys might want. Soda, lemonade, juice, you name it. Who's thirsty?"

Caleb immediately says, "Not me!"

Hayley rolls her eyes. "He's worried because in the car, he—"

"Are you thirsty, Hayley?" Talia asks, shooting her a pointed look.

"I'll have lemonade."

Kelly pours some into one of the margarita glasses and hands it to her.

"Careful with that, Hayley—it's fragile," Talia warns.

"I *am* careful!" She drains the glass and plunks it down on the granite counter.

Talia winces.

"Don't worry," Kelly says. "It's not that fragile, and I won't care if it breaks."

"I won't break it. I drink out of real glasses all the time, even though my mom thinks I need a plastic sippy cup."

Kelly laughs. "More lemonade?"

"No, thanks. I think I'll go out for a walk," she says casually, with a sidelong glance at Talia as if daring her to protest.

Rising to the challenge, Talia responds with a curt, "Oh, no you won't."

"But—"

"Hayley, there's nowhere to walk around here."

"I can walk in the woods."

"Not by yourself, you can't." Talia turns to Ben for backup.

"You can't," he agrees. "We'll all go for a walk in the woods tomorrow."

"I don't want to walk in the woods," Caleb says.

"Why not?"

"There are bugs. And bears."

"And bees, and boogeymen, and bad guys . . ." Hayley says, adding, at Talia's look, "What? Aren't we playing the alphabet game?"

As they settle in the parlor with platters of decadent hors d'oeuvres and cocktails, Caleb sits close to Talia on the velvet sofa, whispering in her ear, "Are there really bad guys in the woods?"

"Of course not."

Ben's sitting on her other side, discussing some television show with Linden. He's coming across as his usual affable, friendly self. But Talia senses that he's slightly guarded, that there's something more possessive than affectionate in the arm he's slung around her shoulders.

Is it because he perceives her friends as rivals for her affection?

Or is he being protective?

Hayley's phone chimes, signaling a FaceTime call. She jumps up. "It's Chloe. I'm going outside to talk to her."

"I don't think that's—"

"Mom! Come *on*!" She turns to Ben. "Daddy? Can I please go outside so that I can have a private conversation?"

"As long as you stay on the front porch."

"Seriously?"

"Seriously," Ben and Talia reply in unison.

Talia sips her margarita. It's strong, as Kelly made it herself.

She can see Hayley through the parlor window, sprawled sideways on a vintage wicker chair, her hair dangling over one arm and her long bare legs over the other.

She reminds herself that her daughter is perfectly safe. There's no danger at Haven Cliff as long as Mary Beth Winterfield stays behind bars.

CHAPTER SEVENTEEN

Lying on the thin mattress in her jail cell, Mary Beth stares at the water stain on the ceiling. Depending on the hour and the weather outside the high rectangular window above the bunk, it sometimes looks to her like the state of Idaho. Other times, she sees it as a man in profile, wearing a stovepipe hat.

Not Abe Lincoln.

No, the man she'd occasionally glimpsed when she was growing up in the house on Fourth Street in Mulberry Bay—a shadowy figure standing over her bed in the night, wearing a tall hat and a cloak of some sort.

A dream, she figured, the first time it happened, even though she was pretty sure she was still awake.

Or maybe a ghost, she decided, the second time he appeared in the childhood bedroom she shared with her sister Caroline. The house had been built way back in the eighteen hundreds. Having lived there all her life, she was too familiar with it to find it creepy, but that's what her friends thought of it.

Or perhaps the Hatman was simply a figment of her imagination.

The terror that accompanied those sightings was all too real. As Caroline peacefully slumbered in the adjacent bed, Mary Beth could only lie there looking up at him, unable to make a sound or move a muscle.

Sleep paralysis.

She learned that years later, in a book she stumbled across in the prison library. The phenomenon dates back to ancient times. The weird thing is that a lot of people who experience it share the same bizarre hallucination: the Hatman.

She found that comforting. It's nice not to feel alone in the bad things that happen to you.

It's also nice that she hasn't seen the Hatman standing over her bed in many years, unless you count the water stain.

She does not. This is more like one of those Rorschach ink blobs that sometimes looks like a man in a hat, and sometimes looks like Idaho, and sometimes, like right now, just looks like a stain.

She can hear the usual din beyond her cell—inmates laughing, arguing, cursing, moaning, crying. Guards talking, shouting; keys rattling, toilets flushing, footsteps echoing, doors clanking.

Her hair is damp with sweat, and her orange jumpsuit is plastered to her body. It's so damned hot in here, not a breath of air.

She reminds herself of how the dead of winter felt in the federal penitentiary where she served ten years of a twelve-year drug-trafficking sentence. She remembers shivering beneath a flimsy blanket, teeth chattering, every muscle in her body painfully clenched. That was far worse.

This is just jail.

She's here because in June, she went to Haven Cliff and threatened Caroline's friends with a gun.

That wasn't her intention. She was armed for her own protection. She hadn't lured them there, as they claimed. She herself had been lured with a text.

Please come to Haven Cliff. Midnight by the statues. I need you.

She suspected it might be a trap, but there was no way she was going to ignore that text.

Of course she went.

It all fell apart so quickly. As Midge, Kelly, and Talia accused her of crimes she hadn't committed, she realized what must have happened, and who was really responsible. For the crimes, and for bringing Mary Beth face-to-face with her sister's friends on that spot on that night—the twenty-fifth anniversary of Caroline's disappearance.

Her sister's little tomboy pal Midge is a cop now, and a powerful one.

Why would she believe anything a convicted felon has to say?

Why would she doubt that Mary Beth lured Gordy Klatte to his fatal fall? Or that she killed another man, a random stranger known locally as the Walking Man, on that same night?

Murder?

Two murders?

If Midge Kennedy has her way, Mary Beth will be charged with both, convicted, and sent away for life.

Mary Beth has made a lot of wrong, selfish decisions in her life. She's pretty much betrayed everyone she ever cared about.

Not this time.

Midge, the lawyers, the judge and jurors, the public . . .

They can think whatever they want about her. Let them.

Let them assume she's a monster. They won't be the first to do so.

Let them believe she's responsible for all of it. Not just what happened to her sister all those years ago, but what happened to Gordy this summer.

Let them.

Because Midge, Talia, and Kelly have no idea who Mary Beth Winterfield really is, or how she got to this place.

And they're not the only ones willing to keep a dark secret for someone they love.

CHAPTER EIGHTEEN

May 10, 1997

In the bedroom she shares with her sister Caroline, Mary Beth crouches in front of the angled bench built beneath the three turret windows. Tugging on the middle section of molding, she removes a section of wood to reveal a hidden compartment.

She's pretty sure her parents don't know it exists. Nor do the twins, Eve and Joanna, nearly six years older than Mary Beth, who moved out and married equally dull guys named Jim.

Only Caroline knows about the secret panel because she's the one who found it when they were little girls, arguing about something. Caroline was probably threatening to tattle on her to their parents about something they wouldn't approve of—which describes many things Mary Beth did back then and nearly everything she does now.

That day, Mary Beth got mad and gave her a shove. Caroline stumbled into the window seat, and her foot hit the molding.

At first, they assumed they'd damaged the wall, and that meant their father was certain to punish them. Mary Beth was usually on the receiving end of his belt lashings—rarely the older girls or Caroline, and only when he held them responsible for some costly repair. The house was old, and everything in it was worn. But if they needed a plumber, their father assumed it was because someone had flushed something that shouldn't be flushed; if the refrigerator went on the fritz, he blamed whomever he suspected of browsing too long with the door open.

This time, though, there would be no punishment. The wall wasn't damaged; it had a concealed panel to a secret cupboard.

Mary Beth and Caroline promised each other they'd never tell a soul about it.

Over the years, it was the perfect place to stash Christmas gifts, candy, flashlights so they could read in bed at night—innocent stuff. Later, Mary Beth hid her diary, her eye makeup and short skirts, and her Daisy disposable razor because she wasn't allowed to shave her legs.

Back in March, she hid the extra pregnancy test she bought after the first one was negative—only because she tested too early, and not because she wasn't pregnant.

She's pregnant, all right. Her waistbands are getting snug, and she's in a perpetual state of nausea.

Nausea, guilt, and terror.

Nobody knows. Certainly not her family. Not her friends. Not the potential father.

There are only two. It's not like she's a slut. But why would she tell them? One is a jerk; the other has a girlfriend. She doesn't love them; they don't love her.

Most of the time, she's pretty sure no one does, with the exception of Caroline, because she loves everyone, and everyone loves her.

The baby, though . . . the baby will love Mary Beth. She's going to be the best mom ever, because her parents have set a great example of what *not* to do.

She reaches into the hidden compartment and takes out the doll she's stashed there. It's an American Girl, once her most prized possession. Now it serves as a hiding spot for something far more valuable.

She twists off the head. Then she reaches into her pocket, fishes out the quarter she found on the sidewalk by a parking meter, and adds it to the stash of cash and coins inside the doll. Every little bit helps, but it isn't nearly enough.

Not for going to Syracuse University, which became her goal after visiting last year for a gymnastics tournament, even with an academic scholarship her guidance counselor assured her was possible if she kept her grades up.

Her grades have slipped this quarter, but it doesn't matter. Even college doesn't matter. Her savings are now meant for something far more important.

She's starting a nanny job as soon as school gets out, working for rich summer people. The pay will get her to her goal, but that money won't start coming in for another six weeks.

She reattaches the doll's head, returns the doll to the cubby, and goes over to the mirror. From the front, she looks like her normal self. But when she turns sideways, she can see that her boobs are getting huge and her stomach is protruding in her jeans. She tries untucking the T-shirt. Now she just looks fat all over.

Time is running out.

She thinks of the Baxters.

Four years ago, when Mary Beth turned thirteen, they were her first babysitting customers. The twins, Erica and Erin, were seven, and adorably so, with missing baby teeth, pigtails, and matching nightgowns. Now they're in that awkward stage, physically and socially. If they pay attention to Mary Beth at all, it's to complain about their designated bedtime or the insufficient snacks their parents provided.

The effervescent and beautiful Mrs. Baxter doesn't work, but unlike Mary Beth's own mother, she'd never call herself a housewife, and neither would anyone else. She has a dressing room full of gorgeous clothes and a busy schedule that doesn't always involve her husband. She has a huge group of friends and often hires Mary Beth to watch the girls during the day while she golfs or goes to lunch, the gym, or the mall.

Mary Beth always imagined herself as the exact same kind of wife and mom when she grew up, but with a loving, fun, and much cuter husband.

Mr. Baxter is an attorney—boring, stern and silent. Mary Beth used to try to make conversation with him whenever he drove her home, but she's long since given up. He always seems to be brooding, and last week, she had to remind him to pay her. When he did, it was short by five dollars, which she didn't realize until she was home.

She thought of calling Mrs. Baxter about it, but that would be awkward. Especially now. The woman has lost her sparkle, like soda that's gone flat. Mary Beth has no idea what's troubling her lately, but she doesn't want to know. That would only make things harder.

Things as in *this* thing. The thing she's going to do to the Baxters on this balmy Saturday night in May.

Well, not as much *to them* as *for* herself, and the baby, and the new life they're going to have together.

This is the only way. They say money doesn't buy happiness, but it can buy freedom, and for her, freedom would be happiness.

She waits until her parents are in bed and Caroline is asleep. It's far from the first time she's stolen out of the house at this hour. It's what got her into this situation in the first place—sneaking around with boys her parents would never allow her to date.

Tonight, she's dressed all in black, carrying a flashlight and the pillowcase she stripped from her bed.

The Baxters used to live a few houses away on Fourth Street. Last year, they moved to Pine Ridge, a private development, where huge homes are set back from the road and away from each other.

Tonight, their house is dark. They're away, visiting Mr. Baxter's mother in Boston for Mother's Day weekend. Mrs. Baxter mentioned the trip Wednesday night, with an eye roll that implied she wasn't looking forward to it.

"*I'm* a mother too," she told Mary Beth as she strapped on a pair of red leather heels that matched her red dress. "Every year, we have to make sure my mother-in-law has a special day, and it's never about me, or what I want."

"What do *you* want?"

Mrs. Baxter hesitated, wearing a sad smile. "You know, I'm not sure. But not sitting in traffic would be nice for a change."

After she and Mr. Baxter drove away, Mary Beth left the girls watching *Sister, Sister* in the finished part of the basement and slipped into the shadowy concrete cavern beyond. It houses the furnace and storage tubs that haven't been touched since the move. There's a door leading out to the side yard, but the family never seems to use it.

Mary Beth unlocked it.

Three nights later, she reaches for the knob.

It's still unlocked, as she anticipated. She opens the door, turns on the flashlight, and descends the steps to the basement.

In the rec room, she feels a twinge of remorse as she disconnects the girls' PlayStation and shoves the console into a pillowcase. Their parents will buy them a new one. New games too. She helps herself to a stack, then makes her way upstairs.

In the kitchen, she opens the drawer where the Baxters keep a wad of cash they use for pizza deliveries, the girls' allowances, and of course, to pay Mary Beth for babysitting. She reminds herself of the time Mr. Baxter shorted her as she tucks it into her sack.

But he only owes her five dollars, not . . . Is this hundreds?

Maybe. She doesn't stop to count it.

Her heart races as she creeps upstairs and opens the door to Mrs. Baxter's dressing room. How many times has she perched on the cushioned bench here while Mrs. Baxter tries on various outfits and accessories, asking her opinion?

She has lots of costume jewelry in a custom-built armoire but keeps the good stuff in a velvet-lined drawer, including the diamond engagement ring she stopped wearing years ago, saying it's too flashy.

Mary Beth takes it, some pearls, gemstone earrings, and a tennis bracelet. She's reaching for a sapphire pendant when she hears something behind her.

It's a small sound—a gasp.

She whirls and sees a woman in the doorway. It takes her a moment to realize that it's Mrs. Baxter, because she's not wearing makeup, her hair is hanging flat and loose, and she's in pink pajamas instead of the lacy lingerie Mary Beth always imagined she'd wear.

But Mrs. Baxter recognizes her. Mary Beth sees her register shock and dismay before she opens her mouth and shouts for her husband.

Later—much later, at the police station—Mary Beth sits in the holding cell, in tears and trying not to vomit yet again. She'd done so in the squad car and again as she was being processed, handcuffed and helpless to even wipe her mouth.

Now the cuffs are off, and she clenches her hands as she listens to the Baxters down the corridor, telling Chief Kennedy they were supposed to be in Boston. Mr. Baxter's mother came to visit them instead, and she's back at the house with the twins, who slept through everything.

No, they say, Mary Beth has never given them reason not to trust her.

No, she's never done anything like this.

No, she doesn't have a drug problem, as far as they know.

Yes, of course they want to press charges.

Then Mary Beth hears other voices—her parents.

Her father, raging. "Where is she? Where's my daughter? You'd better have her locked up, because if I get my hands on her, she's going to wish she was behind bars, or worse!"

Her mother, carrying on as if someone has died.

Hearing her plaintive sobs, and her father's sharp admonishment to his wife, Mary Beth stops crying.

Not because her father ordered her to pull herself together, but because she isn't weak. Not like her mother. She'll never be the kind of woman who obeys a man and doesn't stand up for herself, or for her children.

She wraps her arms around her stomach.

She doesn't regret the pregnancy, or what she's done to provide for her child's future—even tonight, at the Baxters'. They have plenty of money. They could have replaced everything.

She only regrets getting caught. Charges aside, her parents are going to make her life miserable every moment she has to spend with them before she can make her escape.

After that, we'll be home free, she tells the baby, as footsteps and voices approach her cell.

They just have to get through this miserable Saturday night, and then—

Wait, no. It must be long after midnight. Sunday morning.

Happy Mother's Day to me.

CHAPTER NINETEEN

Present Day

Sarah Greene remains missing as the sun sinks toward the mountains in the western sky. It's growing more orange than yellow gold by the minute, but its heat is just as oppressive.

Midge sits with her left signal flashing, waiting to turn into Haven Cliff. There's a steady stream of oncoming traffic on Route 28. If she were in the police cruiser, oncoming drivers would probably slow down, and someone would undoubtedly flash headlights and wave her to make the turn.

But she's in her own car now, wearing shorts and a tank top, blasting the air-conditioning and the radio. It's tuned to the 1990s station she likes, and they're playing Britney Spears's ". . . Baby One More Time."

Ordinarily, Midge might have changed the station—not just because bubblegum pop was never her cup of tea, but because it's a reminder of Caroline. She was a huge Britney fan.

Midge thinks of the pink Walkman, now bagged, tagged evidence at the medical examiner's office, with a Britney Spears CD still inside.

Right now, though, about to reconnect with Kelly and Talia at Haven Cliff, she decides the song is fitting. She leaves it, surprised to find she still knows all the words. She can hear Caroline's sweet, melodic soprano singing along.

She remembers the four of them, packed into Kelly's red BMW convertible, cruising around town singing, laughing, bickering, gossiping the way teenage girls do. How many idyllic summer days, summer nights, had they spent together?

And then it was over.

The end hadn't come without warning. But when you're seventeen, you don't spend a lot of time worrying about what lies ahead. Midge hadn't, anyway.

She thinks of Caroline.

Of Sarah Greene.

Sarah. Where are you?

Amid wrapping up the day's reports at the office, she touched base with the other law enforcement agencies now involved in the case, as well as the state's Missing Persons Clearinghouse. Sarah's mother had provided recent photos for the database and media.

The woman remains distraught, but at least she's no longer home alone. Ginny is there with her now, and she said Rebecca and a few friends are checking out various spots Sarah frequented around town. Between their efforts, the press, social media, and the BOLO, Midge is confident that if Sarah's nearby, she won't go unnoticed.

Before leaving for the evening, she briefed everyone who will be handling the case while she's off duty and extracted promises that they'll let her know if there are any overnight developments.

She makes the turn off Route 28 and passes between massive stone pillars connected by an arched iron banner that reads HAVEN CLIFF.

The sign has been here since Asa Winterfield built the place, rusted but never relegated to ruin as everything else was.

She follows the long, shadowy driveway that's really more of a dirt road, rutted and bordered by woods on either side. It looks exactly the same now as it did back when Midge and her friends started exploring Haven Cliff as children, searching for the lost Winterfield treasure.

The rest—lawns, gardens, walkways, and trails—has now, like the house itself, been restored. All but the pool.

When the contractor began the job last spring, he promised Kelly it would be up and running by the Fourth of July.

Now it's in limbo. They can't move ahead with the excavation and restoration until they have more information about the skeletal remains unearthed there.

As if there's any doubt about who it is.

Back in June, questioned by a local reporter, Midge confirmed that they were human bones, but added, "We have to assume that this is part of that old cemetery we've all heard about."

The reporter asked if there was any connection between the remains in the pool and the nearly concurrent discovery of a deceased man elsewhere on the Haven Cliff grounds.

Midge sidestepped the question, emphasizing that the remains in the pool were skeletal and had been there for a very long time. The corpse in the woods was fresh and belonged to an unhoused loner who'd been in the area for many years.

He was well known to locals as "the Walking Man," but his death didn't cause much of a stir. It might have if Midge had released more information. Like that he'd died of a gunshot wound to the back, or that his suspected killer was in custody, and that his death was likely tied to Gordon Klatte's—also a homicide.

None of that is public knowledge—yet.

It's all going to come out sooner or later. Then there will be an investigation and a trial.

"Not the best publicity for Haven Cliff," she warned Kelly. "People will say it really is cursed."

"Maybe it is, Midge."

"You don't believe that any more than I do. There's nothing mystical about what's happened there. None of this, past or present, has anything to do with vengeful spirits. Crimes happen because bad people do bad things—or occasionally, good people do bad things. It's that simple."

As she rounds a last curve, the trees on either side open to a broad emerald lawn that stretches to the surrounding woodlands. The rutted dirt lane gives way to pavement, winding to a circle in front of the granite mansion.

Kelly's car is parked beside the wide front steps. Behind it, Midge recognizes the SUV Talia was driving back in June. Nearby, she sees a Prius that belongs to Linden, Kelly's decorator.

He's become something of a fixture at Haven Cliff even now that the house is completely done over. Midge enjoys his company, for the most part. He can be a lot of fun.

He can also be . . . *a lot.*

A self-proclaimed drama queen thrown into the mix with Kelly, Talia, and Talia's family?

She parks beside a splashing fountain that glistens in the sun and turns off the engine, silencing Britney.

Needing a minute to decompress and put the grueling day behind her, she leans her head back, eyes closed.

She breathes deeply. In, out, in . . .

Her phone buzzes.

She's tempted to ignore it.

But what if Mrs. Greene is calling to say they've found Sarah?

With a sigh, she opens her eyes and reaches to answer the phone, then hesitates when she sees the name on caller ID.

It's the medical examiner, Nap Moreau.

She's off duty. Whatever it is can wait till later, or tomorrow.

Even the forensic test results?

Even that, she decides.

But then she remembers his earlier text. With a guilty twinge, she realizes that she completely forgot to respond.

Maybe he simply intended to wish her a nice holiday weekend. He's polite that way, Nap. A Southern gentleman.

The least she can do is answer his call and wish him the same.

She picks up. "Nap?"

"Hey, Midge. How've you been holding up in this heat?" he asks in his languid New Orleans accent.

"Oh, you know . . . about as well as a Popsicle on the sidewalk. How about you?"

He chuckles. "This is nothing. Where I come from, a summer day like this would be downright refreshing."

"Well, then, remind me never to visit where you come from on a summer day."

"Come on, now. You're made of tough stuff."

Her phone vibrates. She lowers it for a second and sees that it's a message from Kelly on their group text.

Everyone's here! Where are you?

She raises the phone to her ear again, asking, "What can I do for you, Nap?"

"Sounds like you're busy."

"A bit."

"I don't want to keep you. I'm getting ready to leave the office, and I'm thinking of stopping by the Dive Inn. That band you like is playing at nine."

"You mean Finding Alice?"

"That's the one."

"I'd go, but I'm actually at a friend's place."

"Oh! I thought when you said you were busy that you were still at work. I'll let you go, then." He sounds a bit . . . disappointed? Wistful?

"I'm just at my friend Kelly's. You know her."

"Kelly . . . you mean Haven Cliff Kelly?"

"That's the one," she says, echoing his laid-back tone. "We have plans tonight with another friend who's here visiting with her family. Otherwise, I'd definitely have been up for beers and Finding Alice at the Dive Inn."

"Okay, well . . . they're also playing in Bearsville Sunday."

"How do you know that?"

"I follow them on social media."

"Wait, *you're* on social media? How do I not know that after all these years?"

"Because you're *not* on social media," he says with a chuckle.

She isn't, officially. Not as herself, anyway. Only when she's working a case.

"Anyway, if you're free on Sunday, we can go."

"I can't. My friend is in town, and I've got a case that might get complicated."

"Right. I get it. Have fun with your friends, Midge."

"I will," she says, then adds, "Wait, Nap?"

"Yeah?" Before she can speak, he goes on, "Any day now, and like I said, I'll call you the second I hear."

Midge blinks at the non sequitur. "What?"

"You were going to ask me about the forensics reports we're waiting on. See that? I read your mind."

"Oh, I . . . uh . . . Thanks, Nap, but . . ."

But she hadn't been about to ask him that at all.

No, she'd been on the verge of inviting him to drop by Kelly's. It's probably better that she didn't, since the last time Nap was here at Haven Cliff, he was removing the skeletal remains from the pool, and the Walking Man's corpse from the woods.

Plus, tonight is about seeing her friends and meeting Talia's family.

Then again, Linden is here.

"*But* . . . ?" Nap asks.

"Nothing, I was just . . . I was going to say something else, that's all."

"You mean I'm not psychic?"

She laughs. "Not in the least."

"Well, then, my apologies for interrupting. What were you going to say?"

"It's not important."

"You sure?"

She shouldn't.

But she does.

"I was just going to see if you wanted to stop by Kelly's for a beer or—"

She cuts herself off, allowing him to jump in with a polite *Thanks, but no thanks.*

Instead, after a moment, he says, "Midge?"

"Yeah?"

"Ah, you're still there. I thought the call might have dropped."

"No, I'm still here."

"Do you *want* me to stop by?"

"Sure. If you want to, on your way to the Dive Inn . . . not that it's on your way, but . . ." This time, she forces herself to finish the sentence. ". . . if you're up for it, that would be nice."

"I'm up for it, and that *would* be nice," Nap agrees. "Do you want to make sure it's okay with Kelly?"

"It's fine. The more the merrier. Come on over."

Midge hangs up, gets out of the car, and heads for the house.

Dusk is falling. The landscape is softly illuminated by posts, sconces, solar path lights, and spotlit trees. The mansion's stone architecture glows with strategically placed fixtures, and lamplight spills from windows on all three stories.

She finds herself wishing she'd gone home to change into something more presentable than the casual clothes she keeps stashed in a drawer at work. It isn't just because the house is so swanky, or because it belatedly occurs to her that Kelly might be serving an elegant sit-down dinner in the dining room.

But now Nap is coming.

Nap, who invited her out tonight, almost like . . .

No. Not like a date. Not at all.

He'd simply wanted her to meet him at the Dive Inn, which they've done countless times since he moved here ten years ago. Back then, he had a fiancée, and Midge had just dumped hers.

That was her second broken engagement. Ever since, she's been content as a single woman. She likes making all the decisions in her life. She doesn't want to take care of anyone—well, other than her parents—and she certainly doesn't want anyone trying to take care of her, including her parents.

She enjoys being self-sufficient.

And she's perfectly comfortable attending social events solo. Yet for some reason, that prospect isn't entirely appealing tonight. She's glad Nap is coming.

About to climb the wide stone steps to the terrace, she stops short. Out of the corner of her eye, she spots movement at the far edge of the lawn. There, a grove of tall, arching mock orange bushes screens the mulched woodland path leading to the pool site.

Midge slowly turns to gaze at the spot. Probably deer.

Just like before, at the church.

She thinks of Joseph Nielson.

Earlier, she told Sarah's mother that she'd gone over and spoken with the pastor filling in for Reverend Parker, and that he hadn't seen her and hadn't been able to provide any info about the Bible study group.

"Did you ask him to pray for her?" Mrs. Greene asked.

"To pray for her? I, uh . . ."

"We need prayers, Midge. Prayers have power. You believe that, don't you?"

"I'm sure the pastor is praying for her," she assured Mrs. Greene, though of course she hadn't asked him to.

But you'd think he'd have mentioned it. You'd think he'd have expressed his concern or asked if there was anything he could do to help the family.

To be fair, this isn't Pastor Nielson's own congregation; he doesn't even know the Greenes. Still—

"Midge!"

She turns away from the woods as the front door opens. Seeing Kelly and Talia, holding margarita glasses and grinning, Midge hurries to hug them, pushing Pastor Joseph Nielson from her mind.

CHAPTER TWENTY

Inching his way through a long register line at Home Depot, he checks his email repeatedly on his phone.

Nothing yet.

He's glad the store is so busy, filled with people shopping for air conditioners and fans, discounted end-of-season nursery plants, bags of charcoal, supplies for weekend home-improvement projects. He's thrown in a few outdoor patio cushions and tiki torch fuel, just in case the other items arouse suspicion. But nobody gives him or his cart a second glance, not even the security guard hanging around by the registers.

Inch forward . . .

Check email . . .

Inch forward . . .

Check email . . .

He didn't see the one she'd sent this afternoon until an hour after she sent it.

> Hey, something came up and I'm running late so I can't meet today after all. Sorry. Another time?

As if it were that simple to change plans.

After he'd gone to so much trouble, taken so many risks, to set the stage.

After he was already there, ready for her, waiting for her.

No problem at all, he'd typed, his hands trembling with rage. How about tomorrow?

She still hasn't responded to that.

What if he never hears from her again? Maybe she got spooked. Maybe she knows, somehow, who he is, what he's done, what he's planning to do to her.

At last, it's his turn at the register.

The cashier, a middle-aged woman with a tight perm and tattoos on her saggy, too-tanned skin, asks, "Hot enough for ya?"

"Plenty," he says, forcing a smile.

One by one, she scans his purchases and returns them to the cart: cushions, tiki torch fuel, coiled rope, shovel, work gloves, a pair of coveralls . . .

They're almost at the finish line when she stops to examine the final item, a large vinyl tarp.

"Leaky roof," he says, thinking fast. "I heard it's going to rain tomorrow."

"Crap, is it really?"

Isn't it? Maybe he imagined he heard that. Maybe she thinks he's lying. Maybe that's why she's turning the tarp over and over, squinting at it.

"I bet it'll hold off," he says, hoping he sounds casual.

"I hope so. I'm off tomorrow." She turns away from the register and looks around, toward the security guard.

Panic-stricken, he knows he's trapped. He can't get away. They've got him.

Either she figured out why he really needs the tarp, or that cop put out some kind of bulletin.

"Jess!" the cashier calls, waving the tarp. "I need a price check!"

Jess, it turns out, is the assistant manager standing *near* the security guard.

Five minutes later, pulse still racing, he's back at the car with his purchases, for which he paid cash.

He checks his email again.

At last, she's responded.

> Tomorrow is great. Same time, same place?

He wants to say yes. It would be easiest to meet her in the church parking lot. Easiest, and most appropriate.

Theoretically, the place should be as deserted tomorrow as it was today.

But now? After what he did? After that lady cop was sniffing around, interrogating him?

Now there's no way.

He writes back with a lie: There's a barbecue at the church tomorrow. It will be busy. I'll find another place and let you know where.

He hits send and pulls out of his parking spot. He'll have to drive around and scout out a new location.

Damn that lady cop.

Church was perfect. As long as it's not a Sunday morning, as long as there's not something going on that will draw congregants. It's easy enough to check the website calendar. That's how he knew way in advance that Congregational would be all but deserted today.

Now he needs another place. It has to be public, where even the most cautious person would be comfortable about meeting a stranger. Not a coffee shop or a restaurant. That would be *too* public. Too many people around. Too much interaction with others. It has to be suitably off the beaten path, but not obviously so.

The problem is, the town is crowded, and more people are arriving every minute, with a steady stream of traffic on Route 28. He might have to resort to a neighboring village that's not as touristy as Mulberry Bay has become.

Which is a shock, because he remembers it as a run-down, forlorn town filled with empty storefronts, potholes, and For Sale signs. Back then, the old people who lived here did nothing but complain and reminisce, most of the middle-aged ones who hadn't left were contemplating it, and the young ones couldn't wait to graduate and flee the area.

When he returned this past spring, he noticed that everything was spruced up and the business district was thriving. But that was ahead of tourist season. He hadn't expected anything like this.

He hadn't expected anything that's happened today.

CHAPTER TWENTY-ONE

Before dinner, Hayley changes into her white eyelet sundress with bows on the shoulders. Mom told her not to even bring it, which shows how much she knows.

Mom has changed out of the khaki shorts and sleeveless white V-neck she wore all day in the car into an identical white top and black capris that are sagging off her hips.

"Is *that* what you're wearing?" Hayley asks when they emerge from their rooms to head downstairs.

"Yes, it's what I'm wearing, since I'm wearing it. Why?"

"It's just kind of . . . boring. Don't you think?"

Mom glances down at her outfit, then at Hayley. "I'm comfortable. And we're not going out to dinner; we're just staying here."

"I know, but still . . . I don't think that fits you."

"It does. My style *is* boring, apparently."

"I don't mean it doesn't fit your *style*. I mean it doesn't fit *you*. Your *size*. Those pants are way too big."

"Then I guess I'll have to have seconds," Mom says with a little laugh.

Hayley is kind of worried, though. Mom's always been thin, but the other day when she had on a bathing suit at the town pool, Hayley thought her arms and legs and collarbone were way too skinny. Since then, she's noticed that Mom hasn't been eating much either.

Maybe it's not just because Dad's been mad at her. Maybe it's because she's wondering about her long-lost father, wishing she could find him.

She heard Dad ask her about it in the car.

Mom acted like it was no big deal, but Hayley could tell she was lying.

She wasn't planning to tell Mom about the DNA test unless her dad turns out to be an amazing guy, like a prince or billionaire or movie star, because then she won't get mad at Hayley for eavesdropping and lying about her age on the genealogy website. She'll just be happy to meet her dad.

Then again, she's making it really hard for Hayley to go looking for him, since she's not even allowed to leave the house.

Maybe she should just tell her now, while they're alone. Maybe they can go find him together.

"Mom—"

"Tal'?" Dad calls from their room. "Have you seen Caleb's sneakers?"

"They're in his bag, aren't they?"

"I don't see them."

"I don't either," Caleb says.

"Be right there." Mom shakes her head. "Go on down, Hayley."

"Okay, but Mom?"

Her mother is already heading back to her room. She stops and looks over her shoulder, distracted. "Hmm?"

Hayley hesitates, then says only, "See you downstairs."

She descends the grand staircase.

In the foyer, high on the wall, there's a framed portrait of a couple she recognizes as Asa and Edith Winterfield from her online research. They're the ones who were axe murdered here in 1894. They look so prim and proper that it's hard to imagine them lying all bloody and hacked to death or hanging around haunting the place.

She's pretty sure they are, though. Earlier, when she was on the terrace talking to Chloe on the phone, she could have sworn she saw a ghost flitting at the edge of the woods.

The dining room looks like a fancy restaurant in a movie, with fresh flowers and lit candles and linen napkins and fine china, crystal, and silver. The chairs are huge and heavy, carved of wood with beautiful beige cushioned seats.

She's relieved her mom's friends turned out *not* to be a bunch of boring old people.

Kelly is a real live celebrity, on the cover of a magazine, which you'd think Mom would have mentioned to Hayley.

Midge is amazing too. She's a police chief who's arrested dangerous criminals, which makes her "a total badass."

That's what Kelly called her.

"You have to be, when you grew up with three older brothers," Midge said with a shrug.

Hayley is a total badass, too, except it's because her own brother is younger and a total scaredy-cat. She doesn't say it, though. It might hurt Caleb's feelings. Also, her parents might yell at her if she uses the word *ass*, and that would be embarrassing.

Linden is super hilarious, *and* he's a famous interior designer who used to date one of Beyoncé's bodyguards. He said there are a lot of celebrities around here because they can hide. A lot of people don't even know who they are, and the ones who do don't bother them.

Nap is from Louisiana, and he's named after the famous general Napoleon, who was his great-great-great-great . . . a lot of greats . . . something. He has spiky black hair and he's really tall, but he shook his head when Hayley asked him if he plays basketball.

"I don't, but Midge does. She made it to the championships."

"You did?" Hayley asks in awe. "You're like Caitlin Clark! That's so epic!"

"Not quite," Midge says with a laugh. "That was high school. State championships. And we didn't win. Now it's just winter rec league."

Hayley asks her about that. She asks them all about their lives, and they ask her about hers. She tells them about her summer job with the Piazzas, who live down the street. She calls herself a babysitter instead of a mother's helper, which makes her feel grown up. The adults seem to think so, too, because they talk to her like she's a real person and not a kid.

She hopes Mom and Dad, who never do that, are noticing. But they're way down at the other end of the table with Caleb, and they mostly seem to be noticing that it's way past his bedtime and he looks like he's going to face-plant in the potato–whatever it's called. It's got a French name that Hayley can't remember, even though she repeated it to herself a few times after Kelly told her.

She wants to tell Chloe all about it, because Chloe is part French, even though it's not like she's ever been there or can speak the language. Not like Kelly, who actually *lived* in Paris. No wonder she's so chic and sophisticated.

Caleb tries to cover a huge yawn with his little hand, and Mom sets down her fork.

"Come on, sweetie, let's get you to bed."

"Are you going to bed, too, Mommy?"

"Not yet, but I'll tuck you in, and you can read with the light on."

"No! I'm scared to be upstairs alone."

Hayley sees Mom look over at her, like she expects her to make a comment, like she did about the bad guys in the woods.

She knew as soon as she said it that it was a stupid mistake. Caleb isn't the kind of brother you can tease about stuff like that.

She turns to Kelly. "This is the most amazing chicken I've ever had. It tastes like oranges!"

Kelly smiles. "It's actually duck. I'll give the chef your compliments."

"Duck! Wow!" Hayley cuts off another piece, trying not to think of the ducks she sees in the park back home in the spring with their fuzzy little yellow ducklings.

"Hayley?" Mom says. "It's getting late. Finish up so you and Caleb can go to bed."

"What? No! I'm not even tired! And I'm still eating my duck. I might have seconds!" She turns to Kelly. "Are there seconds?"

"Of course. And there's dessert. Do you like chocolate soufflé?"

"Yes!"

Dad pushes back his chair. "I'll take Caleb up, Talia. Come on, buddy."

Caleb shakes his head. "I want Mommy."

"Mommy is still eating. I'm done, and you're done, and we're both tired. Let's go."

"Are you sure?" Mom asks him.

"Positive. If you'll all excuse me, it's been a long day."

When he and Caleb have said their good nights and left the room, everyone is quiet.

"Sorry," Mom says. "Caleb has a hard time in unfamiliar settings."

"Plus, Dad's allergic to chocolate," Hayley points out. "So it's not like he can have dessert anyway."

"You can have his share, then. I'll go see if it's ready." Kelly gets up, smiling at her. "By the way, kiddo, every time I look at you, I see your mom. You look exactly like her. Doesn't she, Midge?"

Midge nods. "*Exactly* like her."

People say that all the time, but Hayley doesn't see it.

Especially not right now. Mom seems lonely at the end of the table, picking at her food. She glances up as if she feels Hayley watching her, and Hayley quickly looks away, across the table, out the window.

It's dark out now.

She wonders if the ghost is still there.

Or maybe it's not a ghost.

Maybe it's her grandfather, because he knows they're here and he's trying to work up his nerve to come to the door and meet them.

Or maybe . . .

Maybe it *is* him, but he's not the kind of man they'd *want* to meet. Maybe that's why Granny Nat never got married to him or even told Mom his name.

For the first time since she mailed her spit to the genealogy website, Hayley wonders if it wasn't such a great idea after all.

CHAPTER TWENTY-TWO

Back in the parlor after dinner, Kelly is still waiting for a chance to talk to Midge and Talia alone.

The caterers are clearing away the dessert plates. Caleb is upstairs with Ben. Nap and Linden are somehow engaged in a political debate despite both being on the same side of the issue. Hayley is back out on the terrace, FaceTiming with her friends back home. Midge keeps looking at her watch and checking her phone, and Talia is yawning.

It's now or never. Kelly gets to her feet. "Midge and Talia, can you two help me in the kitchen for a few minutes?"

They follow her. Midge is humming to herself.

"Wow, something has *you* in a chipper mood tonight," Kelly comments.

"Or some*one*," Talia says. "I bet it's—"

"I'm not chipper. I just heard a Britney Spears song on the nineties radio station on the way over, and now it's stuck in my head, and I keep picturing that CD at the morgue with . . . the remains."

"That's definitely not chipper." Talia shudders. "It was Britney Spears? The CD in the player?"

"Yes. It was *Oops . . . I Did It Again*."

In the kitchen, Midge points at an array of blades in a wooden case on the counter. "Those are some serious knives."

"They're Marcel's." Kelly indicates the adjacent butler's pantry, where the staff is cleaning up and conversing in French.

"He brings his own?"

"Most chefs do. Especially when they're left-handed."

"Like Caroline. Remember how hard it was for her to use regular scissors when we were kids?"

Kelly nods. "I was her partner on a paper snowflake project. I was afraid she was going to cut herself, so I made a big stink until the art teacher gave her a special pair of lefty scissors."

"You always had her back."

"I still do. That's what I wanted to talk to you about."

Talia's hands shake a bit as she clasps them in front of her on the gleaming black granite surface. Midge's gingery brows are furrowed above blue eyes zeroed in on Kelly as if she's just taken the witness stand.

"The thing is, I've been feeling sick every time I think about what happened to her after she left us that night," Kelly says.

Midge nods. "You're not alone."

"Definitely not," Talia agrees. "I think it's hardest on you, Kelly, because you live here at Haven Cliff. But all summer, I've been wishing we'd never found out the truth. I wish I could go back to assuming she was out there somewhere, living her own life. I don't need to know any more."

Kelly shakes her head. "I do. I want to know the whole story. How about you, Midge?"

"I just want to make sure Mary Beth Winterfield pays for what she did to her sister. And that's exactly what I'm going to do, the second we have an ID on those remains."

"I can't believe it's taking so long," Talia says. "What's the holdup? Did Nap say?"

"This is how it always goes. Forensic test results aren't instant, like on TV. There's nothing to do but wait."

"Well, we all know what they're going to tell us," Kelly says. "That's Caroline. We know it is. But I need to know more."

"About her death?"

"And about her life. So I hired a private investigator to look into it."

Midge gapes. "You *what*?"

"I hired a—"

"No, I heard you. But why? It's not like we don't know what happened to her."

"It isn't that. I just wanted to understand how we could have missed what was really going on with her. I keep going over all the things that led up to her winding up in that hole in the woods, and I know we can't undo any of it, but . . . I guess I need to blame someone."

"You can blame Mary Beth," Midge says.

"I mean someone other than Mary Beth. And other than ourselves."

"Ourselves?" Talia echoes. "Why us?"

"Because we were her best friends. We were supposed to have her back," Kelly says. "We should have been paying more attention to what was going on with her those last few months."

"We tried. But her parents didn't want her hanging around with us. They pushed Gordy on her. She was always with him or involved in some church activity."

"Speaking of that, I was over at Congregational today," Midge says. "Remember the purity ball?"

Talia groans. "I do. Caroline seemed like she was so into it. And since she and Gordy had taken a vow of chastity, I never would have imagined that they . . . you know. But she was pregnant, so I guess you never can tell what's really going on with someone, no matter how well you know them."

"Or *think* you know them," Kelly says. "What if it wasn't Gordy? What if she was involved with someone else?"

Midge nods. "I've wondered that myself."

"Same," Talia admits. "Like . . . maybe she was secretly in love with another boy she knew from church—or even someone from school, someone her parents would oppose."

"*Exactly,*" Kelly says, and turns to Midge. "Why were you at Congregational today?"

"I was on a case. As soon as I walked in there, I had a flashback, and when the pastor came out to talk to me, I thought for a second it was Caroline's Reverend B. Remember him?"

Heart racing, Kelly says, "Reverend Bauer? I can't believe you said that, Midge, because that's what I wanted to talk to you about."

CHAPTER TWENTY-THREE

Mary Beth's leg throbs where the bullet struck, even though it's been a few months and the wound is nearly healed.

Stripped down and soaked in perspiration, she's being roasted alive in a cinder block oven of a cell.

Lights out isn't for another half hour, but she's been lying here since she returned to the housing unit after a supper she hardly touched. It's much too hot to eat steaming food, much too hot to hang out in a common area with a bunch of sweaty inmates, too hot for reading, for lamplight, for sleep.

She doesn't have enough money in her incarcerated account to afford a small fan at the commissary. She's been saving up to buy earbuds and an MP3 player, but that's a long way off. She can rely only on the funds from her work here; no friends and family are making deposits for her on the outside.

For her, there will be no reprieve from the heat, or the noise.

If days on the cellblock are loud, nights are far worse. The only real quiet comes in the hour or two before dawn, but even then, it can be fleeting. You never know when there will be a burst of commotion, some fresh hell playing out for everyone to hear.

After all those years in federal prison, Mary Beth became desensitized to it, but this time is different.

This time, despite her commitment to living a straight life, she's being held on a felony she never intended to commit, and likely facing far more serious charges for murders she didn't commit at all.

Midge and the others will never know that it wasn't Mary Beth who posed as Caroline, luring them into the woods. That she was only back in Mulberry Bay this summer, back at Haven Cliff, because she, too, had been lured.

Yes, she was armed, but because she feared for her own safety, not because she wanted to harm her sister's friends. Yes, she tried to go along with their assumption that she was Caroline. She was so filled with shock—and dread—that she didn't know what else to do.

She realized then—realizes now—that only one person in the world would hold Mary Beth, Talia, Midge, Kelly, *and* Gordy Klatte responsible for what happened at Haven Cliff on that terrible summer night so many years ago.

Gordy, most of all.

Just as Mary Beth is being wrongfully blamed for his death, he died because he'd been blamed for something that wasn't his fault.

The moment she learned he was dead, she knew who was behind it.

That's when she snapped.

Once again, she'd been betrayed by the person she loved and needed most. She wanted to die. It wasn't the first time she'd considered taking her own life, but until that night, she'd had something—someone—to live for.

Now there was nothing left. No one who mattered. No one to whom she mattered.

She was sure that Midge Kennedy was also armed. And that if she felt threatened, or if she felt that her friends' lives were in danger, she'd have no choice but to turn her weapon on Mary Beth.

That's how it was supposed to play out.

What happened instead . . . well, that was a blur.

Some of it still is.

She knows she was shot by a bullet that didn't end her living nightmare.

Now she's resigned to her fate.

Her court-ordered attorney, aware that she intends to plead guilty for the assault on Midge, has been working to ensure that she understands the consequences.

She understands. It doesn't matter.

Very soon, she'll also be facing charges for the murders of Gordon Klatte and the Walking Man, while the real killer is out there somewhere . . .

Where?

Hopefully, far from Mulberry Bay, no longer hungry for revenge.

If not, Mary Beth is certain the nightmare will continue to play out. Not just for her, but for everyone who ever played a role in the tragedy that befell Caroline Winterfield.

CHAPTER TWENTY-FOUR

December 24, 1997

The first pain comes suddenly, jolting Mary Beth from a dead sleep.

She sits up with a gasp.

The room is dark. Hearing soft, steady breathing from the adjacent twin bed, she thinks for a moment that it's Caroline. That she's home.

But she hears a train rattling through the night, and there are none in Mulberry Bay.

Here, she often sits in the window and watches the freight cars fly along the elevated tracks across the street. They never stop. If one ever did, she'd hop on and stow away, allowing herself to be transported to some other, distant place.

The destination doesn't matter. Just somewhere, anywhere but here.

Six months ago, she thought anything would be better than spending another moment under her parents' roof. Even jail. The Baxters must have figured that out after meeting them on that awful night she was arrested, because they dropped the charges. She was a juvenile offender, so her name was never made public, and her records were sealed. No one would ever have to know.

She spent the rest of May and half of June grounded in Eve and Joanna's old bedroom, homeschooled for what was left of her junior year. Her parents told Caroline, and the school, and presumably anyone else who asked, that she was quarantined with mono.

Then her parents figured out that she was pregnant and sent her here—blindsiding her, leaving her no choice whatsoever.

The name *Midwest Golden Bridge Maternity Home* might conjure a sunlit farmhouse beside a babbling brook, but the reality is a converted warehouse in a Rust Belt city where the sky is overcast even when it's not raining, or snowing—which it usually is.

It's a depressing place run by oppressive women overseen by oppressive men, populated by oppressed, depressed, repressed teenage girls in various stages of pregnancy.

At first, Mary Beth made friends easily, as she tends to do in the real world, gravitating toward the ones who are older and more seasoned—thus, later in their pregnancies. One by one, they disappeared into the basement "birthing suite" to have their babies, never to return.

Mary Beth learned to keep to herself, focused on her high school coursework, college essay, and applications. The one good thing about being here is an incentive program for paid college tuition, and her grades are well within range.

Last month, she earned her diploma. Phone calls are forbidden, but letters are allowed. She never receives any, even from Caroline, but she writes to her from time to time.

Hey, guess what? I'm a graduate! And I didn't even have to wear that dopey cap and gown and listen to speeches! Guess there's one good thing about being stuck here . . .

No reply.

Then, when she got her early-decision letter, she sent a postcard:

I got in! Syracuse University, here I come!

Again, no acknowledgment.

She sent Caroline a Christmas card, though she's beginning to suspect that her parents are intercepting the mail. But would they really do something illegal?

Maybe it's just that her sister is as disappointed in her as they are. They've probably brainwashed her into thinking Mary Beth is a sinful loser.

Whatever. She's never going back there. She doesn't need any of them anymore.

The home is preparing her for her baby with classes focused on healthy pregnancy and delivery. Some are geared toward what happens afterward, with a strong focus on adoption options.

Attendance is mandatory to all classes, and to the weekly "mixers" where the girls mingle with childless couples. At every one of them, Mary Beth presents her surliest self, and the staff reprimands her for her "attitude problem."

"I don't see why I have to meet all these people if I'm going to keep my baby," she frequently complains to anyone who will listen. It seems as though nobody ever does.

She attends optional workshops for girls who intend to go the single motherhood route. So far, they've made it seem like a daunting and perhaps insurmountable challenge—physically, emotionally, and financially.

Maybe it is, for some people. But Mary Beth has it all figured out. She still has a big wad of cash hidden in her doll in the secret cubby. It will pay for rent and diapers and food while she goes to college, and she'll get a part-time job. She has it all planned out.

Even labor.

But she thought she had another couple of weeks, at least. First babies are often late, Astrid warned her.

She's Mary Beth's "guidance counselor," like in high school—only the women assigned to you at Golden Bridge aren't trying to help you with schedules and SAT prep and college applications.

"I'm here to answer any questions you have about anything at all," Astrid told Mary Beth on her first day. "Really, you can ask me anything, okay?"

"Okay. Why do round pizzas come in square boxes?"

"I'll get right on that," Astrid replied, straight faced, but Mary Beth saw a twinkle in her eye.

Astrid, too, is from upstate New York, only a few years older than Mary Beth. She attends a nearby college, majoring in nursing, and volunteers at the home. In another setting, they might have been friends.

Seized by another stabbing pain deep in her womb, Mary Beth cries out.

In the next bed, the snoring stops. "Leigh, go get someone."

Her roommate props herself up with a groggy "Huh? What?"

"*Get help*! Hurry!"

There's no need.

On Christmas morning, thirty excruciating hours after that first contraction, a sweating, freezing, sobbing Mary Beth bears down with every ounce of energy and courage she has left. She expected the pain to be more significant than the "discomfort" they described in her childbirth class, but it's far worse than anything she ever imagined.

Astrid promised Mary Beth she'd find out about pain medication, an epidural. When the time came, she said, she'd see to it that Mary Beth got something to ease her labor.

But Astrid isn't here. She's home with her family through New Year's.

And none of the scrubs-clad strangers in the room have offered anything more than coaching and prayers, even when she begged.

"That's right," one of them says, perched between her legs at the foot of the bed. "Come *on*, Mary."

"I'm . . . not . . . freaking . . . *Mary*!" she bites out. They keep calling her that—why? Because it's Christmas and she reminds them of the Blessed Virgin?

Yeah, she doubts Jesus's mother cursed up a blue streak in the manger as she has, eliciting admonishments from everyone in the vicinity.

"You need to calm yourself down right now, young lady! You're hysterical!"

"I am not hyst—aaaaahhhhh!" she screams.

"*Push*. You can do it."

Hell yes, she can. She can set herself free. She can walk out of here with her baby and never see any of them, or this hellhole, ever again.

She pushes with an unearthly grunt that becomes a screech before giving way to a high-pitched wail and collapses, panting. But the wail continues, and she realizes it's coming from a goo-covered thing the doctor is holding, still tethered to her by a bloody gelatinous cord.

Her child.

I did it.

We did it.

I love you so much.

Swept by an overpowering urge to take her child into her arms and never let go, she chokes out words. "I . . . want . . ."

But she's too weak to say it, too weak to reach for the baby, too weak to do anything but watch, helpless, as a latex-gloved hand comes at her with enormous scissors.

The cord is severed.

The baby is gone.

"Wait . . . I want . . ."

"Hush. You need to deliver the placenta, and then we have a lot of repairs to do."

"But . . . my . . . baby . . ."

A nurse in bloody scrubs and glasses hands a metal pan to the doctor, still positioned between her legs, and says, "The baby's fine. Beautiful and healthy, getting cleaned up and ready to meet Mom and Dad."

"No, there's no dad. It's just . . . me."

She sees the confusion register in the nurse's eyes.

A man's voice says, "She hasn't decided yet."

She turns to see Mr. Kendall, the school's president, standing in the doorway.

It's wrong, him being here, wearing a suit with a green-and-red plaid tie, while she's completely exposed, blood-smeared legs splayed. She attempts to adjust her gown, but the doctor barks at her to lie still.

Her hands clench into fists, because there are still contractions, and because Mr. Kendall is dead wrong.

She *has* decided.

She isn't giving up her baby, and there's nothing anyone here can do or say that will change her mind about that.

CHAPTER TWENTY-FIVE

Present Day

The duck and potatoes and chocolate soufflé are churning in Midge's stomach, and there's a massive lump in her throat. She's going to vomit, or cry, or both.

Because the thing Kelly just told them . . .

Talia repeats it. "Reverend B. was a *pedophile*?"

"Yes."

"But . . . but . . . how do you know?"

"Toby found out. She's the investigator I hired to look into Caroline and her family. She's an old friend, actually. I've known her since my law school days, but I don't think you've ever met her, since . . . you know."

Right. Law school was a time when the three of them weren't friends at all.

Everything had fallen apart a year after Caroline disappeared, because Midge thought they should come clean with what they knew, and Kelly and Talia thought they should keep Caroline's secret, as promised.

Majority ruled.

Friendship splintered.

They lost touch.

Midge wasn't the least bit surprised when she heard through the Mulberry Bay grapevine about Kelly's first divorce. But she was shocked—and yes, very glad—to later hear her former friend had since gotten her undergraduate degree and was at Stanford Law.

"Kelly," Talia says, "are you saying . . . Do you think Caroline and Reverend B. . . . ?"

"I don't want to think it."

"Neither do I," Midge says.

"Maybe it's not true."

"Oh, it's definitely true," Kelly tells Talia. "There are too many accusers and reliable witnesses who claimed there was something off about him, and apparently there's some concrete evidence, as well."

"That's not what I meant," Talia says. "I believe that Reverend B. was a disgusting pervert, but maybe he didn't hurt Caroline that way?"

"Talia—"

"No, Kelly, wait—I mean, how could we not have suspected if she was dealing with something like that? We were so close! We saw her every single day, and she was always so sweet and sunny. If that man was—"

"Talia, she wasn't," Midge cuts in. "Those last few months, before she vanished, she wasn't herself. She was quiet, and she pulled back from all of us. I was so busy with spring sports, but I noticed it."

"So did I," Kelly said, "even though I was so busy with . . . well, partying it up."

"We were all caught up in our own stuff," Talia says. "I was obsessed with my role in the spring musical senior year."

"You had the lead," Kelly says. "I remember that. You were Lady Macbeth."

"Kelly! Macbeth wasn't a musical; it was our sophomore play. Senior year, we did *Grease*, and I didn't have a lead. I was a Pink Lady!"

"Okay, do I look like IMDb? All I know is that you were in some show that we all went to see."

"Not Caroline," Talia says. "I thought it was because I kept trying to convince her to audition for Sandy, but when I found out she was pregnant, I assumed that was the reason."

"Maybe the pregnancy was just the tip of the iceberg," Kelly says. "When I remember how that man acted so concerned after she went missing . . ."

"He led a candlelight vigil," Talia says. "We all went. And I remember him joining the search parties combing the woods and fields around Haven Cliff too. How could he have done that if he did . . . well, what you're saying he did?"

The knot in Midge's stomach tightens. "We were a part of all that too. And *we* knew we weren't going to find her."

"Are you defending him, Midge?"

"No! It's just, the more I find out about Caroline's past, the more I hate what we did."

"I hate what we *didn't* do," Talia says.

"We were kids being kids," Kelly points out. "And this isn't about us. This is about Bauer."

"When was he accused?" Midge asks.

"The first one was in 2013, and by then he'd left the ministry, but I'm sure it was going on long before that."

"Where was he in 2013?"

"Teaching theology on the adjunct faculty at a college near El Paso. The news got out, and others came forward from other places where he'd been teaching and ministering. Students, and former congregants."

"Including here? At Congregational?" Midge asks.

"Not that I can tell."

"Why didn't we even hear about this until now?" Talia asks. "About him, I mean?"

"Maybe it's just too pervasive," Kelly says.

Midge nods. "Cases involving schools and churches and sex abuse were exploding in those years. I've investigated a few. There were massive cover-ups, victim shaming, scandal, and repercussions for educators on every level and organized religions of every denomination."

"There's plenty of denial as well," Kelly adds. "Especially when it comes to church leaders. Misguided people are willing to protect them from what they perceive as unfounded attacks. Some of those people are powerful enough to succeed in that effort."

"Or in covering up crimes they're aware of." Midge's voice is tight. "What happened to him?"

"To Reverend B.?"

"Yes." She braces herself for the answer, wondering if she might actually have seen him today after all, back at the church office.

Intellectually, she knows that's impossible. Of course it was the substitute pastor, Joseph Nielson.

But when you're working a missing person case involving a pretty teenage girl and you hear the word *pedophile*, well . . .

That's just where your mind goes.

"He was eventually indicted in Texas," Kelly says. "There was a trial."

"Good!" Talia says. "I hope this monster was convicted and he's rotting behind bars somewhere."

Kelly shakes her head. "He isn't. The case finally went to court just last year. There was a hung jury."

"So it was a mistrial," Midge says.

"Yes. And then it was dropped."

"But how is that possible?" Talia asks.

"It happens a lot, unfortunately. I didn't practice criminal law, only corporate, but I know that in cases like rape and sexual abuse, victims are already traumatized, and then they have to relive it all in court. The defense can be brutal toward the victim. Sometimes it's in their best interests not to be put through hell yet again."

"But you mentioned that other accusers had come forward," Midge says. "What happened with those cases?"

"Nothing. I think he disappeared before they went anywhere."

"What do you mean, he disappeared?"

"I have no idea, Midge. Apparently, no one knows."

"What about his family?" Talia asks. "Wasn't he married?"

"His wife claims she has no idea where he went. They have grown children, and they all say the same thing."

"I don't buy that. I bet they know something," Talia says. "I bet someone does."

"You said he was living in El Paso?" At Kelly's nod, Midge goes on, thinking out loud. "I've been there. It's a border city. You can stroll across a pedestrian bridge to Juárez the way you'd walk a few blocks somewhere else."

"So you think Reverend B. took a stroll to Mexico?"

"It's certainly a possibility. If he was lucky enough to get off the hook for that first trial, it would have to be pretty tempting to escape another one."

"And another, and another, and so on," Kelly says. "According to Toby, accusers were coming out of the woodwork. Look, I know it won't bring Caroline back, but if he hurt her in any way . . . don't we owe it to her, and to everyone else he might have abused, to find him and keep this from happening again? Midge, can you look into it? I know you have resources you can use."

"I'll do whatever I can, but it's difficult to find someone who doesn't want to be found. Send me whatever you've got from Toby."

"I will. There's a lot of background information about him. His family too. You can see in the old photos that everything was staged to make it look like they had a perfect, wholesome life. But then you see his mug shot, and all the stuff from the trial, and wow, what a difference."

"I feel sorry for his wife and kids," Talia says. "I remember them."

"Why don't I remember them?" Kelly asks.

"Because they were younger, or because you only noticed the cool kids, or because you didn't take piano lessons. They had the same teacher I did, so I used to see them."

"What were they like?" Midge asks.

"The girls were quiet. Kind of shy. Really polite. The boys—"

"Hey, Midge? Where are y'all?" Nap calls from the front of the house. "I've got to get going."

"Be right there!" she calls back and climbs off the stool.

"Sorry, we're coming!" Kelly follows her, saying in a low voice, "Please don't tell him about this."

"Are you kidding? I would never."

She turns to Talia. "And Tal—"

"Never. Right now, all I want to do is wrangle my daughter to bed and go to sleep myself. But before we go in there, I have to ask, Midge . . . what's up with you and Nap?"

"What do you mean, what's *up* with us?"

"She wants to know if you two are having a torrid fling," Kelly says. "And so do I."

"Sorry to disappoint you two, but we're just colleagues."

"What I'm hearing is that it just hasn't happened *yet*," Kelly tells Talia.

"You might want to have your hearing checked," Midge says.

"Oh, come on, admit it, Midge," Talia says. "You know you like having him around. He fits right in with all of us."

"I'll admit that. He does. And okay, I do like having him around. He's interesting, and he has some good stories. He gets my job; I get his. But we're both too busy for . . . *torrid*."

Five minutes later, Midge, Nap, and Linden are walking toward their cars.

"I really appreciate your inviting me, Midge," Nap says. "It was fun."

"It *was* fun," she agrees, and she means it. Torrid or not, busy or not, she was glad to have him here tonight.

"You have my number in your phone now, Nap," Linden says. "Text me and I'll send you that info on Slovenia."

"Slovenia?"

"I'm going next month on vacation," Nap tells Midge. "Linden was just there in April."

"That's some coincidence."

"Not really. We both listened to the same podcast about underrated travel destinations," Nap says. "And it's a use-it-or-lose-it situation—the time off and an airline credit that expires at the end of the year."

"I think my vacation days are all going to be in the lose-it category this year." Lest he think she's hinting for him to invite her on the trip, she adds, "But if I can take some time off when Walt's back, all I want to do is hang around here and relax."

"Come on, Midge, you need to live a little. And poor Nap is going to Slovenia all alone."

"Linden! A lot of people enjoy solo travel."

"Take it from me: It's overrated. You should tag along," Linden says in his Linden way, unaware—or not caring—that she and Nap aren't *together*, together.

"You know what's *underrated*?" Midge asks with a yawn. "I mean, besides Slovenia? *Sleep*. I've got a long day tomorrow. Good night, guys."

CHAPTER TWENTY-SIX

With the car engine running and the air-conditioning blasting, he sits in a McDonald's parking lot, eating a cheeseburger and fries, checking his email, and trying to ignore the stench in the air despite the closed windows.

It's from the dumpster a few feet from his car. The restaurant is as crowded as everything else in town, so he parked way back here, where he can eat his meal without being noticed.

He shouldn't have stopped for food at all, but he exerted so much energy today that he's feeling depleted. He needs to fuel up for the unpleasant task he's created for himself, all because of her.

And now she's sent a new email: I can meet you sooner if you want—tonight, maybe?

"Tonight!" He shakes his head, muttering to himself. "No . . . no."

He has to stick to his plan. It can't wait.

In heat like this, the car will start to stink quickly. It's a rental he picked up at the airport. He can't return it smelling like a carcass, and once that stench seeps from the trunk into the upholstery, there's no getting it out.

It's almost dark now. Almost time to head way up into the mountains.

When it's over, he'll get some sleep.

He writes back, I'm sorry, I can't tonight. I have other plans. Tomorrow.

He sends the message and sits holding the phone, troubled.

First she wasn't available today. Now, suddenly, she is? What kind of game is she playing?

What if it's a trap?

What if she isn't who she says she is?

He pops the last bite of his burger into his mouth, licks his finger to get the salty bits at the bottom of the carton of fries, and drains the chocolate milkshake.

He can't take any chances.

He'll go up to the mountains as planned, empty the trunk, and then keep right on driving. North, maybe up to Canada. He'll leave the country for a while, just in case. He'll have to make up a story . . .

But then, he's always been good at that.

About to close out the screen and put away his phone, he sees that another email has come in from her.

> Tomorrow is fine. I have a place to meet. It's called Haven Cliff.

CHAPTER TWENTY-SEVEN

Even at this hour, there's traffic on Route 28. Waiting to make her turn, Midge places a call to Sergeant Renee Michter.

She answers on the first ring. "Hi, Midge."

"Hi. Just checking to see how things are going?"

"Hot time in the old town tonight. Two pickpocketing reports from the band concert, one drunk and disorderly, and we broke up a domestic altercation at one of the picnic pavilions."

"Has the Greene girl turned up?"

"Not yet."

Clearly, Sarah didn't just stop for ice cream on her way home and lose track of time. Still, that doesn't mean she's in serious trouble. Maybe she was just hot and cranky and frustrated with rules and chores, so she decided to go off and have some fun. Maybe she'll come back when she's good and ready.

"Where are you?" Midge asks Renee, hearing background chatter.

"Standing in line to get ice cream at Get the Scoop, along with everyone else in town. Where are you?"

"Heading home from Haven Cliff."

"If you're up for ice cream, meet me here. They've got a two-for-one special. Do you like chocolate fudge chip?"

"I like chocolate anything," Midge says.

"Girl, I've got you. Get on over here."

"I shouldn't, but I will."

She isn't planning to park in her spot behind the police station since she's off duty, but nothing else is available. Shops and restaurants are open late, and plenty of people are still out and about. She hurries toward the ice cream parlor's pink-striped awnings, expecting to see Renee out front holding two drippy cones. But there's a long line out the door even at this hour. Her uniformed pal is easy to spot among the T-shirts-and-flip-flops crowd, right up front but still waiting to order.

"Hey, Midge, thanks for saving me. I don't need two cones if I want to fit into my wedding gown, and I've got a fitting on Saturday."

Renee is getting married in October. She was a cop in the Bronx before moving to the Hudson Valley a few years ago to live with her fiancé, Darius, a local firefighter.

"The invitations are going out next week," she tells Midge. "I'm giving you a plus-one in case there's anyone you want to bring."

"There isn't, but thanks anyway. I'll save you a chicken entrée."

"It's filet mignon."

"No way!"

"Hey, you only get married once. If you're lucky, anyway." Renee points at the menu board. "We're almost up. You want a sugar cone or a cake cone?"

"Sugar," Midge says.

"All I need is another single so I don't have to break a twenty," the man in front of them tells his wife as she digs through her purse with one hand, holding her ice cream cone in the other.

"Oh, come on, really?" a young voice grumbles behind Midge. "Break the damned twenty, dude. I want my ice cream!"

"The line would be moving a lot faster if the kids who work here spent more time scooping and less time chitchatting," an adult voice returns.

Midge sees four teenagers behind the counter, all wearing white uniforms with pink-and-white-striped aprons. She recognizes the girl behind the register from this afternoon. It's Taylor, of the unwashed uniform, pool-hopping brother, and weary mother who could strangle her, but not really.

She's waiting for the couple to pay as another girl and a boy painstakingly scoop ice cream from the round cardboard containers in the glass freezer compartment. Another boy isn't doing anything at all, just having what appears to be an ongoing serious conversation with the others.

"Yeah, well, I bet she ran off with some guy," he's saying.

"Her?" The female scooper pauses midscoop, shaking her head. "No freaking way."

"You're right. If anything, she ran off to join a monastery."

They're talking about Sarah, Midge realizes.

The girl at the register snorts. "Ryan, you idiot. Girls can't be monks."

"Really? How come?"

"No singles, Bob," the woman in front of them tells her husband. "You're going to have to break the twenty."

"Fine." He hands it over.

The girl takes it and punches register keys, telling her friends, "You guys, she didn't run off to do anything. She's probably, like, dead. I heard—"

She breaks off, noticing Renee standing there in her law enforcement uniform.

"You heard what?" one of the coworkers asks.

She just shakes her head, counting Bob's change into his hand, right down to the penny. He pockets it all, plucks a huge pile of napkins from the holder on the counter, and follows his wife out the door.

"Way to ignore the tip jar," the girl grumbles under her breath—though loud enough for waiting customers to hear, and heed. "Next?"

Stepping forward, Renee orders their ice cream.

Midge pulls out her wallet. "My treat."

"Don't be silly."

"You need to save up for all that filet mignon at your wedding," Midge tells her, and holds out a bill. "How's it going, Taylor?"

The girl frowns, taking the money. "Um, great?"

"We met earlier today."

"We did?" She looks up from tapping the register keys. "Where?"

"Your house. I was in my uniform, and you were . . . *not.*"

"Oh! You're the cop who arrested my brother!"

"Tay! Your brother got arrested?" her female coworker asks. "What'd he do?"

"Some dumb thing. Whatever." She hands Midge her change with a fake smile. "Here you go."

Midge drops the coins into the jar, pockets the bills, and looks at Renee. "Can you wait here for our cones while Taylor and I have a little chat?"

"Sure thing."

"Wait, what? I have to watch the register."

"Ryan will take over for a few minutes," Midge says. "Ryan?"

"But I'm supposed to be scooping."

"*He's* taking over the scooping." She points at the kid who's doing nothing at all. "Taylor?"

"Is this about Jacob? Because seriously, I had nothing to do with whatever he did."

"Not about Jacob." Midge steps around the corner. "Is there a place back there to talk?"

Taylor nods and leads Midge into a small storage room. She's trembling.

"Hey, Taylor, relax. You're not in any kind of trouble."

"I'm not?" She leans against a stack of boxes. "What is it, then? You're a cop, right?"

"I am, and I'm looking for Sarah Greene."

"Oh. I, uh . . . I barely even know her. We're not, like, friends or anything."

"But you heard something?"

She gives Midge a blank look, which seems about as genuine as her thick black lashes and polished oval fingernails.

"You said you heard that Sarah is dead."

"Oh! That. I didn't actually *hear* she's dead. I just think she might be."

"Why?"

"My boyfriend's the one who said it. Plus, she kind of looks like the girl who disappeared from Elizabethville a few months ago."

"Junia Stanton?"

"Yeah."

Midge nods. She hasn't seen a photo of Junia in a while, but as she recalls, she and Sarah do look somewhat alike.

"That's what these crazy serial killers do," Taylor says. "They go after girls who all look alike, right?"

"I don't know about that."

"Trust me, they do. I listen to a ton of true crime podcasts," she tells Midge with the confidence of someone who just revealed she has a PhD in criminology.

"Uh-huh. Taylor, does your boyfriend know Junia?"

"No, but he, like, went to football camp with her cousin. He thinks there's a psycho stalker hanging around, and that he got Junia, and now Sarah."

"Your boyfriend thinks that? Or the cousin does?"

"I'm not sure."

"Well, did someone *see* a psycho stalker hanging around?"

"I don't know. Jaret's just, like, really worried about me. He told me to be careful walking home after work tonight. He's super protective," Taylor adds, with a hint of pride.

"What's his last name?" Midge asks.

"Buckley."

"Does he live over on Chestnut Street? Is his dad's name Chuck?"

"Yes. Why?"

Midge knows him from her softball rec league. Nice guy.

“Do you know where Jaret is right now?” she asks Taylor.

“Home sleeping. He has practice at seven thirty tomorrow morning.”

“Okay. Did he tell you anything else about Junia? Or about Sarah?”

Taylor shakes her head. “I don’t think he really knows anything else. I think he’s just, like, guessing.”

“Just like you.”

“Right. Just like me.”

“Let’s hope you’re both dead wrong, Taylor.” Midge gestures at the door. “Come on. You need to get back to work, and I need my ice cream.”

CHAPTER TWENTY-EIGHT

Somehow, he'd assumed it would be easy to find the spot again.

But last spring, things looked different up here in the mountains. Some of the trees were still just bare branches or merely budding, so the trail markers were easier to spot from the car. Now everything is overgrown.

He drives slowly, higher and higher into the wilderness, scanning the sides of the narrow road.

He chose the spot the first time because he remembered that it was blessedly remote.

There used to be a small campsite with a couple of cabins up here, years ago—that's how he knows it—but they've long since burned down. Now there's nothing but wilderness and a few trails that are not for the faint of heart. Nor is this road. One wrong move and he'll wind up stuck in a ditch, or worse.

Rounding a steep uphill curve, he spies an oncoming headlamp. Seized by panic, he hits the brakes hard. The tires go into a skid. He clutches the wheel, regaining control, bringing the car to a stop. Heart racing, gasping air into his lungs, he braces himself for whoever is going to approach and rap on the window.

Nobody does.

Looking up, he sees that it wasn't a headlamp after all. Just the moon, big and round, beaming through the trees up ahead.

But what if it had been a hiker?

Or a forest ranger?

What if they'd come up to the car? What would he have done?

Run them down? Driven on past? Stopped and talked to them as if nothing was amiss?

He's wearing the gloves and coveralls now. Would that tip them off that he's up to something?

He has no idea, and he doesn't want to find out. He's beginning to think this was a big mistake.

Logically, at this hour of the night, no one is out hiking. There's no real reason for rangers to patrol this lonely stretch, is there?

Maybe.

Maybe he should choose another place.

But where?

He remembers the girl in the river.

She was the first.

She was unconscious when he heaved her over the bridge rail into the murky water far below. He figured the gators would devour her.

They did not.

He heard the news on the radio a few days later.

"Authorities believe that the remains of a young woman pulled from the Savannah River yesterday may be college student Sienna Harmon, reported missing last week and believed to have taken her own life."

He'd been careless. Lucky for him, he wasn't caught.

He's learned a lot since then.

Today, he was careless once more. He hadn't meant for it to happen.

Not to *her*.

She was simply the wrong girl in the wrong place at the wrong time; the girl who came along just after he read the last-minute email from the other girl, the one who was running late and had to cancel.

It's a shame, but things happen. All he can do is get rid of her up here, where no one will ever find her. Or at least, not for a long, long time.

After all, they still haven't found Junia Stanton.

August 30

CHAPTER TWENTY-NINE

Kelly begins each day with a predawn hike along the woodland trail to the lake. At the beginning of the summer, she was always out here before five. Some mornings, she still is.

But on the heels of a late night and tequila, she slept a little later than usual. It's nearly six when she steps out the kitchen door in her sneakers and workout clothes, stainless-steel coffee go-cup in hand.

It's like walking into a steam room after the air-conditioned house. The sun has yet to rise, and the temperature might have fallen a bit overnight, but the air is oppressive.

She checked the forecast before bed. Tonight's low is expected to drop into the fifties—hard to grasp at the moment, but she's lived here long enough to believe it, especially with thunderstorms rolling in on a Canadian cold front this afternoon.

That may put a damper on the beach day she planned with Talia and her family. Midge is working but said she'll try to get back here in time for dinner.

Tonight, for better or worse, there will be no Linden, who has tickets to a concert, and no Nap.

Kelly sets out across the lawn, sweat already beading on her face. She strips off her hoodie, tying the sleeves around her waist.

The balmy air is scented with dewy grass and mossy earth. Early birds twitter in towering branches as she reaches the path that was once a walkway linking the mansion to its outbuildings.

Back then, it wound past stables, a carriage house, storage sheds, a greenhouse, even a mansard-roofed Victorian playhouse built to scale for the youngest Winterfield children. She's seen it all in old photographs in the family albums and at the Historical Preservation Society. They helped her restoration team map out the property, guiding them to the sites where the structures had been located. Splintered wood, bricks, and shards of glass, buried in rocky soil and weeds.

It's all been reconstructed.

All but the pool.

She'd been prepared to restore it to the lovely oasis she'd seen in vintage photos, with a diving well and an intricate mosaic border. The pool was surrounded by lounge chairs, potted plants, and cabanas, and bordered by a brick colonnade. Beneath each of its four arches, a statue of a Greek water god stood atop a stone pedestal.

In Kelly's childhood, the pool was a deep, weed-ridden chasm of broken tile and cracked concrete, cordoned off and posted with WARNING signs. The statues were long gone, and the colonnade had been reduced to rubble. Only the pedestals remained, etched with the names of the carved gods that once stood there: Poseidon, Oceanus, Hydros, and Ceto.

Each of the girls claimed her own pedestal. Kelly was Poseidon, Talia was Oceanus, Midge was Hydros, and Caroline was Ceto.

Kelly had the colonnade rebuilt from the original bricks, and the pedestals remain. She debated replacing the statues and decided against it even before the pool work halted. It didn't seem right. When she looks at the pedestals, she will forever see four young girls perched atop them, laughing and talking, carefree in the sunshine.

After the skeleton was discovered, Kelly was tempted to forgo the hikes and avoid the area altogether.

"I wouldn't blame you," Midge said, when Kelly mentioned that to her and Talia. "It's not easy for any of us to deal with, but you're the one who has to live in the shadow of that burial spot."

"It might get better in time," Talia said. "Then again, what do I know? I couldn't even deal with being in Mulberry Bay after Caroline was gone. I'm the one who ran away."

"So did I," Kelly admitted.

"At least you came back."

"Not by choice."

In February 2020, she was living abroad in a belle époque *maison* overlooking the Seine when Mrs. Verga summoned her because her mother was hospitalized. Lousy timing, Kelly thought, when the pandemic stranded her stateside.

Quarantined alone in her childhood home, she faced COVID that nearly killed her, isolation that nearly broke her, and memories she could no longer outrun.

So many memories . . .

Among them, the time she overheard her mother tell her father, "Stop trying to make her into the son you always wished you had."

"No child of mine is going to be a helpless candy-ass," he replied. "She's going to know how to be strong and defend herself."

Kelly Barrow has never been without her faults, but fragility and powerlessness aren't among them.

She survived. COVID, the isolation, the memories, her mother's dementia diagnosis, the news that the pandemic had claimed her closest French friends and that her beloved cat, Bijou, had run away.

By the time lockdown lifted, there was nothing left for her in Paris.

She wasn't sure there was anything for her in Mulberry Bay either. But her mother needed her. Still needs her. Always will.

She's not proud of how she handled loss when she was young. First Caroline, then her friendship with Midge and Talia a year later. After that, she had to deal with her first divorce, her second divorce, her father's death . . .

Every time her life fell apart, she turned her back on the memories and moved—or maybe ran—away.

New York, San Francisco, Paris . . .

She did her best to make all of those cities into her home. Looking back, she can see that none of them ever was.

Only Mulberry Bay and Haven Cliff will ever be home. Now she's not going anywhere, not even with dementia slowly robbing her of her mother.

For the first time in her life, Kelly is tackling loss head-on. It's not easy, but it is empowering.

That's why she continues to follow the familiar path to the lake every morning, even though it leads her past the pool. Even today, having learned what she learned last night from Toby about the man Caroline had known and trusted.

Wildflowers are naturalized in sun and shade along her route. She pauses to gather a stem or two whenever she sees a splotch of pink—phlox, cosmos, hyssop. When she reaches the clearing, she has a full bouquet.

She walks slowly toward the heap of dirt and gaping hole that had been Caroline's grave for all these years.

The pool contractor removed his excavating equipment when the job stalled, saying he needed it elsewhere.

"Just tell me when the cops give you the green light to move ahead again," he said, "and I'll get you back into the schedule as soon as I can."

Kelly thanked him and told him she would, but she no longer wants a pool.

She's decided to have it filled in again, as it had been the summer after Caroline disappeared.

Now she thinks maybe she'll create a beautiful flower garden on the spot.

"That would be nice, K. K.," she hears Caroline's sweet voice saying in her head. "Plant lots of pink. Pink flowers are my favorite."

Pink—never Kelly's style.

Looking down at the wildflower bouquet in her hand, she whispers, "Anything for you. I'm sorry I wasn't paying enough attention. I was so self-centered. If I had known . . ."

In her head, Caroline responds with forgiveness. That's who she was; it's what she would have done.

It's just going to take a while before Kelly can forgive herself.

Head bowed, eyes closed, she promises Caroline, "I'll try to do better."

"You *have* done better, K. K. Look how far you've come."

The voice is only in her head. But she hears something—a soft swishing and snapping back in the trees, as if someone is there.

Her eyes pop open. She half expects to see Caroline standing beside her, alive again, young, sweet, smiling.

She does not. But she can feel the presence. She turns toward the trees and calls, "You're there, aren't you? I know you are."

In response, there's a rush of receding movement, as if Caroline really is there, and is running away.

"Caroline! Wait!"

All is still again. But she knows what she heard.

She used to fear that she was just like her mother, delusional, hearing things, seeing things. Then she attributed it to the neurological effects of her Lyme disease.

Now, though, she thinks it's just grief. Just missing the people she knew and loved, just keeping them alive in her memory.

With a sigh, she turns away from the trees, tosses the flowers into the hole, then continues on toward the lake as the first glow of daylight kisses the mountains in the distance.

CHAPTER THIRTY

Midge was too exhausted when she got home to give Sarah Greene and Reverend Bauer any more thought.

Now it's morning, and she's padding around the kitchen making coffee, and there's still no sign of Sarah.

Remembering the crowded waterfront and all those out-of-state license plates, Midge is well aware that Mulberry Bay is filled with outsiders on this holiday weekend.

What if Sarah crossed paths with some opportunistic stranger who saw a pretty, naive girl and took advantage of her?

Where? At the church?

Okay, then what if . . .

No.

Midge's brain wants to connect her to Bauer, but it doesn't make sense. She attributes the instinct to link him to the missing girl to the fact that the man was on her mind the second she walked through the door at Congregational.

Phone pressed between her shoulder and ear, she measures coffee grounds into a filter as Renee fills her in on the night's developments.

Word is getting out, and several people have reported seeing Sarah yesterday afternoon. They all confirmed that the girl was alone, and walking toward the church.

"So no one saw her leaving and heading back home?" Midge asks.

"That doesn't mean she didn't."

"No, I know. It's just . . . I keep thinking about that predatory pastor."

Last night, in between licks of dripping ice cream, she told Renee about Reverend Bauer, not mentioning that when she visited the church, she hadn't yet been aware of Bauer's criminal history. Renee might ask her how she'd since found out, and she needs to keep the Greene case separate from Kelly's private investigation and her own past, for professional reasons and for personal.

"Bauer? Yeah, I looked into that," Renee says. "Horrible story. He was here in Mulberry Bay from 1998 through 2000. The Winterfield girl went missing from Haven Cliff in 1999, and I saw that she was a member of Congregational, just like Sarah."

Midge fumbles the coffee scoop, dumping grounds all over the countertop, and lets out a curse.

"Midge?"

"Sorry, I just spilled something. It's okay. What were you saying?"

"Nothing that matters. The Winterfield disappearance isn't relevant to Sarah Greene. I just mentioned it because your dad was the chief back when she disappeared, so you must be familiar with it."

"Yes. And she was a friend of mine."

"Caroline Winterfield? Oh, I'm so sorry."

"Thanks. It's . . ."

No, it's not okay. It will never be okay.

Midge says, instead, "It's been a long time."

"Twenty-five years. But a girl who drowned in 1999 wouldn't be connected to a girl who didn't come home from Bible study yesterday. And Sarah wouldn't be connected to Reverend Bauer unless he's still lurking around Congregational. But all signs indicate that he fled over the border to Mexico."

"Exactly." Midge presses the brew button on the coffee maker and grabs a sponge to wipe the counter. "So do you have any theories about where Sarah might be?"

"Absolutely. I mean, you met the mother."

"Sadie. Yes. Why?"

"Sadie?"

"She told me to call her Sadie."

"Funny. She told me to call her Mrs. Greene. I checked in on her, just like you asked, and I know she's going through a lot right now, but . . ."

"Renee, that's an understatement. Her daughter is missing."

"I know, but I'm pretty sure she doesn't want a Black detective on the case."

"Oh no. What did she say to you?"

"It's not what she said, it's how she . . . *is*. Believe me, I can always feel it."

"I'm sorry."

"Yeah," she says around a deep yawn. "I'm used to it. But look, I don't think she has anything to do with Sarah being gone in a nefarious way. I just wouldn't blame Sarah if she decided to get away from that horrible mother and have some fun."

"Let's hope that's what she did."

"I'm sure it's what she did."

"Good. I was planning on stopping over at the Greenes' on my way to the office, but maybe—"

"Don't bother. She just went upstairs to lie down. She has a friend with her. Virginia Livingston, who said she'll let us know if anything changes, but she wants Sadie to get some rest. Oh, and Sarah's father is on his way back from Georgia, but he's driving, so he won't be here until late tonight or early tomorrow." Renee yawns again.

Midge takes a go-cup from the cabinet. "Go home and get some sleep."

"I plan to. And when I check in with you later, I expect you to tell me Sarah Greene turned up in Vegas."

"I really hope that happens." Midge hangs up, doubting that.

Her gut says Sarah, like countless innocent crime victims, was doing what she was supposed to be doing when she crossed paths with something—or someone—dangerous.

Her gut has a lot to say, dammit.

What if Reverend Bauer isn't really in Mexico?

What if he's back in Mulberry Bay?

What if he hurt Sarah?

CHAPTER THIRTY-ONE

"You know, your friends are pretty great."

Surprised, Talia turns away from her open suitcase to see Ben, sleep tousled but awake, watching her from the bed.

She smiles. "Yeah? You liked them?"

"I did." He sits up, stretching. "What time is it?"

"About eight thirty."

"Eight thirty! Is everyone up except me?"

"Caleb is brushing his teeth and washing up. Hayley will probably sleep till noon if we let her. And I'm going to go downstairs and find Kelly just as soon as I throw on some clothes."

"Or you could come back to bed," he suggests, patting the pillow beside him, looking like his old self—the Ben who was playful and flirty, even after all these years.

"Now?" She shakes her head and points at the closed bathroom door. "Caleb."

He sighs. "Rain check?"

"Definitely."

Ten minutes later, she's dressed and in the sunny kitchen with Caleb, pouring coffee from a steaming carafe bearing a Post-it note in Kelly's black Sharpie scrawl: *Help yourself. Be right back.*

Caleb browses nearly a dozen full-size cereal boxes they found lined up on the breakfast bar with another note: *For the kiddos.*

"I can't decide, Mommy!" Caleb says. "Should I have Cocoa Pebbles or Lucky Charms?"

"How about shredded wheat? You love that."

"Not when there's Cocoa Pebbles and Lucky Charms. Shredded wheat is boring."

"Good morning! And I agree." Kelly is back, breezing in the door with a white cardboard go-cup and a white bakery box tied with string. She's wearing a coral sundress, heeled sandals, a broad-brimmed hat, and gigantic sunglasses, looking like she belongs on a yacht on the French Riviera.

"What do you agree with?" Talia asks as Kelly sets the box on the counter and tosses her hat and sunglasses alongside it.

"That shredded wheat is boring. Caleb, I only got it because your mom claims it's your favorite."

"Mom!" Caleb turns an accusing look on Talia.

"You eat it every morning."

"That's because you only buy shredded wheat."

"Blech." Kelly grabs the cereal and tosses it into a garbage bin disguised in a row of lower cabinets. "I just picked up some stuff from the French bakery. There's a fruit salad in the fridge and quiche in the oven. Or I can make chocolate chip pancakes. Do you like those, Caleb?"

"Yes!"

"No pancakes," Talia says. "Choose your cereal."

Caleb stands on his tiptoes, surveying the lineup of boxes. "Which kind should I have?"

"How about Caleb Crunch?" Kelly says.

"What's that?"

"Whatever you decide. Mix a few kinds together and see what you come up with." She hands him a bowl and measuring cups and spoons.

"Yay!" Caleb reaches for a cereal box.

Kelly smiles sweetly at Talia. "Who says Auntie Kelly doesn't know anything about kids?"

"I just hope Auntie Kelly plans on footing his dental bills, because that's all sugar."

"That's why it's not boring." She sips her coffee, makes a face, puts it in the microwave, punches the quick start button, and moves on as if to the next agenda at a meeting. "So I checked the forecast, and we'd better head to the beach right after breakfast. The weather's going to turn this afternoon."

"We can save the beach for tomorrow."

"Tomorrow's going to be worse."

"We don't have to do the beach at all. There are plenty of other things we can—"

"But I want to go!" Caleb protests. "You said we could, Mommy! I want to find sharks' teeth and build sandcastles like we used to do with Granny Nat."

Florida. Granny. The beach. She can still see Caleb in his bucket hat, holding a plastic shovel in one chubby little fist and her mother's hand with the other, both of them barefoot and wading in the shallow surf, leaving sets of wet footprints for an instant before the tide washed them away.

"This beach isn't like Florida, sweetie. There are no sharks' teeth here, and there's really no sand."

"But we have stones instead, and I can teach you how to skip them," Kelly says. "And we have little fish that tickle your toes if you wade in. It's the coolest thing. You can catch some."

"Do I have to eat them? Because I don't really like fish."

She laughs. "These are just minnows. We'll bring a glass bowl, like I always did with my dad. We'd watch them swim around and then put them back into the lake. And he taught me how to skip stones. He was always such fun at the beach."

"Can he come with us today?"

"Oh . . . he passed away."

"Like my granny. How did he die?"

"He had a heart attack."

"Was he old?"

"Not old enough."

"But *old*," Talia says quickly, shooting a look at Kelly.

"Granny Nat wasn't that old," Caleb says, "and she didn't have a heart attack. She—"

"You know, she was a great lady, your granny," Kelly says.

"You knew her?"

"Of course! She was everyone's favorite mom. The other moms were, you know, kind of like shredded wheat."

Caleb giggles. "Boring?"

"Yes. And they all thought I was a little too, you know . . ."

"Not boring," Talia supplies with a smile, opening the bakery box and perusing the contents.

"Right! I was not boring. I thought boring was the worst thing in the entire world."

"I seem to recall you thought *good* was more boring than boring," Talia reminds her.

"Well, isn't it?"

"Don't listen to Aunt Kelly, Caleb!"

"Listen to me, Caleb! I'm wise," Kelly says, laughing. "And Natalie—that's your granny—she liked me. She once said I reminded her of herself when she was young."

"Did she?" Talia selects a blueberry muffin and closes the box. "I don't remember that."

"You weren't there."

"Where were you, Mommy?"

"Probably at play practice—she was always starring in some play. Or, oh, you were probably out with Paul," Kelly says.

"Who's Paul?"

"Just an old friend," Talia tells Caleb.

Paul Liccione. Her first love. Last she knew, he was married with children and living in the Pacific Northwest. They follow each other's social media.

Kelly continues her story. "And *I* was out with an old friend of mine who . . . let's just say we had a fight. Anyway, I saw Natalie's car at the Landing, so I walked over there, and she gave me coffee and a ride home after she finished her shift. I remember it like it was yesterday. She said she liked that I was a straight shooter. Most people did not appreciate that quality," she adds with a chuckle. "I could be a bit much, right, Talia?"

"You were the gutsiest girl I ever knew. Still are."

"That daughter of yours would give me a run for my money."

"True." Talia peels the fluted paper from her blueberry muffin. "I'm glad my mom was there for you when you needed her."

"Oh, she was. I could never talk to my mother about stuff like that. She was way too perfect for bad boys and messy breakups. But *your* mom?"

"Definitely imperfect."

"In the best way. That night, she gave me a little pep talk about how it's way better to be single and take care of yourself than get stuck with some loser. I got the feeling she was mostly talking about your dad."

Talia sets down her coffee and muffin.

"Wow. Really? She never wanted to talk to me about him."

"That's understandable. I mean, he was your dad."

"*Birth father* is more accurate. A dad is someone who's there."

"You're right. That was her point. You don't want to be with a guy you can't count on. Maybe she was talking about bad boyfriends in general."

Talia nods, telling herself that her mother wouldn't have shared more about her father with Kelly than she'd ever told Talia. She was good at girl talk with Talia's friends, and she was obviously just trying to help Kelly get over the jerk who'd hurt her that night.

Talia's birth father fell into the "jerk" category. Natalie met him when she was sixteen, and he was a few years older. It was a summer fling. When fall came, he went back to college, and they lost touch—until Natalie tracked him down to tell him she was pregnant. He wanted nothing to do with her or the baby.

After that, Natalie wanted nothing to do with him. Talia didn't either.

Not when she was growing up.

"I've been wondering about him lately," she tells Kelly.

"You should find him."

"How? She never even told me his name, or where he was from."

"When I put my DNA sample into that genealogical website to see if I'd inherited the Alzheimer gene, it gave me biological connections too."

"It would only work if my father gave his DNA, though."

"Not necessarily. If someone connected to him did, you'd see that. You'd be able to build out a family tree and figure out who he was."

"How likely is it that someone connected to him did it, though?"

"Come on, Talia. Pretty much everyone I know has done one of these things."

She nods. Pretty much everyone she knows has done it as well.

"Maybe I will," she says, and sets down her coffee. "If we're going to the beach after breakfast, I should let Ben know, and Hayley needs to get up and get moving. She takes forever to get ready."

"Ah, just like her mom," Kelly says.

"Not true!" Talia says.

"Well, it was true when you were . . . How old is Hayley? Thirteen? Fourteen?"

"Twelve," Talia says. "And I didn't—"

"Come on, do you know how many times Midge and Caroline and I had to wait around while you tried on a million outfits and did your hair?"

"I did not!"

"Sure, you did! You put on a full face of makeup just to go ride bikes!"

Talia laughs, throwing up her hands in protest. "Well, you never knew who you were going to run into."

"Pretty much just Melvin Warner."

"Melvin . . ."

"The old guy who worked at the Shell station where we used to—"

"Oh! With the vending machine and the Crystal Pepsi!"

"Crystal Pepsi!" Kelly says the two words in unison, and they laugh.

Then Caleb asks, "Who's Caroline?"

Talia's laughter evaporates.

"She was our friend," Kelly tells him. "Like Midge."

"Is she coming over tonight for dinner?"

"Midge? Yes, she'll be here."

"No, Caroline."

Kelly looks at Talia.

"Caroline is . . . she's . . . not alive anymore," Talia tells her son.

"Like Granny?"

"Like that."

"She was an old friend?"

"Yes. Another old friend of ours."

"Did she have a heart attack, then? Like Kelly's dad? That happens to old people."

"Oh, Caroline wasn't old when she died," Kelly says.

"How old was she?"

Kelly says nothing.

Caleb turns to Talia. "Mommy? Was she a little girl?"

"No, not a *little* girl. She was an older girl."

"What happened to her?"

"She, uh . . ." Talia can't tell him the terrible truth. Nor can she tell him the lie they lived with for all those years when everyone thought she'd drowned in the lake, because that will be it for their beach day. Or any beach day, ever, because he's Caleb.

Kelly speaks up. "You know, I can't remember what happened. It was such a long time ago."

"It was," Talia agrees. "I can't remember either."

"But—"

"Hey, you know what I think that Caleb Crunch needs?" Kelly asks, going to a cabinet. "Sprinkles."

"You mean like ice cream sprinkles?"

"Yep. Talia, you'd better go wake Hayley. We'll have the Caleb Crunch ready to serve for breakfast."

Talia shoots her a grateful look and hurries from the room.

CHAPTER THIRTY-TWO

On the way to work, Midge visits the McDonald's drive-through for an Egg McMuffin and a couple of hash browns, one of which she gobbles as she exits the parking lot.

At this early hour, the traffic on Route 28 is mostly landscapers and contractors clogging up the turning lanes near the intersection shared by Home Depot and Lowe's. There are commuters as well, many heading for Albany, or the train stations across the river in Poughkeepsie or Rhinecliff. The rail trip to Manhattan is just under two hours.

There was a time when very few people would consider that a manageable daily commute. Postpandemic, with so many New Yorkers relocated to this area, many seem to think nothing of it. Midge doesn't get that, but then, she's lived here all her life, and her house is a mile from her job.

The most direct route takes her past the high school football field. She sees that the team is there, running drills in the sticky heat. She considers stopping to have a word with Jaret Buckley but decides against pulling him off the field in front of everyone. It can wait. The McMuffin cannot, filling the car with its savory scent.

In the business district, she ignores the illegally parked commuters in front of both Center Street Grind and Lakeside Coffee Roasters. She has more important work to do this morning than issue traffic summons.

The commons is dotted with white awnings and stalls for the weekly farmers' market. She skirts around pickup trucks loaded with produce and a couple of Amish horses and buggies. Spotting a familiar bearded man in a broad-brimmed hat and dark suit, she rolls down her window to call, "How's it going, Josef?"

"Good morning, Midge. Very well, thank you." He indicates a wooden crate in the back of the wagon. "Ruth's apple fritters. I know you've been asking."

"Yes!" Midge fist pumps, grinning. "I'll run over later and get one."

"They'll go fast. Do you want to wait a minute while I unpack them for you?"

She's tempted, but anxious to get to work.

She parks in her spot, tucks her iPad under her arm, grabs her coffee and breakfast, and heads inside. The reception area is deserted, the air wafting with some kind of solvent.

"Allie?"

The girl pops her head up behind the desk, looking guilty. "Hi, Midge."

"What's going on? What's that smell?"

Allie sniffs. "What smell?"

"Like paint, or . . ." Stepping closer, Midge sees that Allie's holding a small bottle. "Is that nail polish?"

Allie follows her gaze as if she, too, has just noticed the object in her hand. "You mean this?"

"Are you giving yourself a *manicure*?"

"No!"

"Then what . . ." Leaning over the desk, Midge sees that her feet are bare, with cotton balls wedged between each toe. Three nails on her right foot are freshly coated in neon-purple polish.

"I'm giving myself a *pedicure*," Allie admits. "I'm sorry. I just didn't have time to get one yesterday, and my boyfriend and I are—"

"Allie, you can't sit around painting your nails! This isn't a salon. You have a job to do."

"I'm doing it, but when it's slow, I get bored, so I figured I might as well just—"

"This is unacceptable. If you're bored, there's plenty to do. There's paperwork to file, and the bathrooms can always stand to be cleaned, and—"

"Okay, okay. But can I just finish my toes really fast?"

"No. Put your shoes on."

"But the polish is wet. Can I—"

"Shoes *on*!"

Exasperated, Midge retreats to her office. Sitting at the desk, she unwraps her sandwich, takes a quick bite, and checks her email.

Kelly has forwarded Toby's reports on Reverend Bauer. All bear the subject line *Confidential.*

Midge starts reading.

Mason Bauer. Born and raised in a small town outside Montgomery, Alabama, became a minister, led congregations in the Southeast and New York state. Married with children. After leaving Congregational, he was pastor at a small church in nearby Phoenicia. From there, he moved back down south, briefly serving as pastor for a congregation in Georgia before leaving the ministry altogether in 2006, for undisclosed reasons.

It's not unrealistic to assume there might have been an incident that was swept under the rug, but she can find no evidence of it in the report.

The first official mention of impropriety came when he was on the adjunct faculty at a community college, teaching theology. A female freshman accused him of improper advances.

He was put on probation.

According to official records, another student filed the same complaint. Her name was later released in relation to a missing person report: Sienna Harmon.

Midge sits up straighter, sets her sandwich aside, and writes the name on a pad.

According to friends and family, Sienna grappled with mental health issues long before her encounter with Bauer.

She'd have been fragile, emotional, vulnerable. A predator's ideal victim.

She wasn't missing for very long. She texted a friend that she was going away to be alone. She seemed despondent.

There was an investigation, of course, when she turned up dead in a river near a bridge. She was presumed to have jumped to her death.

Bauer was said to have no connection, with a solid alibi. He lost his job anyway.

The headlines spurred a former congregant to accuse him of molesting her when she was a young teenager. That was the case that went to trial.

There's plenty of coverage. The courthouse was surrounded by throngs of media and protestors supporting or condemning the man. Photos and video footage depict crowds held back by police barricades, holding signs and waving crosses, shouting at each other and at Bauer himself as he's led to and from the hearings, handcuffed and surrounded by deputies. He looks much older in the photos than he did when she knew him—very thin, with gray and gaunt features.

As Midge suspected, the defense ripped the accuser to shreds on cross-examination. No wonder the charges were dropped after the mistrial. They wouldn't have a case without her testimony, and in a statement through her attorney, she said she couldn't endure taking the stand again. Midge wonders where the young woman is now. She seems to have maintained her anonymity.

One of the accusers who came forward in another state gave a number of interviews in the press. She outlined in harrowing detail how he'd arranged to meet with her alone, with her parents' blessings, under the guise of one-on-one "counseling." He was supposed to help her work through various academic, domestic, and behavioral conflicts, and instead won her trust and gradually seduced her.

"I didn't think it was wrong at the time," she said. "He made me feel like everything everyone said about me was wrong. Like he was the only one who really understood me. When I was with him, I felt like I was a good, worthwhile person. He always knew exactly what to say. I thought I was in love with him. He said he loved me too. He apologized, you know, afterward. He was crying. He said it had never happened to him before, and that we both needed to pray for forgiveness."

Reading that, Midge tosses the rest of her sandwich into the trash can under her desk and leans back in her chair, hugging her stomach.

She looks at the name she wrote on the legal pad.

Sienna Harmon.

She types it into a search engine and finds herself looking at a photo of an attractive young woman with pretty features and long brown hair. She isn't a dead ringer for Sarah Greene or Junia Stanton by any means, but when it comes to victimology, there are similarities.

Most of the hits are news accounts detailing what Midge already knows about her life, and her death.

Social media tells a different story, rampant with rumors that Bauer had something to do with it. There's a large Facebook group devoted to the case: What Really Happened to Sienna Harmon?

Midge has seen this kind of thing before, typically with high-profile cases. Members consist mainly of strangers playing armchair detective, along with trolls and conspiracy theorists. Pages are often rife with outlandish speculation and law enforcement bashing.

This one appears to be no exception. The majority of posts are set to private, and activity has dwindled over the past few years.

Midge applies for membership using the profile she maintains for investigation purposes. One of the moderators, whose profile name is Kimberly Zee, was an acquaintance of Sienna's. Midge writes her a private message explaining that she's a police detective investigating a missing person case with ties to Sienna Harmon and provides her contact information.

She rereads it, inserts the word *possible* before *ties*, and hits send.

There's a strong chance that Sienna Harmon was simply a troubled young woman who took her own life. Sarah Greene's connection to Bauer, and thus to Sienna, is tenuous.

But when you throw Junia Stanton into the mix . . .

Three missing women with a connection to Bauer.

Four, if you include Caroline Winterfield.

CHAPTER THIRTY-THREE

On foot, dressed in a heavy parka and boots on a hot summer day, he lugs a heavy suitcase through crowded streets, trying to find the airport in some foreign city. He tries to flag a taxi, but they all drive on past, and he tries to ask for directions, but no one speaks English. There's nothing to do but keep walking.

Every part of him aches with the effort, and the more he walks, the more lost he is. Day turns to night; the pavement and streetlights and traffic disappear, and somehow he's in rugged, forested terrain. He's dogged by panic, certain he's going to miss his flight, and he has to get away because—

A harsh bleating wrenches him from the nightmare.

It's the alarm.

He isn't in the woods or in some foreign city. He's in bed in the room he rented at the Super 8. The ache is real. So is the heat. He isn't wearing winter clothes, but he is fully dressed, shoes and all, beneath the thin bedspread. He'd been utterly exhausted when he got back here last night.

No, this morning. Just as the sun was coming up.

He *had* lived through a nightmare—the steep mountain road, searching, finding the spot at last, getting down to work with the shovel.

Digging was much easier back in April, when the air was cool and the soil was soft and spongy after weeks of spring rains. Now the air felt warm and sticky even at that altitude, and the ground was dry and hard, strewn with rocks . . . He doesn't remember so many rocks the last time. He couldn't dig nearly as deep a grave as he had for Junia Stanton.

In the end, he dragged the tarped corpse into the hole, along with the cell phone, and covered it with a few inches of dirt and stones, telling himself that it would be fine. It's not as if someone is going to come along and notice that something is amiss.

Now, though, he suspects he was too careless.

He sits up and throws off the covers. The white sheet's underside is streaked with dirt and a bit of blood.

Hers, somehow?

No, it's his own. His palms are raw and blistered from gripping the shovel. His pants are torn and his shoes caked in crumbly soil. He can smell the earth, mingling with his own sweat and putrid breath and the stale hotel room.

He gets up and finds his phone on the table beside the door. He hadn't bothered to turn it on when he got back. Now he does.

There are a number of missed calls. Text messages too.

Yesterday, he answered her Hey, babe, how's the trip going? with a quick Fine, working, will call you later.

He never had. Before he left home, he'd warned her that cell service might be sketchy where he was going.

She'd texted several more times.

Miss you! Still working?

Everything okay?

Getting worried!

Hey, where are you?

Going to bed, just let me know you're alive!

That was the last one.

He responds now with a thumbs-up emoji and a cheery *Good Morning! Sorry, late night.*

He hits send.

His phone rings almost immediately.

He sighs and answers it. "Hi, sweetie."

CHAPTER THIRTY-FOUR

Midge is still at her desk, immersed in the Sarah Greene case. She hasn't heard back from the moderator of the Sienna Harmon page, but there are plenty of other leads to follow.

As Renee mentioned, several reliable witnesses spotted Sarah on her way to Congregational, but no one saw her heading home.

She could have been planning to run away and disguised her appearance somehow, escaping unrecognized. She might even have gone to Pennsylvania to reconnect with Michael Klatte, regardless of her mother's claim that she's no longer in touch with him.

Midge finds his cell phone number in the case file for Gordy's death.

The line rings directly into voicemail.

She debates leaving a message, opts against it, and hangs up.

She debates calling Amy Klatte, opts for it, and dials.

Gordy's widow answers on the first ring.

"Mrs. Klatte, this is Imogene Kennedy with Mulb—"

"Midge! Do you have news? Are the forensic tests back?"

"Not yet. This is actually unrelated. It's about Sarah Greene?"

"Sarah! What about her?"

"I understand she and Michael are no longer in touch?"

"No, they aren't. Why?"

"Sarah's mom is trying to find her, and I thought Michael might have some idea where she is."

"I doubt that. We've been here in Pennsylvania all summer. Is Sarah . . . Why can't Sadie find her? What's going on?"

"She went out yesterday and didn't come home. I thought maybe she'd headed your way, to see Michael."

"*Sarah?* Oh, no. She definitely wouldn't have done that, even if they were still . . . you know. That's not like her."

"That's what I hear. I was wondering if Michael might have some insight."

"I'm not sure he would, but either way, he's away until Monday. My brother and sister-in-law took my boys on a cruise with their family. Gordon and I always wanted to do that with them, and . . ." Her voice breaks, but she regains her composure far more quickly than she did the first few times Midge spoke to her, when her grief was raw. "Anyway, they were excited to go on vacation with their cousins."

"I'm sure they were. I'm sorry to have bothered you."

"It's not a bother. I'll pray that you find Sarah. Please keep me posted, about that and about my husband's case."

"I will," Midge promises, and hangs up.

Ten minutes later, Allie sticks her head in. "There's a call for you from someone named Kim."

"Kim who?"

"Reynolds. Should I put her through?"

"Please."

The Sienna Harmon Facebook group moderator is named Kimberly Zee, but Midge had provided her cell phone number.

She answers the desk phone with a brisk, "Detective Sergeant Kennedy."

There's a pause, and then a female voice asks, "Hi, I . . . uh . . . Did you message me about Sienna Harmon?"

"Is this Kimberly Zee?"

"Kim Reynolds now, but my maiden name was Zakowski, and I went by *Kimberly Zee* on Facebook."

"Then yes, I messaged you."

"Oh, good."

Midge hears a male voice in the background, and Kimberly tells him, "Yes, it was really her." Then, to Midge, "My husband thought I should call police headquarters directly, to make sure it was legit. There are a lot of crazy people out there when it comes to true crime stuff. You wouldn't believe the messages I used to get."

"I'll bet. I'm working on a missing persons case involving a young woman named Sarah Greene, and I'm investigating whether there's a connection to Sienna. Do you mind if I ask you a few questions?"

"Not at all."

Midge opens a new document. "How did you know Sienna?"

"We were in a few classes together."

"Was theology one of them?"

"No. I knew who he was, but . . . no."

"He—you mean, Mason Bauer."

"Yes."

"Did Sienna ever discuss him with you?" Midge asks, typing the information into the report.

"Yeah, she thought he was great, you know, at first. Her grades were suffering because she was going through a rough time—her parents split up, and her grandma died, stuff like that. Professor Bauer was super helpful. She'd go to office hours, you know . . . that's how it started."

"The inappropriate relationship?"

"Yes. I mean, she never told me anything about that. She, you know . . . she kind of changed, and she . . . well, she didn't want to talk about him much anymore."

Yes. Midge knows.

Her hands clench into fists over the keyboard.

"How did you find out about what happened between them, Kimberly?"

"When I heard about the allegations with the other girl, I put two and two together, and I asked Sienna about him. She denied it, defended him, but eventually, she reported him. I was really proud of her. She said she wanted to make sure he didn't pull that stuff on anyone else. She was really determined. Then she just . . . she fell off the face of the earth, basically. Out of nowhere."

"When she went missing."

"Right. She told her roommate she was going out on a date with some guy one night, and she just didn't come home."

"And the roommate reported her missing?"

"Yes, but not for a few days. I think she thought she and this guy just hooked up. It wasn't unusual . . . you know. It was college."

"Right. Who was the guy?"

"That's the thing. Apparently, there *was* no guy. I mean, she didn't mention him to me. And they couldn't find anyone. A lot of people thought it was Bauer, even though a bunch of people vouched for being with him the night she went missing."

"Right. He had a solid alibi."

"I know."

"What's your theory?"

"I honestly thought at first that she just wanted to take off, get some space, get her head straight after everything that happened. I mean, that's what she said in her text."

"You're the friend she contacted?"

"Yes. I had texted her that day, asking her about some assignment, and she never answered. So later that night I asked if she was okay. I asked a few times, and she finally got back to me."

"What did she say exactly?"

"Just that she needed some space because she just couldn't deal with the stress anymore. When I heard that they found her body, I was shocked. I mean, I didn't think she was suicidal. And when I looked back at that text . . . it just didn't sound like her."

"How so?"

"She always texted in shorthand—like the letter *u* for *you*, that kind of thing. And she made a lot of typos because she was always in a rush. That last message was perfect. Everything was spelled out, like she was the grammar queen. I don't know. It kind of made me wonder."

"About whether someone else had her phone and sent the message?"

"Exactly. But the police didn't really seem to think so, and they cleared Bauer, and, you know, I guess it was easier for them to just go with the fact that she killed herself. Sorry," she adds. "I don't think all cops are like that. But sometimes, they don't take young people that seriously, you know?"

"I do know."

She hears a wail in the background on Kimberly's end. "Oh, that's my daughter. My husband has her, but she wants to nurse, so . . ."

"Go take care of her," Midge says. "If you don't mind, I'll take your number. I'm going to look into a few things and may have more questions."

"Sure. Why do you think Sarah Greene is connected to Sienna?"

"Her parents may have crossed paths with Mason Bauer, years ago. I'm just looking into every possibility."

"I really hope you find her."

"So do I."

She hangs up and finishes typing the information into her iPad. Then she pulls up Sarah's photo, enlarging the image.

Staring into the girl's clear-eyed, wholesome, smiling face, she whispers, "Where *are* you?"

CHAPTER THIRTY-FIVE

Hayley has been awake for a while, but she's still lying in bed, just relaxing and thinking about stuff.

Sometimes she does that at home, but it's way better here.

The bed is huge, with silky white sheets and plump pillows and a comforter that feels like a fluffy white cloud. Overhead, there's a carved plaster medallion with a beautiful light fixture hanging from the center. It has frosted glass globes that are painted like flowers.

She took a picture of it to show Chloe, who loves floral things. She'll tell Chloe that it's from Paris, because it probably is.

When she grows up, she's going to have the same light in her house. And the same bed. And she's going to live in a mansion. Chloe can come over for sleepovers any time she wants.

But not Maddie Miller.

Last night, she was there when Hayley was FaceTiming with Chloe, acting like she's slept over at Chloe's house a million times, which she has not.

Hayley has. Not a million, but a lot.

It bothered her to see Maddie in Chloe's room, with the trundle bed pulled out and Maddie's stuff all over it in a messy way, which isn't polite when you're company at someone's house. It bothered her almost as much that Chloe didn't seem to mind that, or when Maddie called her "Chlo," which no one ever does. And it *really* bothered her when Maddie said that Chloe's mom is taking the two of them back-to-school shopping today in White Plains.

"Wait, are you going to Nordstrom Rack?" Hayley asked, because she and Chloe wanted to go there before school starts. They'd seen outfits on the store's website that would be perfect to wear the first day, and Hayley has saved up all her babysitting money to get hers.

"I don't know. We're going to Target, for sure, because the middle school sent out a supplies list and there's a lot of stuff on it that we never had to get for elementary school," Maddie said.

"Right?" Chloe said.

"Right?" Hayley said, like she was aware.

She would have been, if she were home. She'd be going shopping with Chloe and her mom instead of Maddie. They'd go to Nordstrom Rack, and she'd try on the jeans she loves that are crazy expensive, and the sweater that will look epic with them as long as it's not a thousand degrees out when school starts.

The thing that bothered her the most, though, is that she really wanted to talk to Chloe about the DNA test. But she didn't want to bring it up in front of Maddie.

"Hey, Hayley, did you find your grandfather yet?"

"You *told* her?" Hayley asked Chloe.

"Yes! Wait, why? Was it a secret? You never said it was a secret."

No, Hayley hadn't, but she'd assumed. Isn't that how it's supposed to be with best friends? You tell each other stuff, and you don't expect the other person to go blabbing to any rando who comes along.

Although Maddie isn't acting like a rando. She's acting like she's best friends with Chloe too.

Hayley hears footsteps outside her door, and then a knock. "Hayley?"

It's Mom.

The door opens.

Normally, Hayley would tell her she shouldn't just barge into people's rooms uninvited, but Chloe thinks she should tell her about the search for her dad while they're here in Mulberry Bay.

She sits up. "Can you come in and shut the door, please?"

"Are you okay?"

"Yes. I just want to tell you something."

"Oh, honey." Mom shuts the door, comes over, and sits on the edge of the bed. "Did you get it?"

"Did I get what?"

"Your first period! Don't worry, I've been prepared for this for years. I've got everything you—"

"What? No!" Annoyed with her mother's eager, girl-to-girl attitude, she flops back on her pillow with her arms crossed on her chest.

"You didn't get it?"

"Geez, no!"

"Well, any day now. And like I said, I'm all prepared. What did you want to tell me?"

"Never mind."

"No, tell me."

Why does it now feel more like she's about to make a confession instead of giving her mother a nice surprise?

Because Mom will know that Hayley's been listening in on her private conversations with Dad, that's why.

But now she has to tell her something, so she says, "Remember how you were saying there are cute little stores in town? I was thinking maybe we could go back-to-school shopping today."

"Maybe later, but right now, we're going to the beach! Come on. You don't want to miss it."

What she didn't want to miss was a sleepover at her best friend's house, and it's all Mom's fault that she isn't there, and that Maddie is. She doesn't care about the stupid beach with her stupid family.

"I just want to sleep. I was up late. I'm tired. Go without me."

"We are not going without you. This is a family vacation. You're part of the family, so you're coming with us. You love the beach."

Hayley can't argue with that. Still . . .

"Who goes to the beach at the crack of dawn? That's crazy!"

"Okay, it is *not* the crack of dawn, and there's a storm coming this afternoon. It's now or never."

"Fine. Never." She rolls back onto her side and pulls the fluffy cloud comforter over her head.

For a second, nothing happens, and she thinks maybe Mom left.

Then the comforter is yanked back.

She lets out a yowl. "Stop! Leave me alone! I'm not going!" She pulls the comforter and holds it tight over her head.

"You're going!" Mom tugs at it.

Hayley refuses to let go. "I want to stay here and sleep! It's my vacation too!"

"You can't stay here alone!"

"That's crazy! I'm twelve years old! I stay home alone all the time!"

"That's different!"

"How is it different?" she shrieks. "Stop treating me like a baby!"

"What's going on in here?"

It's Dad, standing in the doorway. He's wearing sunglasses, running shorts, and sneakers.

"Mom won't let me sleep!"

"Because we're going to the beach," Mom says, then, "Ben, I was just coming to tell you too. You need to change and get ready."

"I'm going for a run."

"In this heat?" Mom asks, like he just said he's going to dive into a spewing volcano.

"Yes, in this heat. I thought we were going later."

"It's going to storm later. We're going right after breakfast. Which is ready, by the way."

"You know I can't eat before a run, Tal'."

"Well, would you rather go for a run, or have a nice breakfast and go to the beach?"

"He wants to go for a run!" Hayley tells her mother. "God! No one cares about the beach except you!"

"Caleb cares! He wants to go!"

Hayley flops over again with a groan. Of course it's about Caleb. It's always about Caleb.

"We need to get there while the weather's still nice so that we can be back before it changes," Mom tells Dad. "You know how storms scare him."

"Everything scares him!" Hayley tells her pillow.

"Hayley! You know he can't help that. It's because he has—"

"It's because you treat him like a baby, Mom! That's why! Okay? You treat everyone like a baby! Including me!"

"Then stop acting like one!"

"*You* stop acting like a complete bitch!"

For a moment, there's silence.

Then Mom says, "You know what? I just can't with this right now. I'm done. I'm going to the beach with Caleb and Kelly."

Kelly's going? Hayley didn't realize that.

She shoves off the comforter and sits up to say she's coming; she just needs some time to get ready.

Mom is already gone.

Dad is standing there, shaking his head. Not at Hayley. Not like he's mad at her. Not even like he's mad at anyone. He just looks sad.

"You can sleep," he tells Hayley, turning and walking away. "I'm going for a run. We'll meet them at the beach later."

She sinks back into the bed, wishing she could undo the last few minutes. It would have been fun to go to the beach. It's probably her last chance of the summer.

They used to go a lot in Florida, with Granny Nat. And last year, they rented a beach house in the Outer Banks in North Carolina, and that was fun. The whole family in a good mood all week. Mom and

Dad laughed a lot and held hands when they walked, and Caleb wasn't scared of everything for a change. Only sharks, and waves, and the wild horses on the beach. But other than that, he was almost like a regular brother for a change.

Now everything is back to the way it used to be, only way worse. Especially today.

But it's too late to fix things.

There's nothing for Hayley to do but go back to sleep or just hang around Haven Cliff by herself.

Well, maybe not totally by herself.

She thinks again of the person she saw in the woods. It would be epic if it turned out to be a ghost, but way more epic if it's a movie star. Or her grandfather. Or her grandfather who's a movie star.

Whoever it is definitely seemed like they were hiding.

CHAPTER THIRTY-SIX

With every hour that passes without a sign of Sarah Greene, Midge is running out of benign scenarios for her continued absence.

She could have taken a different route heading home—say, a shortcut through the woods. Maybe she got lost. Maybe she passed out from the heat, hit her head. Far-fetched, but it could happen.

More likely, though, she never left the building. She'd have been hot and tired when she got there. If she knew the door code, she'd have let herself in to get some water or take a rest out of the hot sun.

Then what? She accidentally got locked in a closet? In the building? Wouldn't she have heard Al or the pastor or the repairmen and called for help?

Maybe she fell asleep or was somehow injured and incapacitated. Maybe she's still lying there.

The only way to find out is to go back over to Congregational to look around, and Midge would prefer not to wait for a warrant.

She finds the church website and dials the office number.

It rings into a robotic voicemail.

She hangs up. Now what?

She can try to track down the custodian, Al, but she doesn't have a last name. He's local, and she can probably make a couple of phone calls to figure out who he is, but it would probably be quicker to find the temporary pastor, Joseph Nielson. With luck, he's already there, or on his way.

She plugs his name into the search engine.

Unfortunately, there are a lot of Joseph Nielsons in the world.

There are nearly as many in the state, when she adds *New York* to the search terms.

He mentioned he was from a church in a neighboring county, but she doesn't know which one.

She scrolls through the first few entries, but this is getting her nowhere. She goes back to the search window to include the words *Reverend* and *Pastor*.

Bingo!

Joseph Nielson is a pastor at a congregational church in Monticello. That's in Sullivan County, which is right next door to Ulster County.

Midge clicks on the website, only to encounter a headshot of a smiling, bespectacled elderly man.

Wrong Joseph Nielson.

With a sigh, she backs out of the website and scrolls on until it occurs to her that his name might be spelled Neilson. Or what if it's Nielsen? Or Nealson?

This could take all day.

She redials Congregational, hoping someone will pick up this time.

Voicemail again.

She hangs up without leaving a message, grabs her keys, and heads for the door.

CHAPTER THIRTY-SEVEN

The sun is shining, and the sky is blue and clear as Kelly, Talia, and Caleb set out for the beach. It's nice to ride around town with Talia in the passenger's seat, just like old times, with Sirius radio tuned to Pop2K.

"He's right about that," Kelly comments, turning up the volume as they stop for a light.

Caleb, strapped in back, wearing light-blue board shorts imprinted with smiling red lobsters, asks, "Who's right about what, Aunt Kelly?"

"Bono. Listen. He's singing about a beautiful day, and that's what this is."

"It is," Talia agrees. "Poor Midge, having to work and miss everything."

"I wonder if—oh no!" Spotting the CVS at the next intersection, Kelly slaps the steering wheel. "I forgot to have my mom's new medication delivered this morning."

"Isn't one of her aides around to pick it up? Or the housekeeper?"

"You mean Mrs. *'I work for Beverly, not you, and my job doesn't include running all over town in the heat'* Verga?" Kelly shakes her head. "What a miserable old b—"

"Kelly!"

"Biddy," Kelly corrects, flashing her a beatific smile. "I'll have to stop and get the prescription and then drop it off at my mom's. But I promise this won't take long, and then we'll get right to the beach so we have enough time before the storm blows in."

"I don't like storms."

In the rearview mirror, Kelly sees that Caleb's eyes are round and worried beneath the brim of his red bucket hat.

"You know what? I forgot. That forecast wasn't for today," Kelly says. "It's probably from yesterday."

"You forget a lot of things," Caleb says.

"I guess I'm turning into an old biddy too. But I really do love this song." Kelly turns the radio up a notch, singing along.

Talia joins in. Even Caleb catches on, bellowing the chorus with them until the song ends.

"That was U2 with 'Beautiful Day,'" the DJ says. "And now for another hit single from the year 2000, here's Britney Spears with the title track from her second album, *Oops! . . . I Did It A—*"

Kelly jabs the button, changing the station.

"Wait, I want to sing another fun song," Caleb protests.

"We will," Talia says. "This is the nineties station. They'll have lots of good songs, right, Aunt Kelly?"

"Right. Just not this one," she says, wincing as Billy Ray Cyrus twangs about his achy breaky heart. "Let's try the eighties."

She presses the button again and grins. "*Now* we're talking. Who likes the Cure?"

"I don't know if I do," Caleb says.

"Listen. They're great. Right, Talia?"

Talia says nothing.

Kelly glances over and sees her friend looking troubled.

"Tal'? Everything okay?"

"I'm not sure. I think . . . either Midge made a mistake, or that DJ did."

"What do you mean?"

"If *Oops! . . . I Did It Again* was released in 2000, then how was that CD in Caroline's Walkman in 1999?"

CHAPTER THIRTY-EIGHT

On her way to Congregational, Midge stops off on Chestnut Street, where Jaret Buckley lives with his family in one of Mulberry Bay's gingerbread Victorians. It's not grand, like some of the neighborhood's restored mansions, but the two-story Queen Anne is painted in vintage shades of burgundy and plum, and the yard is well kept.

Midge has been here several times. Chuck and his wife always host the softball team's season-ending picnic. This year, she missed it, along with most of the season itself.

Chuck's car isn't in the driveway. Just a beat-up Jeep with an MB Summer Recreation Employee parking pass taped to the back window, which is colorfully painted with *Seniors* and *MBHS Class of '25*. Midge parks behind it, grabs her iPad from the dash mount, and heads toward the front porch.

The morning is warm, filled with the vibrating hum of the boxy metal air conditioners mounted in several windows here and in neighboring homes. It's expensive to add central air ductwork to old houses, and heat waves like this are rare in this area. But as Midge stands on the Buckleys' porch waiting for someone to answer the doorbell, she spies the Hot Cool Guys HVAC van across the street, alongside a contractor's pickup in front of a house that's being renovated.

The Buckleys' door opens, and Jaret regards her warily.

She remembers him as a younger teen, cute and freckle faced. Now he's tall and strapping, tanned and bare chested, wearing only Nike shorts and a towel slung around his neck.

"Jaret?"

"Yeah?"

"Midge Kennedy." She shows him her badge. "I'm a friend of your dad's. From rec league?"

"Oh . . . yeah," he says as if he remembers. That's doubtful, but he seems to relax a bit. "My dad's at work."

"I'm here to talk to you. Do you have a few minutes?"

"Uh . . . my mom isn't home, either, so if . . ."

"You're not in trouble, Jaret. You don't need a parent present to talk to me . . . unless you'd feel more comfortable?"

"What's it about?"

"Your girlfriend mentioned something to me last night, and I wanted to follow up."

"You talked to *Lauren*? About what?"

"I talked to Taylor."

"Oh. Taylor's not my girlfriend. She's just . . ." He shrugs. "You know."

Midge nods, getting the picture. "Anyway, she was working last night at Get the Scoop, and she mentioned that you—"

"Wait, sorry, but I have to ask. Did Taylor literally say she's my girlfriend? Because that's so messed up."

"I might have misunderstood," Midge concedes, feeling a bit sorry for Taylor. "Anyway, she mentioned Junia Stanton?"

"Who?"

"She's a missing person. From Elizabethville?"

"Oh. Yeah. What about her?"

"Taylor said you're friends with Junia's cousin."

"*What*? Man, Taylor sure makes up a lot of sh—"

"So you *didn't* go to football camp with Junia's cousin?"

"No. I went with her *neighbor's* cousin."

"Okay, well . . . did he mention any details about Junia?"

"What kind of details?"

"Did he tell you Junia was being stalked, Jaret?"

"*Stalked?* Is that what Taylor told you? Man."

Midge says nothing, waiting for him to go on.

"Yeah, no, he didn't say anything about her being stalked. He just said he heard she was talking to some guy online."

"Talking . . . like, on social media? Or a dating site?"

"I have no idea."

"Did he tell the police about that? After she went missing?"

"I don't know. Probably."

"And how about Sarah Greene? What do you know about her?"

"I heard she's missing?"

"She is. She didn't come home from Bible study yesterday. I'm looking into it. Do you have anything to share about her?"

"*Me?* No. I barely know her."

"You don't think she was being stalked, like Junia? Or that she may have been talking to someone online?"

"I never said that. But if you heard it from Taylor, she obviously just makes stuff up, so . . ."

"You didn't tell her you thought there might be a connection between Sarah Greene and Junia Stanton?"

"I didn't tell *her*, no."

"You told someone?"

Jaret shrugs. "My friend and I were talking about it when we were getting ice cream. I guess she probably could have heard us, but I didn't say it *to* her."

"What did you say to your friend?"

"He mentioned that Sarah's family's really into church stuff, and I said yeah, that's what I heard about the girl who disappeared from Elizabethville."

"Junia Stanton? You heard that from her neighbor?"

"From her neighbor's *cousin*. That's it. That's all he said. Can I, uh . . ." He gestures at himself, half dressed. "I need to go shower and get to work."

"Where do you work?"

"I'm a lifeguard."

"Over at the town beach?" At his nod, Midge says, "I had the same summer job when I was your age. It's the best, isn't it?"

"I guess. Sure, it's pretty good."

She gets his cell phone number, along with contact info for the friend he was with at the ice cream parlor last night, and for Junia's neighbor's cousin, which he's reluctant to provide.

"Are you going to call them or something?"

"No. I'm going to pass it along to a colleague who's working on finding Junia. You might want to give them a heads-up that they may hear from her."

"They don't really know anything."

"That's probably true. But what if there's a chance that some tiny detail can help find Junia?"

Regardless of whether she wants to be found.

Heading down the porch steps, Midge sees that the HVAC van's back doors are now open, and a young man in coveralls is rummaging inside.

She walks across the street, calling, "Excuse me?"

He looks up. Stops rummaging, straightens his posture, and glances around as if she might be talking to someone else. Then he points at his chest wearing a *Who, me?* expression.

Midge shows him her badge and introduces herself.

"Johnny," he says, pointing to the name patch on his uniform. "What's up? Am I parked too close to the hydrant?"

She glances at it. "Maybe by a few inches, but it's not about that. You were over at Congregational Church yesterday, right? To fix the air-conditioning?"

"Oh! Right."

"Can I show you something?" On her iPad, Midge quickly zooms in on the file photo of Sarah Greene and tilts the screen toward him. "Any chance you saw this young woman on the premises?"

He peers at it and shakes his head. "Only person I saw was the minister."

"You wouldn't happen to have his contact information, would you?"

"No, sorry."

"How about the custodian, Al?"

"You mean Al Novak?"

"I do if he's the custodian at Congregational."

"Yeah. You want his number?"

"If you have it."

"He's not in any trouble, is he?"

"Not with me."

"Okay, good." He takes out his cell phone.

"Were you able to get the AC back up and running over there?" she asks.

"Oh, yeah, quick fix. Some idiot messed with the thermostat." He chuckles, scrolling through his contacts. "Probably a kid trying to get out of going to Bible class, you know?"

"Really? You think someone sabotaged it on purpose?"

He looks up at her. "Hey, I'm not trying to get anyone in trouble or anything. I was just kidding around."

"Oh . . . good. I mean, I'm sure a kid couldn't actually take down the whole system, but . . ."

"You'd be surprised. If you take out the backup battery and pull out the wires, the thing is cooked."

"And that's what happened?"

He shrugs. "As far as I can tell. But if it was some kid . . . hey, you didn't hear that from me."

CHAPTER THIRTY-NINE

Talia takes in Kelly's childhood home, a stately brick Colonial with hunter-green shutters and arched, paned windows. The house is set back from the road beyond low cobblestone walls on an exquisitely landscaped property. Vibrant flower gardens border the plush lawn. Pachysandra rambles beneath towering shade trees, and ivy scales their massive trunks.

"This is like stepping back in time," Talia says as Kelly parks by the front door.

"Isn't it? Do you want to come in and see my mom? She pretty much looks exactly the same, too, and I know she'd love to see you and meet Caleb if she's in a good place this morning. But her moods change from day to day. Sometimes from minute to minute."

"That's okay. We'll wait here. I'd love to see her, too, but if this is a bad day, I wouldn't want to stress her out or confuse her."

"My concern is the opposite." Kelly nods toward Caleb, contentedly absorbed in the coloring books she bought him at CVS, along with three packages of colored markers.

Talia warned her that it wasn't a good idea to hand a six-year-old ink pens in the white leather seat of a nice car, but Kelly shrugged it off.

"My mom can be so sweet on her good days," Kelly tells her. "But on her bad days? Look out. She can be really angry. I know it's part of the disease, but when she lashes out, I have to steer clear."

"I'm so sorry, Kelly. I hate that you're going through this."

"I just hate that *she* is." Leaving the car running, she sighs and grabs the drugstore prescription bag from the console. "Okay, I'll be right back. Then, the beach! I promise!"

Talia watches her hurry toward the house. On the doorstep, she pauses for a moment, hand on the knob. Then she straightens her shoulders, holds her head high, and steps inside.

Poor Kelly. She rarely talks about her mother's illness, but it's obviously taking a toll.

Growing up, Talia occasionally related to her as a fellow only child, but more often, she was envious. Kelly had two parents and plenty of money. But in adulthood, she lost her doting father as unexpectedly as Talia lost Natalie, and all the money in the world can't halt Beverly Barrow's agonizing march into oblivion.

Hoping this is one of her good days, for Kelly's sake, Talia notices the security camera mounted above the door.

On the night Gordy Klatte died, Beverly had told Kelly that Caroline had come to the house looking for her. They'd attributed it to her delusions before discovering that the camera had captured the visitor.

The footage was grainy, but the woman certainly looked like Caroline. She was left-handed, as Caroline was, wearing Caroline's charm bracelet.

At first, they believed it was Caroline, still alive. Caroline, back in town . . . to kill Gordy Klatte?

Yeah, that hadn't seemed likely at the time. The Caroline they knew and loved was incapable of violence.

Later, they realized that it was Mary Beth, posing as Caroline. Wearing Caroline's bracelet. They'd always looked alike, and left-handedness is genetic, so . . .

Of course it was Mary Beth.

The Caroline they knew and loved was long dead.

Grief washes over Talia as if she's just heard the news. There are too many memories in Mulberry Bay. It's time to make some new ones. Happy ones.

Maybe Ben is back from his run and getting ready for the beach. Maybe Hayley is up and in a better mood. Maybe they can have a fun day together—or at least, a fun morning, before the rain begins.

She takes out her phone to check her messages.

There's no word from Ben. That's not surprising. He seemed eager to take a long run, something he rarely has time to do at home.

There's nothing from Hayley either. She had yet to emerge from her room when they left the house.

"I was sure she got her period," she told Ben. "PMS would explain the mood swings. Especially the way she's been treating me."

"Teenage girls are always hard on their mothers," he said mildly, lacing up his running shoes as she threw things into her tote bag for the beach.

"She's not even a teenager yet."

"Then we'd better brace ourselves for a decade-long Hayl-storm."

Talia must have had her share of blowups with Natalie at this age—but right now, she only recalls the good times.

It was just the two of them, and they were so much closer in age than Talia and Hayley are. So much closer, period. Is it possible that they didn't experience the same friction?

If only she could pick up the phone and ask her mother how to navigate this.

It's unfair that she was taken so soon; unfair, too, that Kelly's father is gone and her mother might as well be. And Caroline . . . Caroline should be here.

On the radio, still tuned to the eighties station, Mike and the Mechanics are singing "The Living Years." Talia reaches beneath her sunglasses and presses index fingers to the inside corners of her eyes to stop the tears.

Okay, this is ridiculous. She flips to the next station.

Ah, that's better. She's in the nineties now, with the Backstreet Boys.

She returns her attention to her phone.

There is one new message. It's from Chloe's mom, Camille.

I know you're away, but when you have a minute, can you give me a call?

With Chloe away at camp all summer, Talia has welcomed some distance from her mom. Now, she supposes, Camille will want to pick up where they left off in June, with Camille constantly inviting her to have lunch or coffee or wine, and Talia trying to make convincing excuses.

It's not that Talia dislikes the woman, but they're circumstantial friends, basically in each other's lives because the girls are inseparable. Camille is the kind of person who asks a lot of personal questions and tends to overshare, especially now that she's going through a difficult divorce.

She ignores the text, opens a Google search on her phone, types in *Britney Spears + Oops I Did It Again + which year album released*, and hits enter.

2000.

So the DJ on Pop 2K had the year correct.

Then Midge must have been wrong that it was the CD in Caroline's pink Walkman.

It's an understandable error. Midge was never a Britney fan like the rest of them.

The Barrows' front door opens, and Kelly steps out. Her mother is in the doorway.

Once a vibrant, athletic, attractive blonde, Beverly is gray and frail now, wearing baggy sweatpants and, on a hot summer day, a cardigan that sags on her skinny frame.

Talia sees Kelly hug her with a tenderness she rarely exhibits. As she starts to step away, her mother grasps her wrist, appearing confused. Kelly seems to reassure her. Then Mrs. Verga appears behind Beverly with a protective hand on her arm and shepherds her into the house as if to extract her from an unwelcome visitor, closing the door without a word to Kelly.

From behind, Talia sees her friend's shoulders slump. After a moment, she turns around, her face drawn and weary. Then she seems to remember Talia and Caleb in the car, pastes on a smile, and hurries toward them.

"Who's ready for a fun day at the beach?"

CHAPTER FORTY

After requesting a criminal background check on Al Novak, Midge dials the number Johnny gave her. It rings, and she puts the line on speaker as she heads down Chestnut toward Shore Street.

"Hello?"

"Al Novak?"

"Yes?"

"Detective Sergeant Midge Kennedy with the Mulberry Bay Police." Hearing his gasp and realizing he thinks the worst about a loved one, she immediately adds, "Your family is fine. It's not about anything personal."

"Oh, thank God. I'm driving, and I about went off the road."

"I'm so sorry. I understand you're the custodian over at Congregational?"

"I am."

"Are you on your way over there, by any chance?"

"No, why? What's going on? Was there a break-in or something?"

"Nothing like that. I'm just trying to track down a young woman who was there yesterday for Bible study."

"Oh, they had to cancel that. The AC was on the fritz. Of all days, right? Crazy that if it was any other time, it wouldn't matter. You'd just open the windows. But on a day like that, the place must have been a furnace."

"Must have been? So you weren't there?"

"No, the kids were supposed to let themselves in. I'm just part-time, and this is supposed to be my vacation week."

"Did someone in the group get ahold of you, then? To let you know the AC wasn't working?"

"No, the minister did."

"Do you mean Reverend Parker?"

"No, he's away. I heard about it from the pastor who's filling in for him this week."

"Really." Midge frowns. That's not what he told her.

"Yeah, nice guy. Seems like it on the phone, anyway."

"You haven't met him?"

"In person? No."

"Do you remember his name?"

"Let's see. It was Joseph . . . Nelson?"

"Nelson? Not Nielson?"

"Oh, yeah, maybe it's Nielson."

"What did he say, exactly?"

"He said he showed up in the morning to do some work in the office, and the air was broken, so he canceled the class and called the repairmen. Everything was under control, and he told me there was no reason for me to be there. He said he wouldn't have bothered me at all, but he didn't want me to hear about it around town and go running over. Like I said, nice guy. We chatted for a bit."

"Do you happen to have his phone number?"

"I don't, sorry. He called me from the office phone."

"Do you know where he's from? His home church?"

"Let's see . . . Mount Vernon, I think?"

"Mount Vernon? That's down in Westchester County."

"Mount Vernon was Thomas Jefferson's plantation house, right? That's how I remember it, because I helped my son build a scale model out of toothpicks for a social studies project last year."

"George Washington's plantation was Mount Vernon. Thomas Jefferson's was Monticello."

"Right! It was Monticello. My son got an A on that thing. Well, *we* got an A, if you know what I mean." He chuckles. "And you get an A-plus for setting me straight."

"So he's from Monticello?" Midge asks, thinking of the church website she found earlier, with a pastor by the same name.

"That's what he said."

"All right, well . . . I hate to ask, but is there any chance you can meet me over at the church office sometime today? I need to have a look around."

"I wish I could help you out, but I'm in the car right now, driving to Utica to visit my mom in the hospital. She's not doing great. I'm not sure how late I'm going to stay, but I can—"

"No, no, I'm sorry about your mom, and I'm so sorry to have bothered you at a time like this."

"No worries. Tell you what. The code to the door is 4113—go ahead and let yourself in."

"It's probably not a good idea to give it out to a stranger on the phone."

"Hey, you're not a robber; you're a cop. Unless you're not who you claim to be?" he adds in a teasing tone.

"Oh, I am." Not everyone can say that, though.

"Four-one-one-three," he repeats. "That's been the door code for as long as I've been there, and it's no state secret. Heck, they pretty much advertise it. It's the Bible verse that's carved on the cornerstone. Isaiah 41:13."

Maybe, but Midge has no intention of using that code without a warrant.

"How long have you been there, Al?"

"Going on twenty-seven years."

"One last question. Are there security cameras anywhere on the premises?"

"Nah. Reverend Parker's old school. No cameras, no alarms, nothing like that. There's nothing anyone would want to steal, unless they're into religious stuff—you know, like Bibles and statues. And people who are into all that are law-abiding citizens, right?"

Not everyone, Midge thinks again.

Reverend Bauer certainly wasn't.

As for Joseph Nielson . . .

Why would he lie to her about Al summoning him to wait for the repairmen?

And if he lied about that . . . what else was he keeping from her?

CHAPTER FORTY-ONE

There's a window seat in Hayley's room, with a thick, comfy cushion and throw pillows. It would be the perfect place to curl up and read if she had a book with her and felt like reading.

She does not, but that's okay.

She likes looking out the window at beautiful gardens flitting with butterflies, the deer that are grazing on the lawn, and the spot in the woods where she saw someone lurking in the dark last night. She's concluded that it was probably a ghost or her grandfather, and not a celebrity from a neighboring estate. Celebrities are super busy at night, going to galas and red-carpet events and posting photos on Instagram.

She looks at the large framed photograph hanging above the dressing table across the room. It shows a pair of sisters with long ringlets, posed in front of the exact same dressing table, except the one in the picture has a bench in front of it. Both little girls are wearing high button shoes and frilly dresses with wide ribbon sashes, and the smaller of the two clutches a doll with a painted face.

Hayley asked Kelly about them. She said they lived here back in the eighteen hundreds, part of the Winterfield family, whose portraits are displayed in frames all over the mansion. Maybe they're the ones who are haunting the woods now.

Or it could be their great-great-great-great—however many *greats* it is, and whatever relationship she is to them—Caroline.

Glancing out the window again, Hayley sees movement.

Someone is there! Is it—

Oh. It's only Dad, walking toward the house, back from his run. He's checking his stats on his watch, and he looks hot and sweaty.

She ducks back from the window, hurries to her bed, and gets under the covers. It's an impulse. It's just easier to avoid interacting with her parents today.

Every day, really. But right now, going on a family outing to the beach is the last thing she feels like doing, even if Kelly is there.

She hears her dad coming upstairs, footsteps in the hall. He knocks on her door. "Hayley? Are you up?"

"What?" She makes her voice groggy.

The door opens. "You're still sleeping?"

"I'm tired." She rolls over to look at him. He's in the doorway, holding his phone and a bottle of water.

"Come on. It's time for the beach. I'm just going to throw on my swimsuit. Mom's waiting for us." He wipes his sweaty forehead and gulps some water.

"Just go without me."

"I can't leave you here by yourself."

"You just did," she points out.

"That's different. I wasn't gone long."

"Dad, this is crazy. I don't need a babysitter. I *am* a babysitter, remember? I worked for the Piazzas all summer. They trusted me to take care of their kids! And you and Mom have left me home with Caleb while you run errands."

"True, but . . ."

Seeing him look at his phone as if he's thinking of checking with Mom to see if that's okay with her, she adds, "I just want to relax. I'll be fine. It's not like I'm going to throw a party or sneak out and go anywhere, since I don't know anyone around here and it's a million miles from civilization."

He smiles at that.

"Come on, Dad. If you make me go, you know I'm just going to be miserable and complain-y."

And that means you and Mom will be miserable too, she wants to add, but she doesn't have to. She can tell by the look on his face that he's imagining it.

"Okay," he says. "It's fine. You can stay here by yourself."

CHAPTER FORTY-TWO

At Congregational, Midge finds the parking lot completely empty, and the building has an air of desertion about it. She parks and walks up to the door anyway, knocking and ringing the bell. No one answers.

She looks at the lockbox, and then over at the cornerstone.

Sure enough, it's etched: *For I, Jehovah thy God, will hold thy right hand, saying unto thee, Fear not; I will help thee. —Isaiah 41:13.*

Circumstances don't warrant her using the code to access the offices. This isn't an emergency, there's no evidence a crime was committed, and the custodian isn't authorized to consent to a search.

She pulls out her phone.

Again, she checks the website for the Monticello church led by a Joseph Nielson who bears no resemblance to the Joseph Nielson she met here yesterday.

But what if there was an online headshot mix-up?

That happens. It happened to her. Someone had updated the MBPD website to reflect her temporary status when she stepped in for Walt but simply put Midge's photo above the caption with Walt's name and title. Someone caught it, and it was immediately remedied.

Maybe something similar happened with Joseph Nielson and no one caught it. This has to be the right pastor—he has the same name, and it's Monticello.

She calls the number listed on the site.

A pleasant-sounding female voice answers, "Northeast Congregational."

"Hello, may I please speak with Reverend Nielson?"

"I'm sorry, he just stepped out for a few moments."

"This is Detective Sergeant Imogene Kennedy with the Mulberry Bay Police Department. I want to confirm that he's filling in for Reverend Parker at the Congregational church here in town?"

"He is."

"He *is*," Midge echoes. Mystery solved; she's tracked down the pastor. "Can you please have him give me a call?"

"Of course."

Midge provides her phone number and hangs up, glad to finally be getting somewhere. Now she just has to wait for him to respond.

She heads slowly back toward the car, scanning the surrounding area. Her eyes return to the spot near the rock garden, where she saw the deer grazing yesterday.

Again, she notes the slight parting in the branches.

Again, she makes her way toward it.

Today, she sees an indentation in the grass.

She didn't notice it yesterday. Maybe it wasn't here.

It's nothing major—just a small patch where the blades are flattened in the same direction, away from the woods, and bare dirt is showing. It looks as if an animal pawed across it in an attempt to dig or perhaps dragged its prey out into the clearing.

Stepping closer to the wooded border, she sees that there is indeed a narrow pathway of sorts. It isn't clearly marked and mulched with wood chips like some forested trails in the area. The ground is thick with dead leaves.

Midge ventures in, wondering if Sarah might have done the same yesterday.

It's cooler here, beneath the thick canopy of trees. Peaceful, not a sound but the birds singing in the trees and a squirrel nosing around a fallen acorn branch.

It's slow going, picking her way around rocks, roots, fallen branches. Her foot catches on a vine, and she stumbles, nearly losing her balance.

Sarah, too, could have tripped. She could have hit her head on a rock or one of the fallen trees along the path. She could be here somewhere, injured.

"Sarah?" Midge calls. "Sarah!"

All is still.

She keeps moving, watching for tripping hazards, poison ivy, snakes . . .

Her phone buzzes loudly, startling her. She pulls it from her pocket and sees that it's from the church in Monticello.

"Detective Sergeant Kennedy."

"Hello. This is Pastor Nielson, returning your call. I understand there's an emergency at Congregational Memorial?"

The voice is unfamiliar.

Taken aback, she clears her throat, trying to corral her thoughts.

"Hello?" he says. "Did something happen to one of the congregants?"

"Pastor, were you here yesterday? At the church?"

"No, I wasn't. I'm on call for emergencies, and I'll be leading services on Sunday, but . . ."

"But you weren't here? We didn't speak?"

"No . . . is everything—"

"I'm sorry. This is regarding a young female congregant who was at the church for Bible study yesterday."

"Bible study was canceled. The air-conditioning system was down. I spoke with Al, the custodian. He was there with the repairmen."

"*He* was there?"

"Yes." On his end, she hears voices in the background. "I'm sorry, do you mind if I put you on hold for a moment? I have someone here, and I just need to—"

"No, that's all right. Go ahead. I'll call back in a bit if I need anything more. Thank you, Pastor."

Hanging up, she stares absently at a patch of ferns, thinking about the man she met yesterday.

She has no doubt now that he has something to do with Sarah's disappearance.

He lied to her, to Al, and to the HVAC repairmen.

He'd almost certainly impaired the air-conditioning system to render the building unusable because he didn't want anyone coming around while he did whatever he was there to do.

Who is he? What is his connection to Sarah?

Does he have one to Junia Stanton as well?

Pondering that, she realizes that she's looking at a disturbed area where the ferns are crushed or trampled, stems snapped.

She quickly pulls on gloves and turns on the flashlight from her duty belt and steps closer. Training the beam, she catches a glint of gold amid the green fronds.

It's a delicate necklace, broken, bearing a small cross.

CHAPTER FORTY-THREE

He remembers Haven Cliff.

He's never been there before, but he's certainly heard of it. Anyone who's ever spent any amount of time in Mulberry Bay knows about the abandoned Gilded Age estate, its ill-fated former residents, and the curse.

He supposes there's a certain logic to her suggestion that they meet here, since there aren't many unpopulated places around here on a holiday weekend.

But she was so specific in her instructions.

Coming from town, follow Route 28 along the lake. You'll see a big intersection where there's a Lowe's on one side and Home Depot on the other.

Yeah. He knows the intersection. He was out there yesterday, buying the tarp, rope, shovel . . .

7/10 of a mile past the intersection on the left, you'll see a big sign that says Coming Soon: Trolley Park Beach 2K. *It's a construction project adjacent to Haven Cliff. Turn in and follow the road down to the lake. Ignore the* No Trespassing *signs. No one's working there.*

He knows the site, a long-abandoned turn-of-the-century waterfront amusement park. Yesterday, he saw tall construction cranes poking up from the treetops and the sign indicating that the park is being rebuilt. He noted that in postmillennial Mulberry Bay, everything old is being made new again.

Park in the empty dirt lot where the dumpsters are. From there, you can walk along the water to the stone steps that lead up to Haven Cliff. Follow the path past the picnic pavilion through the woods till you come to a clearing. You'll see tennis courts and a swimming pool excavation. I'll meet you by the brick colonnade. There's a map attached.

He studied it, a printout of an online terrain map electronically marked up with red arrows and a circle. Then he compared it to the area on his own map app.

Considering the furtive, roundabout, specific path she designated for him, if he didn't know better, he might think he was being set up.

But no, he confirmed the match on the Lost and Found website. They share 25 percent DNA. He may not know her name, but he's certain that she is exactly who she says she is.

Still, he's not about to follow her convoluted route to Haven Cliff. He'll need to park as close as possible to the meeting spot because he'll have to get her into his car trunk afterward. He's going to arrive early, set the stage, get acclimated.

He passes the Trolley Park Beach site, slows, and turns into the old estate itself, marked by a scrolled iron sign that reads HAVEN CLIFF. He knows the dirt lane will lead to the site where the house once stood. From there he can find his way along the trail to the tennis courts and pool. The clearing in the woods was plainly visible in the terrain shot on his map app.

He rounds a bend and sees not the overgrown ruins of a stone mansion, but a broad green lawn and the mansion itself, resurrected and quite clearly occupied.

He hits the brakes and gapes at the blooming gardens, bubbling fountain, and SUV parked beside the portico. No wonder she told him to take the back way onto the property.

Belatedly, he sees the man about to climb into the driver's seat. He's wearing sunglasses, a pink polo shirt, madras board shorts, and flip-flops.

It's too late to make a U-turn and get the hell out of here. He's been spotted. The man waves and stands expectantly beside his car, watching him. There's nothing to do but move on into the circular drive, pull up alongside him, and roll down the window.

Hoping it's not obvious how hard he's clenching the wheel, he pastes on a friendly smile and speaks first. "Hey, there. Sorry, I think I'm lost."

"What are you looking for? Not sure I can help you—I'm not from here—but I'll try."

Now the smile is genuine, because this guy just made the ruse a whole lot easier. He can make up any old address and it won't be an obvious fake to a nonlocal.

"I'm trying to find 123 Mason Road?"

"You got me there, but I'll look it up for you." The man pulls a cell phone out of his pocket and starts to approach.

"Oh, that's okay; I'm pretty sure it's over by Home Depot. I was just looking for a place to turn around, if you don't mind?"

"Have at it." The guy steps back, tucking his phone away.

"Thank you, sir. Have a great day now." He waves, rolls up his window, and makes the turn.

As he drives away, he checks his rearview mirror and sees the guy watching him until he's out of sight.

CHAPTER FORTY-FOUR

Midge immediately called for backup after finding the gold cross in the woods behind the church. Investigators from the State Police and County Sheriff's Office, along with K9 and drone units, are now combing the wooded area for Sarah, or another sign that she was there. The necklace has been photographed and collected as possible evidence.

If it does belong to Sarah, it doesn't mean something terrible happened to her in the woods. There's a chance she might have snagged it and dropped it as she was hiking through.

But it's a remote chance.

Foul play is looking far more likely now that Midge knows the man claiming to be Pastor Nielson was an impostor.

Midge contacted the State Police Special Victims Unit to activate an Amber Alert, and a BOLO has been issued citing the man she met as a person of interest in the Sarah Greene case. She provided a detailed description, including the fact that he spoke with a slight twang, was wearing a fishing hat that seemed a size too large, and may be driving a dark-colored sedan.

She cited possible ties to the disappearance of Junia Stanton, along with the remote connection to Sienna Harmon, Mason Bauer . . . and Caroline Winterfield. Facts are facts. It's her duty to provide every possible lead.

The search warrant application for the church and offices depends on judge availability on a holiday weekend, but she's put in a couple of calls, hoping to expedite the matter.

Leaving the investigators to their work, she drives back along Shore Street.

At the town beach, she spots Jaret's Jeep in one of the employee parking spots and recognizes the luxury sedan parked alongside it.

Kelly.

Midge dials her cell phone. No answer.

She tries Talia, who picks up right away. "Midge?"

"Hey. Are you at the beach with Kelly?"

"Yes. It's beautiful here. Can you get away? We brought extra chairs."

"Thanks, but I'm really busy with a case. Can you put Kelly on the phone for a second, please?"

"Sure."

She hears Talia say, "Midge. She wants to talk to you."

In the background, she can hear happy chatter, splashing, a lifeguard's sharp whistle.

Then Kelly is on the line. "Hi, Midge."

"Hi. I just tried calling you, but you didn't pick up."

"I must have left my phone in the car. What's going on?"

"I didn't know you passed the test."

"What test?"

"Red Cross Water Safety."

"What are you talking about?"

"Your car's parked in the employee lot. So you're a lifeguard? Or maybe you're just working at the snack bar?"

"What—oh. Very funny."

"You can't park there without a sticker, Kelly. You need to move the car."

"*Fine*. Bye, Midge—oh, wait, hang on, Talia wants to tell you something."

Talia comes back on the line. "I tried to tell her not to park there."

"I appreciate your trying to make her a fine upstanding citizen, Tal'. Listen, I'm sorry I'm working today, but I'll see you tonight, as long as I can—"

"Wait, Midge. I know you've got to go, but something's bugging me. Remember when you mentioned that Britney Spears CD that Caroline had?"

"In the pink Walkman?"

"Right. Are you sure it wasn't . . . *Baby One More Time*? Because that was the album Caroline was obsessed with. Don't you remember that time she dressed up like Britney in the video, with her hair in braids? The naughty schoolgirl thing."

"Talk about playing against type."

"Right? Anyway, the next album was *Oops! . . . I Did It Again*, but it didn't come out until 2000, after she . . . was gone."

"Are you sure about that?"

"I looked it up. So you must have gotten it wrong. I'm sure it's no big deal, but I thought I should mention it."

In the background, Midge hears Caleb call, "Mommy, come on! I want to go in the water!"

"I'll let you get back to work," Talia says. "And I'll try to keep Kelly in line, but I can't promise you anything."

"Just get her to move her car before I have to have it towed."

Midge hangs up. She must have been mistaken about the CD she saw in the Walkman. She does clearly remember the night Caroline imitated Britney in the video. The four of them were together for a sleepover at Talia's. It must have been before Reverend B. got involved with Caroline, because the subdued young woman she became seemed incapable of letting go and having silly, carefree fun.

We should have known something was really wrong. We should have asked what was going on. We should have helped her.

Now she can only focus on helping Sarah.

CHAPTER FORTY-FIVE

October 25, 1998

Fat, wet flakes are falling as Mary Beth hurries along the sidewalk, crunching through dead leaves.

This isn't the first snow of the season here. That came on Columbus Day, in a storm that toppled trees that were heavy with dazzling foliage.

Autumn was always her favorite time of year back in Mulberry Bay.

Autumn in Syracuse has been miserable. Not just the weather. When you've flunked out of college after only one semester, you're surrounded by students living the life you were supposed to be living, unless you move away.

Mary Beth has nowhere else to go.

She had nowhere to go on Christmas night. It was snowing then, too, beyond the glass door at Golden Bridge. She remembers gazing out at the stormy dark, standing there with a suitcase of her belongings someone had packed for her, and a newborn screaming in her arms. She was raw and limp from the birth, still bleeding heavily. She didn't have a coat. The baby was wrapped in a thin receiving blanket.

The home provided nothing else. If her decision was to raise her baby on her own, then this was the beginning. There would be no tuition money—it turned out that was conditional, a gift provided by grateful adoptive parents, as the home explained it.

They weren't *selling* babies, of course. That was illegal.

She longed to march out that door and never look back.

But where would they go?

It was a crime-ridden, drug-infested industrial neighborhood on the outskirts of a city she'd only seen from her window: broken glass and garbage. That night, the graffiti-covered, boarded-up buildings seemed deserted, as if even the junkies had better places to be on Christmas night.

Mary Beth and her baby did not. If they ventured out, she was pretty sure neither of them would survive until daybreak.

It was no longer a choice. She did what any mother would do: She saved her child's life.

When she signed the papers, she was promised that it would be an open adoption with visitation rights.

Armed with tuition money and living expenses, she arrived here in January determined to pick up the pieces and make something of herself. She intended to become worthy of a role in her child's life. She had contact information for the adoptive parents in Cleveland, but she'd agreed to give them a few months to settle in before reaching out.

She took on a demanding courseload and part-time waitressing job, stashing her tips away for the future—visits, toys, Disney World . . .

Yes, someday, she'll be able to shower her child with gifts, attention, so much love.

Someday.

But exhaustion and depression caught up with her quickly last winter. Rundown, she caught the flu in February, and it lingered into April. She lost her job. Failed every one of her courses. Her college life was over before her Mulberry Bay High School classmates donned caps and gowns and received their diplomas.

If things had been different . . .

But there's no going back.

No moving ahead either.

Mary Beth remains in limbo.

Just before she was kicked out of her dorm, she was sitting on a stool in Joey Jay's, a dive bar. It was nowhere near campus and hardly the kind of place where students went to mingle; it was a place where you went to numb the pain. There, she met some people who became . . .

Friends is a generous word. They're fellow lost souls. Swept into the fold, she moved in with them, in this neighborhood that reminds her of the one she left behind in the Midwest. Her share of the rent is dirt cheap, as it should be for a shared room in a dilapidated yellow brick duplex with plywood over the broken windows.

She quickens her pace as she passes a group of men loitering outside the OTB. They eye her and look away without even an obligatory wolf whistle.

She hacked off most of her hair one night in a stoned stupor, leaving lopsided tufts. She's emaciated, having lost all her pregnancy weight plus an extra twenty, maybe thirty, pounds she couldn't spare. She doesn't have a mirror, much less a scale. Glimpsing her reflection in a store window, she sees a Dickens orphan, enveloped in a moth-bitten men's coat that's much too big.

She rounds a corner. Up ahead, she sees her destination beneath a burned-out neon Joey Jay's sign. It's just past the twenty-four-hour diner with the sign that reads just 24-Hour Diner, as if the owner couldn't be bothered to give it a name.

Somewhere, church bells are clanging.

It's Sunday.

Sunday . . .

The twenty-fifth? Yes, it must be.

Her child is exactly ten months old today.

She wonders what babies do at this age. Walking? Maybe not yet, but probably crawling, and starting to talk.

Calling another woman *Mama*.

Every day, Mary Beth faces pain she can't numb with any amount of booze, with anything stronger. Her heart, her empty arms, her entire being aches for the child who might as well be lost to her forever.

How can she reach out to the adoptive parents when she's like this? She doesn't trust herself to speak to them without breaking down or lashing out. And even if she managed to keep her composure, she can't visit. She can't send anything. She has nothing to offer.

She's gone through the last of the tip money except for a bit of loose change in her pocket.

That's why she needs to go back to Mulberry Bay—not to stay, or even to visit. She doesn't want to see her family. Doesn't want them to see her. She just needs to get the doll she stashed in the cubby.

If only she had a way there and back—a real friend, someone with a car, someone who would do her a favor, no questions asked.

There's only one person in the world who might be willing to help.

Caroline.

Mary Beth has to call when her parents are guaranteed not to be home. That means a Sunday, when they spend mornings at church and afternoons teaching Bible study.

That means today.

She ducks into Joey Jay's. It smells of morning after: stale cigarettes, fruit-scented cleaning solution, and vomit. A few stools are occupied by regulars—not together, not speaking, just drinking, all eyes on the small television mounted above the bar, where the Buffalo Bills are beating the Carolina Panthers.

The owner, whose name is *not* Joey Jay, greets her with a "Hey, M. The usual?"

That's what they call her around here. Just M. And "the usual" is well vodka, straight up.

"No, thanks, I just need to use the phone."

It's in the dim recesses, between the bathrooms, one of which is perpetually out of order, and the cigarette machine, which is always working. So is the pay phone, which receives far more incoming calls than outgoing. This is that kind of place in that kind of neighborhood, but few dealers are doing business at this hour on a Sunday.

Mary Beth fishes the loose change from her pocket. Mostly pennies, but there's one quarter.

She drops it into the slot and dials.

It rings once . . . twice . . .

"Hello?"

Caroline.

She'd been expecting her sister to answer yet is somehow caught off guard by the lilting sound of her voice, even more girlish and sweet than she remembers. Her voice is trapped in her throat.

"Hello? Hello?"

"Wait, don't hang up," she manages to say. It was her only quarter. This is her only chance.

"Who is this?"

"Car' . . . it's me. Mary Beth."

There's a gasp. "Where . . . where are you?"

"How much do you know?"

"Only that you ran away."

"That's what they told you? That I ran away?"

"Yes. Isn't that—"

"No."

"That's why," Caroline says softly.

"Why what?"

"Your doll—it's in the cubby. I figured you forgot it, but . . ."

"So it's still there? The money? And nobody knows about it?"

"It's still there. Nobody knows. What happened, Mary Beth? Where did you go?"

"You didn't get my letters."

"Letters? You wrote letters?" Caroline sounds like she's crying. "I didn't get them. I was so scared you might be . . . But you're alive. Are you okay? Where are you?"

"You have to promise me you won't tell them. Do you promise?"

She hears only sniffling.

"Caroline, if you can't promise, then I'm going to hang up, and I swear to God you'll never hear from me again."

"Yes! Don't hang up! I promise. I won't tell."

"Okay. I have to make this fast. I need you to write something down."

"Hang on."

She hears Caroline rummaging around and pictures her in the kitchen, where the phone is. Not cordless, unless things have changed since Mary Beth left.

Of course things have changed. Everything changes.

A lump rises in her throat. She isn't homesick—she isn't. Not for that somber house, or for her parents. It's just . . . their lives have gone on without her. Even Caroline's.

So will her son's. The difference is that he can't forget her, because he's never known her at all.

Caroline is back on the line. "Okay, I found a pen and paper. What do you want me to write?"

Mary Beth rattles off the address. "Got it? Read it back to me."

Caroline does. "Is this where you're living?"

"It's where you're going to meet me tomorrow."

"Tomorrow's a school day!"

"So play hooky."

"I can't! I have a test."

"Then come after school."

"But how am I supposed to get to Syracuse?"

"Don't you have your driver's license yet?"

"I do, but it's not like I have a car."

"Do your friends?"

"Yes, but I can't just—"

"Yes, you can. For me, Caroline. I need you to do this for me. Please."

"Why? Are you in some kind of trouble?"

Mary Beth isn't sure how to answer that. "You're the only one I can trust. You won't let me down. I have to go."

"But—"

"I'll see you tomorrow."

She hangs up quickly, before the tears fall.

CHAPTER FORTY-SIX

Present Day

Pulling up in front of the Greene house, Midge finds a second car parked in the driveway. It's too soon for Andrew Greene to have driven all the way back from Georgia. It must be one of the friends Renee mentioned, here to support Sarah's mom.

A tall, thin brunette with a tired-looking face opens the door almost immediately. Midge recognizes her from their school days—she used to be Virginia Shade, now Ginny Livingston.

"Midge!" She steps outside and pulls the door nearly closed behind her, keeping her hand on the knob as she asks in a low voice, "Did something happen? Did you find Sarah?"

"Not yet. Is her mom here?"

"She's upstairs sleeping. Poor thing. We were up all night, and I want her to get some rest. I'm afraid she's going to need her strength, because this whole thing is reminding me of when Caroline went missing. I'm sure it must bring back difficult memories for you too. I remember how close you were to her."

Midge nods.

"I was behind you at school, but I got to know her through church. I always looked up to her. She was the sweetest girl, and so cute, the way she was with Gordy. I thought they were the perfect couple." Ginny sighs. "And now he's gone too. But you know that. I remember seeing you at the house that day. What a terrible thing that must have been for you, since you knew him."

"It was."

"And then there's Caroline. Even after all these years, I've never stopped wondering what happened to her. I just pray things will end differently now, for Sarah. I mean, with Caroline, it never ended at all. She just vanished into thin air, you know?"

"I know."

"Sometimes I see her parents at church. I just can't fathom their pain. It's a blessing that they've been away all summer on a mission, what with Mary Beth being arrested for assaulting a police officer."

Midge says nothing. She remembers, now, that Ginny is one of those people who has a lot to say about everything. Kelly used to call her Patty Simcox, after the busybody character in *Grease*.

It may be childish and unprofessional, but Midge feels a prickle of resentment toward Ginny for even bringing Caroline into this conversation, as if they're bound by grief and loss.

"Right now, Ginny, we need to focus on Sarah. I know you and your daughter were at the church yesterday, before you found out Bible study was canceled. Did you happen to see anyone around when you were there?"

"Do you mean, did we see Sarah?"

"Sarah, other students, the pastor? Anyone at all?"

"No. We were the only ones there. We were early. We saw the sign about the cancellation, and we went right back home."

"You didn't open the door and go inside, then?"

"Go inside? No."

"But you do have the keypad code?"

"Of course. Why would we go in, though, with the meeting canceled and no air-conditioning?"

"Were there any other cars in the parking lot?"

Ginny considers that, head tilted. “I think there might have been one. Yes, there was. Parked way back in the corner. I remember thinking that’s because it was the only spot of shade. The car was dark blue, or maybe black.”

“Did you notice the make or model? The plate?”

“It was a Ford Focus. Why? Do you think that was a kidnapper’s car?”

“I’d just like to track down anyone who was in the area and might have seen anything,” Midge says. “Do you happen to have a list of Bible study group members who aren’t away at the retreat and were planning to be there yesterday?”

“I don’t, but my daughter probably knows.”

“All right, if you can get that information for me, I’d appreciate it. And I would like to speak with Sadie.”

“Do you want me to go get her?”

“No, just have her give me a call when she wakes up.”

Midge is expected to use her discretion on how much to share with the family about the progress in the case. There’s no urgency in getting a positive ID on the necklace to confirm its evidentiary value.

And Ginny is right. Midge, too, suspects that Sarah’s mother is going to need her strength in the days ahead.

“Are you sure? You’re welcome to come in and wait if you like. I was just about to make some tea.”

“Thanks, but I can’t.” Midge starts to turn away, then pivots. “Oh, there is something . . . Do you remember Reverend Bauer? He was the pastor at Congregational years ago.”

“I remember him. Reverend B., everyone called him. What about him?”

“What ever happened to him? Do you know?”

“He moved to another congregation after ours.”

“Do you know where?”

“Not far away. Teddy would know. He was friendly with one of his sons. The family used to come on the retreat.”

"In the Adirondacks?"

"Back then it was the Catskills. But there was a fire, and the camp burned down, so now it's way up north."

"Is your husband still in touch with the son?"

"No. I think they eventually ended up moving back down south. That's where Reverend B. was from. He said his wife didn't like the weather up here. Why do you ask?"

"Just curious. When you mentioned Caroline, I thought about him."

"He was such a rock for everyone during that awful time, wasn't he? What a wonderful man."

Hmm. Not only is Ginny unaware of his recent troubles with the law, but she seems oblivious to the man's predatory nature.

Midge would like to believe that her hunch about what might have happened between him and Caroline is wrong, just as she was mistaken about that CD title.

But something tells her it isn't. She's seen it countless times. People don't just turn a blind eye when it comes to a man in a respectable career, a position of power. Sometimes they're truly blind.

CHAPTER FORTY-SEVEN

Mulberry Bay's municipal beach is tucked between the pier and waterfront park. It's small, with a pebbly, grassy shoreline in lieu of sand, and you have to bring your own chairs and umbrellas. The water is more gray than blue even on a sunny, cloudless day, dotted with a few fishing boats well out beyond the roped-off swim area.

It's been years since Kelly has spent any amount of time here, and decades since she did anything other than kick back and bask in the sun on any beach.

That's what she was planning to do today, but she's learning quickly that relaxation can be challenging when you have a six-year-old in tow.

Caleb questions everything in his sight line—who lives in the vacation homes around the lake, why the old sleepaway camp on the opposite shore is called Woody Lo-Hi, which kinds of fish the fishermen might be catching, how many boats can tie up to the pier, whether there's a playground in the park, when the old houses in town were built, what mulberries taste like . . .

Sitting in chairs on either side of him, Talia and Kelly tag team on the replies until Caleb says, "I'm hot. I want to go swimming."

Talia looks at Kelly. "I don't suppose you want to—"

"No, thanks. Have fun."

Talia heads to the water with Caleb, sticks a toe in, and screams, "It's freezing!"

"Oh, come on. It's refreshing!" Kelly calls.

"How would you know? You're warm and toasty on dry land. Wait, Caleb, stay close to shore!"

"Don't worry, Mommy, Aunt Kelly said there are no waves and sharks!"

"Thanks a lot, Aunt Kelly. He still can't swim alone."

"He's not exactly alone, Tal'." Kelly gestures at the hordes of people splashing around in the roped-off area. "There are lifeguards, and he seems to be a good swimmer."

"He is. He's always loved the water. My mom made sure of that, but—Caleb! Come back here by me!"

He either doesn't hear her or chooses to ignore her. Good for him. It's nice to see him loosen up and have some fun.

"Caleb!"

"Shh, you'll embarrass him." Kelly joins Talia at the water's edge.

"He's out way too far."

"He's knee deep."

"Ben is supposed to be here. He's the one who does water stuff with him. Where is he?"

"I'm sure he's coming soon."

"I hope so. Sometimes he gets me so . . ." She shakes her head.

"Feel like talking about it?"

"Not even a little bit."

Kelly nods. "Don't worry. I'll go in with him."

"You don't have to—"

"I know. I want to."

"You're the best. Thanks."

Kelly wades in, remembering how difficult it is to navigate the slippery rocks without water shoes. She gives up, pulls off her sunglasses, and thrusts herself into the water. It's bracing, but it feels good to be drenched in something other than sweat on a day like this. She emerges, puts on her sunglasses, and floats through the shallow water to Caleb.

"Aunt Kelly! You can swim!"

"So can you, kiddo! You're like a fish."

"That's what my granny used to say. She was like a fish too. She could even do somersaults in the water. I wish I could do that. Can you?"

"I used to be able to, but it's been a while."

"Try!"

Turns out it's one of those childhood skills you don't forget. She hands Caleb her sunglasses and demonstrates it for him. Pretty soon he, too, gets the hang of it. It's nice, romping in the water like a kid again, being on the receiving end of unabashed admiration.

"Look, there's my daddy!" Caleb says, and she sees Ben on the beach, talking to Talia.

Perhaps arguing with Talia.

Kelly can't see their expressions, but Talia is shaking her head at him and doing a lot of talking. Hayley is nowhere to be seen.

"Hey, Daddy! Daddy! Watch this!"

Ben hears Caleb and turns away from Talia, shading his eyes with a palm.

Caleb plugs his nose and turns a perfect underwater somersault. Ben gives him a thumbs-up, says something to Talia, kicks off his shoes, and strips off his shirt.

"Hey, my daddy's coming in!" Caleb says.

Kelly takes that as her cue to get out. Passing Ben as she paddles toward the beach, she asks, "Where's Hayley?"

"I couldn't get her to come. My wife is acting like I abandoned a toddler in Times Square. Can you please tell her she's being ridiculous?"

Yeah, that's not going to happen in a million years, Kelly thinks. There's no way she's taking sides in a marital spat. Though if she *were* going to take sides, it would have to be Talia's, because . . . solidarity. Even though when it comes to her kids, Talia might be a tad overprotective. Or maybe a lot overprotective.

Midge might disagree. As a cop, she sees the worst of what can happen when parents are negligent or kids have too much freedom.

Midge . . .

"Crap!" Kelly forgot about her car, still parked in the employee zone.

"Is that a good idea?" Talia asked when she left her purse there.

"It's a great idea. We have enough to carry, and I don't need it at the beach."

"No, I mean . . . anyone can walk by and see it. What if someone steals it?"

"From a locked car in broad daylight in Mulberry Bay?"

"Are there robbers here?" Caleb asked.

"Nope, no robbers. This is the safest town ever," Kelly assured him, having figured out that information sharing with children is on a need-to-know basis.

Kind of like marriage.

Her failed ones, anyway.

Back at the chairs, she finds Talia on the phone. ". . . but this isn't just down the street at the Piazzas' house, Hayley. It's Haven Cliff!"

The beach is noisy with splashing kids, lifeguards' whistles, speakers blasting music, but as she stands by her chair, toweling off, Kelly can clearly hear Hayley on the other end.

"So what, Mom? It's just a house. You're acting like it's dangerous or cursed or something."

And Hayley's acting like she might know a bit about Haven Cliff's past. It almost seems like she's baiting Talia.

"I'm not acting like anything!" Talia tells her daughter. "It's a strange house in a strange place where you don't know anyone."

"So what? I'm twelve."

"Exactly. You're *twelve*."

"You can't treat me like a little kid! Dad said it's fine!"

"Dad should have checked with me first."

"Maybe he doesn't like being treated like a little kid either!"

Kelly pulls on her cover-up, shoves her feet into her sandals, and grabs her car keys from her beach bag. Catching Talia's eye, she mouths, *I'm going to move my car.*

Talia nods at her, saying into the phone, "Dad and I make parenting decisions together, Hayley. He isn't . . ."

Kelly walks toward the parking lot, eager to escape the domestic drama.

She may have felt a tiny pang of regret over missing out on motherhood when she was out in the water with Caleb. Now she's pretty sure she dodged a bullet.

Two bullets. It's her lucky day. Her car is right where she parked it—not towed away, not even ticketed, her handbag visible on the floor of the back seat.

About to climb in, she hears someone say, "Excuse me, ma'am?"

She turns to see a uniformed female state trooper, her face flushed and sweat beaded beneath her broad-brimmed tan hat.

"Oh, sorry, Officer," Kelly says. "I was just about to move it. I didn't realize this was an employee spot."

Even after all these years, white lies flow easily off her tongue when she's in a bind—not that a parking citation is a big deal, but don't the local police usually handle that?

"Wait," she says, "did Midge send you over?"

"Midge Kennedy? You know about the case, then."

"I know Midge. She's my best friend. I live here in Mulberry Bay. Which case?"

"The missing girl?"

Caroline?

What's going on, here? Have the authorities somehow found out that Kelly, Midge, and Talia covered up her disappearance?

"I'm sorry," Kelly says. "I don't think I understand."

"Sarah Greene." The trooper holds up an iPad. "She's missing."

Ah—so this has nothing to do with Caroline. It must be the case Midge was working on yesterday.

"We're canvassing the area for anyone who might have crossed paths with her. Mind taking a look?"

"Oh . . . sure." Kelly leans in and cups her hand to block the sun's glare from the photo of a fresh-faced, long-haired teenager. She shakes her head. "I haven't seen her. She's missing?"

"Since yesterday afternoon." The woman tucks the iPad under her arm again and hands Kelly a paper flyer. "Since you're local, can you please share this and spread the word?"

"Sure."

"There's a phone number there, in case you or anyone you know have helpful information. Have a nice day."

She moves on to question a couple of passersby.

Kelly gets into the hot car, rolls down the windows, blasts the air, and scans the information on the flyer.

Sarah Greene . . . sixteen . . . last seen . . .

Bible study at Congregational Memorial!

The words jump out at her.

Does this have something to do with Caroline?

Or . . . with Bauer?

She grabs her phone and calls Midge.

She answers immediately. "Hey, Kelly. What's up?"

"Got a minute?"

"Make it seconds. I'm driving back to my office and I'm almost there."

"Okay, so I'm in the parking lot, moving my car, and I got stopped by a cop who—"

"Sorry, you're on your own with this one, Kel'," Midge says. "You should have moved it sooner, and you shouldn't have taken an employee spot in the first place."

"No, listen, it was a trooper questioning people about a missing girl. Sarah Greene? Is that your case?"

"Yes."

"She was on her way to Congregational Memorial, Midge."

"I'm aware."

"What if Bauer did something to her too? Because Caroline—"

"Caroline was twenty-five years ago. It just doesn't make sense."

"It does if he's back."

Silence on the other end.

"Midge? Are you there?"

"I'm here. And I'm looking into every possible angle."

"Including Bauer?"

"Including Bauer. If you hear anything more from your pal Toby, send it my way, okay?"

"Definitely. Good luck."

Kelly hangs up, folds the flyer, and tucks it under the sun visor.

Beyond the windshield, the sky remains blue, but a milkier shade now. She recognizes the distant shelf cloud above the mountains as an ominous harbinger.

There's a storm coming, all right, and it looks like it's going to be a big one.

CHAPTER FORTY-EIGHT

The title track from . . . *Baby One More Time* is on a replay loop in Midge's head as she descends the steps to the police station, thinking about Kelly's call and about Caroline, about Sarah, about Junia and Sienna, and about what a dangerous place the world can be for the sweet and innocent.

As for the not so sweet and innocent . . .

She finds Allie at the desk, in the midst of a call that appears to be business, as she's taking a report.

Midge waves at her, heading for her office, but Allie holds up a finger for her to wait.

"All right, we'll send someone over as soon as we can," she's saying. "Yes, I've got the address . . . right . . . right. Just as soon as we can. Yes, we will. Thank you."

She hangs up, tosses the pen aside, and heaves a sigh. "Wow, *that* was an ordeal."

"What's going on?"

"Some old guy, complaining that there are too many people staying at the Airbnb next door to him. He said there should only be six, and he counted at least seven. But one is a baby, so . . . Do babies count?"

"Depends on the rental agreement. Send someone over to check it out. What else?" she asks, impatient to get to her desk.

"Some Amish guy dropped this off for you." Allie opens a drawer and pulls out a white paper bag. "It smells amazing, whatever it is."

The bag is heavy for its size and smudged with sugary grease. Midge peeks in. Seeing two enormous glazed apple fritters, she starts to offer one to Allie.

"Oh, and one more thing!" Allie says, snapping her fingers. "I totally forgot to tell you earlier, and then I was going to call but I didn't have a chance."

"What is it?"

"Nate somebody was here to see you."

"Nate who?"

"Or maybe it was Matt."

"Matt . . . Wait, was it *Nap*? Nap Moreau? The medical examiner?"

"Probably."

"Probably?"

"I'm pretty sure." Allie gives a decisive nod.

"When was he here?"

"This morning."

"*When* this morning?"

"Just before you got here."

"You mean the first time? Or now?"

"The first time. Early. He said for you to give him a call."

"Allie! Why didn't you tell me?"

"I forgot. I was busy."

"With your pedicure?"

"I'm sorry, Midge. I—"

"You're on thin ice, Allie," Midge snaps. "You'd better shape up, fast."

She turns on her heel and strides to her office. Most likely, Nap was just popping in to say hi. He does that sometimes. Maybe he wanted to check with her about going to the Dive Inn.

She reaches into the white paper bag, breaks off a chunk of apple fritter, and shoves it into her mouth before licking her sticky index finger and dialing Nap's number.

It rings into voicemail.

She leaves a message, hangs up, and breaks off another piece of fritter.

Before she's even swallowed it, the phone buzzes with an incoming call.

Wow, that was fast.

But it isn't Nap. It's Ann Webster, the Elizabethville detective on the Stanton case. Midge put in a call to her earlier, after speaking with Al Novak.

"Hi, Midge. I had a message to get in touch as soon as possible. Is your dad okay?"

"Yes, he's fine."

"Oh, thank goodness. When I saw you'd called, I got worried."

"No, it's nothing like that. I wanted to ask you about the Junia Stanton case. We've got a missing teenage girl here, and there are some similarities in victimology."

Her father's term is a deliberate choice now. It's increasingly unlikely that either case is without victims.

"You're talking about Sarah Greene? I heard about that this morning. You're right, they're around the same age, and they're somewhat similar in appearance. And they both left home alone, in the middle of the day. By any chance, is Sarah an adoptee?"

"No, she isn't. Her mother specifically mentioned getting her nickname when she was pregnant with Sarah. There is another connection between the girls, though. The Greenes belong to Congregational Memorial Church, and the Stantons were members years ago."

"So the girls know each other?"

"I don't think so. But it's where Sarah was headed yesterday afternoon, and when I went over to see if I could track her down, I met a man claiming to be the minister."

"Claiming?"

As Midge quickly fills her in, she hears Ann clacking a keyboard.

"I see the BOLO here . . . white man, clean cut, medium build, wearing a hat, driving a Ford Focus," she says. "Talk about a needle in a haystack. Any leads yet?"

"Not yet. I'm hoping he's still in the area. There's one other thing . . ."

Midge tells her about Jaret and his friend's speculation that Junia might have been talking to a strange man. Again, Ann is typing, taking down notes and asking for the boys' names and numbers.

"Thanks, Midge. I'll reach out to them and see if they have anything for us. We've been trying to get access to Junia's phone, email accounts, social media, all of it. But you know how that goes."

"Yes. It takes a while. Her parents don't have access to anything?"

"Her parents aren't cooperating."

"With the investigation?"

"Not with anything they see as a violation of their privacy or Junia's."

"Are you suspicious?"

"Do I think they had something to do with Junia's disappearance? No. Do I think they're not sharing everything they know? Absolutely. One of her friends reached out to tell me Junia had recently learned she was adopted. Apparently, it caused a rift, because it was something the Stantons intended to keep from her."

"I'm guessing the records are sealed?"

"They are. Junia's friend said that the Stantons refused to answer any of Junia's questions about the adoption or what they might know about her biological parents. They certainly didn't answer any of ours."

"Even if it might help find their daughter?" Midge exhales through puffed cheeks. "Never mind, don't answer that. Okay, so without any records or anyone willing to talk, DNA testing would have been Junia's only means of tracing her biological family. That's what she was doing when she disappeared?"

"She was. Her friend said Junia had provided samples to more than one genealogy site, and that she was communicating with someone from her birth family, possibly making plans to run away."

"But you can't access her records directly on the site to see who it was?"

"She didn't use any of the sites that cooperate with law enforcement. We need a warrant or a subpoena. The thing is, Midge . . . knowing what I know now, I'm not convinced there's any foul play involving Junia. She's a legal adult. She has a right to live wherever she wants to live, and to cut off communication with her adoptive parents. Sarah's a different story."

"I agree. It's just, when I heard about Junia's connection to Congregational . . . it's hard not to think it might be relevant."

"I understand, and you *are* your father's daughter. Bobby's never been big on coincidences. But sometimes, they do happen, Midge. On the job, and in life. I'm sure that's all this is, but I'll text you her parents' contact info so that you can talk to them yourself, if you'd like."

"That would be great, thanks."

A moment after they hang up, her phone lights up with a text from Ann.

As promised, she's sent phone numbers for Junia's parents, Brian and Astrid Stanton.

CHAPTER FORTY-NINE

Hayley cannot *believe* her mother.

On the phone, she thought at first that Mom was just disappointed about her not going to the beach with Dad because it was supposed to be a family thing.

But apparently, that's not it. She's all freaked out about Hayley being here alone.

She should just *tell* Hayley that she thinks Haven Cliff is cursed or haunted, and about her friend Caroline who vanished after the prom in 1999. But no, she has to act like Hayley is just a little kid, too young to understand, too young to be left without adult supervision.

She actually wanted to drive back and pick her up. "Just put on your bathing suit and be ready when I get there."

"Don't come. I'm not going to the beach."

They did a few rounds of *yes, you are* and *no, I'm not* before Hayley said, "I'm just not comfortable in a bathing suit right now, *okay*?"

It isn't true.

But it worked as intended.

"Fair enough. But I'll come back and stay with you."

"Why?"

"You know why!"

"Seriously? You're going to ruin Caleb's only beach day of the whole summer to come back here and babysit me?"

Invoking Caleb is genius, because they both know he won't want to stay there without Mom.

"He loves the beach, Mom. It's not fair to make him leave if he's actually having fun for a change. And you've been looking forward to it, too, to spending time with Aunt Kelly. And I know how to take care of myself for a little while. Didn't you, when you were my age?"

Her mother agreed to let her stay. "You're right. Okay. But you have to make sure all the doors are locked. And you can't let anyone in if they come knocking."

"Who's going to come knocking?"

"You never know. A chef, or a delivery, or a neighbor, or—"

"Or an axe murderer?"

"Hayley—"

"Relax, Mom. I'm just kidding around. But what am I supposed to do if, like, the chef shows up to make dinner?"

"If *anyone* shows up, just call me immediately. You are not to open the door for any reason."

"Can I open it to sit on the porch and read, or do you want me to, like, climb out the window?"

"I want you to stay *in* the house. No going outside for any reason."

Hayley rolls her eyes. She can't resist asking, "What if the house catches on fire? Do you want me to burn to death?"

"You know what I mean. Oh, and I don't want you turning on the stove or oven either. Got it?"

"You want me locked up and starving to death like a prisoner. Got it."

"This is your choice. I can come get you if you want—"

"I don't," Hayley says. "I want to stay here. I'll be fine. Have fun. *Bye-eee*."

She drifts downstairs, pretending she's the lady of the house and wishing she were dressed in a sweeping ball gown, or even the white eyelet dress she wore at dinner last night.

That was her plan, but unfortunately, she must have somehow sat on a crumb of chocolate soufflé, and it left a brown smudge in the back. She left the dress in a heap on the floor. Maybe Mom has OxiClean with her, or Kelly has some she can borrow to remove the stain. She just hopes no one noticed it last night, because that would be totally embarrassing.

She's not going to waste time worrying about it now, though, because she wants to enjoy her time alone. Well, alone except for Kelly's cat, Bibi. But Kelly said she's shy and mostly stays on her bed, so Hayley hasn't even seen her yet.

She keeps an eye out for Bibi and an ear out for ghostly voices as she makes her way through the first-floor rooms, noticing that the house is much quieter than her own house. No creaky floorboards, squeaky door hinges, or dripping faucets. She hears only clocks ticking, appliances humming, and her sandals flip-flopping across the marble, wood, and carpeted floors.

In the kitchen, she finds a white bakery box with a scrolled blue label written in French. It's full of pastries that look like miniature works of art. She chooses a chocolate tart-type thing and gobbles it down while she's standing at the counter, because there's no one here to tell her to sit down and get a plate.

Thirsty, she opens the fridge, bypassing the lemonade for a pretty blue bottle of sparkling water. It kind of looks like champagne. She pretends that it is, and it's half gone before she wishes she'd poured it into a stemmed crystal flute.

If only Chloe were here. Hayley snaps a few selfies to send her, making sure to get the beautiful cabinets and black granite counters in the background.

Noticing the half-full coffeepot, she sees that there's a Post-it stuck to it. It says, *Help yourself.*

Kelly probably meant that for Mom and Dad. But then again, maybe it was for Hayley too. Kelly treats her like a real person.

The thing is, Hayley doesn't really drink coffee. Unless you count the time when Mom ordered something at Starbucks called a macchiato with whipped cream and caramel drizzled on top and she let Hayley try it. It wasn't bad, but it was nowhere near as good as hot chocolate.

She looks through the cabinets for a cup. There are mugs, and a lot of stainless-steel ones with lids. Mom would probably tell her to use one of those so that she doesn't break or spill.

Annoyed, she closes the cabinet and goes into the dining room. There's a glass-fronted cabinet filled with elegant dishes and stemware. She sees a whole set of the gold-rimmed china they used at last night's dinner, but there are other kinds too. Some of it looks really old, like the set with the scalloped edges and little roses. Taking out a plate, she sees that it says *Haviland Limoges* on the back, which sounds classy, maybe even French.

She'll use this for her breakfast. Kelly won't mind. She won't even have to know. Hayley will wash it and put it away as soon as she's done eating and FaceTiming with Chloe.

She stacks a plate, saucer, and cup and steadies it with two hands as she carries it to the kitchen. Opening the bakery box, she selects the prettiest pastry, a flaky confection filled with cream and dotted with sugary flowers and cherries and chopped nuts. She doesn't like nuts, but they look nice, and she'll pick around them.

She puts it on the fancy plate, then pours some coffee into the fancy cup and takes a sip. It's hot and bitter and awful. All the whipped cream and caramel in the world couldn't make it better, but that's okay. She doesn't have to actually drink the stuff.

She balances the cup on the saucer in one hand and carries the plated pastry with the other, walking very slowly to the dining room table. She sits with the elegant marble fireplace behind her and holds up her phone, reversing the camera so that she can see how she looks.

Perfect, other than the bright-green T-shirt. She considers borrowing something from her mom. Or better yet, from Kelly. But it's one thing to help yourself to food and nice dishes and another to go into someone's closet without asking.

She lifts the cup in her left hand as if she's drinking, and she holds her phone in the other, holding it high and at an angle. Then she uses her thumb to FaceTime Chloe.

The first thing she'll do is sip her coffee. Then she'll be sure to mention that she's here alone, just to remind Chloe that she's not a child of eleven, like Maddie is.

Then maybe she can take Chloe on a tour around the mansion. She can tell her that it's haunted too. Chloe knows a lot of ghost stories from camp. Most of them are just silly, but there's one that still gives Hayley the creeps, about a strange figure called the Hatman who haunts people in their beds at night. Chloe showed her an article about scientific research claiming it's an inexplicable phenomenon tied to something called *sleep paralysis*.

The phone keeps making its vibrating FaceTime ring sound. Chloe always answers right away. This time, she doesn't answer at all.

She can't already be out shopping with her mom and Maddie, can she? Even if she is, why wouldn't she pick up? Unless she's in the shower.

That makes sense.

Then again, she always has her phone with her, even in the bathroom. Once when Hayley tried to call her, Chloe stuck her hand out of the shower to send one of those auto-reply messages about *can't talk right now*. And she called back even before she dried her hair.

So, yeah. No. There's no good reason she's not picking up. There's a bad reason, and that reason is Maddie.

Hayley disconnects the call, tosses the phone on the table, and plunks the cup down in the saucer, forgetting that it's fragile, old porcelain. She hears a loud cracking sound.

"No!"

Looking down, she sees that the saucer has broken in half.

Alarmed, she snatches the cup and jumps to her feet. Hot coffee sloshes over the gold rim, burning her hand. She drops the cup.

It doesn't shatter, because it bounces off the cushion of the chair beside her and lands on the plush rug under the table. Brown liquid spatters over the polished wood surface and pools on the pale upholstery.

"No! Oh no, please, no!"

Oh yes.

Hayley jumps up and gapes in horror at the mess.

Snapping out of it, she races to the kitchen, grabs a huge wad of paper towels and some cleaning spray from under the sink, hoping it's OxiClean or something like it. She races back and sprays it all over the table, then the chair, then the rug, and begins wiping it all up with paper towels.

The cleaner is leaving a white film on the dark wood surface and splotchy white marks on the cushion and rug. Crying now, she rubs harder, but that only makes it worse. Realizing that her shirt front is covered in little white dots, too, she looks at the spray bottle.

It isn't OxiClean at all. It's bleach.

CHAPTER FIFTY

Midge's investigation continues to unfold, as so many do, with placing phone calls, leaving voice messages, and searching the internet for additional information while waiting to hear back.

Where the Stantons are concerned, she's aware that might not happen, but she left a message anyway.

As Ann mentioned, there are no accessible records about Junia's adoption, which isn't necessarily a red flag. Checking into the parents' backgrounds, she finds basic biographical information.

Brian was born and raised in Elizabethville, majored in business at SUNY Albany, and is a financial planner. Astrid is from Utica and went to college in Ohio and became a nurse. Early in her career, she worked for an infertility center in Albany.

Was it for personal reasons? Was she infertile?

According to their wedding announcement, they were married in 2003 at a church in Phoenicia with pastor Mason Bauer officiating.

Searching for church records from that time, Midge finds an account of a purity ball in 2005. It's accompanied by photos of a beaming Bauer and teenage girls in white dresses. She scans their faces for signs of distress, but most appear serene, and a few are even beaming like brides. She's about to click on to the next photo when a face jumps out at her.

Junia Stanton!

No—according to the caption, her name is Hannah Fletcher.

But she bears an uncanny resemblance to Junia.

Midge googles her.

Hannah Fletcher was sixteen at the purity ball. She appears to have been a wholesome young woman, active in her church and with school extracurriculars, including the National Honor Society. She began her senior year as student council president in the fall of 2005. But there's no mention of her graduating with her high school class the following June.

June 2006 . . .

Which is when Junia Stanton was born.

Was Hannah Fletcher her birth mother?

It takes some digging, but Midge picks up her trail in Ohio.

Ohio, where Astrid Stanton went to college.

Hannah earned her GED and went to Ohio State, graduating in 2010. She now lives in Akron, is married with children, and works as a dental hygienist. Her contact information isn't hard to find.

Midge places a call to her cell phone.

A pleasant-sounding female voice answers with a cheerful, "Hello?"

"Hannah?"

"Yes?"

"This is Detective Sergeant Imogene Kennedy with the Mulberry Bay Police Department."

"Mulberry Bay?"

"In New York state. Ulster County."

Silence on the other end of the line.

"I'm looking into a Mason Bauer who was the pastor of a church you attended."

Silence.

"I'm wondering if you remember him?"

Her tone is flat. "Sorry, I don't."

Midge doesn't believe her.

"There may be a connection between Bauer and a missing persons case we're investigating out of Elizabethville. A teenage girl named Junia Stanton?"

Midge hears a gasp, barely audible, but Hannah doesn't say a word.

"Do you know her, by chance? Or her parents, Astrid and Brian?"

"No."

"Are you sure?"

"Sorry, but I haven't lived in Ulster County since I was a kid. I left in 2006."

"Why did you leave?"

"Excuse me?"

Midge repeats the question.

The woman lowers her voice, as if not wanting to be overheard on her end. "Look, I have no idea why you're asking me about these people, or even if you're an actual cop, but this is ancient history, okay? I'm just living my life. I haven't done anything wrong. And if you think I have, then you'll have to subpoena me."

She hangs up.

She didn't directly answer Midge's question, but she didn't need to.

Midge pulls up a photo of Hannah as a teenager, alongside a photo of Junia at the same age. They could be the same person.

And when she adds a headshot of Mason Bauer, there's a strong resemblance to Junia as well.

Did he get Hannah pregnant? Was she sent away to have her baby? Did the Stantons know about that in advance and arrange to adopt her?

She's pondering those questions when Nap calls.

"Hey, Midge. Thanks for getting back to me."

"Allie said you stopped in."

"Yeah, I was in the neighborhood. I got coffee at Center Street Grind because Linden mentioned they have a good chicory blend."

"Ah. Is it 'so underrated'? Or maybe it's even epic?" she asks, channeling both Linden and Hayley.

He chuckles. "It's totally *overrated*, and in my book, only Café Du Monde is epic. Well, that, and your basketball skills."

"Right. Just call me Caitlin Clark."

"So, Midge, what I wanted to tell you was that I got the DNA report," he says, getting back to business. "Want to come over here and take a look?"

The medical examiner's office is over in Kingston. Only a few miles away, but with traffic, it could take a lot longer than it should. Weighing the wisdom of dropping what she's working on to make the trip, she asks, "Do you expect it to give us a positive ID?"

"On the Walking Man?"

"I meant on the skeletal remains, but . . . is this about the Walking Man, then?"

"No. It's for Gordon Klatte, and there's something pretty . . . unexpected."

She pushes back her chair and grabs her keys. "I'm on my way."

CHAPTER FIFTY-ONE

Back on the beach after moving her car, Kelly finds Ben and Caleb still splashing around in the lake and Talia reclined in her beach chair, scrolling on her phone. She looks so relaxed that Kelly wonders if she should even mention Sarah Greene's disappearance.

"Have you heard from Hayley?" she asks, settling in her own chair.

"No, but I can see her."

"What do you mean?"

Talia tilts the screen so that Kelly can see it.

She peers at a map with a pulsating red dot in the center of a square. "Hmm . . . Are you sure it's her? I don't see much of a resemblance."

Talia laughs. "It's a locator app."

"Seriously? So you . . . what, did you have her ear microchipped like a pet?"

"No! Ben and I can track her phone. Which is pretty much as attached to her as her ear is."

"I'm glad they didn't have technology when we were her age. My parents didn't trust me as it was."

"It's not that I don't *trust* her."

"Oh, come on, Tal'. Of *course* you don't trust her. She's twelve. Remember what we were doing when we were twelve? Sneaking around, making out with guys, smoking cigarettes in the gazebo . . ."

"That was just you, Kelly. The rest of us were playing Polly Pockets."

"You're right, it was me." She grins. "I wouldn't change a thing, though. I had a damned good time back then."

"You've had a damned good time all your life. Just please don't share the details with my daughter."

Kelly draws an *X* over her heart with her finger. "Not until she's eighteen."

"Twenty-one."

"Deal. So does this give you peace of mind? Is she where she's supposed to be?"

Talia zooms in on the pulsating dot that indicates Hayley's location and again tilts the screen toward Kelly. "She is, see?"

"Wow. That's pretty precise. She's in the house. What a good, obedient daughter you have."

"She really is." Talia smiles and closes the app.

Kelly leans back in her chair, again weighing whether to say anything about the missing girl. If she does, Talia will probably overreact and want to rush back to Hayley, thinking there's a crazed kidnapper on the loose in Mulberry Bay.

What if there is?

What if it's Bauer?

Either way, she reminds herself, Hayley is safely ensconced at Haven Cliff.

Opening her phone to see what she can uncover about Sarah Greene, she finds that Toby has sent her another email. The attachment is titled *Bauer Family*. She forwards it to Midge and is about to open the file when Talia groans.

"Again?"

Kelly glances over to see that she, too, is holding her phone.

"What's wrong, Tal'?"

"Just . . . this friend of mine back home keeps texting me. Well, she's not really a friend, but . . . this is the third time she's asked me to call her."

"About what?"

"She's going through a divorce. She probably just needs someone to talk to."

"Block her."

"Kelly! I can't do that."

"Why not? You just said she's not a friend."

"Her daughter is Hayley's best friend."

"Chloe? The sleepover kid?"

"How do you know?"

"Hayley mentioned it yesterday."

"'Mentioned'? You mean she didn't rant about the unfairness of it all?"

"Oh, she ranted."

"I hope you told her she was being unreasonable."

"I thought she was being perfectly reasonable," Kelly says. "Don't worry. I kept that to myself. But if my parents dragged me away for the weekend when you or Midge or Caroline were having a slumber party, I'd be acting just like Hayley is."

"Yeah, well . . ." Talia shrugs. "Caroline never had slumber parties. She wasn't even allowed to come to ours."

"True. But her parents had no problem letting her hang out with Gordy, or with Bauer the pedophile."

"Right. And one of them got her pregnant."

Kelly nods. "I wish I could believe it was Gordy."

"You don't?"

"Do you?"

Talia hesitates. "I want to. But no."

"Same. And if I ever see that man again, I might strangle him with my bare hands."

"Unless you're planning a trip to Mexico, I doubt you'll see him again. But I feel the same way. I could kill him for what he did to Caroline."

"I know that's why Mary Beth went after Gordy," Kelly says. "Because she loved Caroline as much as we did. And she thought he was the one who ruined Caroline's life."

"Yes, but Gordy was Caroline's boyfriend, not some sick predator."

Kelly nods. "Imagine if Mary Beth knew about Bauer and could have gotten her hands on him; he'd be dead right now instead of poor old Gordy."

"We could be dead right now too. She blamed us as much as she did him. That night in June . . . she had a gun. She was going to kill us."

"She could have. But she didn't. I know it sounds crazy, Talia, and I know she's done a lot of terrible things in her life, but I kind of feel sorry for Mary Beth."

"How can you, after what she did to us, and to Gordy?"

"I just think there's a lot more to her story than we'll ever know."

CHAPTER FIFTY-TWO

June 13, 1999

The 24-Hour Diner is relatively quiet as Mary Beth pours herself yet another cup of coffee, making sure it's not from the green-rimmed decaf carafe.

She started her twelve-hour shift at three in the morning, just in time to serve the drunks, followed by the early-morning senior citizens who nurse fifty-cent cups of coffee and leave nickel tips, then the Sunday after-church crowd.

Most have dispersed, as have the other waitresses, leaving just Mary Beth and the cook, Edgar, who's having a smoke and reading the paper. The remaining few hours should be slow, especially on this sunny afternoon. Unlike her, people have better places to be.

She's getting her life together, though, at last. It's been over six months since she landed this job and moved into a tiny place of her own. She's done her best to distance herself from bad influences—people, places, substances.

Every day is a lonely struggle. Every day, she's aware of her empty arms and the ache in her soul.

She leans against the counter, clutching her coffee cup in both hands, remembering the day she finally worked up her nerve to call the adoptive parents.

A man answered.

For some reason, Mary Beth was expecting the wife.

She said, "Hi, this is Mary Beth Winterfield . . . ?"

It came out like a question, and clearly he didn't have the answer, because he said, "*Who*?"

"I'm the mom."

"Who?"

"The birth mom," she clarified. "From Golden Bridge?"

He murmured something that sounded like *uh-huh* or maybe *aha*, and nothing else.

"I was just checking to, you know, see how the baby is doing?"

"Fine. Just fine."

"Okay, well . . . that's good. That's great. Do you think maybe I could . . ."

Silence.

She cleared her throat, started again. "I thought maybe I could . . ."

Not *visit*. There was no way she'd suggest that.

"Get a picture?" she asked.

"Oh. I, uh . . . I guess you can. I mean, that's how this works, right? I'll have to talk to my wife. She's out. If you give me your number, I'll have her call you."

She wasn't about to tell him she didn't have a phone or give her the number for the pay phone at Joey Jay's, which is how she usually tells people to get in touch with her.

"I'll call back when she's home," she said, thanking him—for what, she didn't know—and hanging up.

She never called back. She supposes she will, but not yet. Not until she can actually give them a phone number and an address in a decent part of town where they can send a picture. Or maybe not until she can actually visit.

She fantasizes about it all the time—about visiting.

With and without their knowledge.

Sometimes she imagines herself stealing into their house in the middle of the night when they're asleep. She pictures herself standing over the crib, seeing the sleeping little angel. She sees herself scooping the baby into her arms and slipping out into the night.

They'll go away, where they can be together forever, just the two of them, the way it should have been. The way it's supposed to be.

The glass door flies open, and a kid bursts in. He's nine or ten, with straggly blond hair, a cute face that always looks dirty, and way too much freedom. His stepdad bartends at Joey Jay's.

"You M.?" he asks.

Mary Beth nods.

"You got a phone call."

"Tell whoever it is that I'm working."

"It's your sister."

She gasps, sloshing hot coffee over the cup's rim. She puts it down and wipes her hand on her apron. "Edgar, cover for me! I have to run next door!"

She's not sure whether he even heard her, and she doesn't care.

Back in October, Caroline's rich friend Kelly drove her to Syracuse to hand over the doll. For Mary Beth, seeing them was the gut punch that, along with the money, set her on the right path.

She hasn't heard from her sister since and figured she never would.

She follows the kid to Joey Jay's and hurries past the barflies toward the pay phone. The receiver dangles from its braided steel cord, and a beefy guy is about to reach for it.

"Don't!" she shouts. "That's my sister."

"Make it quick. I need it."

Ignoring him, she answers the call with a breathless, "Caroline?"

"Mary Beth!"

"Are you crying? What's wrong? Did something happen to Mom or Dad?"

In the split second it takes for the answer to come, Mary Beth realizes she doesn't want that news. As much as she loathes what they did to her, as much as she blames them for what her life has become, there's a part of her that loves them despite everything; a part that still longs for them to love her.

"No, they're at church. It's me, Mary Beth. You said if I ever needed help, I should call you . . ."

Did I?

It was Kelly who demanded that Mary Beth provide Caroline with a way to get in touch with her.

"You call her, and she comes running," she said, eyes blazing, defiant, disgusted with Mary Beth. "What happens if she needs you? Doesn't it work both ways?"

She grudgingly gave the pay phone number, never imagining that she could do anything to help her little sister. But if there is, hell yes, she's going to do it, whatever it is.

"What's wrong, Caroline? What do you need?"

"I need a place to go. I can't stay here."

"You mean, after graduation? Aren't Mom and Dad sending you to college?"

"I'm pregnant."

"What?"

"When they find out, they'll send me where they sent you. I can't let them take my baby."

"No! I'll help you! You can come here, and have the baby, and stay . . ."

"Are you sure? You have room for me and the baby?"

She does not. But she can't let it happen again. Never, ever again.

"We'll figure it out, Caroline. The only thing that matters is that we'll be together, the three of us. You, me, and the baby. We'll be a family."

CHAPTER FIFTY-THREE

Present Day

The door slams behind Hayley as she flings herself down the wide stone steps and across the lawn, racked with sobs, trying to catch her breath.

She's ruined it. All of it. Kelly's antique china, the elegant table, the white silk chair cushion, the beautiful rug . . .

That's bad enough. That's *horrible.*

She'll have to use her babysitting money to pay for all the damage. She has almost $200. She definitely won't be able to get the jeans at Nordstrom Rack now, and maybe not even the sweater, depending on how much is left over.

But that's not even the worst thing.

She cries harder, blinded by tears and wiping her nose on her forearm, which is disgusting, but she doesn't even care.

The worst thing of all is that she's ruined any chance that her parents will ever, ever trust her again. Especially Mom. Especially since she made Hayley promise not to even unlock the door or go outside.

She hadn't meant to. She couldn't help it. When she saw the mess, she panicked, and all she could do was escape. She ran to the front door, threw it open, and rushed out of the house without realizing what she was doing.

Now, though, it sinks in. She goes absolutely still.

What if Mom doesn't even have to know about this part?

What if Hayley goes back to the house right now, and locks the doors, and stays there, just as she promised?

Maybe the mess isn't even as bad as she thought. Maybe she can clean it up. Most of it, anyway.

Maybe Mom and Dad will understand that it was an accident. They'll have to see her as an adult if she offers to pay for it, because that's what adults do, right? They take responsibility for their mistakes.

And *everyone* makes mistakes. Nobody's perfect.

Hayley turns and heads back to the house. Seeing movement in a second-floor window, she stops short.

Oh—it's a cat, looking out as if expecting someone.

"Hi, Bibi! It's okay! I'm staying here," she calls. "I'll be right in."

She climbs the steps and crosses the stone terrace to the door. It's huge and carved of dark, heavy wood, the knob attached to a scrolled iron plate.

For some reason, it won't turn.

Probably because it's so old. Or maybe it's sticking in the heat. One of the closet doors back home is hard to open when the weather is like this.

Hayley dries her sweaty hand on her shorts and grabs the knob again, twisting harder.

Still, it refuses to open.

It takes a moment for it to dawn on her that she's locked out.

There must be a key hidden out here someplace.

At home, they used to keep one under a big clay flowerpot. But then one day the key disappeared, and they had to change all the locks, mostly because Caleb was scared that a robber had stolen it and was going to come back when they were sleeping.

Hayley is pretty sure that's not what happened, because the key was lost on a rainy day when she and Chloe were playing on the porch and moved the flowerpot out of the way. She didn't mention that to her parents when they figured out that it was gone, but she did look around on the muddy ground by the porch just in case it had fallen down there. It hadn't.

Well, maybe it had, because she only looked for, like, a minute before she saw a snake. Which might actually have been a worm. She's not afraid of slithery things, but she doesn't want to touch them either.

Okay, so where would Kelly hide a key on her porch?

Hayley looks around, then down at the welcome mat beneath her flip-flopped feet. She steps off it, reaches down, and lifts the corner. No key.

There are big stone planters on either side of the door, but they're either really heavy or they're bolted down, because there's no way she can budge one.

She looks all over the rest of the terrace, lifting seat cushions and poking around the potted palms. No key.

Now what?

She's going to have to call Mom and tell her what happened. That's the grown-up thing to do.

Mind made up, Hayley reaches into her back right pocket for her phone.

It isn't there.

She checks her back left pocket.

No phone.

But she'd just had it . . . when?

In the dining room, when she was trying to FaceTime Chloe. She was so annoyed when she didn't pick up that she threw the phone down on the table. Then she must have been too busy breaking the saucer and spilling the coffee and trying to clean it up to grab her phone again before she ran out the door.

"Stupid. You're so stupid!"

Stupid, and trapped.

Maybe Haven Cliff really is cursed.

CHAPTER FIFTY-FOUR

Midge hurries along the familiar corridor toward Nap's office, tucking her frizzled hair back under her cap. His door is open, and she can hear him on the phone as she draws near.

"Okay, that's great," he's saying.

Midge peeks through the doorway. He's behind the desk, wearing blue scrubs and reading glasses, phone pressed between his shoulder and ear as he types on his desktop computer keyboard. Midge catches his eye and points to the hall to let him know she'll wait till he's finished. He shakes his head and gestures for her to take a seat.

You sure? she mouths.

He nods. She sits.

"Okay, I'd be much obliged if you can," he says into the phone, leaning back and picking up a pen. "And if you can't—"

He pauses, tapping the pen in an impatient rhythm on the desk.

"Yes . . . right . . . yes. Of course you are. I understand. Busy time of year. Just let me know. All right. Much obliged. Bye, now."

He hangs up. "Sorry about that."

"Oh, it's fine. *Much obliged* to you for inviting me over here, kind sir."

"You can pop in anytime you like, Midge. It's always good to see you."

"Most people think the opposite."

"Maybe the perps, but not the people who know and love you."

"Oh, you'd be surprised," she says wryly. "By the way, after this, can I take another look at the physical evidence we found with the skeleton in the pit?"

"Sure. What's going on?"

"I'm just wondering which CD was in the Walkman. I thought I remembered, but I'm feeling a little scatterbrained."

"It happens to the best of us." He leans forward, eyes on the screen, typing on the keyboard. "That call you just walked in on was me doing my best to expedite the rest of the forensics tests we're waiting on."

"For Gordy Klatte?"

"For the Walking Man, and for the skeletal remains."

"And . . . ?"

"And they're not making any promises. Okay, here we go." He turns away from the keyboard and grabs a rolling chair a few feet away, pulling it up beside his. He pats it. "Come on over here so that I can show you."

"Sure you can't just tell me? Autopsy photos before lunch is . . ." She wrinkles her nose.

"No photos. Just a report. This is the DNA testing on the skin particles under Gordon Klatte's fingernails and some microscopic blood we found at the scene that didn't belong to him. The results were entered into CODIS."

CODIS—Combined DNA Index System—is an electronic national database of criminal offenders.

Midge goes around the desk to sit beside him, asking, "Did we get a match to Mary Beth Winterfield?"

"That's the interesting thing."

"It's *not* a match?"

He scrolls through the report, past written paragraphs and a chart. "Oh, it's a match. In fact, we've got two matches."

"Two! One is Mary Beth, then. Who's the other?"

"Back up, Midge. See this?" He points to the screen. "One is *connected* to Mary Beth. It isn't hers."

"What?" She glances at the cryptic codes on the screen, then at him. "Nap, what are you saying?"

"I'm saying that the genetic material under the victim's fingernails doesn't belong to Mary Beth Winterfield. It belongs to someone who shares significant DNA with her."

"I don't . . . I don't understand."

"It isn't hers, Midge. It's from a close female relative."

"A close female relative."

Nap nods, allowing her to digest the information.

She's doing her best, but . . .

How is this even possible?

Gordy engaged in a physical struggle with someone before his fatal fall. It stands to reason that the genetic material under his nails belongs to the person who lured him outside in the dead of night and is responsible for his death.

If not Mary Beth, then who could it have been?

Before he died, Gordy was receiving texts from someone claiming to be Caroline.

Beverly Barrow's doorstep camera captured someone who looked like Caroline.

Caroline is dead, so it *had* to be Mary Beth, unless . . .

"How close a relative are we talking about?" she asks Nap.

"*Close*. I won't get into the science of it, but you're looking at about twenty-five percent shared DNA."

"Her daughter! Mary Beth had a child in the late nineties and she was forced to give it up for adoption. That has to be it."

"That *can't* be it, Midge. A child would share fifty percent of her DNA. Twenty-five percent is going to be a half sister, an aunt, a grandmother, a granddaughter, a niece."

Familiar with Caroline's family history via their childhood friendship, Midge knows that both Mary Beth's grandmothers are long dead. There were a couple of aunts, but by marriage, not blood.

Mary Beth can't possibly have a granddaughter . . . can she?

She might, if her child, now an adult, has become a parent. But the grandchild couldn't possibly be old enough to have somehow found her way back to Mulberry Bay and killed Gordon Klatte.

Midge considers the other possibilities.

The oldest Winterfield sisters, twins Eve and Joanna, had children, so Mary Beth may very well have a niece. But the twins left the area years ago, and why would their children have motive to kill Gordon?

That leaves a half sister.

Could one of her oh-so-proper and judgmental parents have had a daughter from another relationship? An affair?

"I can see the wheels turning," Nap comments. "What are you thinking?"

"I'm thinking that this doesn't make sense. Are you absolutely positive that DNA doesn't belong to Mary Beth herself?"

"Science doesn't lie, Midge."

"No, I know."

People do, though.

Regardless of whether Gordy was actually responsible for getting Caroline pregnant, Midge believed Mary Beth killed him because she blamed him.

What else would motivate *anyone*—other than the unhinged Mary Beth Winterfield—to kill him?

Nothing in his background suggests that he led anything but an honorable existence, unless you consider that his high school girlfriend disappeared on prom night.

On paper, that fact would cast a shadow on Gordy's sterling reputation, but if you know what Midge knows about it, it's all but irrelevant.

Who else might have cared about Caroline enough to seek that level of vengeance against the man presumed to have gotten her pregnant?

Who else could have been wearing Caroline's T-I-C-K charm bracelet, found clenched in Gordy's dead hand?

Who else might have blamed Midge, Kelly, and Talia as well? Who else might have shown up at the Barrow home looking for Kelly, left-handed and looking so much like Caroline? Who might have known about the pedestals in the woods? Who might have lured them there, calling herself Ceto?

A half sister, an aunt, a grandmother, a granddaughter, a niece.

"The DNA under the victim's nails wasn't just a partial match to Mary Beth Winterfield, Midge," Nap goes on. "It was a partial match to another sample in CODIS. His name is Mason Bauer."

Mason Bauer.

Reverend B.'s DNA was under Gordy Klatte's fingernails.

"*Mason Bauer* is the DNA match?"

Nap nods. "I take it the name is familiar?"

"Yes, it's . . . yes."

She explains that he was the pastor of a local church back in the late 1990s, and Nap tells her what she already knows—that he was arrested on felony charges years ago in Texas but disappeared after the mistrial.

"Lucky for us, he didn't file to expunge his genetic record from the database." Nap taps the screen. "That's a solid match right there."

"So someone who matches Mason Bauer's DNA was here in Mulberry Bay in June, someone who was with Gordy Klatte right before he died."

"Someone who *partially* matches his DNA was here. A female."

"A female—who has both Bauer's DNA and Mary Beth's."

"That's right. But the connection to Bauer is even closer. The subject shares more than thirty-three hundred centimorgans with him."

"Meaning?"

"Meaning she can only be his mother or his daughter."

Mason Bauer's mother, or Mason Bauer's daughter . . .

Midge thinks of Junia Stanton.

Is she missing and endangered? Or is she the female who lured Gordy Klatte to his death? Is she related not just to Mason Bauer, but to Mary Beth Winterfield? Is she the daughter Mary Beth gave up for adoption?

No. She can't be Mary Beth's daughter.

Only her half sister, aunt, grandmother, granddaughter . . .

Niece.

CHAPTER FIFTY-FIVE

"Looks like your monsoon's on its way," Talia tells Kelly, pointing at the sky.

The bright, hot morning sunshine has given way to muggy gray. Bruise-colored storm clouds are pushing past the mountains in the northwest.

"It's fine with me," Kelly says with a stretch and a yawn. "I've had enough beach to last me till next summer."

Ben, too, seems to have noticed the changing weather. He and Caleb are finally making their way to shore.

"Mom, did you see me turn two somersaults in a row?"

"I did. Very impressive." She wraps her son in a beach towel. "Your lips are blue, and your fingers are prunes, kiddo."

"I'm starving. Did you bring Goldfish?"

"I'm sorry, sweetie, I didn't think of it."

"But Granny Nat always brought them to the beach!"

"Your mom brought goldfish to the beach?" Kelly asks Talia.

She laughs. "Not live ones. The crackers."

"Goldfish crackers? Huh. Are they made out of goldfish?"

Caleb finds that hilarious.

"The kid's a great audience," Kelly tells Talia. "This isn't even my best material."

Ben finds *that* hilarious.

Kelly points at him. "*Also* a great audience. Why don't we go to lunch at the Landing? I don't think they have crackers made out of goldfish, but they have real ones in a huge aquarium, and minnows and catfish and tetras too."

"Do you think they have french fries?" Caleb asks.

"In the aquarium? I don't think french fries are great swimmers."

That earns her another big laugh from Caleb.

"Yes, of course they have french fries. Great ones. *And* ketchup. And your mom used to work there."

"Really, Mom?"

Talia nods. "So did Granny Nat."

"And it's right over there, so we can walk, see?" Kelly points at the gray-shingled structure by the pier. "But we'll have to put all the beach stuff in your car, Ben, because thanks to our friend Midge, I had to move mine to East Bumf—"

"Kelly!" Talia says.

"—fonia. East Bumfonia," Kelly repeats with a wink at Talia.

She shakes her head and takes her phone out of her bag. "I'll text Hayley and see if she wants to come."

Ben pulls his pink polo shirt over his head. "How is she going to come? We're walking over, and she's not here."

"If she wants to, we can go pick her up."

"By *we*, you mean me."

"I can do it," Kelly offers.

"Thanks, but as far as I'm concerned, if she didn't want to come to the beach, she's going to have to miss out on lunch at the Landing."

Talia ignores him. She sends her text and holds her phone in her hand as they start packing up.

All around them, others are doing the same. A resigned melancholy has settled over the crowd, as summer seems to have drawn to a premature close amid the washout weekend forecast.

Talia checks her phone yet again as Ben dumps the melted ice out of the cooler. "Well?" he asks.

"I bet she hasn't seen my text. She might be in the shower, or taking a bubble bath . . . She was really excited about the bathtub, remember? I should probably call her."

"No, you shouldn't. You know how she is with that phone. There's not a chance in hell that she missed a text, even if she's soaking in a tub. She's just ignoring you."

"Maybe, but . . ." Talia looks at Kelly. "Maybe we should go straight back to Haven Cliff."

"Whatever you want, Tal'."

"But I really want to see where you and Granny used to work, Mom. And I really, *really* want to see the giant fish tank," Caleb says as she fastens the Velcro straps on his little sport sandals. "And really, really, *really*, I want to eat a lot of french fries, with a real lot of ketchup."

"So do I. We're going to lunch," Ben says firmly, juggling the folding chairs and cooler as they join the mass exodus toward the parking lot.

"Tal'?" Kelly asks. "Is it really unusual for her to ignore her phone for this long?"

"It is, but she's probably still angry with me."

"I'm sure that's it, but—"

Talia's ringing phone cuts her off.

"Ah, there she is! See?" She answers it without checking the screen. "Hayley?"

There's a pause. "Talia? It's me, Camille."

"Camille! Hi!"

Kelly wags her finger at Talia.

She mouths, *I thought it was Hayley.*

"I hate to bother you with a phone call on vacation, but I tried texting a few times and didn't hear back, so . . ."

"You did? Sorry, I've had sketchy service here," Talia tells Camille, slowing her pace and falling behind the others. "In fact, I might lose you any second, so if I disappear . . ."

"I'll be quick. I just thought you should be looped in on something Chloe and Maddie told me."

"Maddie?" she asks, drawing a blank.

"Maddie Miller. She's a good friend of the girls'."

"Oh, right," Talia agrees, though the name isn't familiar. Rather, it's too familiar. There are several Maddies in Hayley's class.

"Anyway, Maddie's here with Chloe for the weekend, and I overheard the girls talking . . ."

Uh-oh. Talia would prefer hearing about Camille's divorce to whatever drama is unfolding among the girls. Remembering Kelly's comment about being twelve, she braces herself for whatever is coming.

Sneaking around, making out with guys, smoking cigarettes in the gazebo . . .

But it isn't any of those things.

Uncertain she heard it right, Talia says, "Wait . . . she *what*?"

"She submitted her DNA to one of those online genealogy websites," Camille repeats. "Since she's underage . . . I mean, if it were my daughter, I'd want to know."

"But why would she do something like that?" Talia asks.

"Apparently, she's trying to find her grandfather. The girls think it would be your father, maybe?"

Talia stops walking, phone pressed to her ear as Camille talks on.

"I'll admit I was a little confused, because I know Ben's dad passed away when the girls were in elementary school, and I thought I remembered that your father died when they were in pre-K."

"That was my stepfather."

"Ah! So she's looking for your biological father?"

"Apparently." She clears her throat. "Camille, I appreciate your sharing this. But I, um . . . I'm at the beach, and the call is probably about to drop, so . . . thank you. Talk soon."

She hangs up and immediately dials Hayley.

The line rings . . . rings . . . rings . . .

Voicemail.

She tries again.

Same result.

She opens her texts. Hayley still hasn't responded.

Talia sends a new message: **Call me right now. It's important!**

CHAPTER FIFTY-SIX

Decades ago on the high school softball field, Midge was tearing toward third base when an outfielder's throw slammed her between the shoulder blades. The sheer blind side stole her breath from her lungs, muffled the din from the stands, and made the field swim before her eyes.

She never forgot what that felt like.

She never experienced it again.

Not until now.

She pushes back her chair. "Thanks, Nap. I'm working a case, so I'd better get—"

"Wait, you said you wanted to take a look at the evidence found with the skeletal remains."

"Oh! The CD in the CD player. Right, I did. It can wait, if it's not—"

"No, it's quick. I can pull up the photo." He beckons her around to his side of the desk.

She leans over his shoulder as he opens a file.

The photos are thumbnails, all images of evidence she saw in real life, on that awful day, staring into the pit.

She looks away, shaking her head, doing her best not to blink and release the tears welling in her eyes.

"Sorry," Nap says, glancing at her, then back at the screen. "I know it's hard. Hang on . . . okay, here it is."

He clicks one of the photos and enlarges it until she can clearly read the lettering on the CD.

Oops! . . . I Did It Again.

She closes her eyes and tilts her head back. Hot tears spill down her cheeks.

Dammit. Dammit!

Caroline didn't die the night she tried to run away.

She lived a whole year.

"Midge?" He touches her arm. "Are you okay?"

"Yes. But I have to go talk to Mary Beth Winterfield. *Now.*"

CHAPTER FIFTY-SEVEN

The midday sun is disappearing behind clouds, but Haven Cliff's stone terrace radiates its heat. Hayley can't even turn on the ceiling fans that kept the wicker seating area nice and breezy yesterday, because the switches are inside.

She'd literally kill for a bottle of water.

And for her phone, not just so that she can call for help, but because she's nearly as bored as she is thirsty. She can't text or FaceTime or listen to music or browse online . . .

There's absolutely nothing to do except sit and stare off into space.

Space being the trees at the edge of the big front lawn.

The lake is back in there somewhere. It must be, because that prom girl drowned in it during the party in the woods at Haven Cliff. She probably didn't know how to swim, or went in too deep, or was wasted, or maybe all of those things. And it was nighttime.

Hayley will be fine. She just needs to cool off. Plus, the lake water is probably safe to drink.

Mind made up, she sets out across the grass and into the woods.

It's much cooler here. The scented air reminds her of fall—of damp leaves on the ground, and of snuggling in her heavy quilt on a crisp night after it's been stored in Mom's cedar chest all summer.

She just wishes she were wearing sneakers instead of flip-flops. In a few spots, there are trailing vines poking through the thick layer of wood chips on the path that might be poison ivy—she's not sure if that has clusters of five leaves or three. Chloe had a bad case at camp. She had to spend three days in the infirmary, and she scratched her face so badly you can still see the scar.

As she walks, Hayley keeps an eye out for ghosts, thinking it would be cool to go home and tell Chloe a true ghost story that actually happened to her, not just some thirdhand tale the counselors share around a campfire.

She'll leave out the part about the mess in the house, of course, and about getting locked out. And she'll change it so that it happens at midnight, because there's nothing scary about walking in the woods in the middle of a sunny day.

Although the day isn't that sunny anymore.

At a fork in the path, she pauses, wondering which side might lead to the lake. In one direction, it goes into a steep climb toward big rock ledges. The other direction isn't exactly downhill, but it looks a little flatter.

If she heads uphill and there's no lake, she's going to be even hotter. The sky is clouding over so fast, she might not have time to backtrack in the other direction for a swim before it rains.

She takes the flat route. It winds through the trees for a short distance, then around a bend into a big open space with a tennis court. Nearby, there's a brick arched wall, with a stone pedestal standing under each curve. Just beyond, she sees yellow tape roping off an area marked by big piles of dirt and rock.

Spotting a big rectangular hole in the ground, she steps closer.

Then, hearing a footfall behind her, she whirls around, expecting to see a ghost.

But it's a man, and he looks perfectly solid, not filmy at all. Wearing a blue hat and a strange smile, he says, "I've been waiting for you."

CHAPTER FIFTY-EIGHT

When the guard informs Mary Beth that she has a visitor, she bolts upright in her bunk, heart racing.

It's Ceto. It *has* to be her. She's come to make amends, or to tell Mary Beth that she's going to turn herself in, or—

Wait, no. It *can't* be her.

You can't just drop by to visit an inmate unless it's visiting hours, and even then, there are procedures.

Requests, forms, approvals . . .

Even if procedures were followed, it's never going to be Ceto. She wouldn't dare show her face here, even if she wanted to see Mary Beth. Which she doesn't.

Not after that last night, at home in Syracuse, back in the spring.

The guard brandishes handcuffs. "Let's go, Winterfield. Your visitor doesn't want to wait all day."

"Who is it?"

"Detective Sergeant Midge Kennedy with the Mulberry Bay PD."

"What if I don't approve the visit? Isn't that my right?"

"Not when it's law enforcement with the warden's approval."

"Shouldn't my attorney be present if I'm going to talk to her?"

"She says she's an old friend, not here to interrogate you. This isn't about your case. But if you want to invoke—"

"No. I'll see her."

The guard cuffs her and escorts her to a visitation booth.

Midge is seated on the other side of the glass partition. Mary Beth refuses to make eye contact as she settles in the chair and the guard removes her cuffs.

Her heart is pounding. She's seen no one from the outside world in ten weeks. There's been no break in the monotony of incarcerated life. And now . . .

Midge Kennedy? Here out of the goodness of her heart?

The guard steps back.

At last, Mary Beth looks at her visitor, somehow expecting the freckle-faced tomboy who was always hanging around Caroline when they were kids.

The woman opposite her has reddish-orange strands of hair poking from beneath her cap and freckles on her face. There are laugh lines around her blue eyes and her mouth, though in this grim setting, she's somber.

This isn't the first time they've seen each other in middle age. But on that fateful June night, they were in the dark woods at Haven Cliff, and Midge wasn't wearing her uniform as she is now. Midge, Talia, and Kelly were simply her sister's old friends, ganging up on her with accusations and assumptions, blaming her for what happened to Caroline, for Gordy's death.

Gordy. Dead.

Blindsided by that news, she reacted—*over*reacted—badly.

"Hi, Mary Beth," Midge says.

"Hey, *old friend*." She gestures over her shoulder, toward the guard. "He said that's why you're here? Not, you know, on official business?"

Midge answers the question with one of her own.

"I know you didn't do it. So who did?"

CHAPTER FIFTY-NINE

April 18, 2024

You'd think Mary Beth would know by now that April weather in Syracuse is never as nice as you expect it to be.

Sometimes God or Mother Nature or whoever's responsible decides to throw in a beautiful day. Even the flowers and foliage are fooled by it.

She hurries toward the door, past ice-glazed forsythia and limp daffodils with their sunny heads half buried in crusted snow. This morning was so balmy that she wore only a light windbreaker over her uniform and didn't bother to put on socks with her loafers. By ten o'clock, it was obvious that boots and a parka would have been more suitable.

Juggling her grocery bags into one hand, she pauses to go through the damp mail poking out of the metal box beside the door.

Flipping through it, she extracts everything addressed to Mary Beth Winterfield and Ceto Winterfield, Apartment 1A. It's all bills, as always. She returns the downstairs tenant's mail to the box and heads inside.

She can smell weed in the vestibule as she unlocks her door. Sometimes it's the teenage kid who lives upstairs, but more often than not, it isn't.

Today is one of those days.

Ceto is on the couch with a joint in her hand, feet on the coffee table still cluttered with the greasy take-out bags she brought home last night. The way she eats and lies around, you'd think she'd have bad skin and be carrying extra weight, but no. For the most part, she looks as wholesome as any other attractive blue-eyed blonde in her mid-twenties.

"Aren't you supposed to be at work?" Mary Beth asks.

"I'm sick."

"Ceto! You can't keep doing this! It's irresponsible! They're counting on you to be there."

"It's Starbucks. They have a million people working."

"Well, they were counting on a million and one. You let them down. And you needed the money."

"How would you know what I need?"

"Because your student loan bill just came in the mail, and I know you can't afford to pay it."

"It's a joke. Why would I pay a loan from years ago when I don't even have my degree?"

"Whose fault is that, Ceto? You're the one who flunked out of school. You still have to pay back what you borrowed."

"I *am* paying it back."

"Whatever. It's your life. It's your problem. Can you at least come help me put this stuff away?"

"What is it?"

"Food. So that we have something to eat. Something other than crap," she adds with a nod toward the bags.

"It's not crap. I like it."

"It's not good for you. It's full of chemicals. Smoking's not good for you either."

"No way, Mom! Where'd you hear that?"

"Why do you always have to be so damned sarcastic?"

"I must have inherited it from you."

Mary Beth turns away, as she always does when Ceto mentions anything like that. She has no memory of Caroline. As far as she knows, Mary Beth is her mother. There was no reason to tell her otherwise. She thinks her father was a deadbeat one-night stand.

She's always been curious about him. Mary Beth has told her she never even knew his last name.

A few months ago, Ceto said she was thinking of doing a DNA test to find him.

"I don't know why you'd bother," she said, keeping her voice level. "He's a loser."

"How do you know? Maybe he's changed. *You* did."

Right.

When Ceto was little, Mary Beth knew of only one way—other than stealing other people's stuff—to keep food on the table and a roof over their heads. That led to the drug-trafficking arrest.

The only thing worse than serving time was knowing that her precious Ceto was in the foster care system, growing up without her.

Mary Beth always intended to tell her the truth about her mother when she was old enough. And her father. She'd never met Gordy Klatte, but she knew Caroline truly loved him. He was no deadbeat loser. He was kind.

"Then why don't you tell him you're pregnant and marry him?" she asked her sister, early on.

"Because I can't do that to him. It would ruin his life. The baby and I will be fine on our own. With you. The three of us will be a family."

And then it was just the two of them. Then Ceto alone, in foster care.

The way she kept getting in and out of trouble, just like Mary Beth . . .

Things could have been different, if she'd known the truth all along—known that she came from something better.

Maybe it was a mistake, but it was too late to change things.

"Just put away the groceries while I go get changed," she says, putting the bags in the kitchen. "Leave the macaroni on the counter. I'm making it for dinner."

"With sauce?"

"With butter."

"You mean that cheap fake margarine crap. Yeah, sounds really healthy."

"If you prefer butter, you're welcome to buy it yourself. No one's stopping you."

In the small bedroom off the kitchen, she kicks off her shoes, swaps her waitressing uniform for sweats, and shoves her cold, achy feet into slippers. Better.

But she needs to hang the uniform for tomorrow. Her other one is in the hamper, and she doesn't feel like doing laundry tonight.

She opens the small closet and grabs a hanger. About to close the door, she sees that the stack of boxes on the shelf is slightly crooked.

She wouldn't have left them that way. All those years in prison hadn't just left her determined to get her life in order—they'd taught her to keep it in order, including her physical possessions.

She hasn't gone through them in a very long time.

But someone must have.

She takes down the one on top, sets it on the bed, and starts going through it.

Five minutes later, she's back in the living room.

Seeing her, Ceto sits up straighter and stubs out the joint. "Okay, okay, I'm putting away the groceries."

"Where's my bracelet?"

"What are you talking about?"

"My silver charm bracelet. Where is it?"

"How would I know?"

But she knows. Mary Beth can tell by the look on her face. She'd probably have seen it on her own face in the mirror, back in the old days.

"I guess you did get something from me after all," she says, shaking her head. "It really does take one to know one."

"One what?"

"Liar. And thief."

"I'm not—"

"Oh please. You are. And I'm not angry. I'm broken, okay? You've broken me. I've been in the federal pen. I've been through a hell of a lot worse. But this? You stealing the one thing that means anything to me in this world? This breaks me."

"A stupid bracelet means more to you than anything? Seriously? It's not even gold."

"So you do still have it. Good. I was going to ask you where you'd pawned it so that I can get it back. Hand it over."

Ceto reaches into her pocket, takes out the bracelet, and hurls it at her.

Mary Beth ducks.

It hits the wall and drops into the trash can beneath it.

Mary Beth fishes it out. It's covered in ashes and coffee grinds. Wordlessly, she takes it over to the sink and cleans it. Her hands are shaking. Her entire body is shaking. She turns off the tap and walks over to Ceto, holding it so that it dangles from her fingers.

"You have no idea what this means to . . ." She stops, choking back a sob. "But how could you know?"

She should have told her.

But it's not too late.

Mary Beth looks down at the bracelet for a long moment. Then she reaches out, takes Ceto's bony wrist, and puts it on.

"What the hell are you doing?"

"Just swear you'll never sell it."

"I told you, it's a worthless piece of crap. I don't know why you're acting like it's the crown jewels or something."

"I should have given it to you a long time ago, because . . ." Mary Beth takes a deep breath. "It was my sister's. And she was your mother."

CHAPTER SIXTY

Present Day

Across the glass partition, Mary Beth stares down at her orange jumpsuit as she seems to mull over the question.

Midge waits.

"I don't know what you're talking about," Mary Beth says at last, looking up with a shrug.

"Gordy Klatte. The Walking Man. If you didn't kill them, who did?"

Mary Beth remains stoic. Silent.

Midge shifts gears. "Let's backtrack. Why were you in Mulberry Bay the night Gordy was killed?"

"Who says I was?"

"You were caught on security camera footage."

"Then I guess I was there."

"I'm trying to figure out why. You were living in Syracuse. You were clean. You had a good job."

"I was a freaking *waitress*, Midge."

"At one of the best restaurants in town."

"Sounds like you've been snooping into my past."

"It's not really considered snooping when it's your job."

"Yeah, well, call it whatever you want. If you know all about me and my life, why are you here asking questions? Oh, right . . . it's a *friendly visit*. I forgot."

"You were doing *great*, Mary Beth. You really were. You turned your whole life around. What went wrong? Why are you here?"

"You know why I'm here. You were there that night. You *put* me here."

"You were willing to take the blame for Gordy's death. You didn't deny it. And you were willing to kill me, Mary Beth, to protect someone. Who is she?"

She flinches. "I wasn't going to kill you, Midge."

"You held me at gunpoint."

"Because I knew you were armed. I was counting on you to use your gun on me. Suicide by cop. Isn't that what they call it?"

Shaken, Midge says, "I don't believe you."

"I really don't care what you believe. It's the truth." She frowns. "But why don't you believe me?"

"Maybe I don't want to. Because it's so much worse."

"Worse than my threatening to shoot you?"

"In some ways. Do you know how traumatic it would be for me to take your life, Mary Beth? I'd be grilled about whether my actions were justified. I'd have to deal with liability, legal issues. I could be suspended or lose my job. Aside from that, can you imagine the emotional burden I'd carry, knowing that I was the instrument of your death? I'd spend the rest of my life reliving it, wondering if I could have done something differently."

"I *wanted* to die, Midge! Don't you get it?"

"Then why did you try to take me down when I went for your gun? Why didn't you just let me take it and turn it on you?"

"I spent years of my life on the street, Midge, then in prison. Old instincts die hard. Someone catches you off guard and makes a grab for you, you don't stop to analyze it. You react. So, yeah. I botched it. It wasn't the first time. You can't sit here and tell me how great I am when you know better than anyone that I never was good at anything." She lifts her left arm, palm facing Midge. The white skin along her vein is marked by slashing scars. "See? Not even killing myself."

Midge stares at the marks. "*You* did that? When? How?"

"A long time ago, and not with kiddie safety scissors, but you'd think so, right?" she says with a bitter laugh.

A long time ago . . . Scissors . . .

Someone was just saying something about that. About Mary Beth?

No, Caroline.

Last night, Talia and Kelly were reminiscing about Caroline needing scissors that were specially made for lefties.

Midge stares at Mary Beth's wrist.

Her *left* wrist, bearing self-inflicted wounds that came from her right hand.

That wasn't her in the security camera footage, wearing Caroline's bracelet. She isn't left-handed, like Caroline . . . or like the person who came to Mulberry Bay to kill Gordy Klatte.

In this moment, the inmate sitting across from her isn't her would-be executioner, or a cold-blooded murderer. She's a girl Midge once knew, a lively girl whose little sister adored her. A girl perpetually longing for fun and for freedom, her spirit suppressed in a lifeless, loveless home.

"Do you remember Mason Bauer?"

"No. Should I?"

"He was the pastor at Congregational."

"When?"

"In the late nineties."

"It must have been after my time. I left here in the spring of '97."

"Because you were pregnant, and your parents sent you away to a place where you were forced to hand over your newborn child."

"Are you asking me, or telling me?"

"I know what they did to you, Mary Beth. It isn't just cruel and reprehensible, it's illegal. And I'm going to look into it. But I need the facts. So is that how it happened? Like I described? They forced you to let strangers adopt your baby?"

"My son," she says softly. "Born on Christmas. He was perfect."

Her sorrow is palpable. Despite everything, Midge pities her.

She waits a moment to ask the next question, as much for Mary Beth to regain her composure as for herself.

"Do you know where he ended up? Your son?"

"Yes. It was an open adoption. I was supposed to be allowed contact. He was in Cleveland."

Midge thinks of Hannah Fletcher, who disappeared as a teenager and resurfaced in Ohio. Of Astrid Stanton, who went to college in Ohio.

"Why Cleveland?" she asks Mary Beth.

"What do you mean, why? It's where I was."

"When you gave birth?"

"Yes. At the Golden Bridge Maternity Home. A lot of the adoptive parents were local."

"You said you were supposed to be allowed contact? Did they go back on that, then?"

"Sort of. It's . . . it wasn't just them. It was me too. Anyway, he's twenty-six now. I just hope he has a happy life. He sure as hell doesn't need someone like me barging into it." She clears her throat. "This isn't why you're here. You aren't asking about my son, offering to look into what happened at Golden Bridge, out of the goodness of your heart."

"I told you why I'm here. I'm trying to figure out who you're protecting."

"I'm not protecting anyone. That's not how I roll."

"It's how you rolled with Caroline. When she told you she was pregnant, you wanted to make sure that what happened to you wouldn't happen to her. You helped her run away so that she could keep her baby. The two of you were going to raise it together. Is that correct?"

No reaction from Mary Beth.

"Caroline had told you about our deal with her—that in exchange for our keeping her secret, she promised to meet us at Haven Cliff exactly a year later, so that we'd know everything had turned out okay for her."

"What does any of this have to do with Gordy Klatte?"

"His killer's DNA was under his fingernails. It didn't belong to you."

No response.

Midge clears her throat. "Remember the pastor I was just asking you about? Mason Bauer?"

"It's *his*?" She looks surprised. Relieved.

"It's his *daughter's*."

Mary Beth's eyes widen, and her jaw drops.

Midge clears her throat. "Mason Bauer has a history of sexual assault on minors. Did you know that?"

The mask of indifference is back. "I didn't know *him*. How would I know that?"

"Right. You weren't around that last year or two of Caroline's time in Mulberry Bay, when he was there. She looked up to him. She was . . . close to him. I'm afraid . . ." Midge can't bring herself to say it.

For a long moment, all is still.

Then Mary Beth says in a whisper, almost to herself, "I didn't know. You can believe what you want to believe, Midge, but I didn't know."

"There's something else. Gordy's killer was also a partial match to your DNA."

Mary Beth looks down. She's trembling.

"The killer is female. It would be a half sister, if you have one. Or your aunt, your grandmother, your granddaughter. Your *niece*."

Mary Beth's flinch at that word tells Midge all she needs to know.

Maintaining her composure, she goes on. "You said that on the night Caroline disappeared, she changed her mind about leaving and letting you help her raise the baby she was going to have?"

Or did she already have it?

Midge doesn't bother to ask the question. She knows the answer. And Mary Beth's lips are sealed between her teeth.

She goes on, "You were losing your sister—the only person who was ever kind to you. And you felt as though you were about to lose *your* baby all over again. The two of you quarreled. Caroline somehow fell—or did you push her in a fit of rage?—into the empty pit where that swimming pool used to be. Is that right?"

Mary Beth shakes her head, tears brimming in her eyes. "I didn't push her! I would never have pushed her! It was an accident! She fell!"

"But after she disappeared, searchers combed every inch of Haven Cliff. You know what I've been wondering? How did they miss finding her in that pool? I think I know now."

She leans close to the partition, gaze locked on Mary Beth.

"The searchers missed her that night because she wasn't there. She *did* leave Haven Cliff on prom night. She was with you. She lived a whole year. She . . ."

Midge breaks off, shaking her head. Compartmentalizing.

"Then, on the anniversary in June 2000, she came back to meet us, just as she promised. She had her Walkman with her, with the new Britney Spears CD in it. Maybe you came with her, or maybe you followed her. It doesn't matter. *That's* when she died. A year after she disappeared."

Midge rests both hands on the table in front of her and leans so close, her cap's brim brushes the glass.

"You didn't mean to. I know that, Mary Beth. It wasn't your fault. You never meant to harm her. She died because you loved her. Because she told you she was leaving you and coming home to Mulberry Bay. Home to us. Talia, Kelly, and me. And you didn't want to let go. So you—"

"Guard!" Mary Beth screams. "Guard! No more of this! Not without my attorney!"

"It's all right," Midge says, pushing back her chair. "We're finished here. For now."

Her heart is racing. Her heart is *broken.*

She knows why Mary Beth is protecting Gordy's killer.

She knows that Caroline lived a year after her disappearance.

She knows that she didn't lose her baby.
Her child was born.
Her child lives on.
Her child is Ceto.
A stone-cold killer.

CHAPTER SIXTY-ONE

Talia catches up with Ben, Caleb, and Kelly as they finish packing everything into the car.

"What's going on with Camille?" Ben asks.

She hesitates. "Oh, you know . . . she and T. J. are splitting up, and she wanted to talk about it."

Now isn't the time to tell him about Hayley and the DNA testing. She's still trying to process the information herself, wondering what in the world possessed her daughter to do such a thing.

Her mother's husband, Oliver, was a lovely man who died back in 2016. Hayley called him *Grandpa*, and Talia saw no reason to explain to a child that age that he wasn't her biological grandfather. Anyway, her mother asked her not to.

"There's no reason to tell her anything different," Natalie said, when Hayley was working on a family tree project in first grade. "She's too young to understand, and I don't want her thinking any less of me for something that happened so long ago."

"Mommy, that would never happen. Hayley worships you."

"And I'd like to keep it that way."

Talia honored her word to her mother, assuming they would revisit the subject when Hayley was old enough to understand. Then Natalie was gone, and there's been no reason to bring it up.

Apparently, she underestimated her daughter's interest in her biological roots.

As they walk over to the Landing, Talia clutches her phone, wishing Hayley would call back, though unsurprised she hasn't.

Clearly, she's giving Talia the silent treatment.

That, or she's fallen in the tub and hit her head and . . .

Don't even go there. She's fine.

There are times when Talia wonders where Caleb got his anxiety. This, however, is one of those times when she knows—and *is*—the answer to that.

According to the locator app, Hayley has kept her promise and is still in the house.

"So this is where you used to work? Pretty fancy," Ben comments, indicating the valet stand in front of the restaurant and the sign advertising KOBE STEAK & MAINE LOBSTER SURF AND TURF.

"It was a dump back then," she informs him as he reaches to open the door for them. "My mom used to say—"

She breaks off, seeing a flyer taped to the glass. Beneath the headline *MISSING*, there's a photo of a pretty teenage girl. Sarah Greene. She's sixteen.

And she disappeared yesterday, in broad daylight, from Mulberry Bay.

Kelly touches her arm. "It's okay, Talia. Don't let this—"

"Did you *know* about this?"

"I just found out a little while ago."

"How could you not tell me?"

"Tell you what?" Caleb asks.

"Because Hayley's safe. She's at Haven Cliff. You can see her on your app."

"But she's not calling me back, and she's not answering texts!"

"Because she's upset with you, Talia. You know how she is. This"—Ben points at the flyer—"has nothing to do with our daughter."

"You don't know that, Ben! You don't know . . . there's a lot you don't know!"

"Who's that girl?" Caleb asks, standing on his tiptoes to see the flyer.

"What don't I know?" Ben asks.

Talia shakes her head, calling Hayley's phone.

The line rings . . . rings . . . rings again . . .

Voicemail.

She immediately redials. "She's not picking up!"

"Because she's ignoring you," Ben says.

"Then *you* call her."

She expects him to protest, but he turns to Kelly. "Why don't you and Caleb go in and get a table."

"Good idea. Come on, Caleb." With a backward glance at Talia, Kelly ushers her son into the restaurant.

Talia can't even look at her.

"She should have told me," she tells Ben as he pulls out his phone.

"Yeah, well, it sounds like there's some stuff you should tell me," he says, placing the call to Hayley.

"I will. Just . . ."

She can hear the line ringing.

Then voicemail.

"Something's wrong, Ben."

"She's probably just mad at both of us."

"No. I have to get to Haven Cliff. Where are the keys?"

He reaches into his pocket. "Talia, don't you think you're overreacting? She's—"

"I'm not overreacting!" She jabs a thumb at the flyer on the door. "*She* disappeared yesterday!"

"Who knows what was going on with her?" He pulls his car keys out of his pocket. "We know our daughter. Hayley's not the kind of kid who would—"

"Yes she is!" She snatches the keys from his hand and heads toward the parking lot.

"You don't even know what I was—"

"Whatever you were going to say, you're wrong! Kids keep things from their parents, Ben. Kids disappear. That girl on the flyer. And my friend Caroline . . . she—"

He's at her side, putting an arm around her shoulders. "It's okay. I know. I'll go. You stay here with Caleb. I'll get Hayley and bring her back here."

"No. I'm going."

"What about Caleb?"

"You stay here with him."

"I'm not letting you take off alone. Not like this."

"You're not *letting* me?"

"You know what I mean. I'm worried about you. And about Hayley. Caleb's fine with Kelly. And I've got the keys to the house. Let's go."

CHAPTER SIXTY-TWO

Midge reclaims her belongings—weapon, radio, phone—at the security checkpoint and powers her phone back on as she heads for the exit. Beyond the glass doors, she can see that the sunny day has given way to dreary rain that matches her mood.

She imagines Mary Beth in her orange jumpsuit and handcuffs, being led back to her cell, resigned to facing charges for crimes she didn't commit.

Caroline's daughter . . . a murderer?

It doesn't make sense, but as Nap says, science doesn't lie.

So.

Caroline's daughter . . . a murderer.

The motive tracks. If Mary Beth believed Gordy was responsible for getting Caroline pregnant and destroying her life, her daughter must have believed the same.

If she knew the truth, she'd have gone after Mason Bauer.

But why would she go after Sarah Greene?

Occam's razor, Midge. The simplest explanation is the best.

The problem: There *is* no simple explanation.

Phone in hand, she hurries through the rain to her car. It isn't far, but she's drenched in the process.

She takes off her cap and turns the air on full blast with the vents aimed directly at her, hoping to dry off while she checks messages and emails.

There are no new leads on Sarah Greene.

The Stantons haven't gotten back to her yet. She didn't expect them to.

There's a text from Nap. Hope you're hanging in there.

She responds by putting a thumbs-up on it. He's sweet, but he can't possibly understand what all of this means.

Talia and Kelly will, but she isn't about to barge into their beach day with a bombshell.

Switching to her iPad, about to look into the Golden Bridge Maternity Home, she sees that Kelly has forwarded another report from Toby with an attachment labeled *Bauer Family*.

Now there's a loaded caption, Midge thinks as she downloads the attachment.

She opens the document and starts reading.

Mason Bauer's elderly mother lives in a nursing home in his small hometown outside Montgomery. His wife is in El Paso. His adult children are scattered from Texas to Alabama, all married with large families.

She flicks through the photos, scanning their smiling faces, looking for—and finding—a resemblance to Junia Stanton in several of them.

Junia disappeared while trying to trace her birth family.

Sienna Harmon disappeared and turned up dead.

Sarah Greene is missing.

Caroline's daughter killed a man.

Four young women whose lives intersect on one point:

Mason Bauer.

Scrolling on through his family photos, Midge stops short.

What the . . . ?

She leans in and touches the iPad screen to enlarge the photo captioned *Mason Bauer Junior*.

He's the same man she met yesterday at Congregational.

CHAPTER SIXTY-THREE

At the Landing, Kelly waits behind several people at the hostess stand, keeping an eye on Caleb. He's nearby, face pressed to the glass on the huge aquarium she told him about. Talia and Ben lagged behind and are still outside, probably having another disagreement over Hayley.

Kelly wishes she'd told Talia about Sarah Greene back on the beach. Yes, Talia would likely have reacted then as she has now. And yes, her intention was to preserve Talia's peace of mind. And yes, she's certain Hayley is safe at Haven Cliff.

Still, when it comes to friendship—any friendship, but especially theirs—withholding information can feel like a lie.

"Table for two?" the teenage hostess asks.

"No, for four."

"I can't seat you until the entire party is here."

"They're right outside."

"Just let me know when they're *inside*," the girl says, and moves on to a newly arrived couple in tennis whites.

Kelly rolls her eyes and turns to Caleb. "Pretty cool fish tank, isn't it?"

"Yep. I'm trying to count how many fish there are."

"I don't know if you can count that high, kiddo." Feeling her phone vibrate with an incoming call, she curses under her breath, certain it's Mrs. Verga.

"That's a bad word," Caleb informs her without turning away from the fish tank.

"It absolutely is. And you have bionic hearing."

The call is from Talia.

Kelly answers with a quiet, "Where are you?"

"Can you please get lunch with Caleb? Ben and I are going back to Haven Cliff."

"Why?"

"Hayley's not answering texts or picking up her phone."

"I'm sure she's just sulking, Tal'. Don't let her ruin your lunch."

"I really hope so, but she's not answering for Ben either. We're worried, and—" She breaks off and says, "No, don't turn here. Up there, at the stop sign."

"Is that my mommy?" Caleb asks. "Where is she?"

"She's just going to check on Hayley."

"I want to go with her!" He starts toward the door.

She goes after him. "Caleb, no, come back here."

"Kelly, please don't take your eyes off him. I need you to keep him safe," Talia says, sounding choked.

"Of course, but—"

"And don't tell him anything that will scare him."

"Why would I—"

"And can you please call Midge and tell her to meet us at the house? I tried her a few times just now, but she must not have her phone."

"She always has her phone." Kelly catches up to Caleb by the door and steers him back toward the fish tank.

"She didn't pick up. Maybe she didn't recognize my number."

Kelly agrees, though they both know that wouldn't be the case.

"I need her, Kelly. I'm really worried. Just get ahold of her, will you?"

"I will. Right away. Just try to breathe."

Caleb grabs her arm. "Mommy can't breathe?"

"Tell him I'm fine. I have to hang up. We're almost there." She disconnects the call.

"Wait! What's wrong with Mommy?"

"Nothing at all, sweetie. How many fish did you count so far?"

"Twenty-nine or maybe twenty-ten."

"Okay, great. Keep going. I have to call Aunt Midge."

It rings immediately, going right into voicemail.

The hostess is back, about to help the next people in line.

"Wait," Kelly says. "There are only two of us now. We can be seated. Come on, Caleb. We can finish counting later."

The girl grabs a leather-bound menu and a kids' menu that comes in a packet with crayons and leads the way to the outdoor dining deck.

She seats them alongside the rail overlooking the water.

Kelly settles Caleb into his seat, shows him the activities printed on his paper menu, and hands him the crayons.

"Can we play tic-tac-toe?" he asks.

"Sure, in a second. I just have to call Auntie Midge again," she says, dialing.

"Where is she?"

"That's a good question," Kelly says.

There's still no answer.

She texts instead.

Meet Talia at Haven Cliff ASAP. Something might be wrong.

She hesitates for a moment, replaces the words *might be* with *is*, and hits send.

CHAPTER SIXTY-FOUR

If Nap's CODIS DNA blind side hit Midge like a fastball between the shoulder blades, her recognition of Bauer's son impacts her like a meteor to the skull.

No wonder her subconscious mind kept trying to link the man at the church to Reverend B., and to Sarah Greene's disappearance.

No wonder.

He fits.

He didn't lie to her about everything. He does have a wife, and six children. They look like the perfect family, on paper and in photos. Even Mason. Especially Mason.

But the sabotage, his very presence at the place where Sarah was supposed to be, the trampled ground, the necklace . . .

Something happened to Sarah Greene yesterday, and he's very likely connected.

Oh, come on, he *is* connected. He did something to her, and to Junia Stanton. He killed Sienna Harmon.

And now it's not just her gut. Now there's evidence.

Circumstantial, yes. Defense attorneys are adept at using it to create doubt in the courtroom. But in Midge's experience, it's a powerful investigatory tool.

Driving back through the rain to Mulberry Bay, she makes the necessary phone calls. Now that the person of interest has been identified and his photo added to the BOLO, Midge is certain that if he's still in the area, it's only a matter of time before he's caught. All available county and state law enforcement resources are now on the case. Investigators are flooding the area. The Investigative Support Unit is at the Greene house and Congregational Church. The necessary warrants have been expedited. It's out of her hands, for the time being.

She parks in the lot behind police headquarters, turns off the car, and leans back in her seat. Just for a moment. Just to listen to the rain thumping a steady rhythm on the car. Just to rest her eyes—and her brain.

It persists, though, working away at a puzzle that almost fits together.

If Mason Bauer Junior is involved in what happened to Sarah Greene—and that's not a huge *if*—then it's not a stretch to assume he's somehow connected to Gordy Klatte's death.

Except . . .

If you force a jigsaw tab into the wrong socket, you haven't solved anything. There can be no gaps, and the fact that the DNA under Gordy's nails belongs to Bauer's daughter and not his son is a huge one.

Her phone buzzes with a text.

Meet Talia at Haven Cliff ASAP. Something is wrong.

Midge turns on the car and barrels out of the parking lot, siren blaring, lights swirling.

CHAPTER SIXTY-FIVE

The man in the woods is definitely a stranger. But not a creepy one. He has really short hair and a face like a dad. He's dressed in hiking pants and boots and long sleeves, even though it's kind of hot for all that. But then, Hayley's wearing flip-flops, so he's probably thinking she's the weirdo.

"You've been waiting for *me*?" Hayley asks, thinking he has her mixed up with someone else.

Then it dawns on her.

"Wait, are you my grandfather?"

He looks confused.

She gets a better look at him and wonders if maybe he's not old enough to be a grandfather. But if he's not, he'd probably say so. Maybe he just forgot. She heard Aunt Kelly talking about her mom last night. Older people get confused and forget stuff, sometimes even their own names.

"Who are you?" he asks.

"I'm Hayley, Talia's daughter."

"Good to meet you, Hayley."

He doesn't say his name, and Hayley doesn't know it, because she hasn't gotten the DNA test results back yet.

She wonders if they're supposed to shake hands or hug or something.

A hug would be weird. And he's not offering a handshake. He's just standing there staring at her.

He's probably thinking she looks a lot like Mom. People always say that.

"I figured you might be around here," she goes on. "Last night, I saw someone out here and I thought it was probably you. Well, my grandfather. That, or a ghost."

"I'm definitely not a ghost."

"But you were here yesterday?"

"Here, in Mulberry Bay? I was. I thought we were going to meet. Like I said, I was waiting for you."

"You should have just knocked on the door or something if you wanted to meet me. And my mom. I mean . . . I'm pretty sure she'd want to meet you. I was actually going to tell her I was looking for you, but I didn't have a chance, and anyway, surprises are nice."

"Sometimes they are." He's smiling, but his voice sounds cold. Like he's angry with her.

Which is crazy, because he doesn't even know her.

"This is a beautiful property, by the way. Are you staying here?"

"Yes. Just for the weekend."

"Can I ask how old you are?"

He can ask, but she's not about to tell him the truth.

"I'm fourteen."

"You're only fourteen?"

Resenting the *only* and the shocked expression on his face, she's compelled to add, "I'm almost fifteen."

"And you're here by yourself?"

"Of course." She shrugs as if this isn't a new thing—being allowed to stay home alone while her family is out.

"How about your dad? Where is he?"

"At the beach."

He nods, almost like he was expecting her to say that. "But does he know about this? About me? The DNA match?"

"You already got the results? That's why you're here!"

Okay, now he looks as confused as she feels.

"Isn't that why you're here?"

"No. My mom doesn't know about the test. I was going to surprise her."

"Your mom? Are you sure we're alone here?" he asks, looking around.

"How would I know?" She, too, looks around.

She isn't scared, exactly . . . She's never scared. She reminds herself of that, sternly.

It's just that her stomach is starting to feel weird and queasy and her heart is thumping hard and fast, kind of like when she went on the roller coaster with her dad at the carnival.

It's probably because she's not used to being in the woods.

Or alone at all.

Or alone in the woods with a strange man, even though he looks like a regular person. Although maybe not a grandpa. But definitely not an axe murderer.

She wishes she hadn't said the words *axe murderer* to her mom earlier, and she *really* wishes she hadn't read all that stuff online about the Haven Cliff curse and the Winterfield murders and the girl who disappeared out here on prom night.

At that thought, she hears a rumble of thunder, like something out of the ghost story she was planning to tell Chloe.

The man hears it too. He looks up at the gray sky.

"Uh-oh. It's about to rain. We'd better get moving."

"Get moving where?" Hayley takes a step back, away from him.

He gestures at the path that leads away from the clearing, into the woods. "The pavilion. We can talk there. We have a lot of catching up to do, right?"

Her hand goes to the back right pocket of her shorts, but her phone isn't there. That's right, because it's locked in the house, and she's locked out of it.

"Come on."

"I think . . ." *No*. Her voice sounds small, almost like a scared little girl. Hayley is not a little girl, nor is she scared.

She clears her throat, lifts her chin, looks him in the eye, and starts over. "I think you have me mixed up with someone else."

He tilts his head and looks at her, like he's trying to figure out something.

Her instinct is to turn around and take off. But she forces herself to stand her ground, not sure how fast she can run in flip-flops. Maybe faster than him, since he's kind of old. But so is her dad, and he can run pretty fast.

Not that she thinks this man is actually going to chase her . . .

Is he?

He takes a step closer to her. One arm is folded across his chest, and the index finger on the opposite hand is pointed to his temple, like he's thinking. "You *are* the one who emailed me? About the DNA match?"

She takes a step back, bending her right leg and plucking off her flip-flop, then taking another step back and doing the same with her left.

He still looks like he's thinking, but he's also watching her.

"Whatcha doing?" he asks in a quiet voice.

Hayley turns and starts to run.

So does he.

He catches her quickly, his strong arm yanking her from behind and his hand covering her mouth, muffling her scream.

CHAPTER SIXTY-SIX

When Talia was four or five years old, she got into her mother's secret candy stash while Natalie was busy in another room. She remembers unwrapping a jawbreaker and popping it into her mouth, remembers the delicious sugary slick, remembers swallowing the whole damned thing . . .

Rather, trying.

It lodged in her throat. She couldn't get it down, and she couldn't get it up. Couldn't breathe. Couldn't make a sound.

Then her mother was there, grabbing her hard from behind, squeezing and squeezing until the candy was ejected.

To this day, Talia refuses to eat hard candy, even cough lozenges, and she never allows her kids to have it. On Halloween, she sorts through their trick or treat bags, confiscating and throwing away anything that might cause them to choke.

Natalie often recounted the episode. She was in the midst of some chore when she was seized by the inexplicable and urgent need to check on Talia. She dropped what she was doing, rushed in, and saved her life.

"I just knew she needed me," she'd say, wrapping up her story.

"But how did you know?" the listener might ask.

"Mother's intuition. Don't ever doubt that it's real."

Talia never has.

Jumping out of the car at Haven Cliff, she wants to believe that her daughter is safe inside, soaking and sulking in the bathtub. But she knows with chilling certainty that she isn't, because nothing is as it seems. Hayley keeps things from her. She has secrets.

Secrets can be deadly.

Talia races through the rain, up the steps, and across the stone terrace. She tries the door, and it's locked. Good. That's good. It's supposed to be locked.

Ben is right behind her, Kelly's spare keys already in his hand. He unlocks the door and opens it.

Talia barrels past him. "Hayley? Hayley!"

The house is silent. It feels empty.

She rushes up the stairs and down the hall toward her daughter's room, her panic mounting when she sees that the door is ajar.

"Hayley!" She takes in the unmade bed, the clothes on the floor. The adjoining bathroom is empty. "Hayley!"

She can hear Ben downstairs, shouting their daughter's name as well.

Then he shouts her own, in a tone that makes her blood run cold.

CHAPTER SIXTY-SEVEN

Enraged, he drags the girl away from the old swimming pool, his left arm crooked around her neck, his right covering her mouth. She writhes and struggles, making muffled sounds against his hand.

She's fierce, this one. Not like the sweet, docile girl yesterday.

Sarah. Sarah Greene.

He'd been heading toward his car in the church parking lot when she trudged into his sight line, looking flushed and sweaty.

"Are you here for Bible class?" he called.

"Yes."

"It's canceled."

"What? Oh no!"

He introduced himself as the substitute pastor and told her about the air-conditioning problem. He fully intended to send her on her way, and to go on his.

But she lingered. Such a friendly young woman. Chatty, even. She was grateful for the cold bottle of water he offered.

"Thank you so much," she said. "It's going to be a long, hot walk back home."

"I'd be happy to give you a ride."

He saw the misgiving spark in her eyes.

"Oh—no, that's all right," she said quickly.

Was it a normal reaction to an offer from a stranger, or did she suspect something?

He really would have simply driven her home. That's what he told himself later. What he tells himself even now.

But that flicker of doubt made him paranoid. Was she suspicious? Did she realize that he was up to something? Was she going to tell someone?

He couldn't let that happen.

He forced himself to stay calm, to keep her talking. Eventually, she seemed comfortable again, especially when he asked her about Bible study. He could tell she was reassured when he quoted passages from memory.

He was patient, steering the conversation from one benign topic to another. Finally, he asked her if she wanted to see a litter of newborn kittens he'd discovered that morning.

"Yes! I love kittens!" she said.

As he led her toward the woods, she told him that she'd always wanted a cat, but her parents said no.

"Maybe you can bring one of these sweet babies home," he suggested. "I bet they'll change their minds."

She assured him that they wouldn't, and then they were in the woods, and he cautioned her to tread quietly and carefully, so as not to disturb the kittens. He led her deeper into the undergrowth, pushing aside vines and holding back branches for her.

"Um, where are they?" she asked, hanging back a little.

He turned to her with a finger to his lips and then pointed at a clump of ferns. "In there," he whispered. "Take a peek. Just don't scare them."

He stood aside and gestured for her to move past him.

She was smiling as she did so.

That's when he grabbed her, in one swift movement, hands around her throat.

In that moment, it didn't matter who she was . . .

Rather, who she *wasn't*.

She didn't deserve it. Not like the others. Sarah Greene wasn't the devil's spawn, born of his father's wicked sins. She wasn't going to bring shame to his family or add to his mother's already unbearable burden of pain. This wasn't divine redemption. When the moment passed and he stood looking down at that girl, the life squeezed out of her, he wasn't filled with satisfaction, but with remorse.

It had happened so quickly and easily. His clothes were unsullied. There was no blood. Not hers, anyway. Just a small spot on his arm where he'd been scratched by a bramble. There'd barely been a struggle.

Nothing like this.

"Shut up!" he snarls at the girl. "Shut up, or I'll kill you right here!"

Maybe he really will kill her here, in the clearing, and be done with it.

He left his car by the dumpsters at the construction site next door, as directed. It was far enough away from the old pavilion where he attempted to lure her. That's where he stashed the tarp and rope he'll need to drag her down to the car.

He's been planning this ever since he read her first email a few weeks ago.

> I'm trying to find my birth family via DNA testing on the genealogical website Lost and Found. My results identify you as a close biological relative . . .

Close? You bet.

It's like Whac-A-Mole with these half siblings. Every so often a new one pops up, searching for their roots, unaware that their biological mothers were teenage assault victims and their biological father was a predator who met his end in the most poetically just way: fed to ravenous bayou gators.

A father-son fishing trip, he'd told his old man, to celebrate the mistrial and release from prison. They could meet halfway between Dad's home in Texas and his own in Alabama.

When it was over, all that was left of his father was the blue fishing cap floating in the shallow green water. He reached a cautious hand off the boat, grabbed the hat, and kept it as a remembrance. Or perhaps a trophy.

His only regret is the lie he told his mother, claiming that his father never made it to Louisiana that weekend. It was for her own good. She was ravaged by the ordeal, and it had only just begun. There were more accusers out there, more indictments looming. Better to let her think that her husband had left the country than to put her through all that again.

He does what he has to do to protect himself. To protect his mother, his wife, his children.

He did that yesterday, with the girl at the church.

He'll do it today, with the girl fighting his grasp as thunder rumbles closer and the first drops of rain begin to fall.

He'll slit her throat right here, right now. The storm will wash the blood into the earth.

He removes his hand from her mouth and grabs the switchblade from his pocket. She lets out a scream. He yanks her head back so that her neck is positioned. Then he presses the button on the knife's handle, popping the blade, and goes in for the kill.

CHAPTER SIXTY-EIGHT

Talia stands in the dining room with Ben, gaping at the broken china, toppled chair, spattered stains, and Hayley's cell phone, lying on the rug.

"It looks like . . ." She swallows hard and recovers her voice. "It looks like there was a struggle."

"I know."

"My phone is in my bag in the car. You have to call—"

"I'm doing it."

He presses three numbers on his phone, and Talia hears, "9-1-1. What is your emergency?"

"My daughter is missing. In Mulberry Bay. At Haven Cliff."

Talia presses a fist to her mouth as he relays the specifics.

She can't believe this is happening. Her worst nightmare has become a reality, and all she can think of is Caroline's mother, standing on the doorstep, accepting that damned casserole.

Outside, thunder crashes, rattling the panes and her nerves.

She walks toward Hayley's phone, about to bend over and pick it up, but he grabs her arm.

"No," he says. "Don't touch anything."

"Why—"

She realizes he's thinking that this is a crime scene. Evidence shouldn't be disturbed.

She steps back from her daughter's phone and buries her head in Ben's shoulder. He wraps an arm around her as he confirms the address for the dispatcher.

Then he says, "I don't know if this is relevant, but a man came by here earlier."

Talia's head jerks back, and she looks at him, mouthing, *What?*

"Probably in his late thirties, early forties," Ben tells the dispatcher. "White, clean shaven, driving a black Ford Focus with rental plates. He said he was looking for an address . . ."

Talia listens in disbelief as Ben relays information he didn't share with her. If he had . . .

"All right, thank you." He disconnects the call and looks at her. "They're on their way."

"How *could* you, Ben?"

He doesn't ask what she means. He knows.

"I didn't think anything of it, Tal'. Not until we saw that Missing poster, at the restaurant. I didn't . . . He wasn't . . . Maybe he was . . ." His voice breaks.

"I *told* you. I told you that she shouldn't have been left alone. Not here! I told you that people disappear! You didn't listen to me! I tried to tell you!"

"Why would I listen to you? You lie!"

"I don't lie!"

"You lied about why Camille called!"

She filled him in about Hayley and the genealogy website as they raced over here, needing him to realize that their daughter doesn't tell them everything. Not by a long shot.

"Because that wasn't the time to get into it, with Caleb there, and Kelly. I would have told you."

"Like you would have told me everything else you've kept from me?" He sweeps a hand around them. "All of this . . . your friends, your past . . . you had this whole life I never knew a damned thing about."

"Did you ever ask me about it?"

"I thought it was too painful, because of your dad."

"It *was*! But you could have asked, Ben."

"Would you have told me?"

She opens her mouth to say yes, but that's a lie. She shakes her head. "No. I just wanted to forget. Especially . . . Caroline. She's dead, Ben. She didn't drown in the lake. She—"

She breaks off at another loud clap of thunder.

But no, it isn't thunder.

It's the door; someone is banging on the door, screaming her daughter's name.

But it isn't Hayley.

It's Midge, with her gun drawn. "Where is she, Talia?"

"I don't know! I don't know!"

CHAPTER SIXTY-NINE

Hayley sees the swirling gray sky overhead as he jerks her head back. She feels the rain pouring over her face like tears. But she isn't crying.

She's too angry for tears, filled with fury that leaves no room for fear.

How dare he?

How dare he do this to her?

How dare he touch her, threaten her, kill her?

She's actually going to die.

This is what it feels like. This is how it happens.

You do one little thing wrong, and it leads to an even worse thing, and then another even worse thing, and the next thing you know, you're in trouble. In *danger*.

You're going to die, and there's nothing you can do about it.

Her parents are going to be so sad, and Caleb is going to be so scared, and it's all her fault.

No, it's really the fault of this horrible, evil man who looks like a normal person and thinks she's someone named Sis, and has a knife and is holding her so tightly she can't move, and she sees the glint of steel blade as it slashes toward her, and she closes her eyes just before it hits her throat—

And then there's a deafening blast, the loudest noise Hayley has ever heard.

All at once, he lets go.

She falls on her back, gasping. She feels him topple to the ground beside her, and she feels a rush of movement.

A voice says, "Run! Go!"

She opens her eyes.

The man is lying there, gaping at her, blood pouring from his mouth. He's making terrible gasping sounds.

Someone else is here, standing over them.

"Run!" the voice says again, and Hayley realizes it's a command meant for her.

She rolls onto her side and sees the girl. She's dressed all in black, wearing a hood and some kind of cloak, and she's holding a gun.

That's what made the noise. She shot him.

She's going to shoot him again. She's leaning toward him, pointing the gun at his head.

Hayley pushes herself up. Her feet are bare, her flip-flops lost in the struggle, but it doesn't matter. She starts running, as fast as she can.

She hears another blast of sound, and this time, she knows it came from the gun. She runs faster, her heart racing as much from the exertion as from shock.

Because she recognized the girl with the gun. The girl who saved her.

It's Caroline Winterfield, Mom's friend who drowned in the lake.

CHAPTER SEVENTY

Midge is trying to understand the rambling details that spill from Talia's mouth, with interjections from Ben. It sounds like Hayley was here alone while they were at the beach. She stopped answering calls and texts. They came back, and she was gone.

Gone, like Sarah Greene and Junia Stanton and Sienna Harmon.

Gone, and Mason Bauer's son is out there somewhere.

So is Caroline's daughter.

Are they working together? Ceto and her half brother Mason?

"Talia, we're going to find her," Midge says. "*I'm* going to find her."

She radios for backup, then opens the door and peers out.

She sees a flash of lightning and hears the wind in the trees as the storm blows in.

Then she hears another sound and knows, with a sickening feeling in her gut, that it isn't thunder.

"What was that?" Talia wails. "Was that a gunshot? Midge? Was that—"

"Stay here!" Midge is already running.

"I'm coming!" Ben is right on her heels.

"No! Stay! With Talia! Do not leave her alone, Ben!"

She races outside, across the terrace, down the rain-slicked stone steps. She couldn't tell from which direction the shot came, but she instinctively heads for the woods. The pool site.

If it's Ceto, that's where she'll be.

If it's Ceto . . .

Why would she hurt Hayley?

Gordy makes sense. If she thought he was her father, she'd have a motive. But Hayley? Hayley isn't—

No. Stop. She's going to be okay.

She needs to believe it. Deep down, she does believe Hayley's fine.

Just as deep down, she's certain that Sarah Greene and Junia Stanton are not.

If Ceto thought Mason Bauer was her father . . .

What if he's the one she's after, just like she was after Gordy?

Or what if Mason's son is after Ceto, who, like Junia Stanton, was the product of his father's bad behavior? Junia went looking for her biological roots.

Maybe Ceto did the same.

Maybe, instead of the father, they found the son.

She hears another gunshot. This time she's certain it came from the woods by the pool site.

She quickens her pace, racing across the expanse of lawn. As she reaches the mock orange bushes that mark the trail toward the pool, she hears thrashing in the brush up ahead. She flattens herself against a massive tree trunk.

The sound comes closer. Someone is barreling in her direction.

She sucks in a breath, poised with her weapon, eyes on the path.

The figure that comes into view isn't Mason.

Nor is it Ceto.

Hayley.

She's barefoot and bleeding. Her expression is sheer terror. But she's in one piece.

Midge steps out from behind the tree. Hayley cries out, then realizes who she is and sobs out her name.

"Shhh!" Midge pulls her off the path, positioning herself as a shield between Hayley and whoever's chasing her. Eyes on the terrain, she asks in a low voice, "Are you okay?"

"Yes!"

"Who's up there?"

"A man. He tried to—" She covers her mouth as if she's just realized what happened, or perhaps what could have happened.

Mason Bauer.

"Shhh, just . . . We need to be quiet, okay? Are you hurt? Did he hurt you? You're bleeding."

"I'm all right. I fell. He pushed me down." She's breathing hard. "He had a knife."

"He's still up there?"

"Yeah, but I think he's dead. He got shot."

"He has a gun, then? Not a knife?"

"He has a knife. *She* has a gun."

"Who has a gun?"

"The girl. She saved me. She shot him."

"Who—"

"I can't tell you. You won't believe me."

"I will, Hayley. Tell me."

"You can't tell anyone."

"Hayley, I can't promise you that."

"But they'll think I'm a stupid little child if you tell them. And I'm not! I know what I saw."

"Are you kidding me? No one could ever think you're a stupid little child. You . . . you're like a superhero. You're one of the most . . . *epic* young women I've ever known."

"Seriously?"

"Seriously, Hayley. Just tell me who it was. Who else is up there? Who shot the man?"

"It was a *ghost*. It was the girl who drowned on prom night. Caroline Winterfield."

No, not a ghost.

Not Caroline.

Her daughter.

Ceto.

"She has a gun?" Midge asks, eyes peeled on the path.

"Uh-huh. I didn't think ghosts needed guns."

"What did she look like?"

"She looked like *her*. Like Caroline Winterfield. I've seen pictures, and I know it was her ghost. I mean, she wasn't white and glowing or anything like that. She was all in black, with a black cape, I think, and a hood over her head. But I could see her face."

"Did she say anything?"

"She just told me to run. So I ran."

"And the man? Did he say anything?"

"I think he thinks I'm someone else. He was talking about a DNA match, and I thought he was my grandfather."

"Why would you think—"

"Because I took a DNA test! But I didn't hear back yet. And he said he did."

A DNA test.

Another piece of the puzzle falls into place.

It's as Midge suspected. Mason Bauer must have matched with Junia Stanton.

And with Ceto.

But this time, it seems, the predator met his match.

"Get back to the house," she tells Hayley. "Run. Your parents are there."

"Wait, Midge, come with me, please?"

"I'll be there in a bit."

"But my parents are going to be so mad."

"Your parents," Midge says, shaking her head, "are going to be so happy to see you that they'll forget all about being mad."

"You don't know my mom."

"Oh yes I do, kiddo. I knew your mom first. Now go."

At that, the girl takes off running.

Midge quietly radios for backup confirmation as she watches Hayley rush back to the house. The door opens before she reaches the porch. Talia and Ben are there. They've got her.

Midge whirls away and darts up the trail.

It's been several minutes since she heard the shot. By now, Ceto will have fled, unless Bauer, too, had a firearm. Or got ahold of hers and turned it on her.

Midge slows her pace as she approaches the clearing, moving stealthily now, weapon in hand. She can see the pool site, still cordoned off with yellow tape, and the newly rebuilt colonnade, and the pedestals carved with names of water gods and goddesses.

Kelly was tempestuous Poseidon, Talia was noble Oceanus, Midge was benevolent Hydros, and Caroline was Ceto.

"A sea monster?" she exclaimed.

"A primordial sea monster *goddess*," Midge reminded her, because she was the one who'd looked up the stories behind the names.

"But why do I have to be the monster?"

"Because typecasting is boring," Talia said.

"I like boring! Boring is good!"

From Kelly, "No, it isn't, Caroline. But trust me, *good* is definitely boring."

They were laughing, all of them. Four friends, laughing in the dappled sunshine of a long-ago summer.

Today, there's no sunshine. There are no carefree young women perched on their pedestals. There's no laughter.

Thunder rumbles and rain pours down. The yawning pit that was once a pool, and then Caroline's grave, fills with mud.

Midge isn't alone here.

Seeing movement, she ducks behind a tree. She waits a moment and peeks out. Someone is beside the stone that belonged to Caroline, the one that bears the name Ceto.

Midge slips closer, moving silently from tree to tree, as the rain falls all around her.

The figure is wearing dark, shapeless, hooded clothing and has its back to Midge, bent over a large object on the ground, poking at it. A clump of leaves? A fallen branch? What is that thing?

No—that isn't a *thing*. That's a *person* lying there, very still. A person streaked with red . . .

Blood.

The figure—a woman, it's definitely a woman—straightens and takes a step back like an artist inspecting her handiwork. She reaches down again as if to make one last tweak.

She isn't cloaked, as Hayley said. She's wearing an oversize black sweatshirt with the hood tied tightly around her head, black jeans, black sneakers, black gloves.

Midge steps into the clearing with her gun drawn. "Mulberry Bay Police! Raise your hands where I can see them!"

The figure remains motionless.

"I said raise your hands! Above your head! Now!"

The woman follows the order, arms up.

"Turn toward me! Slowly!"

She pivots with painstaking care until she's facing Midge.

Midge's breath snags in her throat and her legs threaten to liquefy as she takes in the young woman's face, with the sweatshirt hood tightly puckered around it.

The first startling glimpse feels like peering through a portal into the past.

This young woman has Caroline's delicate features and pale complexion. She's virtually identical.

Then Midge meets her gaze, and . . .

No. The eyes are strikingly different from Caroline's. They aren't a soft, velvety blue. They're a much paler shade, cold and hard as ice.

"Ceto."

Midge sees her flinch, barely perceptibly. A slight lifting of the chin, as if she's determined to maintain her composure.

"You figured it out," she says, with a hint of amusement.

It isn't the sweet, soft laughter that often rippled in Caroline's voice in the early years, before her parents sent Mary Beth away, before Gordy came along . . .

Before Bauer.

This is derision laced with mockery. "You're the brilliant detective, though, aren't you? Detective Sergeant Imogene Kennedy?"

"Call me Midge. You know who I am as much as I know who you are."

"All right, Midge. I understand you knew my mother. And my father." She tilts her head to indicate the prone figure on the ground.

Midge knows better than to shift her own gaze in that direction. It, and the gun, are fixed on Ceto.

"Wow. And here I was all set to say, 'Made you look.' Very impressive. You must be well trained. But then, of course you are. *Your* father was the police chief, right?"

Midge says nothing, fighting the urge to look over at Bauer. He's motionless. Hayley said he was shot; she thought he'd been killed.

If he's still alive, every second matters.

Midge hears sirens in the distance.

"It's just too bad your father didn't do his job when my mother disappeared. I wonder if he was protecting you and your friends? Or was he protecting him?" Again, she indicates the bloody man. "I hear he was a good guy from a good family."

"No, Ceto, that man isn't Mason Bauer," Midge says. "He's—"

"His son," Ceto says. "I know exactly who he is. Mason Bauer Junior. My half brother. Do you read the Bible, Midge?"

"I have."

"I guess we do have something in common after all. Do you know John 5:19?"

"Refresh my memory."

"'The Son can do nothing of himself, but what he seeth the Father doing: for what things soever he doeth, these the Son also doeth in like manner.' What does that tell you?"

"It tells me you decided to find him and punish him for his father's sins."

"And vice versa."

"Meaning . . . ?"

"Meaning, we found each other."

"How?"

"How does anyone find anyone these days?"

"DNA. And you arranged to meet?"

"We did. Yesterday. I canceled. I don't think he liked that very much. He likes to have the upper hand. So do I. It must run in the family. It was just a matter of who was going to beat the other to the punch." Again, she gestures at the wounded man. "I won, obviously. I always win."

"What about Gordy Klatte?"

"Oh, he lost. That was unfortunate. When I asked him to meet, he was expecting my mother, and—"

"He was expecting your mother because that's who you claimed to be."

"Very good. He didn't even know I existed. When he saw me, he was shocked . . . I think he thought I was her ghost."

"When he saw you . . . that night in June? The night he died?"

She ignores the question, talking on, but Midge knows the answer.

"He kept saying he couldn't possibly be my father, and boy, did I believe him. You've met the man, haven't you, Midge?"

"I have."

Another derisive chuckle. "Then you know there's no way he was the one. He was so lame, so dull—"

"You killed Gordy."

"—so *clumsy*." She shrugs. "After that, I knew I had to find my real father. The closest I could get was Big Brother here."

The sirens are much closer now. They're here.

Ceto turns her head, listening. "Time for me to go, Midge."

"Don't move."

"Oh, come on. You're not actually going to shoot me. I'm Caroline's daughter. See ya." She lowers her hands and turns away.

"Stop right there!"

Ceto whirls back toward Midge. She, too, has a gun. Midge sees it the instant before she fires.

If Midge wasn't anticipating it—if she didn't see the weapon the instant before Ceto fired—if Ceto had a decent shot . . .

So many ifs.

But the bullet misses. Midge takes cover behind the colonnade and fires. Too late. Unscathed, Ceto ducks into the woods and is gone.

Chasing after her, Midge is quickly overtaken by the arriving backup officers.

"Up there! She's armed!" she shouts, and they fan out into the woods ahead of her.

"Detective Sergeant Kennedy!"

She turns to Lieutenant Carlos Figueroa, an investigator with the state SVU. He's been working the Sarah Greene case.

She briefs him, matching his long-legged stride as they return to the clearing and come to a stop a few feet away from the man on the ground.

"Is he—?"

"Yes," Figueroa says. "He's got multiple GSWs, one through the heart. No pulse. Any chance you can make a preliminary ID?"

"Yes. Mason Bauer Junior."

He radios it in. "We've got a 10-66 . . ."

It's a summons for the medical examiner, meaning a dead body has been discovered.

As he asks for further assistance, investigators, forensics, Midge takes in the scene.

It's clear that Mason Bauer didn't die on the spot where he lies.

He's been dragged here.

He's posed, lying on his back with his legs out in front of him and his hands folded over the bloody hole in his stomach, clasping a blue hat. The granite pedestal etched *Ceto* is at his shattered head like a tombstone.

Like a signature.

Ceto . . . Caroline's child.

Ceto . . . a monster.

Figueroa's radio crackles. She hears confirmation that the ME is on the way.

Nap was here at Haven Cliff just last night, enjoying a meal, some laughs with friends.

Nap was at Haven Cliff on that terrible night in June, when they found skeletal remains in the cordoned pit just steps away from where Midge now stands.

She thinks of the lost summer that lies between that day and this one. Of other summers. Of sweet childhood summers.

Of Caroline, long gone.

Of Kelly and Talia, returned to her, and Hayley, safely in her mother's arms.

Midge walks back toward the house to find them as the cold, hard rain scrubs sweat and tears from her body, and blood from the ground.

September 2

CHAPTER SEVENTY-ONE

Mary Beth saw him again last night.

The Hatman.

Not a water stain over her bed, but the silhouette of the man. He just stood there watching her, the way he used to when she was a little girl, and she was unable to move or speak.

He's been here the last few nights, ever since Midge Kennedy visited her, talking about the past, her lost son, her lost sister, and Mason Bauer.

Reverend B.

Mary Beth remembers Caroline bringing him up a time or two, during the year they spent together in Syracuse, but she never said much about him. She said even less about Gordy. She seemed resigned to leaving her past in Mulberry Bay behind. At first, anyway.

But toward the end, Mary Beth felt her pulling away from the new life, wistful for the old. Not for their parents or sisters; not for their childhood home. For her friends.

Midge, Talia, Kelly . . .

They were her family. They were her home. She was determined to go back. Mary Beth should have realized that nothing she could say or do was going to stop her.

But she held on. She tried.

In the end, she lost the sister she loved not to the life Caroline planned to reclaim but to the Haven Cliff curse.

The baby, though . . . Ceto . . .

Ceto was spared.

Mary Beth now knows it was wrong to flee that night, wrong to raise her niece as her own daughter. But she was just a kid herself, reeling with the shock and grief of Caroline's death.

When the enormity of what had happened settled over her, she grasped that if she ever told anyone, Ceto, too, would be lost to her. She'd be adopted by strangers or turned over to Gordon Klatte, or far worse, to Mary Beth's parents.

She couldn't let that happen. Caroline wouldn't want that. Caroline would want Mary Beth to raise her child, even now. Caroline would have forgiven her.

But Mary Beth will never, ever forgive herself.

Ceto never knew the whole story until that night last spring, when Mary Beth gave her the charm bracelet, and the truth.

She told Ceto about Caroline, and Gordy Klatte, and Mulberry Bay. She told her that her mother's death was an accident. That she fell.

"How could you?" she screamed at Mary Beth. "How could you lie to me for all these years?"

"Because I loved you. Because if you knew . . . if anyone knew . . . I'd have lost you forever."

"You lost me anyway. When you went to prison, you lost me."

"But that wasn't forever."

"It might as well have been. I was alone for all those years in foster care. I didn't understand—"

"I know that, and I'm sorry. I'm so sorry. But I promised you that we'd be together again one day, and I'd make it up to you. I promised I'd never leave you again."

"Well, I'm leaving you."

Those were the last words Ceto said that night before walking out the door.

Mary Beth was certain she'd be back.

The night passed. The day passed. Nights, days. Weeks. Months.

Then came June, and the cryptic text from Talia Shaw asking Mary Beth to meet her at Haven Cliff.

Why? What's this about? Mary Beth asked.

The one-word reply was the only thing guaranteed to get her to show up: Ceto.

She had no way of knowing that the text was from Ceto herself, that she'd stolen Talia's phone. Or that she'd been texting Gordy from her own phone, posing as Caroline.

She had no way of knowing that Gordy was dead. That Ceto was responsible.

Mary Beth knew none of it the night she returned to Haven Cliff, but that doesn't matter. She'd have gone anyway. If Ceto needed her anywhere, anytime, under any circumstances, she was going to be there. She was going to keep the promise she'd made to herself, and to Caroline, and to her daughter, so many years ago.

Someone is at the door to her cell. Keys jangling. Door unlocking.

A guard.

"Hey, Winterfield. Is this feeling like your lucky day?"

"No."

It's feeling like anything but. It's feeling like her luck ran out a long, long time ago. It's feeling like the Haven Cliff curse will follow her to her grave.

"Well, it is. You made bail."

She gasps, sitting up. "Who . . . ?"

He consults the papers in his hand. "Someone named Kelly Barrow."

CHAPTER SEVENTY-TWO

June 14, 2000

Mary Beth has long known about Caroline's promise to Midge, Kelly, and Talia.

The sisters had agreed, early on, that Mary Beth would return to Haven Cliff alone on this night, the one-year anniversary of Caroline's disappearance. She would leave four pennies on the pedestal marked *Ceto*—Caroline's spot, and the source of her daughter's name. The pennies were a secret sign her friends would understand. They'd know Caroline was okay. They'd be able to go on with their lives, and Caroline would go on with hers.

But Caroline has changed. The plan has changed. Everything has changed.

Yes, Mary Beth still makes the long drive back to Mulberry Bay. But Caroline is in the passenger's seat. Ceto is in back, asleep in her car seat—six months old now, a cherub of a child with golden ringlets and big blue eyes.

Tonight, unlike last year, it's raining.

Tonight, a sick feeling has replaced the butterflies in her stomach.

Tonight, she isn't embarking on a mission to rescue her sister. She's losing the only two people who have ever truly mattered to her.

She parks at Woody Lo-Hi, the abandoned camp across the lake, just as she did on this night last year. Again, she borrows a canoe from the half dozen stored in the crafts shack with the broken lock.

Paddling across the shadowy, ripply lake, she kneels in the middle facing the stern, doing her best to keep herself low to distribute the weight.

Caroline is behind her in the bow, holding Ceto, who's still strapped into the car seat that doubles as an infant carrier.

"Careful!" Caroline cries out every time the boat wobbles.

"Don't flail!" Mary Beth barks. "You're making it worse!"

"I can't help it! I'm afraid! I feel like we're going to flip over and die!"

"So do I!"

"What? But I thought you knew how to—"

"I do know how to paddle a canoe! I got us back across the lake last year after you ran away, remember?"

"I don't remember it being this scary."

"It wasn't pouring out! And it was just the two of us, and we can both swim! We didn't have to worry about a helpless little baby! She shouldn't be here! Neither of you were supposed to be here tonight!"

Caroline weeps softly until at last, they make it to the opposite shore. Mary Beth ties the canoe to an old fishing pier piling poking up from the shallows.

They disembark in silence. Caroline covers the baby's carrier with a blanket and hands Mary Beth the small satchel containing a few items for the baby. For herself, she has only the clothes on her back, and the treasured pink Walkman clipped to her jacket. She's left all her other possessions behind in Syracuse, discarded remnants of a life she no longer wants.

Now Mary Beth herself has become one of those castoffs. Unwanted, unneeded. Raindrops and teardrops run down her cheeks as they make their way along the pebbly beach, up the steep stone stairs to the old woodland trail.

Last year, she took a roundabout route through the woods to her designated meeting spot with Caroline, dodging raucous postprom kids. But the days of illicit parties amid Haven Cliff's ruins ended when Caroline Winterfield went missing.

Tonight, the sisters have the deserted grounds to themselves.

"What in the world?" Caroline murmurs when they reach the old pool site.

It's cordoned off. Heavy equipment is poised nearby.

Mary Beth steps closer to a permit posted on a tree and shines her flashlight on it.

"What does it say?" Caroline asks.

"They're going to backfill the pit."

"When?"

"June 15, 2000."

"That's tomorrow. I wonder why they're doing that?"

"Who knows? Who cares?" She clicks off her flashlight and turns away.

"I care," Caroline says, after a moment. "This used to be our family's home. I'll bet it was beautiful back then."

"Yeah, well, now it's decrepit and run down. Oh, and cursed."

"I don't believe that."

"Well, I do."

They duck under the ropes and make their way to the heap of bricks where a colonnade once arched above four stone statues.

Mary Beth sets the satchel on the ground and feels for the four coins she tucked into her pocket this morning, before her sister dropped the bombshell.

She shows Caroline the pennies. "It's not too late to change your mind."

"It is, Mary Beth."

"But we can leave these here for your friends, see? Just like you promised! Just like we said!" Mary Beth places the coins on the pedestal. "Come on, Caroline. This is crazy. We're getting drenched. It's not good for the baby. Let's get out of here and go home."

She turns back to her sister. Even in the dark, she can see that her hair is plastered to her scalp. Her eyes are rimmed by dark circles and filled with tears. She looks utterly miserable.

"I can't go back! Don't you see? I tried. For a whole year, I tried! But for me, *this* is home."

"Haven Cliff?"

"Mulberry Bay! I've missed it so much. I've missed my friends."

"But you can't just show up at Mom and Dad's with a baby! You disappeared! You can't just reappear like magic! They think you're dead! That's what you wanted! Everyone thinks you're dead!"

"Not *everyone*. My friends will help me figure out what to—"

"Your friends have moved on, Caroline! They're in college now. I'm sure they've got better things to do. They probably won't even show up tonight!"

"Yes they will!"

"How do you know?"

"Because I know them."

"You *used to* know them. It's been a year!" Mary Beth shouts, incredulous.

The baby lets out a muffled whimper.

"Shh," Caroline says. "You're scaring Ceto."

"*I'm* scaring her? She should be at home asleep in her crib, not out here at night in the rain in the middle of nowhere! This is *your* decision, not mine!"

"I know, and I shouldn't have involved you. I'm sorry. You can go. They'll be here soon."

"I can *go*? Do you really expect me to just leave you here alone and hope that a bunch of strangers come and rescue you?"

"My friends are *not* strangers. They're more like family than Mom and Dad ever were."

"What about me? I'm not *like* family. I *am* family. I'm the one who saved you!"

"I know that, and I'll always be grateful for everything you did for me. For us." Caroline looks down at the baby. "But I can't hide forever. It's time for me to come back. I have to figure out my life. For her sake."

"What about *my* sake?"

"Mary Beth—"

"Please don't leave me, Caroline!"

"Oh, Mary Beth . . . I have to!"

"But what about me? What about me?" She screeches it over and over, racked in sheer anguish.

The baby is howling now as well, like she, too, is aware that this is wrong.

"Do you hear her?" Mary Beth screams at Caroline. "Do you hear what she's saying? She's begging you not to take her away! She knows she belongs with me!"

"She's crying because of *you*, Mary Beth! You need to calm down! You're hysterical!"

Mary Beth flinches, squeezing her eyes shut and shaking her head.

You need to calm yourself down right now, young lady! You're hysterical!

She's back at the Golden Bridge home, surrounded by strangers in scrubs, her body tense with agony, struggling to bring her child into the world. It's been so lonely and difficult for so long, but it's almost over. The pain, the loneliness, all of it.

The pain is excruciating. Her body, her heart, especially her empty arms that have ached for so long to hold her baby.

And he's here! He's here at last! Her son! She can hear him wailing.

Her eyes snap open. The glaring delivery room lights have been extinguished—why?

Because they're trying to hide the baby from you. They're trying to take him. You can't let them take him!

There's a shadowy figure before her. One of the nurses. She has the baby in a carrier. She's going to leave with him.

"Give me my baby!" Mary Beth reaches for him. "I want my baby!"

The nurse backs away, sounding frightened.

"No! Mary Beth, what are you doing? This isn't *your* baby!"

"Stop!" Mary Beth moves closer, again reaching for the child. "You can't take my baby! I won't let you!"

"He's gone, Mary Beth! Your son is gone! And I'm so sorry for that, but this is my child!"

"How dare you?" Again, Mary Beth attempts to grab the carrier. "Give him to me!"

"Stop! What are you—"

She wrenches the handle from the nurse's grasp.

The nurse loses her footing.

She falls backward into the chasm with a high-pitched scream.

Mary Beth hears her land with a sickening thud. She hears her own screams, hears screams from the baby. She unstraps him and holds him against her breast.

"Shh! It's okay, sweetheart! It's okay. Mommy is here. Mommy's got you."

He's crying, his lungs loud and strong.

"What is it? Did she hurt you? Did that mean old nurse hurt you? Shh, here, let's take a look . . ."

She finds her flashlight in her pocket and flicks it on, careful not to shine it in her son's eyes.

In horror, she sees that the child in her arms isn't a newborn baby boy, but a little girl with blue eyes and blond ringlets. She looks like Caroline, and Caroline is . . .

With a strangled cry, Mary Beth trains the beam into the yawning pit. She must have imagined it. Of course she did. This is just a terrible nightmare, not—

But it is. It *is* real.

She sees the broken body in the muddy pit far below. Her neck is twisted at an unnatural angle. Her blue eyes are vacant, staring at the heavens.

She isn't the nurse.

She's Caroline.

CHAPTER SEVENTY-THREE

Present Day

It isn't unexpected—the news Nap just delivered.

Yet Midge finds herself unable to push words past the lump in her throat as he goes on, referring to his computer screen and the forensic testing results that landed in his inbox this morning.

The skeletal remains found at Haven Cliff do indeed belong to Caroline Winterfield.

"You okay?" Nap interrupts himself to ask, peering at her across the desk.

She nods.

He invited her to come around to the other side and sit beside him, as she did when he showed her the genetic results pertaining to Gordy Klatte. Today, she declined. She doesn't need to see the report. There's nothing here she doesn't already know. In her gut. In her heart.

Nap, however, begs to differ.

"There's something here that doesn't quite match what we know about the victim's personal history. But at that age . . . well, at any age, I guess . . . we all have secrets, don't we?"

Midge pushes the lump from her throat, leaning forward in her chair, hands tightly clasped. "What is it?"

He focuses on his screen again, tapping it with the eraser end of a pencil, using it like a pointer. "There are parturition scars on the pubic bone, and there's an indentation in the ilium. It's not definitive, but this evidence does suggest that she was pregnant and delivered a child."

Midge nods.

Ceto.

She evaded capture after disappearing into the woods at Haven Cliff, where she'd killed Mason Bauer Junior.

The SVU investigators accessed his electronic records and learned that he and Ceto had made plans to meet after she contacted him via the genealogy website on August 16. She wasn't the first DNA match to reach out to Mason Bauer.

Junia Stanton had indeed arranged to meet him the day she disappeared.

As for Sarah Greene . . . it appears she was simply in the wrong place at the wrong time, crossing paths with him at the church after Ceto canceled their meeting.

In the wee hours after she disappeared, Bauer's phone pinged off cell towers in a remote part of the Catskills, and his vehicle was captured on a surveillance camera at a service station on a nearby highway. Soil that might have come from the area was found on a shovel in the trunk of his rental car, along with blood and hair strands that might be Sarah's. All are being tested.

Midge remembered what Ginny Livingston had said about retreats the Bauers had attended up there, and the campsite that had burned down. She suggested that the search focus in that area.

Midge is certain it's only a matter of time before they find Sarah's remains. Junia's as well. Perhaps others. Investigators are tracking down everyone in the site's database who contacted him after learning they shared his DNA.

Meanwhile, Ceto remains at large.

The FBI is involved. The manhunt extends far beyond Ulster County and New York state, but Midge worries that Ceto, like Mason

Bauer Senior, might never be found. She worries that she'll be looking over her shoulder for a long, long time, remembering what Ceto said about her, and her friends, and her father . . .

But now isn't the time to think about that.

"I have to get over to Haven Cliff for breakfast," she tells Nap. "It's Talia's last day. I promised I'd spend some time with them before they head home, and now I need to tell them . . ."

He nods. "Go. Tell them."

She sighs, stands, and heads for the door.

"I'll forward this report to you. We're still waiting on everything else. But I figured you should be told. And, Midge? I'm sorry."

"Thanks. But I knew . . . We all knew."

"Does this make it easier?"

"Easier?" She shakes her head. "Until it's confirmed, there's always hope. Once you know for sure . . . it's gone."

"Right. But sometimes closure can—"

"Nap?" Midge cuts in. "Sometimes closure is overrated."

He meets her gaze and nods. "Got it. I'll be around if you need me."

"Thanks, Nap."

Driving back to Haven Cliff, Midge thinks of the Greenes. For them, hope is quickly running out.

She thinks, too, of the Winterfields. They'll need to be informed that Caroline's remains have been found.

So will Mary Beth, though she already knows. Has long known. But not now. Not this morning. Not when she's about to taste freedom for the first time in ten weeks.

Posting bail was Kelly's idea, after Midge shared what she'd learned. Mary Beth will still face the assault charges, but it's pretty clear she wasn't responsible for Gordy's murder, or the Walking Man's. Nor, Midge is certain, for Caroline's death.

For Kelly, money is no object. And she always had a soft spot for Mary Beth and her devil-may-care attitude.

Caroline loved her, and she loved Caroline.

Midge brushes tears from her eyes. It's so unfair. Bonded sisters, desperate to escape the fate laid out for them by a tyrannical disciplinarian father and a subservient mother. Caroline, naive and vulnerable. Mary Beth, filled with spitfire. If things had been different . . .

But you can't move through life dogged by what-ifs. You can't move through it at all if you're mired in the past, rewriting in vain stories that have already been told.

"You have to get on with it," Midge tells herself sternly, but her voice sounds small and hollow to her own ears.

She swipes her eyes and reaches to turn on the radio, wondering if it's still tuned to the nineties station. In the moment before she flips the knob, she knows, with absolute certainty, that she's going to hear Britney Spears. Yes, and it will be a message from Caroline from beyond the grave, telling Midge it's time to lighten up and let go.

The radio is still tuned to the nineties station, all right; "Who Let the Dogs Out" blasts through the car.

So much for her detective's intuition. Laughing, Midge cranks up the volume and sings along, tapping the steering wheel in time to the beat. The song ends just as she makes the turn off the highway to pass between Haven Cliff's stone pillars.

She lowers the volume at the opening chords of the next song—a ballad, not bubblegum pop. Sarah McLachlan, not Britney Spears.

It's fine. She doesn't really believe in spirit communication from the great beyond anyway. She's all about facts and evidence and—

Then she realizes which song it is.

"I Will Remember You."

A choked sob escapes her throat. She pulls off to the side of the drive, crying, laughing through tears.

Maybe there's room for one more little what-if.

When the song ends, she wipes her eyes with a McDonald's napkin, pulls herself together, and drives the last stretch along the tree-shaded lane, emerging to see the stone mansion's turrets towering against a clear blue sky. Ben, Caleb, and Hayley are out on the broad lawn in the sunshine, tossing a Frisbee, laughing and teasing each other.

Midge waves at them, glad they're outside so that she can break the news to Kelly and Talia in private.

She finds them in the kitchen, standing at the stove, shoulders touching. A pair of crystal flutes is on the counter on either side of them, filled with mimosa, and a pitcher of orange juice sits beside an empty flute and an open bottle of champagne in an ice bucket. Sunlight streams through the tall windows. The air is fragrant with coffee, butter, and . . . is that chocolate?

"No, you don't just drop them *wherever*!" Talia is saying. "You only need six!"

"Come on, that's ridiculous. I promised your kids I'd make them chocolate chip pancakes, and I want to do it the fun Aunt Kelly way, not the boring, stingy Mom way."

"I'm not boring and stingy! I just don't want them throwing up in the car on the way home."

"Hi, guys."

They turn, seeing Midge.

"Midge! You're missing the mimosas. Where have you been?" Kelly asks.

"I was with Nap. He—"

"Wait, Midge, you have to tell her!" Talia says.

"Tell her? You mean Kelly? Tell her what?" Has Talia somehow already heard about Caroline?

But then Talia goes on, "Tell her the chocolate chips are supposed to be a face! Two for the eyes, one for the nose, and three for the mouth. Kelly's just dumping them on willy-nilly."

"'Willy-nilly'?" Kelly echoes. "Who the heck is Willy Nilly?"

"It's an expression!"

"All right, *Grandma*." Kelly fills the empty flute with orange juice and champagne and hands it to Midge. "We need a toast!"

"Wait, first, tell her, Midge!" Talia says.

Tell her . . .

Tell them.

Yes. Midge has to tell them.

"Tell *her* that it's always the more the better when it comes to chocolate chips, right, Midge?" Kelly prods.

She hesitates. The last thing she wants to do is ruin this lighthearted moment.

"Right. Sorry, Tal'. You know me and chocolate. I'm with Kelly on this." Midge sips the mimosa. "And, Kelly . . . this morning . . . did you take care of it?"

"Yes. I went over and posted bail for Mary Beth first thing. By now, she's probably out."

"Where do you think she'll go?" Talia asks, with the batter bowl poised over the sizzling griddle.

"Home to Syracuse, I guess," Midge says.

"I wonder if she'll ever come back here."

"She'll have to. She still has to answer to the charges," Midge tells Talia. "Unless she jumps bail."

"She won't. I know she won't. But if she does . . ." Kelly shrugs. "It's only money."

"I meant, I wonder if she'd come back here to live," Talia says. "Ben and I were talking about that this morning."

"About Mary Beth?"

"Not Mary Beth." She pours a dollop of batter on the griddle. "And not for good. Maybe just . . . you know. For the summer. Next summer."

"Wait, you and Ben and the kids? You'd come back here?"

"Maybe. We could rent a cottage."

"That would be amazing!" Midge says. "Exactly like old times. *That* should be our toast."

"Wait, we need to top off the drinks." Kelly grabs the champagne. "And you don't have to rent a place, Tal'. You could stay here at Haven Cliff."

"For two months? Come on, Kelly, you'd get sick of us."

"No, I'd love it. It's been nice having you all around. I kind of like it."

"Even the kids?" Midge asks.

"*Especially* the kids. Caleb is such a sweetheart, and Hayley . . ."

"*Not* a sweetheart," Talia says with a laugh. "But a self-proclaimed badass superhero. She's so *you*, Kelly. She's you, too, Midge."

"And she's *you*, Tal'." Kelly shrugs. "She's all of us. She's who we used to be. I miss that *me*. I miss that *us*."

"How is she holding up?" Midge asks Talia.

"Like it never happened."

"And Caleb?"

"We told him as little as possible. And I told Ben as much as possible. So that he'll understand."

"And does he?" Kelly asks.

"He's starting to. And there's something else. Don't get me wrong—I'm still furious that Hayley took it upon herself to put her DNA out there. I've just been too busy being glad she survived to punish her for it. But if it comes back with a match . . . maybe I'll see if I can find him."

"Are you sure you want to do that?" Midge asks.

"I think so. I'm just not sure my mom would want me to." Talia pours more batter on the griddle.

"For what it's worth, I think Natalie would say that's your decision." Kelly dumps a handful of chocolate chips on the new pancake.

"Hey! Willy Nilly! Willy Nilly!" Talia slaps Kelly's hand, but she's laughing.

"You're *such* a boring mom!" But Kelly, too, is laughing. She grabs a chocolate chip from the bag and surreptitiously throws it at Talia, hitting her on the nose.

"What the . . . Kelly! Did you just *throw* something at me?"

"No! It was Midge. She's the one with the great pitching arm, not me."

"Midge!" Talia grabs a chip and chucks it at her. "What kind of behavior is that for a dignified officer of the law?"

"Kelly started it!" Midge throws a chip at Kelly, who ducks so that it hits Talia.

"Hey!" Talia lobs it back.

Midge catches it in her mouth like a trained seal, and they dissolve in laughter, all of them.

"So, getting back to Nap, what were you saying?" Talia asks her, grabbing a dish towel and wiping a glob of melting chocolate off the stove.

"Yeah, Midge, spill it. Why were you at his place this early in the morning, hmm?"

Talia swats her with the towel. "Kelly! A lady never kisses and tells."

"Oh please. Midge is no lady. Right, Midge? What's up with you and Nap?"

"Sorry . . . if I *was* kissing, I'm not telling."

No, she's not telling them that, or anything else. The news can wait.

If somewhere deep down inside, Talia or Kelly or both still cling to a shred of hope . . . well, let them, for just a little longer.

Closure, as she told Nap, is overrated.

But *this*?

This moment? This last morning together with treasured friends who were almost lost, celebrating with champagne and chocolate the last bit of a summer that was almost lost?

To quote the girl who reminds her of all the things that she, Kelly, and Talia once were, still are, and always will be . . .

This moment is *epic.*

It was a long time coming; someday, all too soon, it will be a long time ago.

And so, in this moment, Midge raises her glass and offers a toast. "To the good old days, to the better ones ahead, but mostly to right here, right now."

Acknowledgments

With gratitude to Laura Blake Peterson, my agent of thirty-five years (!); to my editor, Megha Parekh, my developmental editor, Charlotte Herscher, production editor Liz Gluck, copyeditor Haley Swan, proofreader Tara Whitaker, and the team at Thomas & Mercer; to Holly Frederick, James Farrell, and the team at Curtis Brown, Ltd.; to Carol Fitzgerald and the team at the Book Report Network; to Alison Gaylin, my indefatigable sounding board and cheerleader; to Alafair, Kellye, Laura, Megan, and Sarah, with whom I try to make sense of this crazy industry and with whom I laugh and/or commiserate when we cannot; to my husband, my sons, and all the family and friends who get me through; and most of all, to the book people—readers, writers, booksellers, librarians, publishers, reviewers, influencers—thank you for continuing to support and celebrate literature in this crazy busy, buzzy world!

About the Author

Photo © 2023 Patti Looney Photography

Wendy Corsi Staub is the *New York Times* bestselling and multi-award-winning author of more than one hundred novels, including *The Fourth Girl*, *Windfall*, *The Other Family*, and *Dying Breath*. She is also the author of the Lily Dale Mystery series, the Foundling trilogy, the Mundy's Landing trilogy, the Nightwatcher trilogy, and the Live to Tell trilogy. Wendy is a three-time finalist for the Simon & Schuster Mary Higgins Clark Award, and she's won an RWA Rita Award, an RT Award for Career Achievement in Suspense, the 2007 RWA/NYC Golden Apple Award for Lifetime Achievement, and five WLA Washington Irving Prizes for Fiction. Born and raised in Dunkirk, New York, Wendy is married, has two sons and three rescue cats, and has fostered for various animal rescue organizations. For more information, visit www.wendycorsistaub.com.